His Best Acquisition

DANI COLLINS

RACHAEL THOMAS

TARA PAMMI

First Published in Great Britain 2017
By Mills & Boon, an imprint of HarperCollins*Publishers*
1 London Bridge Street, London, SE1 9GF

HIS BEST ACQUISITION © 2017 Harlequin Books S. A.

The Russian's Acquisition, *A Deal Before the Altar* and *A Deal with Demakis* were first published in Great Britain by Harlequin (UK) Limited.

The Russian's Acquisition © 2014 Dani Collins
A Deal Before the Altar © 2014 Rachael Thomas
A Deal with Demakis © 2014 Tara Pammi

ISBN: 978-0-263-92990-4

05-1217

Printed and bound in Spain
by CPI, Barcelona

THE RUSSIAN'S
ACQUISITION

BY
DANI COLLINS

Dani Collins discovered romance novels in high school and immediately wondered how a person trained and qualified for *that* amazing job. She married her high school sweetheart, which was a start, then spent two decades trying to find her fit in the wide world of romance writing, always coming back to Mills & Boon Modern Romance.

Two children later, and with the first entering high school, she placed in Harlequin's *Instant Seduction* contest. It was the beginning of a fabulous journey towards finally getting that dream job.

When she's not in her Fortress of Literature, as her family calls her writing office, she works, chauffeurs children to extra-curricular activities, and gardens with more optimism than skill. Dani can be reached through her website at www.danicollins.com.

To the editorial team in London, especially Suzy Clarke and Laurie Johnson.

Suzy because she fell for Aleksy early and told me to keep him on the back burner (that's why he smolders), and Laurie because she fell for him as soon as she met him (and then told me how to make him even more brooding and irresistible).

Thanks, ladies!

CHAPTER ONE

I miss waking up with you.

THE NOTE STRUCK a pang of wistfulness in Clair Daniels's chest. She wondered if anyone would ever write something so romantic to her. Then she recalled the waves of emotional highs and lows Abby had been riding for months, all under the influence of that elusive emotion called "love." Being independent was more secure and less hurtful, she reminded herself. And the roller coaster she'd been through in the last two weeks, after losing a man who was merely a friend and mentor, was brutal enough.

Still, she had to hide envy as she handed the note back to Abby and said with a composed smile, "That's very sweet. The wedding is this weekend?"

Abby, the firm's receptionist, nodded with excitement as she placed the card back in the extravagant bouquet Clair had admired. "I was just saying to everyone—" She waved at the ladies gathered with their morning coffee. "I texted him that after Saturday, we can wake up together forev…" She trailed off as it struck her who she was talking to.

The horseshoe of women dropped their gazes.

Clair's throat closed over a helpless *I wasn't waking up with him*. She'd never slept with anyone but couldn't say so. Her confidentiality clause with Victor Van Eych had made such confessions impossible.

Still, she knew everyone had thought her relationship to the boss went deeper than merely being his PA. The gossip had eaten her up, but she'd let it happen out of kindness for a man whose self-assurance had been dented by age. Other people's opinions of her shouldn't matter, she'd told herself. Victor was nice to her. He had encouraged her to start the foundation she'd always dreamed of. Letting a white lie prevail in return had seemed harmless.

Then his family had refused to let her into his mansion to so much as share condolences, turning their backs and pushing her to the fringes like a pariah.

She wasn't someone who wore her heart on her sleeve, but the one person she had begun to count on had *died*. Shock and sorrow had overwhelmed her. Thankfully she'd had a place to bolt to for a week and absorb her loss. Ironic that it had been the orphanage, but what a timely reminder how important the home and foundation were, not just to her, but to children as alone as she was.

Now she was feeling more alone than ever, trying not to squirm under the scrutiny of her colleagues, not wanting to reveal that her chest had gone tight and her throat felt swollen. It wasn't just Victor's unexpected death getting to her, but a kind of despair. Would anyone ever stick? Or was she meant to walk through life in isolation forever?

Into the suffocating moment, the elevator pinged and the doors whispered open. Clair glanced over her shoulder to escape her anxiety, and what she saw made her catch a startled breath.

A hunting party of suits invaded the top floor. It was the only way to describe the tribe of alert, stony-faced men. The last off the elevator, the tallest, was obviously their leader. He was a warrior whose swarthy face wore a blaze of genuine battle injury. At first that was all Clair saw: the slash of a pale scar that began where his dark hair was combed back from his hairline. It bisected his left eyebrow, angled from his cheekbone toward the corner of his mouth, then dropped off his clean-shaven jaw.

He seemed indifferent to it, his energy completely focused on the new territory he was conquering. His armor-gray suit clung with perfect tailoring to his powerful build. With one sweep of his golden-brown eyes, he dispersed the clique of women in a subtle hiss of indrawn breaths and muted clicks of retreating heels.

Clair couldn't move. His marauding air incited panic, but her feet stayed glued to the floor. She lifted her chin, refusing to let him see he intimidated her.

Male interest sparked to life as he held her stare. His gaze drifted like a caress to her mouth, lowered to her open collar and mentally stripped her neatly belted raincoat and low-heeled ankle boots.

Clair set her teeth, hating these moments of objectification as much as any woman, but something strange happened. Her paralysis continued. She wasn't able to turn away in rejection. Heat came to life in her abdomen like a cooling ember blown into a brighter glow. Warmth radiated into her chest and bathed her throat.

His attention came back to her face, decision stamped in his eyes. She was something he would want.

She blushed, still unable to look away. A writhing sensation knotted in her stomach, clenching like a fist when he spoke in a voice like dark chocolate, melting and rich, yet carrying a biting edge.

She didn't understand him.

Clair blinked in surprise, but he didn't switch to English. His command had been for one of his companions, yet she had the impression he'd been talking about her if not to her. He swung away, moving into the interior offices as if he owned the place. One of the men flanking him murmured in a similar language.

"Was that Russian?" Clair asked on a breathless gasp as the last pin-striped back disappeared. She felt as if a tank had just flattened her.

"They've been coming in all week. That tall one is new." Abby dragged her gaze away from the hall and became conspiratorial as she leaned over her keyboard. "No one knows what's going on. I was hoping you could enlighten us."

"I wasn't here," Clair reminded her. She hadn't even been in London. "But Mr. Turner told me before I left that everything would carry on as usual, that the family were keeping things status quo until they'd had time to settle his private affairs. Are they lawyers?" She glanced toward the hall but was certain that man wasn't anything as straitlaced as a lawyer. He struck her as someone who made his own rules rather than living by any imposed on him. Her skin still tingled under the brand of ownership he'd imprinted on her.

"Some are, I think," Abby answered. "Ours have been meeting them every day."

"Our—? Oh, right." Clair forced herself back to the conversation. Lawyers. Not just her friend deceased but the boss and owner, leaving the place on tiptoes of tension. She'd noticed the mood the second she returned. Having strangers prowl like bargain hunters at a fire sale didn't help. Clair decided she didn't like that trespasser of a man.

Abby glanced around before hunching even closer. "Clair? I'm really sorry for what I said. I know losing Mr. Van Eych must be hard for y—"

"It's fine. Don't worry about it," Clair dismissed with a light smile. She stepped back to freeze out the empathy.

Putting up walls was a protective reflex, an automatic re-action that probably accounted for why no one ever sent her flowers or love notes. She wasn't good at being close to people. That was why she'd let herself fall into a fake romance with Victor. He'd offered companionship without the demands of physical or emotional intimacy, protecting her from anyone else trying to make a similar claim. No risk, she'd thought. No chance of pain.

Ha.

That Russian would make incredible demands, she thought, and her stomach dipped even as she wondered where her speculation had come from. No way would she let someone like that into her private life. He was a one-way ticket to a broken heart. Forget him.

Nevertheless, trepidation weakened her knees as she looked toward her office, the direction he'd taken. Silly to be afraid. He would already have forgotten her.

"I'll check in with Mr. Turner," Clair said, holding the smile of confident warmth she'd perfected as Victor's PA. "If I'm able to tell you anything, I will."

"Thank you." Abby's worried brow relaxed.

Clair walked away, determined to push the Russian from her mind, but she'd barely hung her coat and bent to tuck her purse into her desk drawer before Mr. Turner appeared in the doorway. Waxen paleness underpinned the flags of red in his sagging cheeks.

Clair stood to attention, heart sinking with intuitive fear. "What's wrong?"

"You're to report to—" He ran a hand over his thinning hair. "The new owner."

Aleksy Dmitriev set the waste bin next to his feet, reached for the first plaque on the wall and tossed it in, taking less satisfaction in the loud *clunk* of an industry award hitting the trash than he'd anticipated. This coup had been too easy. *Clunk.* The bastard wasn't alive to see his world collapse. *Clunk.* Van Eych had succumbed to the lifestyle he'd enjoyed at the expense of men like Aleksy's father rather than face the revenge Aleksy had intended to wreak. *Clunk.*

The blonde in the foyer was that filthy dog's mistress. *Smash!*

A delicate crystal globe shattered in the bottom of the can, leaving a silver heart exposed and dented.

"What on earth," a clear female voice demanded, "do you think you're doing?"

Aleksy lifted his head and was struck by the same kick of sexual hunger he'd experienced fifteen minutes ago. The part of his anatomy he couldn't control suffered another tight, near-painful pull.

At first sight he'd judged her snowflake perfect, delicate and cool with creamy, unblemished skin, white-gold hair and ice-blue eyes. As potent as chilled vodka with a kick of heat that spread from the inside. He'd demanded her name and details.

Now the dull raincoat was gone, revealing warmer colors. Her peach knit top clung to slender arms and hugged smallish but high breasts, while her hips flared just enough to confirm she was all woman.

He smothered reckless desire with angry disgust. How could she have given all that to an old man, especially *that* old man?

Under his stare, her lashes flickered with uncertainty. She turned one boot in before setting her feet firmly. Her fists knotted at her sides, and her shoulders went back. Her chin came up in the same challenge she'd issued when they first came face-to-face.

"Those might have sentimental value to Mr. Van Eych's family," she said.

Aleksy narrowed his eyes. The heat of finding the fight he'd been anticipating singed through his muscles. She was an extension of Victor Van Eych, and that allowed him to hate her, genuinely hate her. His sneer pulled at his scar. He knew it made him look feral and dangerous. He was that and more. "Close the door."

She hesitated—and it irritated him. When he spoke, people moved. Having a slip of a woman take a moment to think it over, look *him* over, wasn't acceptable.

"As you leave," he commanded with quiet menace. "I'm throwing out all of Van Eych's trophies, Miss Daniels. That includes you."

She flinched but remained tall and proud. Her icy blue eyes searched his, confirming he was serious.

As the heart attack that killed your meal ticket, he conveyed with contempt.

She turned away, and loss unexpectedly clawed at him.

He didn't have time to examine it before she pressed the door closed, remaining inside. Inexplicable satisfaction roared through him. He told himself it was because he would get the fight he craved, but what else could he expect from a woman of her nature? She didn't live the way she did by walking away from what she wanted.

Keeping her hand on the doorknob, she tossed her hair back and asked with stiff authority, "Who are you?"

Unwillingly, he admired her haughtiness. At least she made a decent adversary. He wiped the taint of dust from his fingertips before extending his hand in a dare. "Aleksy Dmitriev."

Another brief hesitation; then, with head high, she crossed to tentatively set her hand in his. It was chilly, but slender and soft. He immediately fantasized guiding her light touch down his abdomen and feeling her cool fingers wrap around his hot shaft.

He didn't usually respond to women like this, rarely let sex thrust to the forefront of his mind so blatantly, especially with a woman he regarded with such derision, but attraction clamored in him as he closed his hand over hers. It took all his will not to use his grip to drag her near enough to take complete ownership, hook his arm across her lower back and mash her narrow body into his.

Especially when she quivered at his touch. She made a coy play at pretending it disconcerted her, but she'd been sleeping with a man old enough to be her grandfather. Acting sexually excited was her stock in trade. It made him sick, yet he still responded to it. He wanted to crowd her into the wall and kindle her reaction until she was helpless to her own need and he could sate his.

Disappointment seared a blistering path through his center. He wanted her, but she'd already let his enemy have her.

Aleksy Dmitriev released her hand and insultingly wiped his own on his tailored pants, as if her touch had soiled his palm.

Clair jerked her hand into her middle, closing her fist over the sensation of calluses and heat. He was hot. In every way. All that masculine energy and muscle was a bombardment. She didn't want to react, especially to someone who wanted to *fire* her.

She dragged at her cloak of indifference, the one she'd sewn together in a school full of spoiled rich kids. "What gives you the right, Mr. Dmitriev, to take away my job?"

"Your 'job' is dead." His curled lip told her what he thought her job was.

"I'm a PA," she said tightly. "Working under the president. If you've taken ownership, I assume you're moving into that position?"

"On top of you? A predictable invitation, but I have no use for his leavings."

"Don't be crass!" she snapped. She never lost her temper. Poise was part of her defense.

He smirked, seeming to enjoy her flush of affront. It intensified her anger.

"I do real work," she insisted. "Not whatever you're suggesting."

His broken eyebrow went up. They both knew what he was suggesting.

"I manage special projects—" She cut herself off at his snort, heart plummeting, suddenly worried about her own very special project. The foundation was a few weeks from being properly launched. After last week, she knew the building she'd grown up in was badly showing its age. The home needed a reliable income more than ever. And the people...

"Clair, are you okay? You're more quiet than usual," Mrs. Downings had said last week, catching her at the top of the stairs where she'd been painting. They'd sat on the landing and Clair hadn't been able to keep it all in. Mrs. Downings had put her arm around her, and for once Clair had allowed the familiarity, deeply craving the sense that *someone* cared she was hurting.

She'd come away more fired up than ever to get the foundation off the ground. She had to keep people like Mrs. Downings, with her understanding and compassion, available to children with the same aching, empty hearts that she had.

"Are you shutting down the whole firm?" Clair asked Aleksy with subdued panic.

He turned stony. "That's confidential."

She shook her head. "You can't let everyone go. Not immediately. Not without paying buckets of severance," she guessed, but it was an educated one. There were hundreds of clients with investments managed here.

"I can dismiss you," he said with quiet assurance.

Another jolt of anger pulsed through her, unfamiliar but invigorating. "On what grounds?"

"Not turning up for work last week."

"I had the time booked months ago. I couldn't have known then that my employer would pass away right before I left." And she would have stayed if Victor's family hadn't been so cutting. If someone, anyone, had said she was needed here.

"You obviously cared more about enjoying your holiday than whether your job would be here when you returned."

The annual blitz of cleaning and repair at the home was the furthest thing from a holiday, not that he wanted to know. "I offered to stay," she asserted, not wanting to reveal how torn she'd felt. With her world crashing around her here, she'd been quite anxious to escape to the one stable influence in her life.

"The VP granted my leave," she continued, scraping her composure together by folding her arms. With her eyes narrowed in suspicion, she asked, "Would I still be employed if I'd stayed?"

"No." Not a shred of an excuse.

What a truly hateful man! His dislike of her was strangely hurtful too. She tried hard to make herself likable, knowing she wasn't naturally warm and spontaneous. Failing without being given a chance smarted.

"Mr. Turner assured me before I left that another position would be found for me. I've been here almost three years." She managed to hang on to a civil tone, searching for enough dignity to disguise her fear.

"Mr. Turner doesn't own the company. I decide who stays."

"It's wrongful dismissal. Unless you're offering a package?" She hated that she tensed in hope. She knew exactly how marketable her skill set was: barely adequate. Going back to low-end jobs, scraping by on a hand-to-mouth existence made her insides gel with dread. This job had been her first step into genuine security.

The Russian tilted his head to a patronizing angle. "We both know you've enjoyed the full package long enough, Miss Daniels. If you haven't set aside something for this eventuality, that's not my concern."

"Stop talking like I was—"

"What?" he demanded, baring his teeth. "Victor Van Eych's mistress? Stop acting like you weren't," he snarled with surprising bite. In a few long strides he was at his desk, flipping open a file, waving a single sheet of paper. "Your qualifications are limited to typing and filing, but you're occupying an executive office." Another sheet flapped in the air. "You're paid more than his personal secretary, but he still needed one because you were dedicated to 'special projects.'" He cracked out a laugh as he snatched up the next record. "You live in the company *flat*—"

"In the housekeeper's wing because it's one of my duties to water the plants," she defended, hearing how weak it sounded even though Victor had made it sound so logical.

"The janitors who dust the place can water the plants. You're a parasite, Miss Daniels. One who's being pried off the host. Take the day to pack your things."

A *parasite*. She was doing everything in her power to pay back the system! This job had been a golden egg, but she'd tried not to take advantage of Victor's generosity. Now she was finally on the brink of being able to help others instead of focusing on her own struggles—something she wanted not for the recognition, but to support

children like what she'd once been—and he was calling
her a parasite?

"You reprehensible, conscienceless…" Her voice dried
up, which was probably best. She was shaking and liable
to get personal. Mention that scar, for instance.

"Conscienceless," he repeated through lips that peeled
back in a snarl. He closed her file and took up a memo of
some kind. "Do you even know what you've been sleeping with? Read that, then tell me who is conscienceless
and reprehensible."

CHAPTER TWO

ALEKSY TOLD HIMSELF he was only confirming that she'd actually left. He was not looking to run into her. Nevertheless, the part of him still prowling with a sense of anticlimax would leap on another chance to verbally tussle with her. Until she'd read the memo, paled, then walked out in stunned silence, Clair Daniels had been—

Forget her, he ordered himself again, but it wasn't easy. Her type was usually fair game. He didn't mess with marriageable women, just the types who enjoyed physical pleasure and material wealth over love. Clair had obviously fallen into that category, asking if he was offering a package. She'd been royally peeved when he turned her down, displaying the kind of passionate anger that suggested an equally passionate—

Stop it. He was here to take ownership of one more acquisition. That was all.

He keyed in the entry code to the firm's penthouse and stepped into generic opulence. The plants looked very well tended. Unfortunately that was the only thing recommending the place. It was the height of modern convenience. No expense was spared in the white leather furniture or silk rugs over marble tiles, but it lacked...

Traces of her.

Absently stroking his thumb along the raised line on his

chin, he strolled through a dining room that held no fresh flowers. The white duvet on the master bed was undented. The bathroom was not decorated with intriguing lingerie. In the kitchen, the pantry shelves were bare of all but the minimum staples. She'd vacated so completely, it was as if she'd never lived here at all.

How, then, would he find—

He caught the faint sound of a feminine voice through a wall and cocked his head, instantly alert. Moving past the refrigerator, he found an unlocked door to a laundry room. On the opposite side another door opened into a narrow kitchen, where the scent of toast lingered. Beyond, in a modest lounge peppered with colorful throws, unopened mail and abandoned shoes, Clair Daniels stood. She had her back to him as she finished a call. Her pert bottom and slim thighs were mouthwateringly silhouetted by clingy yoga pants.

The internal wolf that had been pacing restlessly inside him leapt to the fore, exploding his heart in his chest and slamming hot blood through his limbs. He was furious to find her here, but he smiled.

She hung up, turned and screamed.

Clair clapped a hand over her mouth as she recognized the Russian. As forbidding as he looked, as frightening as it was to have a man appear in her private space, she instantly knew she wasn't in real danger. At a very deep level, she'd been expecting him. *That* unnerved her, but she ignored it.

Dropping her hand, she accused, "You scared the life out of me!"

"It wouldn't have happened if you'd left as you were told." He no longer wore the suit jacket and tie from earlier. His fog-gray shirt strained across his chest, barely containing his big shoulders and thick biceps. He'd turned up his sleeves, revealing strong flat wrists and a ruthlessly simple gold watch.

She had an urge to touch his arm to see if it was as hard as it looked, which was ridiculous. Men fell into two categories for her: *Get lost* and *Friends is friendly enough*. She'd never been silly over boys and had always found women who went hormonal a bit irritating. She was capable of noticing a man with nice abs or a handsome smile, but she didn't get hot and weak-kneed. Ever. Especially over men who came on so strong. This quivery, oversensitized version of herself was not her.

And yet she watched with fascination as he moved with masculine grace, bending his arm and glancing at his exclusive watch, then flicking his gaze toward her bedroom door where her unpacked suitcase stood against the wall. "You've packed at least."

"I haven't *un*packed from being away." She shouldn't take such pleasure in throwing defiance at him when she was falling into desperation, but it gave her ego a boost to let him know she wasn't bowing and scraping under his every word. She didn't like what he was doing to her and wanted to make it stop. Under no circumstances did she want him to know how much power he was wielding over her.

"Well, that saves time, doesn't it?" he said with false pleasantry.

"Whose? Yours? Are you here to throw me out?" It wasn't even five o'clock. She'd started calling hotels but had wasted precious hours trying to find a workable solution for the foundation first. She had survived starting with nothing before, but she couldn't bear to let down people whose hopes she'd already raised. The trustees needed to run the home, not spend all their time scrambling for funding. She was stuck, but she didn't want him to know how desperate she was. "Why didn't you just send the clown who threw me out of my office?"

His arrogant head went back. "You can't mean Lazlo?"

"The lowbrow who said, 'I'm to assist you if you require it'? He might as well have grabbed me by the collar and thrown me into the street."

Although she had to admit it had been less humiliating to stuff her few personal items into her laptop bag and make a quick exit than try to explain while saying goodbye to everyone. She'd been shaken by what she'd read in the memo and hadn't wanted to speak to anyone while it sank in. Victor, the man she'd put so much stock and trust in, had put on far more fronts than having a young blond mistress.

"I'll remind him to be more sensitive next time," Aleksy said.

"Next time?" she repeated with a kick in her heart. "He's here?"

"No, we're alone."

Her stomach quavered. She folded her arms over her middle, trying to project confidence when she felt gullible and stupid. "Well, I'd rather deal with him. At least he doesn't sneak up on a person like a thief."

Aleksy's golden-brown eyes flashed a warning. "I bought the company fair and square and entered a flat I now own. You're the one with no right to be here."

"It's a job perk!"

"It's a love nest. One the firm will no longer support."

So this was about money. She had deduced as much. He must have bought the firm believing its worth to be higher and only learned that Victor had falsified returns after the purchase went through. He didn't have to take out his bad luck on her, though. They were both victims of Victor's ruse.

"You know, if you let me keep my job, I could pay rent

and this unused apartment could generate income, rather than be an expense," she suggested.

He narrowed his eyes, displaying thick eyelashes. "How long have you been here?"

"Over a year."

He moved through her small lounge with calculating interest, probably adding up the value of her few possessions. The place came furnished, but the faded snapshot of her parents in the cheap frame was hers. Her father's pipe stood on the mantel above the gas flame fireplace. The items were all she had and didn't come with real memories.

He jerked his chin at the pipe. "I'm surprised you let him keep you in here. A woman with your *assets* could have pressed for the main prize." He turned his head.

She ought to have been offended, but her body betrayed her. Heat flooded her under his lingering stare. Her breasts became tight and sensitive and her thighs wanted to pinch against a sweet tingling sensation high between. She was compelled to wet her parted lips with a stroke of her tongue.

His cynical lift of an eyebrow stabbed her with mortification.

"That pipe was my father's, not Victor's." She moved to snatch it up, as though that were all it would take to whisk away the pulsing attraction disconcerting her. "I never—" She cut herself off and tightened her fist around the pipe. "I signed a confidentiality statement," she finally said, lifting her chin to see him better.

He was so looming and intense with not a shred of compassion for a naive young woman who had wanted to believe she'd been noticed because she worked hard. Aleksy Dmitriev was far above her, not just in wealth and education, but in confidence and life experience. Part of her was intrigued, but their inequality raised her barriers. It killed her to beg guidance off him, but she had to.

"I'm sure you would know better than I whether such agreements are meant to be binding after a death. With your being the new owner, are you in a position to insist I disclose—"

"I insist," he commanded, flat and sharp. "Tell me everything."

"Well, I don't know anything of national import. Don't get excited. I'm just sick of you accusing me of sleeping my way to the top when I didn't. Victor was impotent."

He took her chin between his thumb and curled finger. "Don't lie," he warned.

She lifted her free hand, intending to shove his disturbing touch away.

He caught her wrist in midair, but what really held her immobile was the ferocious flare of gold in his eyes. His irises glittered with more demand than this situation warranted. It made her still out of curiosity.

"Why would I lie?"

"Because you know I don't want you if he's had you."

She sucked in a shocked breath and instinctively tried to pull away.

His grip on her wrist flexed lightly to keep her close. "That wasn't really what he was hiding, was it?"

Clair was plunged out of her depth, body reacting with alarm, mind splintered in all directions by what he'd said about wanting her.

"I—I didn't know until today that Victor was hiding anything," she stammered, trying to ignore the detonations of nervous excitement inside her. "I thought he was exactly what he looked like. A successful businessman." She tried to resist looking into his eyes, but once his stare caught hers, she couldn't look away. Her nerves seared with something like fight or flight, but it wasn't fear. The danger here was subtle. Sexual.

"How did you meet him?"

"Who are you? Interpol?" She longed to move away, disturbed beyond bearing.

"Tell me," he insisted, not releasing her.

"He needed something after hours. I was working late in the file room." She begrudged making the explanation but wanted him to believe her. Sort of. *You know I don't want you if he's had you.* It was such a Neanderthal thing to say, but it made her insides quiver. "I found it and he said I was the sort of person the top floor needed."

"I bet he did." His thumb moved into the notch below her bottom lip. He tilted her face up, into the fading light from the window. His gaze stroked her face like a feathery caress, taking in features she knew men found attractive, but she sensed evaluation, not admiration.

It shouldn't matter, but it undermined her confidence. Her looks were all she had unless she managed a miracle with the Brighter Days Foundation, and losing her job had quashed that.

"I didn't think his motive was romantic. He was old." She tested his grip on her chin, but he held fast, making her vibrate with nerves and awareness. It took everything in her to suppress her shivers and pretend she barely noticed his touch. "When I did realize he wanted people to believe we were together, I told him I wasn't interested and he said I didn't have anything to worry about. He wasn't able to make it with any woman, but he didn't want people to know. He said if I was able to keep a confidence, I'd have a good career ahead of me as his PA. I needed the money and it wasn't like he was grabbing me all the time or anything." She pointedly moved her fist with the pipe into the center of his chest and pressed. "Unlike some men."

His touch on her face changed. His fingers fanned out and he stroked his palm under her jaw to take possession of the side of her neck, thumb lightly grazing her throat.

The tender touch stilled her, not just because it was unexpected but because it felt so nice. She didn't encourage people to touch her and hadn't realized how cherished and important it could make her feel. Her lashes wanted to blink closed so she could focus completely on the lovely sensation.

"So you took him for all he'd give you and never put out for any of it."

"It wasn't like that." He made it sound ugly when she hadn't taken anything. "The raise and job title were his idea. He suggested I move into this flat because he held receptions and cocktail parties in the main suite. If people thought we were together, that was their assumption. Maybe neither of us corrected it, but all I did was work for him."

"What kind of work? Hostess duties? Attending functions as his escort?" His lip curled. "Why on earth would people get the wrong impression?"

"He was a widower, so yes, I was his date. But he also put me in charge of forming the firm's charitable foundation."

"Ha!" He released her with a lifting of his hands in rejection. "Van Eych help the less fortunate? Now I know you're lying."

"I'm not." The words rushed out, but a sense of loss washed over her as well. *Let him believe what he wants to believe,* she told herself, but if she was allowed to set the record straight, she wanted to, especially if he'd fired her because he thought she was involved with Victor. Maybe he would reconsider if he believed she hadn't been. Maybe that's what he'd meant when he'd said he didn't want her if Victor had had her.

Dismay squirmed through her. She didn't want him to

want her physically, did she? No. She was trying to rescue the foundation. If there was even a remote chance of keeping her job, and keeping the foundation alive, she had to try.

Veering from him on shaky legs, she found her laptop bag and unzipped it. "You won't have seen it on the books because it's not up and running, but I can show you…"

Most of her records were on her laptop and it took forever to wake up, but she had a slender file with proof of the logo she'd recently approved. It wasn't the fanciest letterhead, but it gave the foundation an identity and made it real. Her heart pounded with pride every time she looked at it. She showed him.

"'Brighter Days'? It looks like a child drew it." He barely glanced at it.

"It's supposed to! It's an organization that provides funding to group homes and offers grants to orphaned children so they can develop independence."

"By underwriting their lives?"

"By providing support of many kinds!" Insulted, Clair whipped the file closed. "You obviously don't know what it's like to be without parents or you'd have some empathy." As she tucked the file back into her bag, she let her hair fall forward to screen how wounded she was by his cynicism.

"Or maybe I do and I didn't have the luxury of handouts to help me find my way. Maybe I managed on my own." His tone was dangerously quiet.

The truth in the hardened brass of his gaze made her hesitate. The thought that he might have shared some of her struggles struck a chord of kinship in her, but he emanated aggression, provoking her defensive response.

"So did I," she challenged. "I'm still capable of wanting to help others."

His hard laugh cracked the air. "Van Eych gave you this

flat, a manager's salary, and countless other favors for *that* face." He pointed at her features, then let his gaze traverse insultingly down her narrow shape. "Among other attributes. Not for any smiley face you drew on the sun. Hardly pulling yourself up by your bootstraps."

He acted as if this illustration was all she had to show for her year of research and meetings and planning. Impotent fury threatened to engulf her, but to let him see he could get under her skin was handing him a weapon he didn't deserve to hold.

"I don't care if you believe me," she said stiffly. "You're obviously a bully who kicks people around for the fun of it. If you'd like to wait in *your* flat next door, I'll clear out of this one by midnight."

Such an ice queen, walking into the bedroom as though she wasn't daring him to follow. Throwing out the bait that she'd never let Van Eych have her. He wondered how she'd homed in on the one reservation he had against her and dismantled it so effectively. A depth of experience in getting what she wanted from men, he supposed. Look at the way she had singled him out as the top dog this morning, making a play with one bold look before he even knew her name.

He almost didn't care whether she had given herself to Van Eych, so long as he possessed her, which left him oddly defeated. Van Eych had stolen everything from him: not just his parents and home, but his youth and looks and his right to a normal life. No matter how Clair was connected, he ought to want to bury her, not bury himself in her.

He told himself her defiance provoked him. A man who'd conquered as many challenges as he had was internally programmed to trim the claws of a spitting cat and show her he wasn't the easy dalliance she was used to. She wouldn't be the biddable sex kitten he was used to either, but that made the thought of having her all the more exciting.

Listen to him. He knew better than to trust her, but he was halfway into bed with her anyway.

Pulling out his mobile, Aleksy texted his PA, then held his breath. He had the truth in seconds and swallowed back a howl of triumph. Her sugar daddy hadn't been capable of making physical demands. That made taking her not just acceptable but imperative.

He pushed open the half-closed door and found more evidence to support her claim. She was moving clothes into a laundry basket set atop a narrow, single bed. There was something very youthful and innocent about her. He imagined Van Eych had been feeling his age—and beginning to feel the pressure of Aleksy's running him to ground—when he'd discovered Clair in the file room.

Clair was just the old man's type: young and pretty, angelic in looks but not in disposition. Van Eych had had women on the side even during his marriage, so it came as no surprise that he'd wanted to maintain the illusion of virility into his later years. The inability to fully enjoy Clair must have churned like bent nails in the old man's gut.

If only he were alive to hate Aleksy for this. A wicked smile of enjoyment pulled Aleksy's mouth. "The medical records confirm what you say. Van Eych was limp."

She sent him a glance that tried for boredom but held an underlying flutter of nervous tension. "I told you, it doesn't matter to me what you believe."

"It matters to me." He hooked a hand over the top of the doorframe, anchoring himself so he wouldn't press forward into the room and take what he wanted before they'd outlined the terms. She had maneuvered a very profitable situation out of a criminal-class schemer. He couldn't underestimate how conniving she could be.

She grabbed a hooded jacket off the suitcase near his feet. As she folded it, she hid her expression and any chance of reading her thoughts, but he heard the wheels turn.

He took in the unpacked case as he waited for her to make the next move, distantly wondering where she'd been for a week. With a real lover perhaps, but other men didn't matter. She had never belonged to Victor. That was the important piece here. The thought of taking her for himself kindled a hungry fire in him. It was an approximation of the victory he craved, and he *would* have it.

With possessive satisfaction, he toured her shape, stoking the heat of anticipation as he hit narrow feet in bronze ballet slippers and climbed up slim but shapely legs. Hips that would fill his hands. A thick pullover sweater that hung loose, disguising whether she wore a bra. He'd bet she wore a snug undershirt of some kind, something that would trap the heat of her skin but still allow him to find and rub her taut nipples.

Her arm came across her breasts, forcing him out of his fantasy. Her blue eyes were wide, her lips parted. A blush of awareness bloomed across her cheekbones. She knew exactly what he was thinking and even though she was acting shocked, she wasn't repelled. Her lashes dropped to hide her eyes, but she flirted light fingers through hair that looked as shiny and silky as gold tassels on a scarlet cushion. Her chest rose in a shaky little pant and she ran her tongue over ripe lips.

It struck him that she wasn't accustomed to wanting the men she used.

He chuckled, delighted not only to have the upper hand, but to have her delectable body fall so easily under him. "Go ahead, Clair," he taunted. "Ask me if offering to share that bed will persuade me to let you stay in it."

CHAPTER THREE

FOR SOME REASON Abby's note from this morning came back to Clair.

I miss waking up with you.

Clair didn't allow herself to be an idealist. She knew better than to wait on Prince Charming, but her insides twisted all over again. She'd had invitations to sex before, even considered a few, but something had always held her back. Fear of letting down her guard. A sense of emotional obligation that wasn't comfortable. Never once had she heard anything so blunt and tactical.

"I thought you believed me when I said I wasn't sleeping with Victor."

"Victor, yes. No man at all?" He was three thousand percent confident, laconically filling her bedroom doorway with his primed body. "You're what? Twenty-five?"

Clair closed lips that had parted with indignant denial.

"Twenty-three," she muttered, which was still long in the tooth to be a virgin, but she was stuck in a catch-22. She had thought she ought to save herself for someone she cared about, but she shied from any type of closeness. Opening up was such a leap of faith. Handing your heart to someone put it in danger of disappointment at the least and complete shattering at the worst. The right man hadn't come along to tempt her into taking the risk.

This man shouldn't tempt her, but sex without the entanglement of feelings held a strange allure. She suspected it would be very good sex too, not just because he looked as though he knew his way around a woman's body, but because her own seemed drawn to his, sense and logic notwithstanding. He made her hot.

It was driving her crazy. She didn't know how to cope with it except to pretend the reaction wasn't there. Shaking out the T-shirt she wore to bed, she folded it against her middle and said frigidly, "What makes you think I want to sleep with you?"

"You've managed to convince me you're capable of honesty, Clair. Don't start lying now. You want me."

He could tell? How? Humiliated, she avoided her own eyes in the mirror opposite, not wanting to see the flush of awareness he obviously read like a neon sign.

"That bothers you, doesn't it?" he mocked. "That you're attracted to more than my fat wallet?"

"What wallet?" she scoffed, ducking an admission that she was reacting to anything. "All I heard was an offer for one night in exchange for what, one more day here? You said I was selling myself short earlier. Surely a man in your position could do better than that."

Her words didn't take him aback, only provoked a disparaging smile. "You want the penthouse."

"I didn't say that," she protested.

"Good, because the sale closes tomorrow."

Her insides roiled. She really was homeless. She didn't let him see her distress, only blurted, "You work fast."

"Believe it."

Her belly tightened at the resolute way he said it, and

quivered even more when she saw the gleam of owner-ship in his eye.

"Well," she breathed. "I can hardly ask you to share this bed if you can't arrange for me to stay in it, can I? Pity." Her false smile punctuated her sarcasm.

"I'll provide you a bed. One that's bigger and…sturdier."

A jolt of surprise zinged all the way to the soles of her feet. He wasn't supposed to take this seriously. *She* wasn't.

She clenched her hand around the edge of the laundry basket as if it were a lifeline that would lift her out of this conversation, but for some stupid reason, her gaze dropped to his open collar where a few dark hairs lay against his collarbone. She imagined he was statue perfect under that crisp fabric, with sharply defined pecs and a six-pack of abs. His hips—

Good grief, she'd never looked at a man's crotch in her life. She jerked her gaze away, mind imprinted with a hint of tented steel-gray trousers. She blushed hard and it was mortifying, especially when she heard him chuckle.

"I don't even know you," she choked, wanting it to be a pithy rejection, but it was more a desperate reminder to herself that this was wrong. She shouldn't be the least bit interested in him.

"Not to worry, *maya zalataya*. I know you."

That yanked her attention back to him and his su-premely confident smirk.

"You're waiting for me to meet your price. Let's get there," he said implacably.

"That's so offensive I can't even respond."

"It's realistic. If you were looking for love, you wouldn't be living off an old man, allowing people to think you be-long to him. I don't need hearts and flowers either, but I like having a woman in my bed."

"Your charm hasn't landed you one?"

He shrugged off her scorn. "I'm between lovers. The takeover has kept me busy. Now I'm tallying up my acquisitions, preparing to enjoy the spoils."

"Well, I don't happen to come with this particular acquisition." She kneed the side of the mattress. "I didn't have to share this bed to sleep in it and I had a paycheck besides. Don't throw that look at me!" she snapped, hackles rising when he curled his lip. "Victor was going to underwrite the foundation, and it—"

"By how much?" he broke in.

"Pardon?"

"How much was he going to donate toward 'brightening your day'?"

"He— You— Oh…" She ground her teeth, glaring at his impassive expression. Planting her hands on her hips, she stood tall and said clearly, "Ten." That ought to make him realize how seriously Brighter Days had been taken.

"Million?" His eyebrows shot toward his hairline.

"Thousand," she corrected, startled. She could dream of having millions at her disposal, but Victor's promised funds would have been enough to keep the doors of the home open until she raised more.

Aleksy removed his mobile from his pocket. "You do sell yourself short. We'll add a zero to that and call it a deal."

"What?" she squeaked, but he was already connecting to someone, speaking Russian, then switching to English.

"Daniels, yes. You have her details through payroll? Perfect." He ended the call.

"What did you just do?" she gasped.

"The transfer will complete in the morning." He pushed his mobile back into his pocket. "Come here, Clair."

She stayed where she was, aghast. Infuriated. Was it

wrong to be dazzled and elated, as well? Oh, what she could do at Brighter Days with a hundred thousand pounds!

"That's—" She cleared her throat, recalling he was under the impression he'd just bought her. Her stomach turned over, except…well, it wasn't with the repulsion she expected. It was like peaking on a roller-coaster track and feeling the car drop away while she hung suspended and breathless. She bottomed out quickly, though, rattled by the way the world began whirring by as the situation picked up speed. She didn't know which way was up. She wanted off.

"That's a very generous donation," she choked, blindly scrabbling up her folded T-shirt. She snapped it out and creased it into a messy rectangle against the bedspread. "I'll issue a proper receipt for the full amount after I've moved it into the trust account."

"Do whatever you want with it. It's yours. Now let's find more pleasant surroundings. I'll send someone to finish packing your things."

"The transfer hasn't cleared." Terror provided the quick retort, but it felt incredibly good to lob it at him. Better than revealing how thoroughly he mixed her up. "And given that you repulse me—"

"Do I?" He launched from his lazy slouch in the doorway. She only had time for one backward stumbling step before he'd clamped hard arms around her, pulled her into the wall of his chest, then crushed her mouth with his.

Claw his eyes out, she told herself, but aside from the fact that her arms were trapped between them, the sensation of his mouth closing on hers was too remarkable to reject. He was domineering and inexorable, but this wasn't punishment or force; it was—

Hot. Sexy. Enticing. She instinctively parted her lips under the angle of his firm ones, and his tongue speared wetly into her mouth, shooting such a jolt of pleasure through her that her knees buckled. She moaned and lifted her chin, seeking another thrust and another. Rocking her mouth against his and moaning again when his hand moved to her bottom, crushing her against the hard ridge at his hips.

It was unfamiliar and overwhelming, but she wanted to cry, it felt so good to be wrapped in strong arms, mind blinded to all but the pleasure flaring up from her abdomen, filling her with a blossoming sense of rightness. She didn't know she was moaning with gratification until he drew away and she heard her own mewl of distress.

With a final nip of his teeth over her swollen lips, he released her, letting her crumple with dazed clumsiness onto the bed's pillows.

He made an adjustment to himself, his stature powerful as a warrior's, his harsh breath moving through parted lips, the grim line softened by the sheen of their kiss. "We can wait until morning if you really want to play hard to get, but I don't think you do."

"I do," she gasped, struggling to sit up. The laundry basket tumbled off the narrow bed, dumping all her packing onto the carpet at his feet. "I don't sleep with men for money. I'll transfer the money right back to you. You can't force me into bed with you."

"I don't have to," he said on a snort, shoulders pinned back in a hard flex. "You just proved you want to." He paused to let her absorb what she couldn't deny.

An awful telltale heat suffused her, making her dig her fingernails into the edge of the mattress. It was true, she wasn't immune to him. He kept effortlessly brushing past the invisible shield that usually protected her and branding himself against her core.

"So what if I do? My instincts are warning me that it

would be a bad idea," she told him, holding his gaze and trying to listen to those instincts even as everything in her reached longingly toward him. She could barely think of anything but sating this unfamiliar hunger when he looked at her as if he wanted to flatten her onto the bed and finish what he'd started. Her breath stuttered and her nipples contracted to tight, painful points. All of her felt magnetized toward him, but she stayed put, maintaining the distance.

Something flashed in his eyes. Frustration maybe, but it had a flicker of desperation that quickly dissolved into triumph. "And of course there's your reputation. Wouldn't you like to preserve that?"

She frowned. "Sleeping with you would ruin it!" Her voice came out throaty and oddly tinged with anticipation. She was struggling for logic, but all she could wonder was, how would it feel to have him on top of her? Inside her? An earthy part of her desperately wanted to know. No one had ever made her feel so much, and the feelings weren't emotional and painful, but physical and exciting. Thrilling. Her lips were still burning, aching for the return of his.

She didn't even know him.

But she wanted to. From the second he'd stepped off the elevator, she'd been wondering who he was. Her online search had turned up dry details about his business interests, nothing about his background. Where had he come from, besides the biggest country in the world? Why had he singled her out? Why did she react to him like this?

"You read the memo," he said, interrupting her thoughts with grating flatness. "A full investigation has been launched at the firm. Anyone found to have colluded with Victor's illegal activities will be terminated. I expect more than a few rats to jump ship before they're fired."

It took a moment for his statement to penetrate. She knew she wasn't a rat, so she hadn't been frightened. Until now. "I didn't know what he was up to," she reminded him, experiencing the stabbing sense of being falsely accused. "You don't think people will say I was fired because— I would never take what I didn't earn!"

"Says the woman who just accepted a hundred thousand pounds for a charity that doesn't exist."

"I didn't ask for that!" She scrambled to her feet. "You'll never prove any wrongdoing on my part."

"Nevertheless, you've been sacked. People will draw their own conclusions. Something you're comfortable with, I believe?"

"That was different! And if I slept with you after seeming to be with Victor, I'd look like—" The biggest gold digger in the world. Her heart plummeted.

"Better to be called what you are than presumed a criminal. I'm well known for drawing a hard line against cheaters and thieves. I wouldn't have one in my bed, and the world knows it. Sleeping with me would clear your name, whereas walking away would heighten speculation. I don't think you'd find another patron after that. Not one able to keep you in the style to which you've grown accustomed."

She wouldn't find a job frying chips with rumors of lawbreaking dogging her. "*You* could clear my name! You only have to speak up."

"Make it worth my while," he countered, not bothering to hide his superior enjoyment at having her exactly where he wanted her. He really was conscienceless.

"Why are you backing me into a corner like this?"

"Why are you fighting me when you know you'll enjoy it?"

"*You* won't," she blurted, shoulders hunching. Her appalling lack of experience would bore him out of his skull before the first act was over.

Triumph flashed in his eyes and a satisfied smile drew

the corners of his mouth back, revealing a wolfish grin. "I have no problem communicating what I like, and you seem receptive. We'll do fine together," he assured her.

She folded her arms, fingers plucking self-consciously at the cables knit into her sleeves. The thought of his laughing at her for being a virgin didn't appeal, but she had to tell him. "Look, I'm not…what you think I am."

"What I think," he said, nudging aside a pile of tumbled clothing as he stepped closer, "is that you're something Victor wanted." He clasped her arms above her bent elbows, gently straining them backward so her breasts arched into his muscled chest.

She gasped, stiffening in shock, hands splaying over the ridges of his ribs, fingertips unconsciously moving to trace the powerful cage beneath warm fabric. Rivulets of heat poured through her taut abdomen to a place where need pooled, making her flesh tingle and ache to be touched. "Wh-what?"

"Victor couldn't have you and that means I must. Do you have a passport?"

She couldn't think when he touched her, but couldn't draw away, trapped by his strength and her own weakness. But he was talking as if she were mere spoils of war.

"Did you travel with him?" he asked with exaggerated patience.

"I was supposed to, but he died before I went anywhere. Go back to that bit about why you…" She couldn't bring herself to say "want" when it sounded as though the sexual attraction drowning her wasn't affecting him. She shivered in a hot-cold shudder of uneasiness while blood rushed under her skin, flushing warmth into her chest, making her breasts feel swollen and sensitized. Her hips longed to press into his, seeking the hard length that had nudged her when they kissed.

He knew what he was doing to her. A smug gleam lit his narrowed eyes as his gaze dropped to her lips. He started to lower his head.

Jerking hers back, she gasped, "I haven't agreed." But did she really want to step onto the street at midnight with her meager possessions and become one of the homeless? Her few shallow friendships were all with people she worked with. They wouldn't take her in for fear of losing their jobs. She didn't have a cushion of savings, just a credit card she couldn't pay off if she didn't have an income.

The direness of her situation began to hit home. At least this afternoon she'd been sure she could find some kind of menial work, but not now. Any character reference out of the firm after today would be career-stoppingly negative. Flicking a look from his set jaw to his penetrating eyes, she whispered, "You're a real piece of work, you know that?"

"I lost my redeeming qualities years ago," he agreed, something dark flickering in his gaze. "Which means there's no appealing to my better nature. Make this easy on both of us and give in, Clair."

She was tempted to. She didn't have anything to lose and no one to answer to while he was dangling—what? A night? A reprieve at any rate, one that advertised a fringe benefit of physical satiation she had never expected to want. The emptiness of a one-night stand was, well, empty enough to make her ache, but she wasn't in the market for a real relationship, so…

"Why extend your takeover to include me?" she asked in a voice more husky than the disparagement she was aiming for. "Didn't you get enough out of scooping up the firm from a dead man?"

"He was still alive when I started proceedings and no, I didn't get anything near what I wanted. Don't make out like you're some kind of prey just because you're used to being the predator. You get to keep the money," he taunted softly.

"No matter what?" The jerky toss of her head was supposed to convey brash confidence. The question was real, though. She couldn't help being seduced by the prospect of running the foundation her way, without needing approval on every detail. Without having to reveal that each of those details touched her personally and that was why she was fighting so hard for them. "I'm not into anything kinky," she warned. "If you're looking for someone to spank you, move along to the next girl in the secretarial pool."

"I'm not the submissive in any relationship," he assured her dryly. "I like straight sex and lots of it. I don't hurt women, ever, if that's what you're dancing around asking. I might play with dominating one, controlling her…" He flexed his hands on her elbows, making her breasts press into his chest.

Excitement returned with a spear of pleasure straight into her loins. She gasped.

"If she likes it," he murmured.

She struggled, but he held fast and to her chagrin the short tussle only caused her heated desire to kindle into a shivery anticipation. His vital strength was incredibly sexy and she must have had a kinky strand after all if she responded to having pleasure forced upon her. No guilt, she supposed.

"Too bad the money hasn't cleared," she said with breathless regret. "Go back to your own suite. I'll talk to you tomorrow." After she'd had time to talk herself out of the rash agreement she was considering.

He slowly let his hands release her, his fingertips oh so slightly brushing the sides of her breasts, making need pierce her belly and leaving her shuddering with longing.

"So you can disappear with my money? I don't think

so. Van Eych might have been teased into giving without
return, but I don't tolerate cheats or thieves. Fetch your
passport and we'll take whatever you've left in that case.
I have properties around the world. Lady's choice where
we go, but by the time we land, you'll have your money
and then—" He skimmed a proprietorial glance over her.
"I'll have you."

CHAPTER FOUR

"I'M LOSING MY home at midnight," her soft lips pronounced before tensing with acrimony. "I need to pack. Traveling will have to wait." There wasn't an ounce of self-preservation in her as she matter-of-factly righted the laundry basket and heaped the tumbled clothing into it.

"Don't test me, Clair. I'm not nice."

She straightened with a flushed face, all out aggression blasting at him in a way that had him planting his feet.

"What do you want me to do? Leave my things for the new owners to throw in the trash? Exactly how much do you want from me besides my job, my home and—" She clamped her lips over whatever else she almost said. Her mouth trembled briefly and for a moment there was a cast of startling defenselessness to her.

It was gone before unease could take a proper hold on him, hidden by the shift of her body away from him. Her stiff shoulders were proud. "You're the one who sold this place out from under me. Stop complaining that it's cutting into your plans."

She was acting like an amateur.

Aleksy narrowed his eyes on her back, always aware when women were trying to manipulate him and occasionally willing to allow it when it suited his end purpose: primarily to get the physical release his body required. If

Clair was attempting to wring guilt out of him, she was being predictable and hopelessly misguided. If she didn't appreciate how powerful and absent of empathy he was, he'd demonstrate.

With one call—in English so she'd understand it—he swept away her stall tactic.

"The brawny and coldly efficient Lazlo again?" she asked without turning.

"He's enlisting a young man you might know. Stuart from accounting? He's proving to be extremely cooperative. A stickler for procedure. Stuart will make an inventory of your property and put it in storage at my expense."

"Stuart from accounting wants to paw through my underpants drawer? And run back to the office with what he found in my medicine chest?"

"Not if he intends to keep his job." Aleksy didn't like the way she paled and liked even less the thought of some flunky fondling her undergarments. His hands tingled to cradle her in reassurance. He shook off the unfamiliar urge. "Gather your personal things if it will put an end to this delay," he muttered. "You have one hour."

In the end she chose Paris, but not for the reason he thought.

"The city of lovers," he'd said ironically, the timbre of his voice stirring her blood. "Of course. A perfect weekend retreat."

Weekend. The word punched low, gushing delicious heat through her abdomen.

She shook off the reaction and bit back an explanation that she'd picked Paris because she could get home on her own steam if she had to. Not that she had a home to come back to, but flying back to London from Cairo or Vancouver or Sydney would destroy her shallow savings.

As they traveled, she focused on budgeting for a new flat and where she'd start looking for a job so she wouldn't recall the way Stuart's Adam's apple had bobbled when he found Aleksy in her flat.

Aleksy had curved a possessive hand against the back of her neck and said, "I don't date my employees. Clair is no longer with the firm."

Clair had lifted a disillusioned *Could you be more blunt?* expression to him.

Aleksy had quirked his split brow in a *Want me to be?*

She'd left without saying a word, her guilty blush burning her cheeks, aware that he'd sealed her fate. Her reputation as a tart was solidified and *so* much better than criminal. That made her squirm, but she'd learned to shield herself against judgment long ago. No, it was the way he'd gotten into her head so easily that really disturbed her. It made her feel vulnerable.

"Clair."

His touch turned her from staring out the car window, once again opening that invisible gateway through her defenses. His intense personality whirled into her psyche like a restless summer wind, scattering her thoughts and inducing an instant, fluttering sensuality that reached toward everything in him.

"We're here."

The lights of Paris came to sparkling life around her. The scent of rain-damp streets smelled promisingly fresh as he left the car. The strength in his hand as he took hers to help her exit made her heart trip in a nervous rhythm against her breastbone.

She paused as he steered her toward a building, turning her face up to the sprinkling black sky to take in the facade of elegantly lit stone. It wasn't a towering structure of glass and steel, but an old-world walk-up with wrought-iron balconies and planter boxes already blooming with spring. "This is very—" *charming*, she almost said "—nice."

"It's a good investment," he dismissed.

The statement chilled her. "If you're so keen on good investments, why did I hear you dumping all of Victor's properties?" He'd been positively ruthless, speaking harshly into his mobile as she'd moved through the flat collecting her few sentimental items. He hadn't taken any losses that she could discern, but he hadn't seemed concerned with making huge profits either. "I'm sure his family would have kept what you didn't want."

"His sons kept enough," he said bluntly, pausing on the top landing to open a door by punching a code into the security pad. "I left them their homes because they have innocent wives and children, but they knew enough about how their father made his fortune that they didn't fight my takeover. I didn't have the evidence to prove Van Eych's crimes until the firm's accounting books were in my hands. Now the truth will come out and his sons will change their names to escape any connection to him."

His mouth curled into a cruel smile as he held the door for her.

Foreboding crawled through her veins. "You think it's funny to cause the severing of family ties?" Everything in her castaway upbringing was appalled.

"Funny? No. Justified? Yes."

She stepped into a room lit with intimate golden pools, but she didn't take it in, too caught up with looking for a crack of humanity in his unyielding expression. Until now she hadn't worried what would happen to her, aware only that if she walked away from Aleksy's money, she'd always cringe with regret. Orphaned children needed a voice and it wasn't as if she could find support for the foundation elsewhere. Victor was gone and who else would sponsor it if rumors started up that its founder had been in collusion with a white-collar criminal? No, if she didn't do this, the foundation was history, but reality hit as the door clicked shut behind them, loud and symbolic.

Aleksy Dmitriev was a hard man. Not cruel; she believed him when he said he didn't hurt women. He'd already demonstrated that he held himself to specific, sharply defined ethics. But he wasn't merely detached like her. She deflected emotions, but he didn't feel them at all. That made something catch in her. Apprehension, but empathy too. What had made him so devoid of a heart? Had he ever had one?

Did it matter? She belonged to him regardless.

Her heart sank, taking her last chance of protest with it, leaving her feeling naked and defenseless. *You're not naked yet,* a lethal voice whispered in her head.

"Dine out or in?" he asked, his accent raspy on her sensitized nerves.

Her breath stuttered and she struggled to catch it, not realizing she'd been holding it. Part of her would rather get the main event over with. It was late enough she was growing tired, but she was also wide-awake with nervous anticipation.

His nearness, the power of his intense glance, stole her voice. His hair had flattened into a dark helmet under the light rain. A shadow had grown in on his square jaw, accentuating everything male in him. She was ridiculously weakened by the sight. Her gaze should have been flashing a back off. Instead she studied his mouth, recalling the feel of those full lips moving with erotic control over hers. Her fingertips itched to trace the smooth curves that were uncompromisingly masculine, yet wickedly sexy.

"This stubble will burn if I kiss you the way you're begging me to," he said in a growled voice that slammed her back to reality.

"I—" She strangled on denial, mortified enough to jerk out of his hypnotizing aura and move across the room.

"I'll shower and shave. You put on one of those cocktail dresses you asked me if you should bring. I want to see your legs."

She threw him a livid glare, but he disappeared down a hall. What did she have to be angry about anyway? She'd sold herself into his control, hadn't she?

Clair gripped her elbows, hanging on to her composure with bruising tightness, taking in her surroundings to turn her mind from her precarious situation. The lounge was enormous, tiled in marble and divided into sections with area rugs and attractively arranged furniture. Everything was decidedly masculine, the writing desk set in the corner surrounded by enough space to accommodate its charismatic owner. The rest of the flat took up the entire top floor of the building, incorporating half a dozen smaller flats into a single sprawling living space that one man couldn't possibly need.

She had thought Victor obscenely wealthy. She shook her head, reminding herself that the real test of a person's class came from his character, not his possessions. Problem was, Aleksy guarded himself even more closely than she did. She wondered what kind of man lurked beneath that polished granite exterior. One who would laugh her to the curb when he realized what a novice she was?

Stop it. Steadying her knees and pulling her shoulders back, she resolved not to be intimidated. He could laugh all he wanted, but she had her own principles: loyalty, a debt of gratitude and a personal honor that demanded she live up to her word.

She was terrified, but she'd sleep with him because she'd said she would.

Her luggage was gone from his room when he emerged from his shower.

It was an unexpected slap in the face for Aleksy. Women never rejected him. Given the math Clair had scratched into a notebook on the plane, he had considered their deal more than sealed; was she now trying to get out of it?

Snatching up his mobile, wearing only a towel, he strode from the bedroom to the empty lounge. Down at the far end of the flat, as far as she could get from his master bedroom, the door was shut. He pushed through it, noted her open suitcase on the bed and heard the hair dryer click on in the bathroom.

The release of tension in him was profound—and aggravating.

Get a grip, he ordered himself as he returned to his room. She was only a woman, the same as all the others he'd taken into his bed. Yes, there was a certain satisfaction in claiming what Victor had wanted, but Aleksy had been patient enough to hunt that man down over two decades. He ought to be capable of waiting a few more hours for this final conquest.

The short flight to Paris had been unbearable, though, the drive from the airport eternal. She'd been quiet, almost as if trying to hold herself behind an invisible shell, while his senses had been homed onto her presence, for once hungry to learn about his partner, but he hadn't wanted to reveal his curiosity.

He didn't want to feel it. She shouldn't be drawing him in this strongly.

When she'd turned that look of longing on him after they arrived in the flat, it had taken everything in him to keep from leaping on her. Whether it had been a tease or real, he had ached to accept her invitation like nothing he'd ever wanted, even his lifetime of revenge. He'd controlled himself because any weakness for women had always been a distraction he couldn't afford. He wouldn't let a habit of a lifetime click off like a switch, but he'd been near panting in London when she'd thrown down her condition that the money had to clear.

His saving grace had been that she had been panting too; it was affecting him. The women he usually went for enjoyed sex, but with Clair the chemistry was notched to maximum. She might have an agenda, but her desire was interfering with it. It was an unbelievable turn-on; it enthralled him.

Surely once he'd had her the mystique would dissolve though. It had to. This obsessiveness was intolerable.

He stepped into black jeans and tugged on a light gray pullover, returning to the lounge, where he made a few calls while pacing off his restlessness, mercilessly tying off his need as he waited for staff from a nearby restaurant.

As he waited for Clair.

Clair forced one foot in front of the other and stepped into the lounge, tensed for the impact of Aleksy's inspection. He was on the phone, his face and body in quarter profile.

She had expected one of his disturbingly penetrating looks, but found herself doing the appraisal, going weak as she took in the length of his back and the way his jeans hugged the shape of his backside and outlined his muscled thighs. He stood with his long legs braced and shrugged a shoulder, drawing her attention to the powerful layers of muscles bulging beneath the wool. She imagined exploring light fingers over the textures of cashmere, swarthy neck and short, damp hair and had to strangle a moan of longing.

He finished his call and turned to strip her deep purple slip dress with hungry eyes. It was the same look he'd given her this morning, just as carnal and without the safety net of an office full of people to prevent him acting on his desires.

The assessment acted exactly as powerfully on her, pinning her feet to the floor and making her realize that for all her rationalizations about helping orphaned children, the real reason she was here was this: she wanted to be with him. It was a frightening admission after a lifetime of convincing herself she didn't want or need anyone.

"Lovely," he said, languidly climbing his appreciative gaze from her exposed knees to her carefully composed expression.

Her stomach contracted under the impact of his undisguised sexual intention.

"Victor liked it." She didn't know why she said it. Perhaps to keep him from guessing how utterly he held her in thrall, but it had a glacial effect on him.

He narrowed his eyes and said chillingly, "Be very careful about throwing his name at me, Clair."

Uneasiness wafted over her along with confusion. She had pushed that "spoils of war" unpleasantness to the back of her mind, but it came flooding forward now.

A knock on the door kept her silent.

He opened it to uniformed staff. They turned one end of the dining table into an intimate candlelit cove, setting out covered plates and pouring wine. Soft music came on and fragrant flowers complemented scents of orange sauce and rich braised duck.

Unsteady in her heels, Clair moved forward to the

chair Aleksy held for her, trying to frame her suspicion in a way that didn't demean her any further than she already was.

When they were alone, she cleared her throat. "You said earlier—" Was it only a few hours ago they'd stood in her flat setting out terms for this arrangement? What was she *doing!* "You said that you'd been targeting the firm for some time. Victor was under considerable stress leading up to his heart attack. Was that from the takeover?"

The implication behind her simple question crashed and reverberated in Aleksy's head, as swift and unexpected as the knife that had cut the line into his face. A dark maelstrom of emotion threatened, the kind he hadn't allowed himself in years. He fought it back, master of everything he felt or didn't feel, but it shocked him that she'd almost pulled something out of him that he no longer allowed. Chagrin. Loss. Rage.

"Are you accusing me of murdering him? Intentionally?" He was able to keep his tone impersonal, but she didn't mistake the threat beneath. She paled.

"N-no." Her voice was weak.

"Because I've been targeted for takeovers many times. It never raises my blood pressure. Van Eych knew what was coming and may have grown hypertensive, but that's because he didn't take care of himself. He lived as if an overweight, sedentary lifestyle would never catch up to him." His entire body ached with tension.

"I know. I told him—"

"I don't want to hear what you told him," he snapped with a slip of control that made her jump. "I know more about the man than I ever wanted to. Now I want to forget him. I want his entire existence obliterated."

He was revealing more than he intended to, but it would put an end to any more infuriating remarks regarding Victor. He glared at the elegantly simple dress that showed her delicate curves to perfection, offended that Victor had paid for it, that anything about the man had ever come in contact with her.

She sat primly, cowed by his temper into holding her hands in her lap, her spine straight, her eyes downcast. He didn't apologize; he wanted the message driven home that this topic would never be revisited again.

"Well," she said with quiet impertinence. "That certainly answers the question I was really asking, which was whether you had a grudge against Victor."

"A grudge?" Aleksy choked on the inadequacy of the word, but what did you call it when you knew a man was responsible for your father's death? For your mother's slow, painful decline? For your own self-destruction? He swept his clogged throat clean with a swallow of wine, suppressing anguished thoughts. "Yes, Clair, I had a grudge."

Aleksy's posture was casual, but his stillness spoke of extreme tension. There was nothing to be read in his expression beyond the startling prominence of his scar.

Clair realized she needed to tread softly, but she had to ask, "Why?"

"He knew. That's all that's important."

"Not to me," she protested.

The corner of his lip quirked. She realized he knew what was really bothering her. "You struck the deal you wanted. Do you hear me asking why it was important to you?"

He'd already made it pretty clear he didn't care about her motivation. This was commerce, not romance, but the worry drilling a hole in the pit of her stomach was that he didn't really want her. Obviously he was attracted to her to some degree, but she didn't want to be a *thing*. She wanted her first sexual experience to at least be sensual, not a twelve-point inspection and a stamp on the windshield. What happened when she turned out to be less than the high-performance ride he was used to?

"I just want to understand. You didn't want anything to do with me when you thought I'd been sleeping with Victor, but when you learned I hadn't, you coerced me into this arrangement. If you're on a mission to collect all of Victor's possessions, why count me among them? And why sell them off as quickly as you acquired them?"

His jaw hardened at the word *coerced*, but he only said bluntly, "To dismantle what he built. To expunge his mark on the world."

"Well, I won't let you dismantle me." She grew hot. "I wasn't his. You don't get to erase *me*."

"He thought you were his," he shot back. "You let the world think you were."

"It doesn't mean you can treat me like—"

"Property?" Bracing his elbows, he leaned forward so she had to jerk back. "Why do you care? You got what you wanted. I'll get what I want. There's no conflict."

There was, but apparently only to her.

Drawing a deep breath, she picked up her fork and said stiffly, "Just so I'm clear…You don't care whether the things you've acquired are to your taste. You only want to hold them long enough to devalue and unload them?" Looking him in the eye was an act of supreme courage, especially since it made him bare his teeth in an uncivilized grin.

"You get to keep the money, Clair. You'll walk away satisfied that your bottom line has benefited, I promise. Now let's change the subject."

"I think you just did," she muttered, staring at food she had no appetite for as she tried to sift through the mixed emotions of being physically infatuated with a man who promised to give her pleasure while only taking a cold helping of revenge for himself.

His attitude hurt her and she didn't want him to have that power. She wanted to be unaffected and remote, the way he was.

"Did I?" he responded with throwaway sarcasm.

"Yes, you did." She set down her fork with a clatter. Trying to eat was pointless when she was so consumed with nerves. She could sit here waiting out the minutes until his stupid money came through, trying to reimagine this into something more meaningful than it would ever be, or she could have sex with him and be done with it. It didn't matter if he didn't feel anything, she told herself. She had always preferred superficial connections over something deeper. Right?

Right?

"Let's do it now," she decided shakily.

Her statement arrested him. "Why the sudden change of heart?" he asked, narrowing his eyes.

Her pulse raced, but she ignored it, determined to be as *cool* and impervious as the women he was no doubt used to. "Because unlike an island villa or a vintage car, which have no say in life, I am a human being capable of making a choice. I want to complete this transaction so I can move on."

She rose and left the table, heading toward his room without looking back, unable to hear if he followed because her ears filled with a whooshing sound. Her whole body trembled. She halted when she saw the intimidating expanse of his bed.

What was she doing? A cold chill of doubt washed through her. She couldn't be so casual about stripping naked and letting a man into her body.

Fingertips grazed her spine, making her flinch. He lowered the zip of her dress before she clutched at the drooping front, panic whirling her to face him.

He scooped her to his chest, trapping her arms between them as his mouth captured hers. One hand streaked from her waist to slide beneath her elbow, where he cupped and firmly massaged her breast.

The dual sensations of fierce kiss and possessive, intimate touch hammered her with a pulse of pleasure so strong it frightened her. The situation was not just flying but exploding out of her control. She jerked her head to the side, gasping for breath, and pressed with her forearms for distance.

"You're going too fast!"

CHAPTER FIVE

HER WORDS RESULTED in a loaded silence.

She used it to gather her composure, shocked by how easily he'd stripped her of it with one soul-stealing kiss. *Compartmentalize,* she urged herself, but it was impossible when the heat of his body melted her bones and his hands flexed restlessly against her back. She had to slow him down or he'd own her completely.

Trying to hide how unnerved she was by her response, she forced herself to meet his gaze. His expression was flushed, his eyes glittering with suspicion.

"A minute ago, I wasn't moving fast enough," he growled.

Her chin automatically came forward, even though challenging him was probably the stupidest thing she could do. "A girl still wants to be seduced." It was the only thing she could think to say.

"Does she?" he asked in a tone that made her belly tremor. He held her chin and stared at her. "Or does she want to see how far she can push a man?"

"I'm not—" She tried to swallow through a dry throat. "I'm not going to back out," she whispered. "I just want a slower pace. Is that so unreasonable?" She wished she had enough experience to know exactly what kind of mistake she was making.

"Are you attempting to keep it interesting or afraid of losing control?"

His guess, so accurate, sent a startled pulse through her. Unable to control how the world treated her, she instead controlled how deeply she felt the ebbs and flows of life—but she definitely couldn't control the way she reacted to him. That terrified her.

He touched her lips. The tickling graze of his fingertip made her mouth quiver. "Tell me when you want me to kiss you, then," he taunted gruffly.

Now. She couldn't deny that she wanted his mouth. And she wanted to make a go of the foundation. If she kept that in mind, maybe she could get through this without giving up too much of herself.

"N-now." The quaver in her voice reflected her inner turmoil.

"Now?" He plucked at her bottom lip.

"Yes. But just a kiss," she cautioned, then added, "Please."

He chuckled in a way that sounded bitter and trailed his calloused fingers along her jaw, into her hair, gently threading his hand into her loose tresses as he tilted her head back.

"Since you said please…" He stepped closer and brushed a light kiss onto her neck.

She shivered as his lips moved under her jaw and up her cheek to her temple.

It was lovely, but she felt unsteady. She set her hands on his hard chest to ground herself, eyes involuntarily closing as she appreciated the patience he was showing, touching butterfly kisses all over her face, pressing the corner of her mouth and drifting away. Giving her the time to absorb each caress, the flutter of reaction it raised, and even anticipate the next.

Before she realized what she was doing, she unconsciously tried to follow him for a real kiss. His grip in her hair made turning her face impossible. The next time his heated breath flowed over her lips, she parted her own in invitation, but he left again. A whimper of dismay escaped her and she realized with a sting of uneasiness that she wasn't setting the pace at all. He was in control.

She ran restless hands over his chest. It was unfamiliar but thrilling. Hard muscle rippled with power beneath soft cashmere as she tried unsuccessfully to convey what she wanted from him.

"Aleksy." That throaty tone did not belong to her.

"Do you want my mouth on yours?" he asked in a husky growl.

She did. For all her misgivings and apprehensions, her lips were hot and sensitized, the waiting unbearable. "Yes."

He rubbed her lips lightly with his own.

A needy ache gathered hotly between her thighs. "More," she breathed.

"Show me what you want," he commanded.

A frustrated sound escaped her. She didn't know! Or did she? She wanted a proper, openmouthed, hot, swirling kiss. As crazy as it sounded, she craved the mindlessness he inflicted on her.

Lifting, she tried to show him, crushing her swollen, aching mouth against his, clinging with her lips and delicately invading with the tip of her tongue.

He stiffened.

She was doing it wrong. Failure and rejection instantly loomed, even more horrifying than the swamp of sexual excitement. She instinctively tried to pull away, but his arm tightened and she felt the answering lick of his tongue against hers. A bolt of sweet lightning flashed through her, a fierce relief followed by a warning of a storm.

She stilled, tried to pull herself together, but he boldly

took possession of her the way she yearned for, sealing their damp lips in a tight fit and thrusting his tongue against hers, spiraling her into the exciting world he seemed determined to pull her into.

Of their own volition, her hands crept up his shoulders, linking behind his neck to draw him down, encouraging him by diving her fingers into his short hair.

His arm stayed locked across her back, but he wasn't pressing her into him. She did that, not even realizing she was doing it until she felt herself plastered against him. Her dress was open, she realized, but she didn't care. Her body badly needed the pressure of his chest against breasts that seemed to swell and reach toward him, aching. A moan of longing escaped her.

"What do you want? This?" He drew one of her arms down and slid her hand beneath the soft knit, guiding her touch up his hot chest.

Startled by this new realm, she explored with rapt intrigue. His skin was like sunbaked satin, his chest hair flat and softly abrasive, his nipple small and pebble sharp against her curious fingertips. She splayed her hand, petting, fascinated, and learned quickly when he taught her the pressure he liked. She circled and flicked, feeling him jerk. Wrong again?

His arm at her back pinched her closer. "Do you want me to do that to you?" His head dipped and he caught her earlobe between his lips, sucking and sending a shocking streak of pure excitement flashing into her loins. "This too?"

She groaned at the thought of his mouth on her breast and curled her fingers against his chest, raking his nipple lightly with her fingernail. *"Yes."*

His breath hissed in. "Take off your dress, then," he ground out, loosening his hold on her and backing away.

Shaking, she dragged her hand free, grazing his abdomen on the way, feeling his stomach contract beneath her touch. He was remarkable. This state was remarkable, feeling all hot and fascinated. *Alive*.

It struck her that he would forever hold a place in her memory for this. The indelible connection was already bittersweet enough to make the backs of her eyes sting. Part of her screamed, *Run away*. The bond was temporary and would hurt to break, but she craved it all the same. Desperately. So much so that she found herself nudging the straps of her dress off her shoulders. They fell down her arms and warm silk dropped into a dark puddle over her shoes.

She was naked but for her bra, underpants and hose, all black but built for function. Her palms shyly covered the clasp between her breasts, forearms shielding the small, pale swells that peeped over the cups.

"Ask me for help with it," he said.

"I—" It wasn't that she couldn't open it. It was how real this was becoming. What if she wasn't enough for him, even for a night?

He commanded her with a look, wanting to gaze on her nude body, do things to it. The unknown scared her, but the thought of stopping was equally frightening. She couldn't move, caught in a trembling paralysis.

He stepped close and sure fingers brushed past nerveless ones. The cups released and her neck went weak. She dropped her forehead onto his chest, aware of her bra skimming lightly over her shoulders and down her back. Her breasts were exposed to cool air while her back was branded by his hot palms. She covered herself with her crossed arms, lacking the confidence to step back and reveal herself.

"Sit on the bed." He curled a steadying hand under her elbow.

She complied because she would fall down if she didn't,

but sitting put her eye level with his fly and she wasn't ready to go that far even with a glance. She looked up at him, but he was no gentleman intending to kneel at her feet. He held a look of detached intensity. A roaring sound filled her ears, the kind that warned of danger. She had inadvertently entered into a power struggle with a man who could overwhelm her without effort, but he wasn't doing it like that. He was turning her against herself. Stoking a hunger that was stronger than her natural reserve.

She clung hard to her shields but sensed he would disarm her without even trying. As easily as he caught a hand behind her knee and stroked tantalizing fingers under her calf, carrying her foot up to his stomach, tipping her onto her back.

Her heart dipped in consternation, and then she squeaked in alarm as the position parted her knees. She shot a hand between her thighs, hypersensitive to where his gaze was traveling, so tangible it was like a physical caress.

Her shoes hit the floor, *thump, thump*, barely heard over the beat of her racing heart. He reached to stroke her knuckles where she protected her most intimate flesh, his touch so personal she almost jerked her hand away in surprise.

"Let me take off these at least." He moved his hand down her thigh, stroking the translucent hose. "You want to feel my hands on you, don't you?"

"Yes, but— You're not going to undress?"

"Eventually. When you're ready." He ran his hand up to the waistband, eyes glittering with challenge while his expression was one of merciless control.

Over her or himself?

Both.

Warring thoughts crashed inside her like storm waves. Apprehension at the reality of being stripped. A moral compulsion to keep her word and go through with this. An underlying weakness of pure want. Terror at the way self-control was slipping away.

He began to draw the hose down and she lifted her hips to help him, eyes closing in denial of what she was doing, but she couldn't ignore that only her panties remained. She hid them behind her palm, knees bent to the side and locked together, breath held as she tried to imagine what would come next. And then after that.

He stood over her assessing her, proud and commanding, all the power in his court. "Do you want me to join you?"

She blew out a breath of wild laughter at his taunt. He must know how badly she wanted him and was only making her ask for it to prove a point. If she could have revealed that she wasn't ready, she would have, but it was mortifying how much she wanted to feel him on top of her. "I do." Her voice broke in surrender.

"Make room, then. When you're ready," he added, raking her body with hot, hungry eyes.

She writhed in protest, wanting mastery over herself and wanting him. Rolling onto her back, she straightened her legs, forcing her hand to fall away from her mound, the other to lift off her chest. She'd never felt so vulnerable in her life.

He set heavy hands on either side of her waist and leaned over her, taking his time studying her breasts, making her breath hitch as she felt a need to shield herself again, but resisted it. She couldn't help watching his face with a timid need for approval. She wasn't voluptuous. Would she be enough to gratify him?

His expression grew tight as he looked her over. A shudder quaked across his shoulders and it was a long time before he finally met her searching gaze.

She couldn't hide how defenseless she felt, splayed before him.

"Nice," he said in guttural English.

Nice? Her stomach plummeted at the bland word. She wasn't even sure he meant it, but was distracted from questioning him when he grasped her wrists and slid her fists above her head. At the same time, he pressed a knee between hers and opened her legs, lowering himself onto her in a blanket of soft, crushing weight.

Clair moaned in startled delight under him, twisting against his grip, but Aleksy kept her firmly clasped.

If he allowed her to touch him right now, Aleksy thought, if he didn't have a barrier between his tight hide and her downy skin, he'd lose it. It had been all he could do to find an English word to describe how exquisite she was.

He forced himself to remember that she was toying with him, trying to win a power struggle he hadn't started, but was determined to win. Stroking his free hand down her arm, past her breast, over her hip and along her thigh, he curled her calf over his lower back, resenting the wool that kept him from feeling the caress of her skin against his own. He shifted and pressed his groin tight to hers, thin layers of cotton and denim between. She was utterly at his mercy and he took full advantage, rocking himself against her, wanting her to lose control before he did.

Acute arousal hued her cheeks and glazed her eyes. Her hips lifted to increase the pressure, almost sending him over the edge, but the helpless noise she made was worth the torture she was inflicting on him by drawing this out. He was winning, but barely.

Scorching excitement seared Clair's breath from her lungs as Aleksy teased her. She couldn't move, couldn't speak, could only whimper in ecstatic sufferance. She'd kept men at a distance all her life, feeling superior to other women because she hadn't believed men really offered this kind of pleasure. She'd never felt this susceptible, but she was caving now. Completely and utterly. Breathing in his aggressive male scent like a drug.

He cupped her bare breast, his palm hot and possessive. Once a month her breasts felt swollen like this, overfull and incredibly sensitive, but never this sweet. His heavy touch assuaged the ache and incited it. Her nipple grew painfully engorged, ripening under his hot stare like a cherry in the sun. He drew circles with his thumb, massaged and shaped the swell, traced the aureole and refused to give her what she wanted. What she instinctively needed.

"Aleksy, please," she begged.

He swooped like a hawk, his masculine groan muffling as he covered the tingling tip with his hot mouth. The erotic pull almost lifted her off the bed. Moist heat flooded into her sex, completely beyond her ability to rule it. All of her became a throbbing pulse of hot need. The power of the feelings daunted her, but she reveled in them at the same time, exalted by the sense of being purely woman. When he moved to her other breast, she arched to offer herself, unable to contain her ragged moan.

His hand caressed the back of her thigh, followed the sensitive inner skin to the leg of her underpants. A sure finger slinked beneath, stroking into folds that were slick and incredibly sensitive. She had thought she knew what her body was capable of, but his touch made her jerk her hips under the intensity of pleasure. The tremendous intimacy, his confidence, the way he pressed to sustain the tantalizing peak—

"Oh, Aleksy…" she moaned.

He skimmed his touch away. "You didn't ask for that, did you?" His eyes had gone black and inscrutable. The cruel curl at the edges of his mouth told her he wasn't as innocent as he was playing. "Do you want me to touch you? Or—" He hooked his elbow behind her knee, hitching her ankle onto his shoulder. "—kiss you?"

A fresh flood of craving poured into her loins. She instinctively tried to close her legs against the betraying reaction, but she met the resistance of his muscled back.

"Yes?" he murmured, touching a kiss to her breastbone, then lower. His hot mouth opened against her trembling belly, lightly biting before he applied suction in a delicate sting of healing. "Shall I remove your panties with my teeth?"

She couldn't be completely naked under him while he was fully clothed. She couldn't. "Take off your clothes first," she gasped.

He slowly pulled away, the retreat of his body a caress that drew out the pleasure and gave her plenty of time to appreciate the cooling pain of losing him. It also brought a moment of clarity. She realized her knee lay crooked open and her panties were wet. Her stomach quivered with tension, her nipples stood taut with arousal on breasts that rose and fell with her ragged breaths.

Inhibition was gone. She didn't care how she looked or behaved, only that he continue making love to her.

Aleksy strained under his self-imposed leash. His blazing arousal burned him alive and every male instinct in him screamed to possess her. *Begged to.*

She twisted her slim body, so graceful and beguiling he had to catch back a groan of pure need. Logical thoughts disappeared from his mind. All he knew was that she tasted like summer, smelled like nectarines and ran like warm honey under his touch. Hands and mouth weren't enough to sate him. His body needed to be inside hers. His erection throbbed harder and thicker than ever in his life, desperate to spear into her.

Her taunt about going too fast was the only thing that kept him standing over her, hiding his ravenous desire behind a stoic mask while her beautiful image slithered on the spread before him. She wanted to make him crazy and it was working, but he wouldn't give her the satisfaction of knowing it. He wouldn't show her any more mercy than she was showing him. She could play games, but he would drive her to a screaming pitch, erasing anything from her mind except the same imperative eating him alive.

"Aleksy?" Her languid eyes darkened with a moment of doubt.

He let a slow grin steer across his face, liking that she wasn't assured of her lead over him. "I was waiting for your command," he mocked, peeling his pullover up and off, tossing it to the floor. There was no relief from the sweat of arousal sheening his back and chest. A conflagration of desire continued to scorch from the pit of his gut to the back of his throat, prickling his skin. Demanding action.

"Oh…" Her weak sigh might have made his lips twist in cynical amusement. It was, after all, a sound he'd heard before when he stripped, but the way she licked her lips sent a rod of need through his hard flesh, swiping other women from his mind.

"What does that mean?" he growled, barely able to find his English. "Do this slower?" He peeled open his jeans, then forced his hands to stop. One fell away to his side; the other dipped two fingers into his pocket, bringing out the condom.

Something flickered in her gaze. Confusion. Recognition. Consternation?

"You don't want me completely naked, do you?" The thought of being uncovered for the first time in his life, in *her* was enough to make him need a moment to regroup. With thumbs hooked in his waistband, he fought a complete loss of control, eyes pinned to the wink and tremor of her navel.

How he wanted her.

"Naked but protected," she eventually said, as if she thought he'd been waiting for her answer. It sounded innocent, almost as if she wasn't confident he'd get there unless she requested it. Her voice made him shudder with hunger.

He would get there. Oh, yes. Definitely.

Carefully he eased his jeans and shorts off his hips, dropping them and kicking them away, forcing his hands to hang loose, revealing none of his excruciating tension as he straightened.

She studied him in a long, taut silence, something he allowed because he was going to look at her the same way very soon. Still, he grew unbearably hard and thick under her gaze. His skin would split if she didn't let him have her soon.

"You're—" she began faintly.

He clenched the packet between his teeth and tore it open, then rolled on the latex, aware of the fine trembling that betrayed him.

"Ready," he said, finishing her sentence. "Are you?"

She didn't say anything, only looked at him with wide eyes, the reflections in them a swirl of emotions he couldn't interpret. Was she trying to tease him into insanity? He reached out to hook a finger in her panties at her hip, giving her plenty of time to slow him down.

She didn't and as he peeled them off, he had one satisfaction at least. Her nest was spun gold, darker blond than her hair, but only a little. In his periphery, he saw her hand move convulsively, but he prevented her from covering herself.

"You're too beautiful to hide, my golden one," he murmured, distantly aware he'd spoken in Russian but what did words matter when the need to touch consumed him? He drew a soft line through her curls, finding slippery silk and—

She arched as though electrified, breath hissing in.

"Yes," he agreed. "Now." He hiked her up the bed as he covered her, spreading her thighs with his own.

She reacted to the touch of his body as if he'd burned her, shrinking into the mattress before squirming to stroke herself against him, a whimper of surrender trembling from her lips. Her hands slid over him, meeting at his spine. Her legs bent to bracket his hips, and her skin was hot and soft. Delicate and feminine and enthralling.

"I didn't know anyone could make me feel like this," she whispered with an ache in her voice.

He didn't want to hear about other men. The mere suggestion shook him out of his blind, ferocious need and brought him back to reality. Was she trying to incite him with jealousy? Well, he would be the *only* man on her mind right now.

"Do you want me?" he growled.

"So much." She pushed her breasts and stomach against him, cheek rubbing his shaved one like a cat begging to be stroked.

"This?" He guided the tip of his erection to part and find the center of her.

She caught her breath and stilled.

He ground his teeth, waiting in agony.

Slowly she slid herself against him, rocking her hips, nearly exploding his mind as she teased them both with a hesitant, barely there caress. "Oh, yes," she breathed.

He thrust.

CHAPTER SIX

HER STARTLED SCREAM was quickly choked off, but it was a cry of pain.

Through his shock, Aleksy recognized that his shoulders burned under the cut of her fingernails. Engorged and rampant, his erection ached at the tight pressure stopping him from finishing his entry. Beneath him, Clair had gone stiff and taut.

For several racing heartbeats, he held motionless with incomprehension.

A strained whisper stirred the air near his ear. "I didn't think it would hurt that much."

Her words didn't fully penetrate, but Aleksy instinctively tried to pull back.

Clair squeaked and clamped her legs on him. "Please don't move."

Understanding hit him in waves. This wasn't a misjudged case of too much too soon. This was— She was—

"You're a virgin?" He was amazed he found the word. And so loudly.

She flinched. Her hands slid to his ribs, and her tangled lashes trembled with uncertainty. "Not anymore?"

"I don't *do* virgins," he bit out, but he was locked indelibly inside one. How? His normally agile brain wanted answers, but sensations crowded his ability to think. She was tight and tense, silky and hot and vulnerable. He was livid, knew this was wrong, but couldn't draw away. His body was shaking, intense sexual arousal riding his pulse, sending all the wrong signals when he was compelled to be still. This couldn't be happening. He had to stop it.

"Please don't ruin it," she said faintly.

It? He was ruining *her*.

The sharp pain was subsiding, leaving a sting and a deep awareness of the hard length lodged inside her, hot and still.

He was furious. There was no hiding from that unpleasant reality, but Clair was more caught up in how her body was trying to accommodate his intrusion. Her internal muscles flexed. An answering pulse, surprisingly erotic, made her melt around him. He settled a fraction more deeply inside her.

Her breath hitched and so did his.

She let hers go slowly, unable to look at him. His harsh *I don't do virgins* was still cutting her in two. She didn't know what to do! Her skin was still sensitized and wanting to be stroked. His penetration transfixed her. It was incredibly intimate but wickedly persuasive. She felt as if she stood in the doorway to a new understanding and desperately wanted to grasp the concept.

While she could tell he wanted to exit stage right.

Tears of frustration gathered in her eyes. "Please—"

"Stop saying that," he rasped, hands moving to cup her head. His thumbs drew circles at the corners of her eyes, rubbing the leaking dampness into her temples. "When you're ready, we'll finish this."

He sounded gruff but almost tender. The kiss he touched to her lips was gentle. Brief but followed by one a little longer. A little more thorough.

She sighed in relief. He wasn't giving up on her. As he took her mouth, she curled her arms around him, pulling him into her, wanting to feel all of him. When she tilted her pelvis, he slid home. There was a final sting, but— *oh*—such a sense of rightness. Too many sensations to pick apart and name. She was all feeling and he was part of it. All of it. She squirmed against him, filling her hands with him, seeking maximum contact while reveling in the fresh magic of being possessed by him.

He kissed her with ravenous generosity, exciting kisses that transmitted joyous signals through her, making her move against him.

Thick Russian words filled her ear as he slid his wet mouth down her neck, tucked his hand under her bottom, carefully withdrew and thrust.

It felt so perfect, so *good*. Clair threw back her head, a lusty groan tearing raggedly from her lips. She couldn't speak, could only embrace this primitive state and encourage him with ancient signals, stretching and arching beneath him, moaning her pleasure.

Urgency built, quickening their rhythm. The sensations were so acute she wanted to scream. She needed more. "Please, Aleksy, please."

With a growl, he thrust faster, offering what she craved, taking and giving, straining over her, driving her to a peak, holding her there, pushing her off...

She fell, but into flight. Breathless, soaring flight. Distantly aware of his guttural yell, she rose to skim the sun, where she burst into brilliant, ecstatic flames. It was the most delicious death until, like the sparks from a spent firecracker, she drifted in pieces back to earth.

Aleksy reeled as he left her. Dealing with the condom was his excuse, not that he voiced it, but he had to get away from her. He was spent, body twitching with exertion and coated in sweat, but he wanted her again. She was like Christmas dinner, when it didn't matter that he'd already gorged himself. Greed for more consumed him.

He splashed cold water on his face, then glared in self-disgust at his reflection, his scar standing brilliant white against his flushed skin.

Incredible, mind-shattering sex that shouldn't have happened at any pace. *You're going too fast.* No wonder she'd been so shy about surrendering to passion. And when she had...

Please don't ruin it. What was he supposed to have done? Left her frustrated and disappointed by her first experience with a man? Would that have salvaged something of the civilized gentleman in him?

As if there'd ever been anything civilized in him, he thought with bitter self-recrimination, old blades of guilt and abhorrence flashing between himself and his image. He was well aware of the primitive forces in him. He held them in check with his rigid standards, always. Shame and contempt filled him for dallying with a virgin. He'd stolen from a man he didn't even know.

How dare she put him in this position?

He moved back to the bedroom to confront his mistake and found her sitting up, the sheet knotted in her fist against her collarbone leaving her pale shoulders bare.

She looked like a bride on her honeymoon, thoroughly tumbled, lips puffy and ripe, hair tousled, expression still retaining some vulnerable innocence while her new knowledge made her skim a hesitant, admiring look over his frame.

That look was a baited hook that caught in his gut. Lower even. The erection that hadn't completely subsided pulsed with renewed life.

He hated the response he couldn't control; he refused to be led by it, especially where she no doubt thought she could take him. Planting his feet hard on the floor, he crossed his arms and stood at his full height.

"I won't marry you." His cold warning grounded out the sexual electricity still crackling in the air.

Her shoulders flinched before she steadied them. "Did I ask you to?"

"It's reasonable to assume you're trolling for a proposal with this little gesture, especially ahead of the money transfer, but forget it. I'm not the marrying kind." She wouldn't have tried this if she knew what a monster he really was.

"What little gesture?" She lifted haughty eyebrows.

"A woman's virginity belongs to her husband." He'd never forgive himself for this. Fooling around with experienced women was one thing. They had the same unclouded views he did. Innocents had expectations he would never live up to. "I didn't ask for your virginity, so don't think you can guilt me into making restitution for it."

She reddened with insult. Or anger. He didn't let himself dwell on what she might be feeling so long as he was driving his point home.

"A woman's virginity belongs to her husband?" she repeated through her teeth. "Welcome to the twenty-first century where a woman's body belongs to *her*. It doesn't look like you're saving *your*self for marriage."

"It's a good thing one of us knew what he was doing." Although he hadn't. She'd neglected to inform him of one very salient detail. She was craftier than he'd given her credit for, coldcocking him with that one.

"We all have to start somewhere. What good is waiting for a husband who hasn't once shown up when I needed him? I'm stuck with taking care of myself, aren't I?"

"And this is how you chose to do it? By throwing away your virginity for hard cash?" Precisely the type of woman he usually dealt with and yes, he supposed they had all started somewhere. He was still left with a pall of disappointment in both of them.

Astonished hurt parted her lips.

Out of habit, he mercilessly sealed over the fissure her crushed expression threatened to make in his conscience, closing himself off to any emotional appeals. Best if she understood he had no heart, but then something in him stirred. Perhaps she really was romantic enough to believe this sort of thing led to a lifetime commitment. The weight of being unable to live up to that expectation settled heavily on his shoulders.

She surprised him by masking her hurt. As though shrugging into a coat, she pulled on an air of dignity. "I made a choice that was mine alone to make. I'm not the marrying kind either."

He snorted. Innocents like her dreamed of a family. If his own family were alive, they'd expect better of him than the way he was behaving right now. Of course, if they were alive, he'd still be an innocent like her.

"You don't know me," she said with quiet assertion. "You don't even want to. I'm only spoils of war to you. I trust your grudge is satisfied and you'll leave me now?"

The cool, pithy words struck his abdominals like punches. That wasn't what this was. Despite hating himself for not realizing sooner that he was her first, the basest male part of him was already anticipating tasting her shoulders and neck again, stroking the warm silk of her back and thighs, making her writhe against him until she was ready to take him into her. And it had nothing to do with revenge.

He didn't want to leave her—which stunned him—but

she had to be tender. He hadn't been as gentle as he would have been if he'd known... if he'd *known*...

His skull threatened to split under the pressure of conflicting imperatives. He had to leave her. For now.

CHAPTER SEVEN

CLAIR WOKE IN an unfamiliar place, mind blanking with alarm before her memory rushed back. She sat up, still in Aleksy's bed, still naked and very much no longer a virgin. Anxiety quickly faded to relief as she saw she was alone. She couldn't have dealt with him *and* her mental disarray. Stunned disbelief bounced off crazy elation and crashed into an inferno of embarrassment.

Hugging her knees, she tucked a hot face into them and tried to countenance how she'd let Aleksy do all that to her. She hadn't grown up with a lot of affection; nor did she possess any long-denied, deep-seated needs for physical closeness.

Yet she'd reveled in Aleksy's caresses, giving herself over to him without inhibition.

Her heart wrenched as she recalled that the singular experience had cost her his respect. What kind of throwback had such archaic views on virginity? His judgment and contempt had hurt, not that she should care what he thought, but a weak part of her did. She wanted to know he'd enjoyed their coming together as much as she had.

Physical satisfaction was secondary for him, she knew. He'd taken her to strike at Victor and he'd walked out right after, his interest in her gone with the same lightning speed he'd developed it. No one had ever wanted her for the long haul. It was silly to imagine that a man like him, who could have anybody, would be any different.

The door creaked, startling her.

He caught her unprepared for the impact he had on her. He was still wearing the crushed pullover and snug jeans from last night, but he wore confidence like a visible aura so radiant she needed sunglasses. His hair was damp, the short cut combed uncompromisingly to the side. She knew how those soft strands smelled. How they felt between her fingers. Against her breasts.

His gaze locked with hers as though he read the memories she tried to repress. She died a little at being incapable of locking him out, nipples hardening with remembrance of his mouth, loins pooling with excitement for him.

It was distressing to react this strongly, to relive these sensations without him even touching her. It was a massive invasion of privacy. Against her will, her mind zeroed in on that safe moment when they'd been unequivocally linked. He'd been a lover then. She'd felt cherished, not bare and self-conscious like now. Everything in her yearned toward that memory like a flower seeking the warmth of the sun.

But that man was gone. This was the man with the grudge. To him she was a pawn on a chessboard to be tipped over and taken with ice-cold deliberation. And he'd done it.

This was the get up and get out moment, she supposed, her pulse racing.

"Hungry?" He sounded ironic, his deep voice abrading her taut nerves.

Was he taunting her for skipping dinner in favor of sating herself with him? It was cruel. She dug into her deepest reserves of composure, the way she'd done when the school bullies had taunted her.

"I could eat." She lifted her chin and kept her gaze steady, ignoring that she was on fire inside. Other women were capable of relegating sex to something as mundane as chatting over coffee. She needed to be exactly that unaffected. She needed to get this awkward morning after finished and get out of here. "Why? Do you not know how to boil your own egg? You need me to do it?"

His eyebrows elevated a fraction at her pert challenge. His golden eyes looked deeply set into hollows darkened by a sleepless night. She was so startled by the thought that this powerful man might have lost sleep over her, she let it go as if it were hot.

The impression dissipated as he said with casual arrogance, "I pay the housekeeper to cook—or in this case deliver pastries."

"Oh. I would have liked to walk to the patisserie."

A flicker of surprise crossed his expression, followed by a purse of his mouth that made her bite her lip. He didn't want to stroll hand in hand down the Champs-Elysées and she hadn't meant to sound as if she was longing for romance either.

"I've never been to Paris. I'd like to visit a patisserie for fresh croissants at least once in my life," she defended, embarrassment stinging her cheeks. "But that's fine. I'll be out in a moment." She shifted her feet to the edge of the bed, signaling she needed privacy to rise and dress.

He didn't move.

Because there were no secrets from him behind this sheet. Perhaps he had sent his housekeeper out and come to wake her for a different reason. Her heart tripped and her fragile poise slipped. She swallowed, mind casting with indecision. She knew she shouldn't want to sleep with him again, but she did. Weak longing stole over her even as she searched his expression for his intention.

He gave nothing away as the silence grew loaded. Finally he entered the room, coming around the bed. She tensed, but he passed her by, stepping into the bathroom long enough to reach for something off the back of the door. When he returned, he draped a pewter-colored robe over the foot of the bed. "Take your time."

He left and she let her breath out in a whoosh, staring at the closed door, wondering why she felt so forlorn. In the space of twenty-four hours the man had completely taken over her world, which was intolerable. She didn't need to be completed. She was already whole. Aleksy might have tapped through her inner walls last night, but she had an infinite capacity for shoring herself up against the world. He'd simply caught her in a moment of weakness. Showered and dressed, she'd be completely unaffected.

She had to be.

Aleksy was not used to sexual denial. If he wanted a woman, he found one. When he had one, he *had* one. Waiting for Clair in the lounge, knowing she was running a soapy cloth over her nectarine-scented skin, was excruciating.

The proximity of her lissome body had burned in him all night as he paced the dark lounge. Taking her should have iced his vindictive cake, allowing him to discard her and move on, but he couldn't stop thinking about how exquisite she'd been. He'd thought he only wanted to mark his victory over his enemy, but she wasn't Van Eych's. She belonged to him, only him.

It was one more twist that caught him unexpectedly. He'd planned to be in London indefinitely as he drew the noose ever tighter around Van Eych's neck, putting him in a cell while stripping him of his stolen riches, but going to London had turned into nothing more than a formality because Victor had died. Aleksy's appetite for steering the takeover was gone. He could leave it to his team and go back to Russia where his own interests had been neglected far too long.

Given Clair's inexperience, he should sever their association. The deepest part of him knew that, but the rest of him rejected the idea. What would be the point in acting gallant now? Her virginity was gone. She'd given it up as a survival tactic in the face of losing her job and home. If she was going to sell herself, it might as well be to him.

It was a rationalization he grasped with surprising desperation, which disturbed him. For two decades his entire life had revolved around one thing: retribution. Taking Clair was supposed to be a facet of that, but instead she'd been an escape from it.

The stark realization unsettled him, agitating him further when he realized he wanted that escape again and again. He told himself it was timing and circumstance, that he would have found extra significance in any woman he'd bedded right now, but he didn't want *any* woman. He wanted Clair.

So he would keep her as long as it took to satiate this inexplicable want, he decided.

His resolve took a hit, however, when she appeared in a filmy white sundress a few minutes later. Her disturbing sense of purity made his heart lurch. It was not unlike the modesty she'd shown in not being able to reveal herself by leaving the bed this morning. She withheld her thoughts behind a mask, but her blond hair was a golden veil and her minimal makeup revealed her natural beauty, fresh-faced and ingenuous.

If this was going to work, she had to fit the mold.

"I'll book you into a salon today," he pronounced with the swift call to action that had made his meteoric success possible. It would also fill her day so her nearness wouldn't tempt him beyond bearing. Women always expected a new wardrobe anyway.

Clair touched her hair, her composed expression denting with confusion. "I had a trim a few weeks ago."

Aleksy resisted the urge to roll his eyes. "A fashion salon," he clarified, then added with irony, "So you can wear what I like." He held a chair at the table for her.

"Why? Taking possession of Victor's trophy wasn't enough? You need to stamp your own engraved plate on it?" A betraying unsteadiness undermined her cool challenge.

He didn't let her remark ignite his temper. "I intend to remove any traces of him from you, yes."

"For whose benefit?"

She seemed genuinely baffled, which was yet another reminder of her unfamiliarity with the way these arrangements worked.

His housekeeper brought their meals at that moment and he watched Clair withdraw even further behind her frustrating shields as she was offered tea and asked if she'd found everything she'd needed.

After Yvette left, Clair muttered, "As if this isn't harrowing enough." Her hand tremored as she helped herself to a croissant, the only betrayal of tension behind an otherwise cool demeanor.

"Harrowing." Aleksy repeated the unfamiliar word so he'd remember to look it up.

"I'm sure mornings after one-night stands are old hat to you, but this is my first. I'm not exactly comfortable with a stranger witnessing it."

He tensed. Was that what she thought? "I don't do one-night stands," he informed her quietly.

"Or virgins, if I recall. Must have been a two-for-one special."

"But you're not a virgin anymore, are you?"

She stilled. Smoldering memories darkened the blue of her eyes, igniting a lovely blush under her skin. She swallowed and looked away.

He didn't like that she would try to withhold any part of herself from him, especially that intriguing response. Forget experience. She had to know that once wasn't enough for either of them. He reached out and drew her chin around to face him.

The look in her eyes was shockingly defenseless, full of anxiety and fear coupled with deep longing. Things that stirred a deep, protective desire to comfort her with tenderness...

She jerked back, blinking away the peek into her soul, turning serious. "I need to return to London."

Her words jolted him with a startlingly strong kick of possessiveness. "Why?"

Clair's heart jammed under his intense regard. She wanted to be as dispassionate as he was, but it was impossible. Her normal ability to hold people at a distance wasn't bearing up against Aleksy's penetrating looks. She didn't even know why she was having a problem with this. She had known she was a conquest, nothing more, but she still felt vulnerable, out of her element and unaccountably lonely. Everything in her wanted to escape before it got worse.

"To find a job and a place to live," she reminded him.

It was amazing how his eyes could harden into inscrutable bronze disks that still managed to pierce like lasers. A muted hum sounded and he glanced at the mobile next to his plate. "Perfect." Turning it, he showed her the message. "Your time is mine now. Along with everything else," he added with silky danger, his gaze sliding over her like loose, velvet bonds.

Clair read the confirmation of deposit, fifty thousand into her account. Her emotions seesawed as all of yesterday's repugnance at the arrangement flooded back.

"We agreed on one hundred," she said, then inwardly shrank from her mercenary retort. But it was for the foundation, she reminded herself. She wasn't putting herself through this emotional wringer for one pound less than what they'd agreed. With a defiant lift of her chin, she used a show of mutiny to mask her shame.

"You don't get where I am without performance guarantees. What if you'd changed your mind?" Aleksy was a study of couched power, ready as a tiger to leap.

"But I didn't. I held up my side of the bargain. I expect you to do the same." She felt like one of those balls on a tilting table, rolling out of control, destined to fall through a black hole any second.

"You'll receive the rest when our affair is over."

She gripped the table. "But— I thought—" Once had been enough for him, hadn't it? Last night he'd certainly left her with that impression. "It is over, isn't it?" The hesitant question came out involuntarily. She held her breath, not sure what answer she wanted to hear. Her ears pounded with anticipation as she watched something stark and fervent flash in his eyes.

"Nyet."

No? Or *not yet*? She was so lost in trying to read his expression, so off balance by the uneven trip of her pulse that she couldn't make sense of what he'd said. And she had prepared herself to walk away today, blasé and sophisticated and only slightly scathed. Her incredulous laugh scraped her throat.

"How much longer do you expect it to last?"

He shrugged laconically. "Until I'm bored."

No. Unpredictability made her anxious. "You can't expect me to put my life on hold indefinitely."

"Consider it a lesson against agreeing to open-ended contracts."

"But—" A panicky lump lodged in her chest. All she could think was how easily he had peeled away her layers of reserve last night. She didn't know if she could withstand further baring of her inner self.

"What's the problem? You said yourself you have no rent to pay or employer to report to. Do you want me to say I'll ensure that those details are looked after before we dissolve our association? Very well. I can agree to that."

"That's not—" She searched the hard angles of his face, cringing from the vague distaste curling his lip, wondering how his twisted brain worked that he could only see her as avaricious and self-serving, not scared out of her wits because she was drifting so far over her head. "What did Victor do to you that you're like this?" she breathed.

The billowing silence told her she'd stepped over a line. "My history with Van Eych is not up for discussion. It has nothing to do with us. You and I have a strong sexual connection that needs to run its course. When it has, I'll release you and the rest of the funds."

His words sent a zing of surprise all the way to the soles of her feet. A strong sexual connection? "I thought I was paying for the sins of a man I barely knew," she charged, hands knotting under the table.

His cheeks hollowed. *"Nyet."* He looked away, fiercely controlled emotion tightening his mouth. "There is no way for anyone to compensate for that. His sins were too great."

He gave off vibes of such deep devastation, such intense pain, an unfamiliar desire to reach out caught at her. He'd only brush her away, she reasoned, startled that the impulse touched her at all. She wasn't the affectionate sort.

And yet she found herself turning over that *strong sexual connection* remark. Was she more than a tool of reprisal after all? Fluttery sensations like a million moths flooding toward a sliver of light filled her.

"Are you saying you want...*me*?" It took all her courage to step into the bottomless chasm of asking him.

He grew guarded and his eyes cut to her with a flinty look. "I want your body."

The inner door that had cracked open slammed shut. "Of course." She removed her napkin from her lap, no longer hungry. But what did she have to be offended about? She wanted him for *his* body, didn't she? Her long-term avoidance of relationships had been an avoidance of the unbearable sea of emotions that came with them. Wanting to be wanted was agonizing. She'd learned early not to let those longings take root. Skimming her gaze over his unabashedly masculine form, she recognized that he was offering her a gift: all the joys of physical engagement without a toll on her heart.

He cocked his head, amusement tilting his mouth. "How is it that a woman as naturally sensual as you are has never taken a lover before?"

Her pulse raced at how easily he'd read her yearning in one brief, unguarded glance. If she continued seeing him, she'd have to learn to keep her thoughts to herself.

"No one ever tempted me." She tried to keep her voice level so he wouldn't guess how unnerved she was at the way his powerful sex appeal kept smashing through her self-protective reserve. "And normal relationships don't interest me," she added.

"Normal?" His eyebrows climbed.

"Dating to find love. Searching for a soul mate." Profound disappointment seemed the inevitable follow-up to those quests. "You were right when you accused me of being more pragmatic than that. I don't want to live in a cave, but most people my age live the other extreme: partying and hooking up. Being Victor's platonic mistress seemed like the happy medium." She sipped her coffee, but it had gone cold and bitter, much like how she felt about her arrangement with Victor, especially now that she'd glimpsed how much pain he'd caused Aleksy. It was yet another harsh reminder that relationships—even ones with seemingly impervious boundaries—could reach inside to wound.

She should take that as a warning sign, but last night had been extraordinary. All her reasons for agreeing to sleep with Aleksy were still there along with memories that made tongues of flame lick down into her pelvis.

"Now you see the advantages in being a real mistress," he murmured in that deadly accent. He reached for her free hand, lightly combing his fingertips between her fingers before tracing a path across her palm. Her entire body jolted and a moist layer rose under his teasing caress.

She tugged her hand into her lap and tried to erase the tingling sensation by rubbing it on her thigh. She couldn't hide that he had a profound effect on her.

As if he read her response as acceptance, he nodded with satisfaction and rose. "I'll call for the car. You'll need a full wardrobe before we leave for Moscow."

"Moscow?" Her composure dropped along with the coffee cup she still held, the clatter in the saucer jarring. "I can't get into Russia without a visa."

"I have your passport. Lazlo will arrange it," he dismissed with a shrug.

"What happened to ladies' choice? I run my own life, Aleksy." She rose to grip the back of her chair.

"I've been occupied with this takeover at the expense of my interests at home," he said stiffly. "I need to return and I want you with me. Is that asking too much?"

I want you with me. Don't, Clair. Don't let that mean something.

"You're not asking," she pointed out, determined to assert herself.

"No, I'm paying for it."

Ouch. Piqued, she threw back, "Yes, you are, because I'm not footing the bill on whatever you expect me to wear."

His scarred face twisted with a smile of patronizing satisfaction that made her want to bite back her words. "I wouldn't expect anything less."

CHAPTER EIGHT

SHE SHOULD HAVE known a man like Aleksy could only come from a city like Moscow. It dominated the way he did. Its weighty buildings with their tall, imposing towers and sharp-eyed windows spoke matter-of-factly of strength and the ability to endure. The facades, scarred by history, told a story she would never fully hear.

Yet there was an unexpected idealism she hadn't expected in the archways and balconies and loving attention to detail. Even Aleksy revealed a streak of sentiment in the way he'd refurbished his living quarters with an eye to art and a respect for the past. The block he lived in had been built for high-ranking Soviet leaders, he told her when they arrived, which accounted for the amazing location on the Moskva River and enormous top-floor mansion, but the original wiring and wooden interiors had made the building a fire hazard. He'd had the entire structure torn apart internally over two years and was rebuilding to original floor plans with upgraded specifications.

That surprised her. He seemed unaccountably merciless in everything he did, utterly focused on his own interests. After their night flight from Paris, he'd spent most of today in his office down the hall, phone buzzing constantly, conversing in half a dozen languages. Yet if he'd only wanted to turn a coin with this building, he could have made simpler choices, punching out cookie-cutter flats for foreign investors. Instead, from the brief glimpse she'd caught through the replicated elevator cage, he was blending modern conveniences with charming vintage elements, offering stylish homes to his countrymen.

Most startling of all was the photograph above the fireplace in the lounge. The bride wore a modest dress, the groom a simple suit and tie. The corner of the small snapshot was burned, the colors faded, but it was set off by a wide mat and an elegant frame, so it took up significant space, speaking of its importance to the flat's owner.

She guessed from his resemblance to the groom that they were his parents. Aleksy confirmed it with a simple *da*, not encouraging more questions, but she'd found herself oddly encouraged by this evidence of a softer side in him.

Such a complex man, just like his city.

And now he'd brought her into it. *Indefinitely.*

She still felt apprehensive about letting him pressure her into going along with his demands. His strong-arm tactics didn't bother her so much as the way she'd folded to them did. She knew how to stand up for herself when it mattered. This mattered. She wasn't a ward of the state anymore and wasn't about to let him erode what autonomy she'd managed to build for herself. It was too hard won.

Nevertheless, she was here. As his mistress.

Until he grew bored and paid her out.

Flinching from that brutal inevitability, she moved away from the window and took up the two gowns again, hands shaking. She was trying to decide which was better suited for seeing the ballet at the Bolshoi Theatre—as if she had the first clue what the well-dressed mistresses in Moscow were wearing.

How infantile it had been to try striking him in his wallet

when it was so well padded. She couldn't imagine what he'd spent on her. Victor had given her a small clothing allowance and she'd bought conservative outfits that helped her blend in with those around her. She liked being unobtrusive.

Aleksy was having none of that. These gowns were daring and sophisticated, the colors bold, the designs requiring confidence to wear them well. She wasn't sure she could pull off a dress like this any more than she could cope with being Aleksy's woman.

Stop it, she ordered herself, refusing to backslide into wanting to belong to someone. He didn't want her soul and she wouldn't give it up. This was a reciprocal exchange of pleasure, unencumbered by demands for true intimacy.

"What are you doing in here?" Aleksy's stern voice made her jump.

"You startled me." Despite her previous affirmations, her knees weakened at the sight of him. Her reaction was a complex tumble of nervous excitement and an inexplicable desire to earn his admiration.

She clamped down hard on those self-destructive emotions but couldn't wholly suppress her physical response. He was still in the casual pants and button shirt he'd worn all day in his office, and his expression was downright forbidding, but her heart raced with appreciation of his fiercely handsome looks. When would he touch her again? The question had been burning in her blood all day.

"You said to be ready for eight," she reminded him, using the gowns as a shield for the lightweight silk robe she wore, glancing down at the drapes of color to keep him seeing her involuntary and immediate desire.

"I meant why are you in this room?" He moved forward and took in the open closet, the myriad empty boxes and zippered dress bags. "I instructed the housekeeper to put everything away in my room tomorrow."

Her heart dropped like a boulder from a rock face. Share his room? After living alone she was finding the idea of sharing a flat—even one as big as this—to be a hard adjustment. She couldn't breathe with him four steps in the door. No, if she was going to get through this in one piece, she needed her own space to retreat to.

"The boxes were in here, so I assumed this was my room and unpacked them." She conquered old twinges of wanting to apologize for occupying any space at all. This wasn't a foster home. He'd brought her here. She'd stay, but on her terms. "I'd like to use it," she said firmly.

He assessed the volume of clothes. "As a dressing room? Very well, but I'm not about to creep up and down the hall looking for you. You'll sleep in my bed."

Conquering a suffocating panic, she asserted, "I don't want to."

"Why not?" He turned the full power of his intense personality on her.

She swallowed, not intimidated by his power and height, but instantly vulnerable to the effects his alpha male nature had on her. At some point they'd have sex again and the recently awakened woman in her craved that so deeply she was a little frightened by the power of it, but sleeping together would have its own way of increasing her reliance on him. That wouldn't do.

"I—" The word was cut off as he drew her into a strong, careful embrace. She automatically tensed and pressed the heels of her hands to his chest, fingers still curled around the padded hooks of the hangers.

He looked down at the way she held him off, not forcing her body into his, but she sensed the firm planes of his stomach and the long, hard muscles of his thighs teasing like a warm breath beyond the fall of her kimono.

He tugged the towel from her head, releasing her damp

hair, and tipped her head back so her gaze tangled with his. He stroked her cheek, then let his caress trail into the sensitive hollow beneath her ear and under her jaw.

"I'm looking forward to tonight. I don't know how I've managed to work when all I could think about was touching you again. Feeling you under me."

Her arms pressed harder as she tried to keep his seductive words from affecting her, but everything else in her melted. This was the sensual heat low in her abdomen she'd looked forward to. She consciously closed herself off to reading any significance in his admission that she'd been on his mind, though. As he lowered his head, a helpless moan escaped her. Her hands released the weight in them and slid up to curl around his neck and into his hair. The first touch of his lips shot a jolt through her. They melded together as the kiss deepened without any insistence from him. She welcomed him with a passionate response, transported to the exciting world he'd initiated her into while trying to hang on to herself, not give him everything—

He lifted his head. They were both breathless. His cheekbones were flushed, but his eyes glittered with aggravation. "What's wrong?"

"Nothing," she murmured, aware of an internal tension that grew as he delved into her gaze. Keeping herself disconnected from the way he made her feel was hard. She looked at the sobering line of his scar to cool her blood, wondering about it.

His expression grew stony as he slid his hands over the silk gown, his palms hot through the slinky fabric, molding her back and fondling her bottom, making her tremble.

She let her head fall forward onto his chest to hide how the sweetness in his caress made her eyes moisten. She felt his hardness against her belly, urgent and thick, and caught her breath in wonder. He wanted her. *Her.*

A burst of relief made her dizzy, unnerving her, filling her with the tautness of wanting him while remaining wary of limitless intimacy. She gathered herself behind an invisible wall, before she followed through on her desire to look up and press her lips to his neck.

Before she could make the move to take this where her body wanted to go, he set her away from him and bent, coming up with the red and the blue gowns. He rejected the red with a toss toward the bed, his expression inscrutable. Holding the blue in front of her, he said with detachment, "This one. Give me thirty minutes. I'll meet you in the lounge."

Her mouth still tingled from the pressure of his. Her whole body felt light enough to fly while bitter disappointment weighed like a rock in her throat, keeping her from calling after him. She refused to beg for affection.

As he dressed, Aleksy was still trying to understand what had transpired in the other room. The fact that he was being so introspective about Clair's behavior was as irritating as her trying to hold him off.

After resisting temptation all day, he'd been unable to help going to her. Finding her in the spare room, trying to keep space between them, was an oddly disturbing rejection. Everyone gave him a wide berth, but Clair's doing it stung unexpectedly. Did she fear him? The thought galled him.

He'd been compelled to close the gap and pull her into his arms with as much gentleness as he was capable of. She had reacted beautifully, her arousal instant and obvious.

When he'd kissed her, her mouth had parted beneath his. The silk of her robe had revealed the tension in her belly and the sharp points of her nipples. Her supple body had even leaned into him. *She*, however, had not been involved.

Why not? She'd called herself practical when they were in Paris, her interest in her financial future blatant enough to assure him they were on well-defined ground. Had she read something about him that had turned her off?

The way she had stared at his scar had seemed to suggest so. Then she'd folded into him, almost as if she was ready to surrender regardless of what she thought of him, but he'd been stinging with disgrace. In one glance, she'd reminded him that it didn't matter how mercenary she was, he still didn't deserve to touch her.

Even she seemed to know it.

From inside the limo, his world gave an impression of chilly silence. The few people on the street wore overcoats and furred hats as they hurried down the street, breath fogging in the frosty air. Yet their very presence in the cold evening spoke of perseverance and a steadfast grasp on life, entrancing Clair into forgetting she didn't want to fall in love with anything, even his country.

How could she stay immune, though, when he'd put her in the center of a fairy tale? The limo stopped and Aleksy left the car, holding a hand to help her stand, so courtly he stole her breath.

He wore a tuxedo with a white bow tie and gloves. It ought to have seemed affected, but his features were carved with masculine perfection, his brow stern enough to make everything about him serious and deliberate. Backlit by an enormous, columned building with a rosy-cream glow, he was devastatingly handsome.

She stood on unsteady legs, taking in the milling crowd streaming around the frozen fountain toward the spectacular entrance of the theater. This was the world he inhabited. Miles above any she'd ever thought to visit. Her treacherous emotions lifted with excitement, caught in a spell of beauty and wonder.

As if that wasn't magical enough, his presence cut a swath through the crowd of people. One glance over their shoulder and people moved aside. Aleksy kept her pressed close to him as they climbed the stairs, coldly ignoring murmurs of "Dmitriev" and Russian phrases she didn't understand, coupled with glances at his scar.

Taking her cue from him, Clair refused to acknowledge the morbidly curious looks, pretending to be absorbed in the grandeur of the theater. She was genuinely awed. The ornamental detailing and painted ceilings looked as if they'd been finished yesterday. For a moment time slipped away and she was a nineteenth-century aristocrat carrying a fan and wearing lace to her throat. The man at her side was an arranged-marriage husband—not a far cry from today's situation at all, she thought with a wry, inward wince. He was supporting her and there was no hope for love.

An attendant approached to take her cape and Clair revealed the modern, off-one-shoulder sparkling blue dress that clung to emphasize her narrow curves and create more height than she really had. Aleksy procured them flutes of champagne and, after a brief consultation with the attendant, told her, "We have the czar's box."

She tried not to drop her drink.

As if this were any casual date, he guided her through a set of double doors that led through an ornate sitting room. Another set of doors ended on a grand balcony fit for, well, royalty.

Red velvet and gold struck her from the row of luxuriant chairs with their gilded edgings to the scalloped curtains framing the box to the auditorium beyond. A wall of balconies stretched away on either side in floor-to-ceiling rows, each separated by low walls decorated with gold leaf and glittering chandeliers. An enormous cake of sparkling crystals cast glamorous winks of light from high above, sparkling off jeweled necks and sequined gowns.

Clair sank weakly into the chair Aleksy pressed her toward. "I didn't think Russia had a czar anymore," she stammered, half fearing they'd be executed for trespassing.

His smile warmed her as if she'd gulped her entire glass of alcohol. "It's actually the president's box now. We could have used mine, but as this one's empty tonight and I'm such a valued patron..." He shrugged self-deprecatingly.

"You must love the ballet. I mean—" The way his eyebrows climbed made her rethink presuming anything about him. "You have your own box and support the company. Everyone seems to know who you are."

"*Litso so shramom.*" His expression altered as he repeated the phrase she'd heard as they entered. The carefully composed lines of his face revealed nothing—which was a revelation in itself. "Scarface."

The bluntness of the moniker made her blink in shock, but she hid it, guessing anger on his behalf wouldn't be welcome.

"I'm hardly anonymous anywhere I go," he said, his jaw tensing. "And no, I don't have a particular love of ballet. Coming here is merely—forgive the ancient metaphor— the quickest way to telegraph my return to the city. Do you like the ballet?"

"I've never been," she answered, lowering her gaze as she absorbed his offhand question. Her preferences had obviously been the last thing on his mind. This was the most exciting outing of her life, yet he'd brought her here for reasons that had nothing to do with her. She had to stop wishing for more! She went back to the nickname.

Irrepressible curiosity made her ask, "Does it bother you that people see the scar, not you?"

"There's no separating one from the other, is there?" His look hit her like a face full of icy slush, his tone chilling her blood.

"I don't know," she replied, ignoring the bite of his hostility, fighting not to take it personally even though she sensed a hint of accusation in his demeanor. "Have you looked into plastic surgery?"

"Why? Does it disgust you?" His fingertip unerringly found the line of raised tissue. He drilled her with his eyes, but she didn't have to lie.

"No. I don't notice it more than any of your other features, like the shape of your nose or color of your eyes." She stopped speaking as she heard how revealing that sounded. She was stunned to realize how thoroughly she had already memorized his face: the hint of a raised bump on his nose, the wicked slant in his eyebrows, the cleft in his chin. She had to force herself not to let him entrance her now.

"It's an advantage," he said flatly. "While people are trying to decide how many of the rumors they should believe, I've summed them up and leapt three steps ahead."

"You like that it makes them nervous. Then they don't try to get close to you," she guessed, earning another baleful glance that made her breath stick. She was certain she was right, though, so much so that parts of her softened toward him as she recognized their similarity. She feared isolation, so she forced herself to find contentment in being alone. What did he fear that kept him holding people off so ferociously? Caring?

The thought was a double-edged sword of understanding and hopelessness so acute it made her head swim.

"This scar reminds me who I am and where I've been,

which is a place you don't want to go, Clair," he said in a gentle warning that made her heart batter her ribs. So he had suffered a very deep wound. Nevertheless, she *would* listen to his story if he wanted to tell her. Had he ever told anyone, she wondered?

The lights faded before she could ask. Faces below rotated to watch the curtain rise. Music swelled as *Petrushka* began to unfold with its tragic puppet, considered cruel but instead capable of emotion, trapped in a cell, unable to reach the ballerina he loved.

Aleksy loathed small talk. It was a step into familiarity that he never encouraged. Clair had been spot-on when she suggested he was happier holding people at a distance.

Scowling, he wondered what had possessed him to talk about his scar. It was a topic he usually shut down outright, but he'd been compelled to learn if it was behind the reserve she'd shown earlier. Clair was exceptionally beautiful tonight, and fresh bitterness had overcome him that he was such an unsightly match for her.

Intellectually they were on an even playing field, which was an anomaly for him. Rather than babbling inanities or barbs, she had a quiet sincerity when she spoke and displayed surprising insight. He avoided women who made him feel. He'd never had one who made him think.

Disturbed by a rush of both anticipation and caution, he forced himself to stop letting her get under his skin and instead focus on their surroundings.

He noted with twisted pride how her smile of pleasure attracted curious, admiring looks during intermission. He detested networking at any level and would have stayed in the private lounge attached to the czar's box if he could, but he succumbed to convention at these things.

With hooded fascination, he watched her greet those

who approached with seemingly sincere warmth, admiring dresses and jewelry if no other conversation presented itself. He was used to his dates sulking, or smiling as if it pained them to make the effort, leaving the weight of social chitchat up to him. Clair put people at ease and he found his own tension ebbing because people weren't so nervous—which, contrary to what she'd said, always made him impatient. Aleksy glanced at the next hovering couple, smiling as he recognized the man behind the gray beard and the woman's twinkling blue eyes. He introduced Clair to Grigori and Ivana Muratov, smoothly forcing those trying to hold his attention to move along.

After brief inquiries about their daughters and grandchildren—he had known their entire family for many years—he and Grigori became caught up in discussing politics.

"That was the chimes," Ivana warned a few moments later, touching her husband to interrupt their conversation. "Intermission is over, but this charming young lady has just told me about the charity foundation she has started. We would like to help her with that, wouldn't we? Aleksy has made a donation."

The unexpectedness of Clair's subterfuge against these of all people made Aleksy's cheeks sting with a rush anger. Thankfully the couple didn't notice, both smiling at Clair's bewildered face.

"Of course we'll match it," Grigori agreed, clapping Aleksy's shoulder with enough enthusiasm to nearly knock him off his unsteady feet. "Send me the details." With cheerful goodbyes, they hurried down the hall toward their own box.

"They seem very nice. How do you know them?" Clair lifted the most guileless eyes to him but sobered as she read his forbidding expression. "What's wrong?"

"Grigori gave me my first real job after my father was

killed," Aleksy answered. He had to school his fury with everything in him as he took her arm and led her back to the lounge. Before she could pass through to the balcony, he cut her off, closing the doors so they were alone in the sitting room.

The music rose in the auditorium and Clair lifted a nervous hand to indicate it. "The show is back on."

Aleksy turned on her. Whatever she read in his grim expression scared her, but she held her ground with more mettle than anyone he'd ever made a point of revealing his fury to.

"Why are you angry?" she asked with rigid dignity.

"Did Van Eych teach you to work a situation like that or is it a personal gift?"

She straightened as tall as she could possibly be, a pale reed so beautifully set off by the deep blue of the gown he nearly had to close his eyes against the temptation to touch her. He focused on the finery of the dress instead, on the fact that the small fortune he'd dropped on her new wardrobe wasn't enough. She was trying to steal from his friend, as well.

"What do you mean?" she asked.

"I won't let you take advantage of Grigori's generous nature." The man had been his salvation, offering Aleksy not just work, but a fresh chance. Grigori had helped a desperate young man put a roof over his mother's head while giving him the opportunity to move up the ladder toward the life he lived now. The life itself didn't mean anything, but Grigori's hand up when no one else had offered meant the world.

"I didn't expect Ivana to offer a donation." Clair managed to sound not just innocent, but hurt. "We were only chatting. She asked how we'd met, so I told her about the charity."

"Which doesn't exist!"

Clair's jaw dropped open. Rather than cower under his blistering gaze, she drew a deep, hissing breath of outrage. "Don't tell me your precious Lazlo failed to advise you of the email I sent him today? I attached the tax receipt. What?" she dared challenge as he narrowed his eyes. "You thought I asked for the Wi-Fi code so I could update my social media status to 'mistress'?"

He ignored her biting sarcasm. "I can check," he warned. "With one call."

"Do it," she choked, acting so offended as she swung away that he experienced a flash of misgiving. He shook it off and scowled at her as he withdrew his phone.

Seconds later a muted buzz vibrated in his palm. Clair's back stiffened as though the sound were the whir of a whip and she was bracing herself for the lash.

The edges of the device dug into his hard grip as he read and reread the message.

"You told him you'd print me a copy if I asked, so he assumed I was aware," he paraphrased, needing to hear it to fully comprehend it.

"You didn't ask," she pointed out, barely able to look at him.

"So it's real, this charity of yours." She even had a registered number.

That swung her around to face him. "Of course it's real! I'm not a liar. You don't truck with those, remember?"

He found himself in the completely unfamiliar state of being at a loss as he let it sink in. "I don't understand," he muttered, voice graveled by his impatience at being faced with something that didn't add up. "You gave me your virginity for *charity?* Why would you do that?"

"People like me deserve—" She cut off her outburst and struggled visibly, jaw flexing as though chewing back words she hadn't meant to voice. Flicking her hair back from her shoulders, she changed tack. "Look. I didn't want all my work to die on the vine. Brighter Days fills a very real need."

"For who?" he asked suspiciously. "Finish what you were going to say. People like you deserve what?"

Clair's jaw ached. She didn't want to tell him. Why? Because she was ashamed? Still? If she wanted to get anywhere with the foundation, she had to conquer this sense of being second class once and for all.

"Support," she answered with a swell of defiance. "When there's nowhere else to turn." She wasn't as confident inside as she acted. It had always been hard to believe she really deserved any such thing when no one else seemed to agree, but she deeply believed children like her deserved a caring home and opportunities to make a secure life for themselves. If she didn't act as their voice, they wouldn't have one, just as she hadn't.

"What kind of people are we talking about?" Aleksy asked. "Orphans?"

"Yes." It was incredibly hard to look him in the eye. Her stomach trembled as she braced herself for how the label would change his view of her.

Aleksy had vaguely absorbed that she didn't have family, but the information had only penetrated distantly. Now he sensed how deeply she felt her lack and was thrown off by her vulnerability. A pang struck him dead center of his chest so hard he wanted to rub it away.

"How old were you when—?"

"Four." She hid her flinch with a shrug, steeling her spine. This was costing her, he could see it, but she said without inflection, "Car crash. I had a broken leg and a dislocated shoulder. They died instantly."

"Why does that make you so defensive?" He had an

urge to take her in his arms, but that wasn't who he was. He didn't coddle, but he still found himself trying to reassure her. "Being an orphan isn't a crime. I'm one."

"You lost both your parents? Not just your father?" Her somber blue eyes softened with empathy, threatening to pull things out of him he didn't want to release. "What happened? How old were you?"

He was instantly sorry he'd mentioned it. "Fourteen when I lost my father. My mother lived until I was twenty. I suppose I wasn't technically orphaned." He glanced away, deliberately not addressing how his father had died. "I'm only saying there's no shame in not having parents who are still alive. It's hardly something you can help."

The irony of his assurance twisted inside him. He suffered deep shame over his father's death and the fact that he'd never been able to provide properly for his mother. He lived daily with the anguished guilt that even if his mother had survived to live as he did now, it wouldn't have cured the broken heart that had been the real cause of her withering away.

Suppressing the agonizing memories, he focused on Clair's circumstance instead, observing, "Four years old is still young enough to be adopted."

Tendons rose in taut lines against her throat as she said with stunned hurt, "That wasn't really in my control, was it?"

He might as well have kicked a puppy. He wished he could take it back, but the damage was done. She was pulling herself inward, composing herself into the untouchable woman he had seen several times now. Her skin was incredibly thin, he realized. He'd bruised her without even knowing he could do so. The way she mentally distanced herself caused an unexpected gap of agitation to open beneath his feet.

He moved forward, taking her arms in a light grip, as if he could prevent her retreat into herself.

She stiffened and her hands came up to his chest. He read the same conflicting signals of resistance and subtle, sensual melting that he'd felt in her earlier in his apartment. She liked his touch but was trying to shield herself at the same time, something he understood all too well, but she didn't have to fear him on this.

"You're right, of course," he murmured, experimenting with a light massage up and down her arms. "I shouldn't have said that. Where did you live, then? An orphanage?"

"Yes." He felt a quiver go through her, one she suppressed as she said with quiet dignity, "The home was the only real one I had. It was stable and I needed that after being in foster situations for the first few years. That's why I'm trying to ensure that it has enough funding to stay open, but I don't need the donation from Grigori. The amount you've promised is so much more than Victor offered that I can keep them going and actually support expansion. Tell Grigori whatever you like. I won't bring it up again. I'll just tell people we met in London and leave it at that." She turned her face away, lips tight.

He had dismissed her charity as a ruse when she first mentioned it, imagining that at best it was the illusion of a bleeding-heart idealist incapable of solving real problems, but the full impact of it being genuine continued to jar through him. She wasn't a gold digger; she was a mother bear fighting to protect children.

The knowledge sliced a fresh cut of ignominy through him, but he ignored it, too caught up in trying to understand her.

"You might have given me some indication," he admonished. "Why let me believe your motivations were shallow?"

"What do you care what motivates me? This isn't the sort of relationship where we talk about our scars, visible or otherwise, is it?" she challenged, pupils contracted with wounded pride.

A knot of complex emotions pulled his gut tight.

"No," he agreed. His hands unconsciously tightened on her arms.

"Good. Because I don't want you in my h-head," she said shakily, but he heard the underlying hurt.

The constant rejection in her life had made her understandably wary of intimacy, Aleksy guessed, but he couldn't stand that chilly shell she was trying to recover. She wasn't just in his head; she was under his skin so deep he could barely breathe without feeling her. Physical intimacy was the salvation for both of them, he told himself.

"How about your body?" he murmured, pulling her hips into a delicate crash against the erection that had rarely subsided since he'd met her. Sex seemed the only way to get past her shields, and he would use it, now, before she'd locked her barriers into place. "Do you want me inside *you?*"

She started with surprise and drew a sharp breath, face flooding with a sexual blush. "I— Well, y-yes. I mean, that's what we've agreed, isn't it? Um." Her words caught and faded into a husky tone of arousal. "Un—um, uncomplicated and…" She licked her lips nervously and the play of her tongue was almost a visceral stroke up his spine.

Simple. Practical. Physical.

He tried to hang on to the words as he backed her toward the divan, the need in him, once acknowledged and released, so intense his muscles began to shake. Every cell in his body ached for the pleasure she promised, but there was a primordial aspect to it that he refused to examine too closely. He wanted more from her than sexual accommodation. He wanted her to give herself to him because she wanted to, not for any orphaned children. He wanted her as ensnared by this wild passion as he was.

He levered her slight body onto the cushions and lowered himself to cover her.

Clair released a helpless whimper as Aleksy's hot mouth touched the racing pulse in her throat. Her overwhelmed senses took in the painted ceiling and the music beyond the doors. Had he locked any of them? The back of the divan offered a bit of protection if someone walked in but not much.

"Aleksy," she choked, voice thick with the conflict of wanting him so instantly she was almost willing to risk discovery and holding back because she was upset. All her internal guards were shattered and in bad need of repair. She should wait until she had a better hold of herself, but he was strangely reassuring in the way he caged her beneath him without crushing her. The way he trailed his lips across her bare shoulder, pausing to drink in the scent of her skin.

"I want everything you'll give me." The statement spurred a light-headed rush, one that nearly lifted her off the divan as he slid his finger under the diagonal edge of her bodice to reveal her breast.

His mouth found the tip and her mind exploded. His urgent demand was as exciting as his mastery, causing a thrilling flood of heat into her extremities. She wove her fingers into his hair, making him lift his head. She was desperate to own his mouth but too shy to say it.

Her body spoke for her, knee bending to bracket him into the space between her legs. He responded by stroking her ankle, her calf, her thigh. With their eyes locked in ever-intensifying connection, he climbed his hand beneath the skirt of her gown until he touched her so intimately she had to close her eyes.

That only made her excruciatingly aware of the deliberate way he tantalized her. She lodged the back of her hand against her open mouth, muffling the cry of pleasure that escaped as he caressed and teased, making her long for more—

"Oh!" He pressed into her wet core and she clenched, surprising herself with an unexpected orgasm that squeezed her eyes shut and rocked her entire body. Jagged moans refused to be suffocated.

"I'm sorry! I'm so embarrassed," she said into the paneled back of the divan, almost sobbing as he lifted her to strip her undies away.

"Don't be," he commanded, his voice thick and fierce. He rose over her, his penetration happening at the same time he took her mouth in a kiss that captured her deep groan of relief.

It was better than the first time. All sweetness as he filled her and paused, giving her a moment to accommodate his thick, hot girth. She grasped at him, certain there could be nothing better than this first deep thrust to alleviate the acute need.

Then he moved and the pleasure storm swept through her.

CHAPTER NINE

ALEKSY SHIFTED, ROLLING onto his back, snapping Clair out of her deep sleep.

Her naked back reacted to the loss of his heat like the cool, raw flesh under a bandage. She fought a foreign desire to turn and burrow into his warm strength.

Smoothing her hair from her eyes, she let her gaze find shapes in the barely discernible pattern of the wallpaper, trying to make sense of what was happening to her. She'd been so angry, so hurt at being misjudged, and positively crushed at his remark about being adoptable. Did he think she hadn't spent her entire childhood waiting for new parents? For someone to want her?

He didn't care about her struggles or pain—he'd more or less admitted it when she challenged him. He only wanted sex from her. That's all this affair was, and it should have turned her off, should have kept her from making love in public at the very least, but his touch had erased all the hurts. She'd forgotten there was such a thing as loneliness.

And the sense of connection had inexplicably remained, even when he'd wryly apologized for being unprepared with a condom and dried her belly with his handkerchief. It should have been a horribly awkward moment, but she'd found herself giggling as if they shared a secret. His tender kiss had tasted like a promise as he solicitously straightened her disarranged clothing and shielded her from the eyes of the wait staff while they slipped out of the theater, flushed and pinned together.

The drive had been a blur. She'd stared out the window without seeing anything, mind reeling, belly still quaking, skin sensitized with longing. There'd been no misgivings, just a glow of joy like an ember inside her.

She hadn't recognized the feeling as a state of sustained desire, but when he'd drawn her to him before their shoes and coats were off, she'd met his kiss with an enthusiasm that had made him groan. He'd scooped her into the cradle of his arms and carried her to this bed. She hadn't given one thought to how long she'd stay here, only that she needed to be naked with him, all of her hurts and worries forgotten.

She very much feared she was losing herself, and that was bad.

Nevertheless, when his big body jerked behind her, her pulse leapt as if they were connected by invisible, electric wires. They'd spent a long time getting to know each other's body. She'd even let him slide down her to arouse her so selflessly she'd almost died, but oh, the deliciousness of that near-death experience. When he'd risen to thrust into her, they'd locked themselves into a writhing knot of ecstasy. She'd been so exhausted and replete after their final, shuddering culmination that she'd fallen asleep without making a conscious decision to stay in his bed.

She should leave now that she'd woken, but she was reluctant, especially when he crooked his leg against hers and renewed desire tingled through her. Would he wake and love her again? Who knew she could be this insatiable?

He muttered something in Russian.

Drawn by curiosity, she rolled to face him and tried to read his features in the dark. His eyebrows were pulled together in a grim line, his jaw clenched. His long body was one taut muscle weighing down the mattress. More utterances pushed through grinding teeth.

A nightmare? Reaching out with instinctive compassion, she lightly touched the tensed muscles of his neck, thumb accidentally lining up with the ridge of his scar on his chin. "Aleksy."

He clamped a swift hand around her wrist, the strength of his grip painful enough to make her cry his name again in a warning.

With a jolt he woke, but his grip stayed locked tight. "Clair." He sounded…fraught, his tone demanding she answer.

"Yes, it's me." She tried to rotate her arm and ease his unbreakable hold. "Where were you?"

He drew a shaken breath, letting his fingers loosen, then just as quickly caught her arm again, closing around her fine bones, exploring lightly for damage. "Did I bruise you? I'll get ice." He released her and started to leave the bed.

"No, I'm fine." She dropped a staying palm on his chest, startled to find it soaked with perspiration. "You're sweating. Do you have nightmares often?"

"Never," he replied shortly, dragging the corner of the sheet over himself, dislodging her touch as he dried himself.

Smarting from his brush-off, she curled her fist into the blankets and drew them up over her chest. "Maybe it was my being here. I was just leaving, so…" She trailed off.

He didn't say anything.

She waited too long. Nausea clenched in her stomach as she realized he wasn't going to protest and ask her to stay. Aghast at herself for making the mistake of fishing for signs she was needed—or at least not unwanted—she forced her stiff limbs to ease toward the edge of the bed. Funny how she had spent years conquering feelings of bereft abandonment, learning never to set herself up for it, yet the tsunami of worthlessness could sweep over her as fresh and coldly devastating as ever.

This was exactly why she avoided intimacy. He was too far inside her if he could bring her to the brink of anguished rejection this easily. This wasn't supposed to happen.

Years of practice allowed her to swallow the lump of unshed tears trying to lodge itself against the back of her throat. She wouldn't cry, refused to. She found her way down the hall to the spare room and crawled into the icy bed with dry eyes, telling herself the ache clawing at her insides was for Aleksy.

What would haunt him so badly he'd have nightmares? She'd been distracted by his misjudgment of her and the foundation earlier, but he'd said Grigori had given him his first job after his father was killed. He had shut down and diverted her by asking about her own history, but she had a feeling the touchy subject of his scar was related. The way he'd just called her name as if he'd been frightened for her stayed with her, filling her with an urge to go back and ask him about it. Offer comfort.

Rolling onto her back, she flung an arm over her eyes and reminded herself not to give or ask too much. This relationship was temporary and if she got any more emotionally involved with Aleksy, she'd be too deeply attached when it ended. Look how she was reacting to being separated by just a wall. She didn't want her heart broken when half a world stood between them.

Better to stay exactly where she would spend the rest of her life: alone.

Aleksy stared unseeingly at the frozen river, still deeply perturbed by his nightmare. He hadn't had one since his mother was alive, yet the dream and the memory it contained had ambushed him with deadly accuracy.

Except this time, when he'd heard his name, Clair's voice had called it and torment had nearly ripped open his chest.

Soft footsteps padded on the tiles behind him. Not the bustle of his housekeeper and he felt Clair's presence like a tangible force anyway. Her sexuality radiated into him, synchronizing to his own. He wanted to touch her with the immediacy that swept through him every time he was near her.

He hesitated to turn, though, dreading what he might see. He had meant to be gone by now, but his driver was caught in one of Moscow's world-famous traffic jams, so he was loitering in his own foyer, mind jammed with unwanted introspection. When he pivoted, he caught her hovering indecisively, showered and dressed, hair glittering like sunlight in icicles. She took in his suit and tie beneath his open overcoat, then the briefcase on the floor. Her eyes were underlined with bruised half circles. No sleep either? Or something else?

Apprehension made his voice unintentionally severe. "Good morning."

"Good morning," she answered. Her cloak of composure slid firmly into place, hiding anything she might have betrayed.

He felt his mouth twist in dismay, but really, it was for the best. He'd saturated himself in her last night, allowing his own well-built defenses to waver so he could draw her in as tightly as possible, but apparently letting down his guard had allowed his subconscious to come out of hiding. That was so disturbing he didn't know what else to do but run.

"You're going out?" she asked without emotion, making it impossible to tell if she was relieved or disappointed.

Her remoteness renewed the fear that had been creeping through him since the early hours. Had he said something revealing in his sleep? Was that why she'd left him for the bed down the hall?

"I'm needed at the office." He scowled at the briefcase he'd filled like a criminal fleeing the country, as if putting off facing her would change anything. There was no changing what she thought of him, only the disclosure of what that might be. "I didn't mean to disturb you last night." He watched her closely, trying to discern what was going on.

"It's fine." Her lightness sounded forced. "I needed to go to my own bed anyway."

He bit back a reflexive *Why?* Her insistence on sleeping apart from him annoyed him and he didn't understand the reaction. He usually gave his women separate apartments and left *them* in the middle of the night, but even that first night when he'd been in a state of utter turmoil, there was something satisfying in knowing Clair was in his bed. He'd looked in on her more than once, baffled by the spell she'd cast over him, but pleased with her presence.

He was a possessive man with possessive urges, he supposed, trying to rationalize how out of sorts he was. But this exaggerated reaction made him more determined than ever to ensure that this arrangement stayed on clearly defined footings. She had a place in his life and it was a narrow one.

"Invitations will be pouring in after last night. I'll call to let you know where we're going and what time to be ready." He collected his briefcase, willing his driver to ring. "I have accounts at all the boutiques on Tverskaya. Ivan will come back after he drops me and you can shop or Lazlo can arrange a private guide if you'd like to tour the city."

Clair tried not to gape, but she was still trying to process her reaction to last night's expulsion from his bed and all she could think was, *So this is what a mistress does with her downtime.*

Logically she understood that a strong man like Aleksy would hate that he'd revealed any sort of vulnerability, so she tried not to let his plan to abandon her cut too deeply. She'd spent hours last night coaching herself not to take any of what happened between them to heart. This wasn't personal; it was convenience. Sex. Good sex.

She licked her lips, trying not to get off track, but memories still crept through, warming her with insidious desire. She suppressed them, considering the shopping and sightseeing offers. Getting out sounded good, but she didn't need anything after the spree in Paris. She just wanted to clear her head and remember how to be herself.

"Don't bother anyone. I'd rather see where my feet take me," she decided.

His macho eyebrows came together like clashing titans. "You want to walk? Alone?"

The incredible sexism in the remark got her back up. "Do you think I'll get lost? I'll print a map before I leave."

"It's not safe," he impressed on her with another stern frown.

Clair dismissed that with a wave. "I've lived alone in London for five years."

"Moscow isn't London, Clair. Kidnappings are on the rise—"

"Who's going to kidnap me?" She splayed a hand on her chest, forcing a laugh, but the need to state the obvious gave a surprising pluck against her heartstrings. "I don't have any family to threaten. Remember?"

"Do you think the paparazzi at the Bolshoi haven't printed photos of the woman with me last night? Even without that you're young, pretty, well dressed. You don't speak the language. Opportunists are out there and you should never, ever underestimate what people will do for money. I don't." His scar stood out stark white against his flush of emotion.

Foreboding slithered through her. She knew then that his scar was not the result of a tragically placed ice patch and a broken windshield. Aleksy had been indelibly marked by violence. Internal brakes wanted to screech the whole world to a stop so she could somehow process that, but how? There was no erasing what had happened to him.

A poignant ache flooded her at the same time. Before she realized what she was doing, she reached out with all the familiarity that had developed between them last night. Cupping his jaw, she lifted herself on tiptoes, aware of him stiffening as she leaned into him. Her lips almost brushed the puckered line before he abruptly set her away, jerking his head back.

"What are you doing?"

His rebuff tore her in two. She winced, regretting the lapse in her reserve, but he had no idea how few people ever showed concern for her—and after whatever he'd been through…

"Thank you for trying to look out for me." She forced the words out.

He tugged the lapels of his overcoat as if he were fitting armor back into place and closed a few buttons. Glancing at his watch, he took a step toward the door, speaking over his shoulder dismissively, "You'll stay in, then? Or call Lazlo for an escort?"

Her silence made him pause. He turned another weighty frown in her direction.

Clair curled her toes in her slippers. It would be so easy to let her self-reliance crumble and allow this protective, strong-willed, incredibly attractive man to run her life.

What about when they were through, though? She'd be back to taking care of herself. She *had* to hold on to her independence.

"I'm not *your* kidnap victim." She tried to sound wry, but for some reason her lips trembled and her heart skipped a beat. "I'll go out if I want to."

"Despite the risk," he snapped, temper sharpening his voice.

"It's not that great a risk!" She folded her arms, stopping short of saying he was overreacting. Obviously his experience had taught him differently. Determined to hold her own, she reasoned, "When you want to do something, who do you ask? No one, right? Same here."

His jaw tightened. He was used to everyone answering to him, that much was clear. The precisely machined, titanium wheels in his head seemed to whir at top speed as he sought a suitable rejoinder.

"I'm not trying to be obstinate," she said, checking her flawless manicure.

"But you won't give me your word."

"It would be a lie."

With a hiss of impatience, he set down the briefcase, its weight hitting the tiles with a hard *thunk*. His mobile sounded and he answered with a staccato burst of Russian before tossing the device on the hall table and shedding his overcoat, his stare holding hers with antagonistic force.

Clair swallowed and fell back a step. "What?"

"You won't stay at home as I've asked, so now I have to take action, don't I?" He began loosening the knot at his throat.

"What does that mean? You're going to tie me up?" Genuine alarm made her retreat several feet in the face of his deliberate advance.

"It means I have to change and go with you." He yanked

his tie free and draped it over her shoulder as he passed, voice pithy and displeased, but he still made her grin as he said, "Save the tying up for after dark."

Clair reminded herself she was not behaving like a spoiled socialite. She was a fully grown adult making her own decisions, and Aleksy could do the same. She wasn't keeping him from his work. His pacing and brooding would not make her feel guilty.

She refused to set herself up for criticism either, so she took the precaution of checking the weather even though the sky was intensely blue and the sun glanced brilliantly off Moscow's blanket of snow. The modiste in Paris had tut-tutted about Moscow's temperatures, taking advantage of Aleksy's open account to empty her winter fashion collection into Clair's possession. After noting the wind-chill warning, Clair pulled on warm socks over the cuffs of her skinny jeans and layered a snug waffle print under a woolen turtleneck.

Her new faux fur boots were adorable as well as functional, their trim matching a smart leather jacket in the same buff tones. She topped it all with a corduroy baker boy hat and a pair of sunglasses worth more than her last pay packet. When she appeared, Aleksy said nothing, only shrugged into a thick ski jacket and laced up sturdy boots.

Clair paused inside the exit doors to check directions with the doorman. His English was excellent, but he stammered as he answered her questions, one eye on where Aleksy waited with detached patience. Clair took care to write down the street names phonetically so she could find her way back—exactly as she would have done if Aleksy weren't coming with her.

"Planning to ditch me?" he asked as they left the building.

"Of course not." Outside, the wind cut like a broadsword, making all her muscles contract and her breath stop in her lungs. She had to clench her teeth against them chattering. "Do you have a preference which way we go?"

"This is your walk."

Clair looked around her, determined not to let his attitude send her slinking back up to the flat. Taking a moment to get her bearings, she started toward the river, not stopping until they were overlooking the frozen water from a bridge twenty minutes later.

As she marveled at the jagged ice squares forming a broken path in front of the Kremlin, Aleksy withdrew a lip balm from his coat pocket and handed it to her.

So she wasn't *completely* prepared. Smoothing balm over her already drying lips, she thanked him and handed it back, getting a funny feeling in her center when she watched him use it too.

"You must be outside in winter often if you're ready for the weather," she said.

"It's still in my pocket from the last time I went skiing."

Oh. Of course. "Do you ski a lot?" Somehow she couldn't connect that detail to a man who was built like an athlete but didn't seem given to using his body outdoors when he could watch the financials from a treadmill.

"When I visit my resort, I do."

"Oh." Of *course*. "Is your ski hill here in Russia?"

"Canada. It's a heli operation. A good investment," he added.

"Of course," she murmured, smiling privately. Heaven forbid Aleksy simply buy something because he liked it. No doubt he thought *she* was a good investment.

That thought pinched enough that she wanted to get away from it. She began walking and he paced her, his formidable presence drawing startled looks, but ones of recognition. The average Russian citizen seemed to know him better than she did.

"What other sorts of enterprises am I keeping you from today? The internet said you got your start in road and rail transport."

He took a moment to absorb that she'd been cyber-stalking him, then answered, "Lumber first, then transport. Other types of manufacturing. Real estate of all kinds. A shipyard." He scowled.

"That one isn't such a good investment?" Clair guessed.

"No, it's very sound." His frown cleared to what looked like pride. "All of my ventures have excellent teams in charge."

"Then why the dismay?" she asked.

Aleksy was frowning because he couldn't think of one thing he was being "kept from" by this stylish blonde in her smart boots and cute hat. The way she was watching him so closely, trying to read his thoughts, was the exact reason he'd wanted to avoid her today. If her penetrating glances weren't bad enough, she was provoking yet more self-examination and he didn't like it.

"I'm thinking of what I would be doing in the office if I were there," he lied.

Her fine-boned jaw tensed, accepting the minor set down without comment as she looked away and walked on in silence.

He'd wanted to seal her lips against further questions, but he hadn't meant to hurt her. The truth was, he didn't know what he'd be doing at the office. His strategy had always been to set the personnel in place so a business ran itself, paying him dividends and allowing him to expand to the next challenge. Each new enterprise had been a step toward overtaking Van Eych, but there were no more steps. He'd reached the finish line. Time to put the game away. The work he'd put into amassing his assets suddenly seemed as pointless as tapping a plastic piece around a cardboard path. Yes, the wealth he'd accumulated would always need direction to keep him comfortable for the rest of his life, but it hadn't accomplished what it was meant to; he was still eaten by guilt.

And still confronting a gaping emptiness in his life that could never be filled.

A bright glint flicked in his periphery, dragging his attention over Clair's head to a man with a camera. He wasn't dressed for the weather and looked miserable. When Aleksy confronted him with a glare, he scurried off, not giving Aleksy the chance to turn Clair and say, *See? He was staked outside the penthouse and followed us.*

Disturbed, Aleksy followed the man with his eyes while he made a mental note to increase his personal security. The typical paparazzo didn't care if his target saw him. That kind of surveillance spoke of someone sniffing out skeletons in closets. A suffocating feeling rose like a band to close around his chest.

Clair's small hand suddenly gripped his down-stuffed sleeve, pouring buoyant lightness into the dark turmoil roiling inside him. Her wonder-struck expression made his heart lurch into a painful, stumbling gallop.

"When you said the streets were dangerous— Am I imagining things or is that a *bear?*" Clair tore her gaze from the astonishing sight down the block to catch Aleksy watching her with an expression of heartrending struggle on his face.

He turned his face quickly to look. By the time he looked back, the only emotion he expressed was sardonic humor. *"Maslenitsa."*

Clair's nerve endings were still vibrating as she searched for traces of what she had thought she'd seen in his eyes, but whatever had been there was gone. She ducked her head so she wouldn't give away how dejected his shift in mood made her.

Get a grip, she ordered herself, and released his arm, repeating the word he'd used. "What is it?"

"A festival to welcome Spring. Like Mardi Gras. Except we have bears, fistfights and troika rides."

"Judging by the first two, I imagine the third is bronco-busting a reindeer? And what makes you think spring has arrived?"

Aleksy chuckled, the rich sound so unexpected Clair had to swallow her heart back to where it belonged. He soon dispelled her misconception by securing them a ride in a sleigh pulled by three horses. Snuggling her into his side, he let the English-speaking driver tuck them under a blanket and educate her on the festival, which was pagan in origin, but also related to Lent. When Clair expressed too much interest in the bear wrestling contest, the old man turned in his seat. "Not for you, *malyutka.* Wrestling is for old men who only have vodka to keep them warm." He winked at Aleksy.

The man ended by fetching Clair a plate of *blini*, round pancakes covered in caviar, mushrooms, butter and sour cream.

"I can't eat all this. You'll have to buy me a whole new wardrobe," Clair protested after a few bites of the deliciously rich food. "Here. Please," she prompted Aleksy.

"No." He held up an adamant hand. "I can't eat pancakes."

"Too many as a child?" she teased, imagining him as a strapping boy gobbling everything in sight.

"Far too many," he said grimly. "If you can't eat it, give it to the dog."

She followed his nod to where a German shepherd was

licking a plate, the owner unconcerned. Clair let the dog wolf down what was left of her *blini* and disposed of the trash, her mind stuck on Aleksy's remark.

They moved under an ornately carved archway built of ice to a park filled with ice sculptures. The angels, castles and mythical creatures were beginning to thaw, their sharpest edges blurred, but they were still starkly beautiful, transparent and glinting in the sun.

"The driver said the festival has only been revived recently. You weren't eating pancakes just for Lent growing up, were you?" she mused aloud, stepping back and hiding behind her camera to keep the question less personal.

"No, we ate them for survival," he said flatly, gaze focused somewhere beyond the stunning sculptures.

"You weren't working for Grigori then?"

"I was hardly working at all. My mother wouldn't let me quit school."

Clair lowered her camera. "Somehow I can't imagine you taking orders from anyone, even your own mother."

"I would have given her anything," he said with a gruff thread of torture weaving through his tone. "I couldn't give her what she really wanted—my father's life back. I worked ahead and was in my last semester when Grigori hired me. My mother still worked at first, and at least we ate something besides pancakes. I gave her that much, at least, before she withered away."

His bitter self-recrimination caught her off guard, making her want to touch him again, but she was learning. He would talk a little, but only if they kept it to the facts.

"Cancer?" she guessed, unable to help being affected by his loss. He gave an abbreviated nod and she murmured, "That's tragic."

"It was suicide," he bit out. "She knew something was wrong and didn't seek treatment. I would have done *anything*—" His jaw bit into the word. "But she felt like a burden on me." His hand opened, empty and draped with futility before he shoved it into his pocket. "And she wanted to be with my father."

Clair caught a sharp breath, frozen with the need to offer him comfort, but very aware she couldn't reveal too much empathy right now.

"She must have loved him very much," she murmured, voice involuntarily husky.

"She was shattered by his death. Broken." His gaze fixed on a sculpture that had fallen over and splintered into a million pieces, its original form impossible to discern. "I hated seeing her like that. Hated knowing I—" He cut himself off and shuddered, looking around as though he'd just come back into himself. "Are you finished here?"

Clair huddled in the constricting layer of her jacket, aching for Aleksy even as she silently willed him to finish what he'd started to say, sensing he needed to exorcise a particularly cruel demon. Yes, she needed to keep from becoming too connected to him, but she couldn't ignore his terrible pain.

Carefully stowing her camera in her pocket, she put her hand on his arm. He stiffened against her touch, rejecting her attempt to get through to him.

"I'm sure you did what you could. Don't blame yourself for something you couldn't control," she said.

"Who else is there to blame?" he countered roughly, utter desolation in the gaze that struck hers like a mallet before he yanked it away.

A name popped into her head and she spoke it impulsively. "Victor?"

"Chto?" The word came out in a puff of condensed breath as he swung his head to glare at her.

"Did Victor—" It sounded stupid as she thought it

through, but she'd been keeping up with the headlines in London. Victor's perfidies were being revealed with glee by the press. Victims were pouring out of the woodwork day by day. Aleksy's hatred of the man was bone deep. His remark from last night, *"after my father was killed,"* still rang in her brain. Perhaps she was being melodramatic, but…?

"Did Victor have anything to do with how you lost your father?" she asked, tensing with dread as she tested this very dangerous ground.

A spasm of anguished emotions worked across his dark expression. There was grief and the reflexive hostility anyone showed when their deepest pain was exposed, but there were other things too. Frustration. Resolve. Remorse?

"It's not a connection I can prove," he said through lips that barely moved.

Her whole body felt plunged into an ice bath. To hear her vague suspicion met with such a condemning remark gave her goose bumps. He believed Victor had played a part in his father's death. No wonder he held her in such contempt for accepting generosity from a man with no right to the wealth he'd used to dazzle and persuade her. She felt sick for letting the advantages Victor offered outweigh a proper examination of the type of man he was.

Clair barely recalled the walk back, lost in absorbing the gravity of the injury Victor had dealt to Aleksy's family. No wonder Aleksy was such a hard, bitter man. The greater wonder was that he hadn't swept her onto the street the way he'd threatened to.

"Are you all right?" he asked when they entered the suite.

She looked up from removing her shoes, startled to see they were in the apartment. "F-Fine." Her lips were numb. "I think I need a warm bath." She could barely face him. "Walking might have been a bad idea after all."

His scarred cheek ticked in silent agreement.

Clair swallowed. "You can go into your office if you want. I won't go out again. I promise."

"You're still here."

Clair's bemused voice startled him, in a good way. She looked better. Her face was clean of makeup, her cheeks glowing from the heat of her bath. She wore yoga pants and a thickly woven pullover that hugged her bottom and clung to her thighs. Gorgeous.

He swallowed.

She'd been so wan after their morning out that he'd been worried about her, which unnerved him; he didn't normally feel more than superficial concern for anyone. She was turning him inside out.

"What do you have there?" he asked, trying to distract himself, rising with the intention of taking her load of laptop and files.

"I was going to work on the foundation in here, but if you'd rather I used the dining room—"

"No, here is fine." He looked at the cover of the laptop balanced on the stack of file folders as he set everything on the desk. The label jumped out at him with the company logo and its scrolled initials: *V.V.E.*

"It…was something he gave me to work on, then said I should keep it." She bit her lip, her upward glance culpable.

Aleksy tensed. The man was dead, but he just wouldn't *die*.

"I'll get rid of it," Clair said flatly. "I just want the foundation files off it. Then I'll throw it in the incinerator. Honestly, I feel so sick with myself!" She covered her cheeks with her hands, her blue eyes clouded with repentance. "I didn't realize he contributed to your father's death. You must be so disgusted with me for having anything to do with him. I am."

Mental walls were clashing into place, trying to lock out what she was saying, but the words were spoken. He couldn't ignore them. All he'd said earlier crept around him like coils of barbed wire, warning him any move would only tangle him up more painfully. He didn't know why he'd let himself delve back into his mother's grief or Victor's role in his father's death. He just wished he could forget them.

He suddenly stopped cold. What was he thinking? For twenty years those horrors had been uppermost in his life, driving him toward making Victor pay for them. To put any of it out of his mind was a betrayal of his parents' memory—but somehow the passionate hatred that had kept him going was now evaporating.

While Clair was seeping in.

His heart gave a hard, uncomfortable lurch—she was starting to mean too much to him.

She inhaled deeply, rousing him from his thoughts. He realized she was interpreting his expression and grim silence as confirmation that he did hold her in contempt. He scowled. "We met because of him. That's it," he tried.

"How can you say that when it's obvious you're angry and hate me for having anything to do with him?"

He was angry. Something was rising in him that he didn't even understand. Clair wasn't stupid, weak or avaricious. Why, then, had she let herself become involved with such a man?

"All right, yes," he ground out with enough fervor to make her start. "I want to know how, Clair. How could you let him near you? How could you not see him for what he was?" Unexpected, bile-green jealousy rose in him. "How could you—"

Not wait for me.

He jerked his head to the side, hands fisting defensively, terrified by what he'd almost said. His heart pounded and sweat broke on his brow and upper lip. He reminded himself that for all his possessive urges, he really had no right to her.

"In part, I was just very naive," she said with quiet self-reproach.

"I know you're naive," he countered, incensed by the reminder. Everything in him was programmed to protect that vulnerability in her, even from—*especially* from—himself. After all, if he'd finished his story earlier, he'd have revealed that *he* was ultimately responsible for his father's death. That his father had stepped into a fight Aleksy had started and that when Aleksy had finished it, he'd walked away with two lives on his conscience. Three if he counted his mother.

He kept looking for qualities in Clair that he disliked so he could feel less disgusted with himself for pressuring her into this arrangement, but she kept reinforcing that he was taking advantage of an innocent. Her next words proved it.

"It was the first time I'd been singled out as special. I was susceptible to that," Clair admitted in a small voice, eyebrows pulling together with humiliation.

Aleksy seemed to freeze into an even stiller statue. Clair experienced that old feeling of wanting to fade into the wallpaper, hiding her flaws so no one would see why she didn't deserve to be chosen and taken home. It was painful to stand tall and own her mistake. She clasped the edge of his desk, drawing strength from its solid weight.

"When I was growing up, the home had an arrangement with the school nearby. If we kept our noses clean, we could attend and have the same chance at scholarships and higher education as the rich kids. I gave it a shot, but I wasn't a genius, just average. And I wasn't rich. I always wore secondhand uniforms, never had trendy shoes, never got invited to parties. The kids weren't trying to be mean. I just wasn't one of them."

Aleksy's intense scrutiny nearly evaporated her voice. It was so hard to crack herself open and reveal this tainted, imperfect neediness inside her.

"When I got to London I wasn't special there either. I worked three jobs to make rent, so I didn't have time to date or party even if I'd wanted to. Then along came Victor. He treated me like I was the only one who could get things right. He needed me to be places for him and when I walked down the hall, people noticed me because they thought I was important." The last part tasted bitter. She'd known she wasn't important, but she'd liked that others had been deluded into thinking it. How pathetic.

Letting her hips rest on the edge of the desk, she gripped it with both hands, shoulders hunching as she spilled the rest. "He gave me things I'd never had, money for clothes. *New* clothes. He said he'd support the foundation."

"*I'm* doing that. Do *I* make you feel special?" His harsh voice grated over her exposed, sensitive core.

It sounded like a trick question. "I realize I'm just another mistress to you. I don't expect you to treat me as anything special," she said.

"You should," he shot back with startling vehemence. "You should expect every man alive to treat you as the smart, kind, remarkable woman you are. Do *not* sell yourself short and fall for scum like Victor." He rubbed his jaw so his final remark came out muffled and almost indiscernible. "Or me."

She took a moment to remind herself she'd only known him a few days, that he might know himself better than she did, but her urge to contradict him pushed her forward a few steps.

"Don't sink yourself into his class," she blurted, her hand going to his arm even though it was a risk of rebuff. "The way you make me feel—"

His arm was iron beneath her touch. She could feel his instant rejection, but his attention fixated on her mouth as though he was willing her to continue.

Clair had thought she'd been cleaved open to her very heart when talking about her secondhand upbringing. What she'd revealed so far was nothing, though, *nothing*, compared to confiding his effect on her.

Especially when he looked so severe, as if whatever she said would be refuted and thrown back at her. He was beautiful and dangerous, clad in black jeans and a black pullover that clung to hard pecs and biceps, someone who could squash her self-worth under a disparaging heel.

"I—" She had to clear her throat. Despite her terror at opening up, she was reacting to his closeness. Heat trickled into her fingers and toes, gathering in her loins. "The way you make me feel isn't some adolescent need for approval or status or…whatever I was looking for then. It's… good. I just feel so good when you touch me."

Her voice dried up and he was talking over her anyway.

"Any man could make you feel like that."

She flashed him a galled glare and snatched her hand back. "I've never reacted to anyone the way I do to you."

Hurt started her pivoting away from him, but he snatched her back to face him.

"You haven't been with anyone else—"

"I haven't wanted to! That's the point. *You're* special. To me. To my body," she clarified. "I don't know why."

He blew out a frustrated breath. "It's the same for me. I don't understand it either."

"Really?" She shouldn't have asked. She should be more confident, not beg for confirmation that he liked to be with her, but she desperately needed to hear it.

He seemed to waver over what to say to that. She might as well have been naked, standing there waiting.

"You must know how you affect me."

She swallowed. His words arrowed sweetly into her heart, even though they only spoke of physical reaction.

"How would I?" she asked with a shrug that tried to hide her defenselessness. "You didn't want me to stay last night. You didn't want me to kiss you this morning."

His cheek ticked in the way she was beginning to know meant his own shell was being penetrated. "Kiss me anywhere," he said gruffly. "*Everywhere*. But not here." He touched his scar lightly.

Her heart lurched while her shield crumbled, leaving her unsteady and weak with longing.

"Do you mean that?"

His stared right at her. "What do you think?"

CHAPTER TEN

SHE BLINKED, TRYING to take in this new information, new freedom, to seek badly yearned for physical contact with another human. With him.

"Like…now?" she asked cautiously, feeling pulled toward him.

The air in her lungs felt sharp as knives. Desire and insecurity ground their rough edges together inside her at how easily he was lifting up her emotions and tossing them around.

He looked at her with the masculine arrogance he wore like a cloak, pure Aleksy, isolated and driven and powerful. She was only Clair, green, overwhelmed and too deeply enthralled by him for her own good. At least when he was the sexual aggressor she knew he desired her. To take up the onus of initiating lovemaking meant doing the unthinkable: asking him to want her.

But she really wanted him to want her. Really, really did.

"Every man enjoys being seduced." He shifted to lean his hips on the edge of the desk, contemplating her with a type of removed curiosity. "I'm no different."

Seduced. She'd meant a kiss, but she was reminded of the care he'd taken when she threw a similar challenge at him.

Acute inadequacy sliced through her at the same time, cutting all the sharper because the longing within it was so honest. She wanted their most intimate connection with all the pent-up hunger that never seemed to dissipate, but she wished she'd kept her mouth shut. Her base need for approval was too bone-deep, the risk too great if she failed to arouse him.

She shook her head and said with a papery laugh of bravado, "As if you'd ever give up control to anyone."

"You don't think you could make me?"

Her heart skipped, teased into hope by the light suggestion. "Could I?"

"Try," he dared.

He was all supreme confidence, and that intimidated her, but a flash of eagerness for the challenge surprised her, making her pulse leap and her nerves flutter. She didn't know what she was doing when they came together, each time so overwhelmed by his experience she lost all conscious thought, but the idea that she might be able to break past his wall of willpower excited her, making heat swirl and tingle into secretive places.

She tried to probe past his burned-gold eyes to the thoughts behind. Need was welling up to tight levels in her. She *wanted* to make him want her.

And he wasn't as detached as he wanted to appear. He was watching her every breath, waiting to see what she'd do.

That gave her the courage to take a few steps toward him, but as his heat and scent surrounded her, all her thoughts short-circuited. Her hands lifted instinctively, greedy to touch, but nerves arrested her.

He was so much bigger than her, his chest a wide plane bracketed by arms hanging with tense readiness, his biceps taut and straining against his pullover. She wanted to kiss his bare wrists, but imagined he'd think that inane.

His rib cage expanded as he inhaled, drawing her eyes to the lift of his strong shoulders, the tendons standing out with strain against his neck. He stared down at her from beneath his thick, spiky lashes, eyes flashing with frustration.

That revelation of want held firmly in check gave her the nerve to take the plunge. She moved to stand between his feet and set her hands on his shoulders.

He jolted a little, as if she'd burned him. She felt the leap of energy as an electrical charge, flaring awake all her senses. With the sort of smooth caution someone used when petting a wild animal, she relearned the familiar shape of his shoulders, hands warming as heat radiated off his muscles. She traced the ridge of his collarbone through the warm fabric of his shirt and when she reached his throat, she crept light fingers under his collar, circling until she found the bump at the top of his spine.

The hollow at the back of his neck was familiar territory. She stroked upward against the short spikes of hair on the back of his head. As she went up on tiptoe, she expected to feel his arms lock behind her, dragging her stretched body into his taut one. Then he would drop his head and kiss her. They'd be in the bedroom in seconds.

He didn't move, only looked at her.

Nobody will ever truly want you, Clair.

Her heart fell and continued to fall, like plunging into an icy crevasse, the descent long enough to comprehend what a mistake she'd made and dread the damage at the bottom. She felt stupid and incapable. A disappointment to herself and him.

Ducking her head, she eased her hold on him and lowered herself to flat feet, body unavoidably brushing his, making her almost cry with denial as she felt the bulge of—

Unnerved, almost fearful, she stared at where his jeans followed the contour of his hardness. Caught in a spell, she slowly reached out and traced the shape with a wary touch, then became aware of the searing affect she had. His breath hissed in and the shape of his erection grew pronounced, unmistakable.

She stared in astonishment. She'd barely touched him! The thrill that went through her nearly melted her onto the carpet at his feet. She wanted him, all of him, so badly. Her gaze skimmed over the wall of him again, starving eyes consuming a banquet. She didn't know where to start. Fear of revealing her extreme need paralyzed her. She didn't want him to see—

But maybe it was the same for him. Maybe it would excite him to know he was wanted, the way she'd just felt a rush of desire from recognizing his arousal.

It took all her nerve, but she lifted her face and let him see whatever was there. A blush of heated excitement, longing in her eyes, admiration for the sheer sexiness of the man he was. Licking her lips, she even told him, "I want to kiss you."

His nostrils flared as he drew in a sharp breath. Color flooded under his skin and his hands came up as though to grasp her hips. He caught himself and clasped the edge of the desk, knuckles white. With a jerk of his head, he acquiesced.

Clair used her hips to nudge his thighs farther apart so she stood right up against his erection. Her heart thundered. Aleksy lowered his head, but that was as far as he went. She had to press her mouth to his and cling to his shoulders for balance as she lifted herself on her toes. She had to open her lips and try to cajole him to do the same. His erection pressed insistently against her belly, but he didn't let go of the desk.

To her chagrin arousal grew in her despite being the one trying to arouse him. Touching him in any way made her body writhe with desire while the taste and feel of his smooth lips against hers clouded her mind. She wanted to lose herself in the kiss. She wanted this to be the kind of all-encompassing kiss he always gave her.

He wasn't cooperating, though. His breathing was erratic, but he didn't seem as overcome as she was. Growing frustrated, she cupped his head and boldly forced her tongue into his mouth.

He grunted and leaned into her. Surprised by her success, she tried again and was met by a welcoming draw and the stroke of his tongue against hers. Now came the drowning pool of pleasure where she ceased thinking about the mechanics of what they were doing and hummed with gratification at the sheer joyfulness of kissing him. Nipping, soothing, consuming. Arching her body, she stroked herself against him, ready to abandon herself completely.

His hard fingers dug into her hips and he straightened away.

She whimpered at the loss and licked her lips where the taste of him still lingered.

"Aren't you going to move this to the bedroom?" he growled.

The fire building inside her was doused, leaving burning hot embers that blistered her sensitive nature. She had thought his innate drive to lead was ready to take over. He was determined to make her work for this, though, and it almost undermined her belief in herself and what she was able to make him feel.

Trying to understand where she had gone wrong, she searched his expression and noted the tension in his face, the tick in his cheek that made his scar pull at the corner of his slightly parted mouth. His chest was expanding in a short hard rhythm.

In a startling burst of clarity she knew why he'd stopped

her. The kiss had started to become more than he could handle. He was cooling the pace so he could remain in control.

A heady sense of power flowed into her, but it was surprisingly tender too. With renewed confidence, she reached out and learned how to open a man's jeans.

"I don't have a condom in here," he warned.

"You don't need one."

Aleksy swore in Russian. Stop her, he told himself. Before she put him over the edge. But he was too hungry to see how far she'd go. The rush of blood in his ears deafened him and the heat of desire threatened to spontaneously combust his soul.

He reached for the soft swells teasingly rising and falling behind a thin layer of wool. She often went braless. He loved it. Those modest, taut breasts of hers didn't need support and he liked being able to find her nipples easily and feel them harden.

Clair stepped back, her light grip catching his thick wrists before he'd barely cradled her soft curves. "No touching. Not yet," she said breathily. She pressed his hands back to the surface of his desk. "You'll distract me and I want to make this as good for you as you always do for me."

Anticipation screamed in him, threatening to make him lose it completely. He instinctively wanted to take over, be the one in control of the pace, especially when her hot blue gaze clashed into his, her enjoyment of having the upper hand obvious.

"I want to suck your nipples," he demanded, balancing on the knife's edge between stealing the dominant role that was always his and letting Clair keep the power she was obviously reveling in.

He almost had her. Her pupils expanded into galactic holes he could have fallen into. Her breath rushed out in a near surrender and her light hands on his thighs grew heavy as she melted closer.

"No," she gasped at the last second, the word driving like a knife into his groin. She dug her fingernails through denim as she firmed her resolve. "Not yet. I want to take off your shirt first."

With hands that betrayed a nervous tremble, she tugged the close-fitting knit up his chest. He lifted his arms, eyes closing as he endured what felt like the loss of his skin. Her lips touched his collarbone.

He caught back a groan.

Another kiss and her splayed hands smoothed across his chest hair. His nipples went so tight they felt pierced. His erection pulsed in the space of his open fly, clawing at his control.

Her hands began to graze with more surety, flowing over his rib cage and abdomen, finding his waistband. Working with awkward inexperience—which was its own delight—she eased her hands under denim, lifting his hips off the edge of the desk to work his jeans down his thighs.

"Finally," he hissed, shaking with need.

She paused and he realized he'd spoken in Russian. She kept going and he kicked out of the jeans, stepping so his socked feet were braced, fingers flexing with desire to catch her up to him and plunder her mouth.

She lowered herself to her knees, hands cool and soft on his calves as she removed his socks. Did she know she was driving him to the absolute edge of reason?

He glared down to see her staying on her knees, gaze coming to rest on his shorts, lips pressed into a line of uncertain study. As she reached out and carefully eased the elastic over him, his vision blurred. He stepped out of his shorts and didn't know if he'd be able to stay on his feet. He was a conqueror by nature and necessity, but at this second he was a slave. A prisoner to each of her incremental movements.

Despite knowing what she was about to do, he was staggered by the first touch of her hands, swelling and hardening to unbearable proportions, filling her palms. Words of protest and abject begging threatened to burst from him, but she was stealing every last thought from him, closing her mouth upon him with untutored, scandalously sexy ardor.

A ragged groan erupted from him. His passion nearly exploded. He wasn't going to last and he wanted, *needed*, to be inside her.

With the very last shreds of his control, he tangled his fingers in the golden silk that brushed her cheeks. It killed him to force her to release him, but he had nothing left. He was about to shock or scare her and he had to have her with him when the last of his restraint evaporated. He wanted to feel each ripple of her orgasm when he came and know she was as insanely lost to pleasure as he was.

"You didn't like it?" she asked anxiously as he drew her to her feet.

"If you don't get a condom on me soon, you're going to have to start arousing me all over again." He couldn't believe the quiet, husked voice was his own. He sounded tender. He even felt a deep, complex stirring inside himself. To say, "I want you" didn't come near to encompassing the expansive need in him.

The phrase still caused her blue eyes to glitter with jubilation. That naked look nearly made him use the desk right there and then.

He cupped her head so he could swoop his mouth onto hers and did everything in his power to convey his desire, to bestow as much pleasure as he could. Her sweet moan, the plaster of her lithe body into his, was his reward.

Swinging her into a cradle against his chest, he made the bedroom in record time, barely able to open the drawer for a condom and get it on without erupting. He removed her yoga pants and the panties beneath with a rending of delicate lace while she pushed off her top, her breasts hot and damp with sweat as he pressed himself over her, crushing her onto the bed beneath him. Using his knees to push her thighs apart, he couldn't resist testing her arousal, finding her so wet and ready she bucked at the first touch of his fingers.

In one triumphant thrust, he filled her. A primal tingling raced down his spine as he made her his, only his, again and again and again.

CHAPTER ELEVEN

ALEKSY TOLD HIMSELF he was allowing the relationship to continue, and deepen, for Clair's sake. Of all the men she'd come across in her life, she found him to be sexually compatible, so he was putting himself at her service. It would be unkind to deprive her of an opportunity to explore her sensual nature. At least he knew she was unique and treated her accordingly. Some might call it self-servicing, but he disagreed. No one had ever gone out of their way to make her happy. She deserved to be spoiled in every way, so he was doing it.

It wasn't his usual exchange of luxuries for sex either. They were both getting exactly what they wanted from that side of things.

His mind drifted to the other morning when his housekeeper had called in sick. Clair had made him breakfast. As her short robe had fluttered around her bare thighs, teasing him with glimpses of her bottom, he'd grown so hard his appetite for food had fallen to a distant second behind his hunger for her. She'd noticed.

Seated on a kitchen chair, he'd pulled her to straddle him and they'd teased and tantalized each other, playing out the lovemaking, holding back even when he was inside her, driving each other crazy until he'd had to knock his eggs to the floor and take her on the table, urged to thrust hard and fast by her breathy pleas. They'd climaxed together, vocal and near violent, and had been equally shaken and quiet afterward.

He'd taken her back to bed, where she'd slept against him, her head a kitten weight on his chest. He had dozed, but mostly he'd berated himself for failing to use a condom.

What was he trying to do, tie her to him forever?

He hadn't brought himself to mention it when she had stretched awake against him, but later in the day she'd shyly informed him she didn't think pregnancy was an issue and that they'd have to curtail their favorite activity for a few days.

A weight of disappointment had settled on him, one he'd blamed on abstinence, but they'd been back to basics this morning and even though he was still fogged with sexual satisfaction, he was also aware of a cloud of unease hanging over him.

Guilt.

The more he learned about Clair, the more he knew how badly he'd taken advantage of her. If he had the least shred of conscience in him, he'd give her up, but watching her natural reserve evaporate was positively entrancing. She had made the first move this morning, rolling atop him and telling him how much she'd missed making love with him. How could any man be expected to forgo waking up to that?

Unable to bring the ends of this particular rope together, he stopped gazing out the window and gave up pretending that he was working. His ambition was nonexistent. He'd only been in the office an hour, but he began to pack up for lunch, excited as a schoolboy for the ring of the bell. Lazlo had inadvertently revealed while arranging Clair's credit card the other day that her birthday was coming up. She had become flustered and dismissive when Aleksy had asked her how she wanted to celebrate, eventually confessing that birthdays had always been a disappointment along with Christmas.

He was determined to turn that around for her, starting with a visit to the city's best jeweler on his way to meet her at an exclusive, sky-high restaurant. Enjoying the way she reacted when he surprised her with toys and trinkets didn't make him selfish, he told himself. It was the opposite.

Wasn't it?

A short time later, however, as he scanned past diamond rings to bracelets and pendants, he recalled the way his father had often taken pains to barter for some treasure or another that his mother had coveted. Once it had been a sewing machine, another time a pair of gold earrings. His father had rubbed his hands in glee at being able to surprise his wife with her heart's desire.

That's all he, Aleksy, wanted to do for Clair, but it felt as if he was making false promises. The sparkling rings mocked him. He couldn't keep this up, keep *her*, forever, even if he wanted to.

Did he want to?

He clenched a fist, aware of a deep need to have her as readily at hand as everything else that was vital to his existence. Air, water. Clair.

Shaken, he dismissed his misgivings and set down a small fortune on a choker with sapphires in graduated shades of blue, brilliant and sparkling as her eyes when she laughed. He *liked* seeing her happy. Provoking her to smile didn't make him a bad person.

His certainty lasted through a pleasant lunch where she practiced her fledgling Russian phrases and he expanded on some of the historical events she'd been reading about. She made him look at his city and country with new eyes, and hers widened with dazzlement when she unwrapped his gift.

"It's too much," she protested in a whisper, then teared up as her cake arrived, topped with half a dozen sparklers. "Aleksy!" Her lips trembled and she threw her arms around his neck, hugging him hard.

The most incredible tenderness infused him as he pulled her into his lap, startled by how much emotion he'd drawn out of her with such a little act.

"Your secret is out now, you know," she said in a strained voice, drawing back enough to swipe under her eyes and offer him a beaming smile.

His heart did a sharp dip and rock in his chest. "Which secret is that?"

"You're the biggest softie in the world. Not nearly as ominous and gruff as you want to appear."

His mouth twitched and his conscience gave him a kick. He was misrepresenting himself if she really believed that.

"Can we keep it between us?" he said lightly, not wanting to spoil the mood, but pressing her back into her own chair.

"Of course," she replied with an enigmatic smile. "I like knowing more about you than anyone else does."

The remark niggled at him as they finished their coffee and left. His security had told more than one parked car to shove off over the last month, but there hadn't been any for two or three days. His real secret was still safe.

Nevertheless, he was so distracted by his inner thoughts as they walked out of the building that they were in the scrum of paparazzi before he realized he was their object, not one of the international celebrities also dining here.

The clamor and flash and jostle was bad enough, especially with Clair to protect. He squeezed her to his side, aware of her hardening into a tight ball as the horrific questions were shouted not just in Russian, but English.

"Aleksy! Are you guilty of murder?"

* * *

After Aleksy's remark about the paparazzi noting whom he'd taken to the Bolshoi, Clair had made a point of searching their names online each day. Sometimes she noticed a photographer aiming a lens at them as they stepped out, but not always. The gossip hunters were sly and determined, however. Every outing was documented whether she was aware it was happening or not, including their impulsive appearance at the *Maslenitsa* festival.

Being stalked unknowingly made her queasy, but until this circus, her main worry had been the helplessly enamored expression on her face that matched the one worn by his previous lovers. So much for her detachment!

But how could she be impassive when he'd made himself into her own personal playground? Each time they came together she grew a little more possessive of the territory she conquered. Now he'd gone out of his way to do something special for her, buying her a ridiculously extravagant gift and—even more precious—revealing a kind of thoughtfulness that made her feel maybe, just maybe, they were forming a connection that went beyond physical.

Still glowing with a sense of being exceptional in his eyes, she let him carry her along to the sidewalk, where they were suddenly mobbed in a way that truly frightened her. Ducking from the chaos into Aleksy's solid presence, she tried to make sense of why this was happening and *what were they saying?*

She realized she understood more than the Russian moniker of *Scarface*, but other names. Victor Van Eych. His son.

"Did you know about the private investigation?"

"How do you respond to the accusation you sent Van Eych to an early grave?"

"You've been arrested for murder before. Are you guilty?"

The words smashed through her euphoria like a rock through a window.

Seconds later, Clair found herself shoved into the back of his town car, jolted by more than the sudden end to the snapping and snarling of the paparazzi frenzy. Aleksy gave Ivan sharp instructions to return them home as he jerked loose his tie and ran fingers into his hair, then made a call in Russian.

She stared at him, conscience squirming at what was going on in her mind, but she couldn't help the reaction. That white line on his face seemed too revealing.

Murder?

His cheek ticked. He knew what she was thinking and his face hardened, but she couldn't help how shaken she was. Adrenaline saturated her blood. She tried to scramble herself together, tried to stop trembling, but she kept asking herself, What kind of man had she attached herself to?

One who bought her a necklace she somehow still had gripped in her tense hands. Also a new laptop, new smart phone, a tablet. Clothes, meals, tickets to shows. There was no end to the generosity he bestowed on her, but he wasn't really soft and kind. He was hard and angry if she cared to remember their first meeting and—her mind tripped to think of it—capable of murder?

No, her heart cried, but his expression wasn't that of someone who was incensed at being falsely accused. There was too much resentment. Too much bitter resignation.

"We'll go to Piter," he said once they'd made it into the safety of his flat. When she only stared blankly, he clarified, "St. Petersburg. Things will be ugly here for a while."

Uglier than right now? He was like ancient iron, all pitted darkness with grim angles in his face. Her mind was grappling to process the impossible. One question burned on her tongue: *Is it true?* Her heart pounded.

"We?" Her lips felt numb.

"You're not going back to London if that's what you're thinking." Implacable.

She gave a near-hysterical choke that wasn't anything like a laugh. "I don't know what I'm thinking." Her gaze circled wildly, searching for a place to land, glancing off the illusion of a home she'd begun to see in these flawlessly decorated walls.

If she hadn't been with him outside and heard those shouts, would he have told her the reason they were leaving Moscow? Or would he be selling this sudden trip as a romantic getaway?

Would she have bought in? Was she that naive and desperate for affection?

"Pack for staying in." Acrid hostility coated each word.

She swallowed, ears ringing. She'd never felt so alone in her life, so aware that her complete disappearance would go unnoticed by the world.

"I need to know what happened, Aleksy." Her stomach trembled, but she managed to keep her voice steady as she met his forbidding gaze.

"I told you that some people will do anything for money." A vilified sneer pulled at his lips.

"Like lie?" *Please tell me it's all lies.*

He stared at her, his gaze not the hard, sharp, dangerous blade she expected. It was supreme blankness. Bleakness. Flat, unpolished bronze.

"Of course lie, but in this case it was a betrayal of official duty, exposing a truth that should have remained buried."

His words knocked the wind out of her. She had to consciously force herself to draw a breath. It seared her throat and made her chest ache. Her skin grew clammy and her stomach tied itself into knots. She had one thought. *Go.*

As she looked past him, gauging her chances, his arm shot out, not touching her, but making clear he wouldn't let her leave. "You're coming with me, Clair. Whether you like it or not."

Everything in her gathered for the fight of her life. Before she could do more than engage his stare in a battle of wills, he ground out, "You have nowhere to hide and they'll eat you alive. I won't let that happen. But I won't touch you either," he added bitterly.

His statement was another shock, so oddly protective when her head was screaming at her that he was a danger to her. For some reason, her stupid brain stumbled on that *I won't touch you* as if it were a trip wire that sent her metaphorically splatting onto her face, pride bruised. She should be relieved, but she just felt rejected. *Again.*

Words crowded her mouth, but her throat was too thick to voice any of them.

"I have security posted at all the doors to keep the paparazzi out." He stepped back. "They'll also keep you in, so you might as well give in. I really don't need the extra humiliation of carrying you kicking and screaming to the helicopter."

He walked away to his room, presumably to pack, leaving his words repeating in her head. *Extra humiliation.* As if *she* were in a position to injure *him.* Cause further injury even, because he was already hurting.

Was he hurting? She rubbed where her breastbone felt as if it were coated in acid. For a long time she stood in the lounge, arms wrapped tight around herself, confused. Frightened, but not by Aleksy. By herself.

She wanted to trust a man who'd just confessed to murder.

CHAPTER TWELVE

CLAIR HAD HEARD Russians talk about their *dachas*. She had gathered they were a type of summer cottage retreat, usually rustic and far enough out of the city to offer a garden plot and a return to nature. The buildings were often little more than shacks, but they were kept in families for generations.

If this was Aleksy's *dacha*, he needed to work on his definition of *shack*. The minute she saw it, her mind heard, *Welcome home*.

They'd flown over nothing but trees once they'd left the outskirts of Moscow, leaving little to distract from her inner turmoil until she'd glimpsed a palace surrounded by a groomed park. The fountains were off, the canals frozen, but she'd realized they were nearing St. Petersburg. This was a place so beautiful even czars chose to summer here.

Far from summer now, the day was overcast, late afternoon flakes beginning to fall. The fresh dust of snow only made the expansive estate they touched down on look fresh and new. Untouched.

It was very new, she realized, looking at the bare, young fruit trees and nut groves that embraced the charming house. The two-story structure was built along old-fashioned lines with a wraparound porch, shuttered windows, pretty gables and a romantic turret. It was big enough to host a crowd, yet cozy and inviting. Not threatening and not something she would have expected Aleksy to build or buy.

As the pilot prepared to lift into the forbidding sky, stirring up a cloud of powdered ice, Aleksy reached onto a porch beam. "The agent said—here." He showed her the key, then opened the door, pressing her inside before the man-made storm hit.

The interior smelled of paint, freshly cut wood and newly laid woolen carpet. All the surfaces gleamed. It was tastefully decorated in masculine colors, spacious and unfussy like its owner, but welcoming.

It struck her as a fresh start. A promising one.

Clair swallowed, reminding herself why she was here and who she was with, but choice and logic had been left back in Moscow where the apartment building had been surrounded by long-lens cameras. She really would rather take her chances with this lone wolf than the pack of coyotes baying at those doors.

And this house felt safe, drawing her in despite her misgivings. The main floor made a circle from front parlor to the dining room, passing a staircase that climbed to an inviting landing. Upstairs, a quaint powder room with a jetted tub overlooked what might be a stream if spring ever did arrive. The bedrooms with their gabled windows begged for cradles and rocking horses and train sets.

Did Aleksy harbor fantasies of a family? she wondered with a clench in her chest.

She silently followed him as he inspected everything, pausing at the threshold to the master bedroom, taking in the huge space and vaulted ceiling from the door.

He noticed her hesitation but covered his reaction with an impassive assessment of the enormous bed, the dark blue coverlet and the walk-in closet. She supposed an equally spacious en suite existed beyond the door on the interior wall.

"What do you think?" he asked.

She thought she was in love but didn't think it would be judicious to say so. "It's beautiful. You've never seen it? Is it yours?" she added as it occurred to her this could be leased as a bolt-hole.

"It is." Aleksy searched for signs of approval in her, not sure why it was important to him. The house was only a thing, and he was past believing the acquisition of things ruled Clair, but he couldn't deny that he wanted her to like his home.

He'd settle for her liking his things since there was no chance she'd feel anything toward *him* except repulsion.

Gut-wrenching loss threatened to breach the walls he'd used to brace himself when she had demanded answers at the penthouse. He'd known his past would come between them eventually, whether he revealed it or not. It was the reason they had no future, but he would have preferred they had separated naturally, before she knew any of this. It broke something in him to see her view of him damaged. To see her fear him.

The woman who'd lately been greeting him with shy smiles and the warmth of her touch now held him off with a white face and mistrust in her eyes. He cringed and looked away.

"Did you design it?" she asked, yanking him back to reality.

"To some extent." Aleksy shrugged out of his jacket and tossed it on the bed. Fantasies of her white-blond hair and peach-flushed skin against the sea of blue tantalized him, but he ruthlessly shut them down. He'd promised not to touch her.

Keeping his voice without inflection, he explained, "My father worked in logging camps when my parents were first married. The accommodations were drafty bungalows. My mother never complained, but when my father was able to buy into a mill and make his own lumber, he built her a proper house. I used that floor plan as a starting point."

Clair cocked her head, her whimsical smile sad enough to puncture the heart he'd hardened to get through this. "You always surprise me when you're sentimental."

"Sentimental?" The word arrested him. He suddenly saw the monument for what it was. He'd told himself he was building a place to go to, anticipating time to relax once he defeated Van Eych, but it turned out this was yet another attempt to resurrect the dead.

"I thought I just lacked imagination," he dismissed, hiding his perturbation by circling a finger in the air, urging her to turn so he could help her out of her coat.

She huddled deeper into the thick folds for a moment, long enough for questions to flash into his mind like so many charges off one fuse. Armor against him? Didn't want him too close? Didn't want to risk his touch? Wanted to be ready to run when he stopped watching her long enough?

With a skittishness she hadn't shown since that first day, she offered him her back.

As he stepped behind her, she tensed and cleared her throat but only said, "It's not a lack of imagination to surround yourself with the familiar."

Her scent clouded around him, so evocative of their closest moments his abdomen tightened. Heat poured into his loins. He ruthlessly controlled himself and drew her coat off her shoulders, focusing on the inane conversation to dispel the sexual awareness overwhelming him.

"Trying to fix the past by using what's left in the present is foolish."

"Don't call it foolish!" She spun. Her hair whipped his knuckles in delicious castigation.

He inhaled and she folded her fingers into fists that she tucked under her bent elbows.

"The trinkets I have of my parents' could have belonged to anyone," she charged quietly. "They don't offer the kind of memories that would let me pay this kind of homage. Your parents loved each other and you cherish that. There's nothing foolish about building that into your home. I'd give anything to have a house built on love."

She really knew how to skewer a man. How did he explain that he'd taken the love in that house and personally caused its loss? He clenched his teeth so hard his jaw ached.

"This was a stupid idea," he muttered in Russian, wondering how he'd imagined they'd be "safe" here. He brushed past her. "I'll get the luggage in and start a fire."

Clair could have walked away. She was half sure Aleksy wouldn't stop her. Bundled for the weather, passport and credit card secreted in her pocket, she even got as far as trudging into the snow off the front porch.

The world was still and quiet. The low clouds had pulled back from the horizon enough to let a glimmer of dying sunlight slant across the pristine blanket that surrounded the house. Instead of forging a path to the road, she was drawn into a bower of trees where the bare branches hung around her like silver-shot lace.

As she absorbed the sight, she conjured a picture of her own face with darker hair behind the curtain. Her own voice said, *Come out, love. Daddy's home.*

In the time it took her gasp to condense on the air and disintegrate, the memory was gone.

Clair brushed at where snow drifted down and left tickling paths on her cheeks, eyes closed now, listening to her own jagged breaths as she tried to decide if it had been real. Why now? What did it mean?

Nothing, of course. It was fanciful imaginings brought on by talk of nostalgia and childhood. She still longed to run inside and tell Aleksy she had remembered her mother.

Oh, she ought to run from him, never mind the fading light and long walk in the cold! *But why?* He'd never once hurt her. Not on purpose. Maybe he'd said some things that were a little too blunt and honest, but he was always conscious of his strength around her. If he found the least little bruise from their intense lovemaking, he berated himself and kissed it better. He wasn't going to turn into some maniac who wanted to harm her.

In fact, what he'd turned into was a man who'd ejected himself from her bed before she'd had to refuse him. His personal code of honor had forced him to. That action didn't fit against one of the most dishonorable things a person could do, and it made her want answers, not escape.

Penetrated by the cold, Clair picked her way back to the house, stepping in her own footprints so she wouldn't further mar the immaculate field of snow. She walked around to the back of the porch, stamping her feet and then sweeping the snow away before stepping into the kitchen rubbing her arms and shuddering.

Aleksy stood pouring vodka into a short glass. He knocked it back before saying, "Finished making snow angels?" through his teeth.

"Are you drunk?" Her equilibrium was yanked by that unexpected twist.

"Russians don't get drunk." He poured another one, then stoppered the bottle and stowed it in the freezer. "They get tough." He moved, loose but steady, to where a tin of cocoa sat on the bench. He spooned some into a cup and poured steaming water from the kettle. Before he handed it to her, he tipped half the contents of his vodka into it. "Warm up. You're not used to this kind of cold."

Clair cautiously put away her boots and hung her coat. The hot mug of cocoa filled her cupped hands with warmth. She let the steam rise to scald her frozen nose.

"Are you hungry?" he asked. "I can make soup."

"Maybe later," she said, faintly bemused at this domesticated side he was revealing. Not exactly the "tough" he was referring to.

He leaned on the refrigerator, staring so hard at her she should have smoldered and caught fire. "I watched you out there, waiting to see if you would run. You looked about twelve with the snow past your knees."

Clair felt twelve again, sinking into a miasma of confusion, hormones flashing like dysfunctional neon lights, the weight of adult emotions threatening to overwhelm her.

"I just wanted to stretch my legs," she lied.

He snorted, swirling the clear liquid in his glass. "There was a time when I took for granted the girls who walked in front of my house. More than one did before I had whiskers and a scar."

"You want me to believe females haven't been falling on your doorstep all your life, scar or no scar?" She forgot about the vodka in her drink until she sipped and it bit back. Heat slid through her all the way to her toenails.

"The young girls were different," he mused into his glass. "They were like you, the kind who knew they wanted to marry and have a family."

"I don't know that," she said, flat but strong, eyes immediately seeking a place to hide. "I might have believed it when I was twelve, but it's not something I still fantasize about." That felt like lying again. She sipped her cocoa, savoring the glowing warmth that spread outward from her midsection. "Too many lessons in remaining realistic," she added, recalling all those childish hopes and adolescent crushes that had amounted to nothing.

Aleksy winced. "You told me not to be ashamed of being sentimental. Don't be ashamed of wanting those things, Clair. I did. Then. I imagined I'd choose one of those girls after I'd made my fortune."

"Were you in love with one of them?" Her heart stilled.

"No," he scoffed, and her knees unaccountably sagged. "But I was arrogant enough to enjoy the idea of them falling in love with me. I was convinced I'd have my pick when the time came."

Clair frowned, hating that word. Pick your teams. Picked last. Never picked.

Skipping over it, she asked, "What made you stop wanting that? Your mother's grief?"

Empathy stole over her like a fuzzy veil, partly due to the vodka slipping into her bloodstream. It made her feel tender, hurting for him when she considered how painful it must have been to witness his mother's heartbreak over the loss of her husband. At least he was there to see it and not locked up in jail....

Clair frowned into her cup, thinking the booze was a bad idea. She was having trouble clicking together important pieces of the puzzle.

Aleksy wasn't speaking, only staring into his glass, face lined with anguish.

She watched him, his powerful shoulders crushed by a weight. He looked...lonely. Inconsolable. She ached to circle his waist with her arms and press her face into the warmth of his chest.

"Aleksy," she began.

"Yes, seeing my mother's pain killed whatever illusions I had of leading that kind of life. Especially since I caused her grief and destroyed the happy life she'd finally been given." The words were dragged out of him and left on the floor like internal organs.

"Finally?" she repeated tentatively. Apprehensively. "Wasn't she always happy with your father?"

"Of course," he conceded with a shrug, "but they struggled for years. Everyone in Russia did. When my father organized the cooperative that bought the mill, it was a chance for a future, but still just a chance. They worked hard for every potato we ate. I should have said she finally had *hope*."

He drew a long breath, seeming to steel himself. His voice hardened.

"The problem was, profiteers were moving into Russia at the same time. One tried to bribe my father into selling his controlling interest in the mill. He refused and we were harassed for months."

Clair closed her eyes as dread stole through her. "Victor."

"He gave the orders. Lazlo has uncovered more evidence and will make it public soon. Victor's son knows what's coming and was trying to discredit me by revealing my past, but the attention will turn back on him once the truth about his father's actions come out. I don't think you'll be bothered too much after that," he concluded without emotion.

When he sent her back to London, she gathered with a little shiver. She was just getting used to sharing her life, and it was almost over. Her feet hurt and she realized she was scrunching them, trying to dig into this place, not ready to be uprooted.

"What exactly did Victor do?" she asked, afraid to hear the extent of it but needing to know before he sent her away. "Did he steal your father's shares? Take the mill?"

"A man came to our house and set it alight in the middle of the night."

Clair gasped and covered her mouth. The house like this one that she adored? "While you and your parents *slept?*" Horror gripped her. "And your father—?"

"Ran outside behind my mother and me. The arsonist was still there. My father told me not to go after him, but I had had enough. I didn't see the knife until he did this." His hand lifted to his face, his expression twisted with old fury and fresh pain.

"Oh, Aleksy," Clair breathed, terrified for him. Everything in her wanted to rush forward in comfort, but he radiated too much pain, as though the least thing would break him. "And you were just a teenager." The pieces were falling together quickly now, forming a tragic, unbearable picture.

He shuddered.

"A boy's temper in a man's body. I would have been killed if my father hadn't intervened. He lost his life saving mine." He slugged the vodka and set down the empty glass with a sharp *clunk*. Then he looked at his hand. His voice seemed to come from far off. "I don't remember doing it, but it's in the statements to police that I killed the other man."

"I can't believe they arrested you!"

"Why wouldn't they? A crime had been committed." He turned to the freezer to retrieve the bottle. "It was ruled self-defense and, supposedly, sealed because of my age."

Ever-deepening levels of dreadfulness rippled over her. A deliberately set fire. A narrow escape. Petrifying violence. Catastrophic loss. His life nearly taken. She never would have known him. The thought pushed tears into her eyes.

And all at the hands of a man she had trusted and relied on. Bile and self-disgust rose to the back of her throat.

Aleksy would *never* pick her. Not to live with him forever. Her awful connection to Victor would always be between them.

"I'm so sorry," she said with remorse, wishing the words weren't so inadequate. "I had no idea Victor could do something so vile." She took a deep swallow of the cocoa, seeking the numbing effect of the alcohol. The sweetness made her gag. She set it away, revolted.

"What about what *I've* done?" A scowl of self-hatred ravaged his expression. "I'm no better than the paid assassin who killed my father."

"You were fighting for your life!"

"I shouldn't have fought at all. I got my father killed and destroyed my mother."

She shook her head. This was why he isolated himself. He thought he was some kind of monster. "You can't punish yourself for a…mistake."

"A mistake that lasts forever."

"If you let it," she asserted. "You can't blame yourself, Aleksy. Victor brought about the tragedy by starting it, not you."

"Stop it." He stepped forward, every muscle bulging in confrontation. "I saw how you looked at me when you realized what I'd done. I know what you really think of me."

"No," she cried, assailed by guilt. "I was in shock from something completely unexpected. I didn't know what to believe—"

"How could it be unexpected? It's right here!" he railed, pointing at his scar. "From the first moment anyone sees me, they know what kind of man I am. You should have run far and fast the first day we met."

"You didn't give me a chance, did you?" she shot back, angry at his rebuke.

"No," he agreed with a bitter bark of laughter. "No, I didn't, but that's the kind of man I am." Snatching up bottle and glass, he elbowed his way out of the kitchen into the lounge.

CHAPTER THIRTEEN

"I'm not running now, am I?" Clair challenged behind him, barreling through the door on his heels.

Aleksy halted, teeth clenching as he searched for patience. Did she not realize his control was hanging by a thread? Without turning back to her, he guessed harshly, "Because you don't know where to go? Call Lazlo. He'll arrange a car and hotel."

"I'm not afraid of you, Aleksy Dmitriev!"

Funny, he was terrified of her. Setting down the bottle and glass with deliberation, he turned and said, "You should be."

"Why? Are you going to hurt me? Kill me?"

He jerked his face to the side, blind to all but splashes of color in his field of vision while he dealt with the sense of being rent open. No, he could never harm her, but he couldn't have her poking heedlessly into his old wounds either.

"Back off, Clair."

"You're not a monster, Aleksy," she said more gently. "You're generous and compassionate and honorable."

"What are you trying to do? Make it okay in your head that you ever let me touch you? I took a virgin for a mistress. I bought you clothes and gave you money for your charity because *I wanted to have sex with you*."

Her breath caught as if she'd taken a stiletto to the lung. "That's not true," she gasped. "It wasn't just sex. Was it?"

He mentally stripped her fleece vest, insulating V-neck and loose jeans, imagining her naked skin catching the glow off the fire, her nipples pulled into dark, shiny points by his mouth, her thighs relaxing open under his hand. "Very good sex," he ground out, dying because he'd never have her like that again.

"Then why are you trying to take a bottle to bed instead of me?" she goaded, angry hurt pouring a wild flush into her cheeks. She had the gall to charge close enough to stand toe to toe with him, breath chocolate-sweet and as innocent-smelling as the rest of her. "You could be sugarcoating your past and trying to seduce me right now. You know you don't have to try very hard, so why don't you?"

His skin tightened and her upper arms were in his flexing hands before he could stop himself. Her slender muscles always shot a warning through him. *Take care.* The protective instinct couldn't be overridden even when he was feeling so threatened he wanted to shake the daylights out of her.

"Don't think I won't give it a shot," he growled. "I'm not in a frame of mind to stop either."

She only dared him with a tiny hitch of her chin.

He searched for vestiges of fear in her expression but wound up homing in on her lips. A tiny shudder quaked through her as temptation crackled in the air.

The weight of his head weakened his neck. "Stop me," he ordered dimly, speaking against the damp, ripe plum of her mouth.

He almost had her. She almost said it. He felt her begin to shape the word, sensed her tongue tucking behind her teeth. If she'd said *no*, for any reason, he would have made himself stop.

Her eyes fluttered closed and she pressed her open mouth to his.

She smelled of snow and chocolate and vodka, sweet and hot. And he was *hurting*. His deepest shame was never meant to be on display like this. He felt flayed to pieces by today's revelations. By her reaction. But when he drew her into him, the pain subsided. The tattered edges of his soul came together and began to mend.

She moaned softly, igniting him. With one step, he had her back against the wall, her neck and the curve of her hip filling his hands, her delicate softness cushioning all his hard angles. Her fingers wove into his hair, pulling him into a kiss he couldn't have ended if the house had fallen down around them. Her tongue stroked his, her throat straining as she reached for the same oblivion he was in. With a growl, he fumbled the fly of her jeans, pushing them down, lifting her as she kicked free and bracing her against the wall so she could lace her legs around him. He needed to be inside her. Needed her.

As he tried to free himself, her fists clenched in his hair, pulling his scalp tight as she dragged him back from the kiss enough to gasp, "Condom?"

It wasn't *no*, but it made him hesitate. He distantly put together that he was about to risk a pregnancy. He couldn't put a baby in her. Him, with his tainted soul.

The deepest agony filled him as he carefully pushed her legs off him and supported her until she stood. Confusion broke through her flush of arousal. "What's wrong?"

"Leave me alone, Clair." He walked outside where the gathering darkness, frozen and harsh, matched what was inside him.

* * *

His rejection devastated her, but, Clair realized, she'd hurt him first.

The knowledge stunned her, hovering like a dark cloud as she took a long bath and tried to sleep. She'd always been the one hurt, always taking it to heart when she was overlooked or misjudged or found wanting. To her knowledge she'd never delivered anything but mild disappointment when she declined a date. The fact that she'd penetrated Aleksy's hard shell was as shocking to her as how deeply she'd stabbed him behind it.

She stared into the dark, her mind unable to stop replaying those few minutes in Moscow when she'd learned about his past. *I saw how you looked. I know what you think of me.* She had let him down when he'd already been feeling humiliated by the uncovering of his deepest pain before the entire world.

Maybe she should have read more into his scar from the very beginning, but even though he was formidable and ruthless, she'd only ever seen that blaze as an injury, never a warning of cruelty or aggression. She'd instinctively understood it was the result of deep pain.

And maybe if they had more going on than sex between them, she might have had more immediate trust! She was nothing to him but his latest mistress, though. He'd made *that* clear while she was performing her little exercise in proving he had honor.

And she had certainly failed to think that through! She clenched her eyes shut, still throbbing with heat between her thighs while the rest of her ached with wounded disappointment and fear. Had honor stopped him or did he not want her anymore? He'd seemed as excited as she was, only stopping because she'd reminded him about birth control. She'd said it because she couldn't bear to trap him into something he didn't want. If they ever married, she wanted—

Clair sat up, instantly shaky and clammy all over. Where had that thought come from? She didn't want to marry anyone.

Did she?

Yes! She curled into a ball, trying to contain the longing that exploded in her like a supernova. Years of denial were blown into fragments as, within seconds, a brilliant future unfolded in her mind: her with Aleksy and children in this house full of affection and laughter and love.

She was falling in love with him and it made knowing he only felt desire—maybe not even that anymore—unbearable. Her mind shot back to Paris and his, *I'm not the marrying kind*. She yearned to believe that was just the self-inflicted punishment he'd hinted at in the kitchen tonight, but even if it was, there was no guarantee he'd ever be interested in marrying *her*. Every solicitous, tender moment he'd shown her had been a prelude to sex. Because he wanted her body, not her. Never her.

With an angry sob, she threw herself back onto the pillows, ordering her longing back into its box, but it was futile. The fantasies continued.

Eventually she quit tossing and turning, sleeping hard from her journey through such taxing emotions and waking to a brilliant day. Coffee was already made when she entered the kitchen and Aleksy's boots and jacket were missing. A quick glance out the window and she spotted him shoveling the snow off the drive.

When he wasn't in his office over the next few days, talking and talking in every language he knew, that's where he was, outside in the cold. She tried to stay busy preparing the final details for the launch of Brighter Days, but Aleksy filled her mind. Every time she saw him, he looked exhausted, as though he was barely sleeping. The media demands were obviously getting to him. She only wished there was something she could do, but he didn't seem to want to share—which was one more layer on the cake of hurt she was carrying inside her chest.

Clair wasn't sure how much longer she could take it. Then her mobile rang unexpectedly. It was Lazlo.

Startled to hear him identify himself, she asked the only sensible question that could explain his ringing her number. "Are you looking for Aleksy? He's upstairs. I was just going to ask him what he'd like for lunch."

"Please don't disturb him. He's doing a live Web conference off his laptop. No, I'm calling for you, Ms. Daniels. I want to discuss the press release on your contribution to our investigation."

"I haven't contributed anything," she broke in.

A significant pause; then, "As it happens, the calendar details you kept of Victor Van Eych's appointments proved very helpful."

"Oh." Clair turned to sit on the stairs.

"We'll be stating that even though you had no knowledge of the misappropriation of investor funds, it was thought you could be in danger from associates who might have feared that you did. This is why, despite any appearances otherwise, you have been the platonic guest of Aleksy Dmitriev since the takeover."

Clair was glad she was sitting. Her blood seemed to drain out of her head, leaving her feeling empty as everything vital in her slithered away.

"Ms. Daniels?" Lazlo's voice came from a long way away.

"Yes, I'm here. Is that what we're stating?" she said, straining not to sound shrill.

"It neutralizes speculation and affords you more privacy in the future."

"When I'm on my own, you mean."

"Exactly," he said without hesitation. "Please respond to any questions or requests for interviews that you aren't at liberty to divulge anything until it has all gone through the courts."

Clair doubled forward, glad she could hear the rumble of Aleksy's voice behind closed doors and knew he wasn't likely to see her like this.

"When do I leave?" she asked tightly.

"To return to London? After the interview today, the worst of the media storm should be over. Everything is in place for when you're ready."

By "everything" she supposed he meant a flat, a job and fifty thousand pounds. Blood returned to her cheeks with hot pressure, sharp with the sting of degradation. Of not even being Aleksy's *mistress* anymore.

"Ms. Daniels? Did you have a comment?"

"None," she choked.

"A perfect response."

CHAPTER FOURTEEN

ALEKSY EMERGED FROM his office with a hole in his belly and an even deeper hunger to see Clair. Her quiet, thoughtful nature had been his salvation through this week of scrutiny, painful questions and trial by public opinion. Each time his mind had been drained of his last wit and his defenses battered to nothing, she'd rescued him by simply being here with fresh-baked cookies, humming to old rock tunes or napping in front of the fire.

He'd offered to bring someone in to cook and clean, but Clair had said she didn't mind doing it and he'd been grateful. He didn't want anyone around. He'd been prepared to send her away, had requested Lazlo to put everything in place for her return to London. He'd thought he wanted to be alone to lick his wounds, but since he didn't have to hide anything from Clair—

That thought brought him up short halfway into the kitchen.

Clair knew his worst secret and she was still here. Through the course of this week, everyone else's reaction had ceased to matter because this one woman, in her tough little way, had skipped the platitudes and supported him with her steady, warm presence in his home.

His soul, locked in a paroxysm of agony for so long, began to unbend, sighing at the release, burning with the return of feeling. It made him wince as he looked at the table set for two. Another stunning realization struck: he was taking her for granted.

"What's wrong?" she asked, turning to catch his scowl.

"Nothing." He shook off his dismay, thinking, *I might ask you the same.*

Clair's hair was loose and she was doing her best to hide behind it as she fussed with putting out salad and hot sandwiches. The little he could see of her face was pale, her lip caught between her teeth, her tension visible in the way she moved.

"You must be bored stiff, locked away like this," he surmised. "Would you like to go into the city for dinner?"

It was an impulsive offer, something he didn't think through, and it surprised her. A sleek decorative bottle full of oil and vinegar dropped from her hand, shattering on the tiled floor. Clair muttered a word her prim lips didn't usually form.

"Stand back," he said, noting her socked feet. "I'll do it."

A few minutes later they sat down to eat. She'd mixed fresh dressing into a measuring cup but was still out of sorts. "I liked that bottle," she groused.

"It can be replaced, Clair." He didn't understand why that made her jaw set and her eyes grow bright. "Look, I appreciate all you've done this week," he tried. "When I brought you here, it wasn't with the intention you'd house-keep for me. I just wanted you out of the line of fire."

She stared for a moment, thoughts contained behind her slightly flushed cheeks and sober expression. "Throwing your jeans into the laundry with mine wasn't exactly a strain. How is…everything?"

Yet again he appreciated the way she took care to probe gently. Many times she'd let him get by with a grumbled

"Fine." He had the strongest urge to lean across, brush her hair back from her cheeks and kiss her.

He hadn't touched her since that first evening when he'd almost taken her in the lounge. In truth, he hadn't trusted himself. His emotions had been all over the place and he'd still been hurting from her initial reaction and angry with her later one. He had needed to shove the entire world away while he dealt with old pain and the lurid interest in his past.

Now he was overwhelmed with a sense of indebtedness along with a desire to be close to one person: Clair. As close as physically possible. He wanted to make love to her, tenderly and thoroughly.

"You don't have to talk about it if you don't want," she said, dabbing a fingertip onto a fallen sesame seed and touching it to her tongue.

Her words snapped him back to the kitchen, but his libido remained transfixed on the action of her tongue, the press of her lips, the faltering curiosity in her gaze as she looked at him.

He didn't disguise the heat rising in him. When she saw it, a flush of desire blossomed on her cheeks, but her eyebrows came together in confusion. She skittered her gaze away and held herself still, not rejecting him, but not screaming with receptiveness either.

Sweat broke out on his brow.

In the space of a few minutes, he'd convinced himself that she'd merely been waiting for him to warm up to her again. She was here, wasn't she? But he hadn't given her much choice in the matter. *At any time*, as she'd ferociously pointed out the other day. Would she even have become his mistress without his high-pressure tactics?

His center of surety, slowly coming back online after this horrific week, backslid a notch. With aggressive determination he leapt to thoughts of how he might continue buying her affections, but that route was distasteful now. He pushed a frustrated hand through his hair, answering her because he didn't know what else to do.

"Today was the worst, but it was my last word on the subject. The result doesn't look like it will be as bad as I feared." He supposed a part of him had expected police to knock on his door to take him away in handcuffs again, but it was all in the past. Just a story that had needed to be repeated until a different story drew interest.

Her expression softened. "You thought you'd be vilified, but two decades of proving yourself as a man of principles couldn't be completely discounted, could it?" she challenged quietly.

He felt cornered by her words. She kept trying to frame him as good and honorable when he had always known he was bad and needing to repent. That was why he didn't cheat or steal, but even at that, he had resorted to bribery with her, hadn't he? He was sitting here plotting how to coerce her to stay in his bed.

Shame pinned his gaze to the food she'd prepared for him. "You're imbuing me with a much higher character than I possess."

"Aleksy, don't. You're a good man. You deserve to be happy. If you cut yourself off from the life you once thought you'd lead, you're letting Victor win."

So earnest. So blind. So determined to turn him into something admirable.

Some of his hopelessness must have shown in his face, because she blurted, "I'm not trying to persuade you into anything, not with me. I'm just saying you shouldn't write off a meaningful relationship because you think you gave up the right."

Not with me.

"What about you?" He felt his blood slowing with time. "Because you deserve to be happy too."

"I know." She swallowed, blinking rapidly, head down. "I've had a lot of time to think since I've been here."

Aleksy didn't understand why her saying that staggered him. He'd already figured out what kind of woman she was. He'd chosen to believe her when she said otherwise, but he'd known. She'd been a virgin. A powerless one that he'd exploited. He was utterly sincere in telling her she deserved everything that her heart desired.

It would come at a terrible cost to him, but he'd pay it. For once, he'd act with the sort of honor she thought he possessed.

Clair held on to her composure with superhuman effort, losing hope as Aleksy's expression grew stonier, washing away the footings of her confidence. She reacted by pulling herself inward, taking refuge behind an air of insouciance that wouldn't betray how much this really meant to her.

"I wasn't lying when I said I wasn't looking for a permanent relationship. When I was a child, all I ever wanted was to be adopted into a family." She set down her fork and folded her hands in her lap, aware of him becoming still, listening so closely the air around them seemed to vibrate. "As the years passed and I wasn't chosen, I convinced myself being part of a family was the last thing I wanted. I really believed it. Self-preservation, I suppose." She shrugged, the movement jerky and not nearly as careless as she wanted to be.

His slow blink was almost a wince.

Clair could hear the voices in her head warning this gamble wouldn't pay off. It made her keep a few cards against her chest, only saying, "But living in this house, thinking about how your parents felt about each other and, I believe, how my parents felt, as well… It made me realize I want a different kind of family. Not parents, but a husband and children."

Her clammy fingers had clenched themselves together under the table and she kept them hidden, fingernails digging into the backs of her hands so she wouldn't betray how anxious she was for him to show some sign he wanted those things too. With her…

"I understand." He sat back, his mouth curling with self-deprecation. "I knew you weren't proper mistress material— Clair, that's a compliment," he hurried to say when she gasped and stood, impaled by the remark.

She began clearing the food they hadn't touched. "No, you're right," she rushed out, clattering dishes. "I know I'm not good at this." She was breaking into pieces on the inside but refused to let him see it. It would only make this worse. "When we met, I was afraid of every type of relationship. I was so terrified I'd get hurt, I didn't let anyone near me. Now I know it doesn't actually kill you to be close to someone. Literally, physically close, I mean." Her smile was brittle. "I'll be able to take that forward…"

She stumbled to a halt, unnerved by the way his eyes went black. Jealousy?

Ducking her head, she let her hair fall forward, hiding her confusion. Hiding the way her face wanted to crumple because she was so full of longing and so unsure.

With a deep breath, she steeled herself and lifted her chin. "Still a long way off before I risk falling in love, but…" She trailed off, bravado tank on empty. "I'm just sorry I'm not—" Her throat began to thicken. *What you wanted.* "I'm going to pack."

She rattled dishes onto the bench and left.

CHAPTER FIFTEEN

IF ALEKSY'S WORK ethic had suffered when Clair was waiting at the penthouse for him, it downright evaporated when she wasn't there at all. He told himself that sinking into new challenges would allow him to leave this gut-knotting anguish behind, but nothing seemed to bury it. He didn't really care about the outcome as his legal counsel cut a deal with a union to keep a factory operating and when a stock market correction dented his worldly holdings. His only concern was whether it had affected the portfolio he'd put together for Clair.

He went through the motions of living, but nothing drove him. He'd never been at such a loss. Genuine hunger, guilt, thirst for revenge… They'd all motivated him to face the next challenge and the next, and now he had no goal. No purpose. The only thing that meant anything to him now was gone.

Clair.

He'd done the right thing, he kept telling himself. She deserved to be loved. He, at least, had known the feeling at one point in his life. He'd subverted his need for it, determined to avenge the lives of his parents, but they'd made sure he knew what it was. Clair hadn't experienced that, and if she could find a man who loved her even half as much as he did—

The thought flashed through his mind like lightning, and then a million others crowded in a rumble behind it.

He loved Clair. He loved her with the kind of devotion that would move him between her and a knife or a gun. He would die for her.

A second jolt of stunned clarity went through him. That's what his father had done. He'd only ever seen his father's death as something he'd caused, but his father had stepped into the fight because he'd loved his son too much *not* to protect him.

No other man would ever love Clair as much as he did.

Did that make him worthy of her? No. But as it sank through him that he hadn't even told her how deeply she was loved, he felt like the smallest man on earth. Her husky "Not with me" continued to ring in his ears all day, every day, but maybe if she'd known how thoroughly she occupied his heart, she would have felt differently. If nothing else, surely she'd realize her own worth and never again settle for anything but wholehearted devotion in a relationship.

Stirred from apathy for the first time in weeks, he sought out her new contact details.

And quickly learned she'd disappeared.

Clair made a note in her calendar, then traced the capped end of the pen over her upper lip, pleased with the number of "yes" responses she'd had to her invitation.

The home usually had a decent turnout for volunteer drives. Clair was one of the diehards. She had expected a few of the people she'd seen during the annual clean to be willing to sit on her committee bridging the foundation funds to the most-needed programs in the home, but she was thrilled to hear all of them eagerly agree.

Things were finally coming together. The home had

cleared out an old cloakroom to make an office for her. One of the cooks had offered Clair the use of her mother's house while the woman visited relatives in Australia. Clair only had to feed the cat and pay the utilities. She wasn't taking a wage from Brighter Days, but she'd interviewed for a clerk position with a notary in the village. It was only a temporary maternity cover, but it would keep her on her feet until she figured out her next step.

She was, if not happy, at least comfortable and rewarded while she nursed a rejected heart from Aleksy's virtually wordless goodbye. He'd driven her into St. Petersburg himself and put her on a private jet back to London, where she'd been met by that dead fish, Lazlo.

She shouldn't be so hard on the man. Lazlo was only doing his job, being attentive to the point of smothering her, ensuring that her boxes had been delivered to the flat in one of the most exclusive buildings in London. *Aleksy's?* She hadn't had the nerve to ask. She hadn't lowered herself to take any of the three jobs he'd secured for her either. As for the credit cards that bore her name but wouldn't send their bills to her, she'd cut them up the minute Lazlo left.

Clair knew it was pigheaded, but she hadn't stayed one night in London. She'd put her things back in storage at her own expense and caught the train here. A clean break, she had decided, smirking a little over using the expression. Look at her, proficient in the vernacular of modern-day relationships after her first one.

Sighing, she flipped the page on her diary to check the time on tomorrow's appointment with an art therapist before she closed the book. This was the part of the day she found hardest—going back to a house that felt like a home and having only a cat for company. Perhaps she'd invite one of the staff and their family to eat with her. She did that now. Rather than forcing herself to tough out the lonely times, she was making real friendships and finding it a confidence booster. It turned out people liked her when she opened up and let them get to know her. She wasn't an awkward orphan any longer. She was an independent young woman like any other.

Fetching her jacket off the hook in the corner, she shrugged it on, flipping her hair out from under the collar with a vague thought to trim it soon. Outside, she noted a stylish car in the drive. Her heart skipped a beat, betraying how many fantasies she still harbored about a certain man, but it was probably just the school trustee who'd promised to pick up the scholarship information Clair had left for her.

Hearing a footstep and a creak of a floorboard behind her, Clair said, "Is that you, Geri? I was just about to hunt you down and ask if you'd like to come for din—" She turned to see a tall shadow filling the doorway. Déjà vu struck instantly.

She couldn't move as she took in tall, dark, scarred, gorgeous Aleksy Dmitriev invading her life again.

"Who is Geri? Is he your colleague?" *That voice*. His rough-smooth accent and deep timbre vibrated through her, making her feel restless and anxious to take flight.

Clair surreptitiously braced a hand on the windowsill behind her. "Geraldine is one of the house parents. What are you doing here?"

"You dropped off the face of the earth, Clair." He stepped into the tiny room and she took in all of him from his uncreased suit to his smoothly shaven jaw. He looked restored to his old self. Better. Like clay that was stronger for going through the fire. Clean, polished and strong. "What were you thinking, disappearing like that?"

Given that her mind was a clean whiteboard at the moment, completely blank of anything but shock, she took a moment to shake herself into a response.

"I wasn't trying to disappear. I only wanted to discuss the foundation with the people it would most closely affect, so I came here to do it. Why?" She didn't like how he put her on the defensive. He'd set her out of his life like bottles for the milkman to collect. She didn't have to answer to him.

At least, she wanted to be that defiant and dismissive, but in reality, her heart was caving in on itself and her entire being was soaking up the effect of being near him again.

"If you didn't want to stay in London, you should have said." His arrogant decree was stated with a scowl of impatience.

"Said to who? Lazlo? Nothing against the man, but he's not my warden and definitely not my bosom chum. He already knows more about my private life than I ever wanted him to. I wasn't about to report my comings and goings to him."

"To *me*." Aleksy loosened his tie, then drove his fists into his pockets, his agitation making her think for a second—

Clair gave her head a little shake, refusing to read in to it. She had let herself get all tangled up in wanting things from him and was still trying to unravel him from her heart. She didn't hate him for hurting her, but she didn't want him to do it again.

Even though she suspected he *was* doing it again and all he'd had to do was step through a door.

"We're no longer involved," she said with as steady a voice as she could muster, reminding herself as much as him. With a flick of her wrist, she prompted him to close the door. When it had clicked firmly and he turned the blinding brilliance of his bronze eyes back on her, she countered it brutally. "You paid me out, in case you didn't know."

His jaw hardened. He leaned into the door, chest rising

as he absorbed her offense. "I'd promised I would. What else would I do? Renege?"

"You didn't have to do all that other stuff." She folded her arms, unable to look directly at him while she relived the sting of being bought off for her sexual favors. She had thought they had shared their bodies with each other freely. Hers had definitely been offered without expectation of compensation.

"I'd promised you that too."

"Well, I didn't have to accept it, so I didn't," she spat out with rancor, hating how cheap he'd made her feel.

"You still could have told me where you were going," he bit out. His voice was so censorious it made her stiffen. "You didn't have to disappear without a word. An email doesn't take any effort at all."

Taken aback by that, Clair choked out a laugh. "Oh, didn't you get my response to yours?"

His eyebrows slammed together. "I didn't email you."

Clair only lifted her eyebrows, waiting for the penny to drop.

With a muttered curse, Aleksy pushed his hand through his hair and tried to pace across the tiny space of her office. He only moved two short steps before swinging back to her.

Clair snapped to attention, aching from the tension of holding herself in this state of readiness. Her palms were sweating within the knots of her fists. "Why are you here, Aleksy?" It seemed rather cruel, quite honestly. She'd managed to move on with her life, not well, but she was doing it. This was going to be a setback of epic proportions. There would be fresh tears she didn't want to shed.

"I'm here to find you." He said it impatiently, as if she ought to know. "I didn't know where else to look, so I came here to ask if they had any contact information on you and they told me you were down the hall. I almost had a heart attack."

Intensity radiated off him, as though he was still keyed up from the discovery.

"There's such a thing as a telephone. You could have called the office," she pointed out. Heat rose on her cheeks and she shifted. The room was too small to contain them both. "Why didn't you put Lazlo on the job? He probably tagged my ear with a GPS when I wasn't looking."

"I was worried." He seemed uncomfortable with the admission, but the words came out of him as though they wouldn't stay inside. "You can't just walk away like that, Clair," he scolded. "I've lost people I loved, and that pain doesn't ever go away. Not knowing where you were or if you were safe was equally as bad."

All her defensive anger fell away, leaving a heart that began beating wildly. She reminded herself that he was just a very protective man with a ferocious sense of responsibility. This wasn't personal.

"Aleksy, I grew up here. Right here." She pointed to the ceiling where two floors up she had shared an attic bedroom with a number of different girls over the years. "To get a workspace in this building, where wards of the state live, I had to pass about a million background checks. That's how serious they are about security. I'm living next door to the police chief. The bus driver greets me by name and his wife sells me eggs. Where do you want me to live that you think I'd be safer?"

He had his unmarked cheek to her and she saw how utterly beautiful he would have been if both sides of his face matched. When he swung his face around, she was almost relieved to see the scar. It made him human and reachable. Mortal.

His jaw worked as though he wanted to say something

but thought better of it. A long minute of silence drew out, pulling her nerves taut.

"You're happy, then?" he finally asked, cheek ticking.

She hugged her coat around her as she shrugged. "It's a little like I've come home, even though…" She frowned, searching for the words. "I feel good because I know I'll make positive changes for the children here, but it's still a place that makes me sad. I wish…" She had to press her lips together to keep them from quivering. "I wish they all had proper homes to go to."

He nodded and the empathy in his expression was more than she could bear. A lump lodged in her chest and she looked away.

After a moment, she found a wry smile even though it was the last thing she felt like doing. "I'm not used to checking in with anyone, you know that. I should have at least told Lazlo not to pay the rent on an empty flat. Sorry about that."

"The money doesn't matter." Aleksy seemed to consume her with his eyes. He'd accomplished his goal, so she wondered why he didn't leave. She was safe here, but the longer he lingered, the more danger she felt. She ached to touch him. Give herself over to him. Again.

Sucking in a breath, he asked a question that shocked her. "Are you seeing anyone?"

"A *man?* No!"

Aleksy's chuckle rasped her nerves. "Why do you say it like that?"

"Because—" Clair's heart clenched. She felt her eyebrows pull together in a pained frown and turned to the windowsill to hide it, tracing some long ago child's initials carved into the wood. She couldn't find her voice to continue.

"You told me that's what you wanted." He sounded confused.

"I did. I do! I'm just not ready yet." She wasn't over *him* yet.

He didn't say anything. She found the courage to glance back at him and found him eating her alive with his eyes, a tortured expression on his face.

He still desired her. It made her insides quiver with yearning. She felt the same way. Pulled.

"Aleksy, don't," she pleaded softly, increasing his agitation.

"I know, I know. *Not with me*." He grimaced.

The bottom dropped out of Clair's world. She wasn't sure if she understood. "Aleksy," she said haltingly, his name like honey on her tongue, "I thought you understood... Oh, I wish I could make you *believe* that you're as entitled to happiness as anyone. Why do you have to say that? 'Not with me.'"

"*You* said that," he countered harshly.

"When?" But even as she said it, she remembered and closed her eyes.

"That last day in the kitchen," he growled. "You went off about how I should subscribe to the Happy Ever After channel, but *not with me*."

"Why on earth would I say *with* me when I'd just gotten off the phone with Lazlo and knew you were already sending me away?" she cried, aghast at how her voice cracked, revealing the stunning pain that still reverberated through her when she recalled it. "You didn't even want me as a mistress anymore."

She clenched her teeth, throat scraped raw as she thought of how she'd laid it on the table as plain as she'd been able. He'd stared at her with that same impenetrable stoniness he turned on her now.

"You spoke to Lazlo that morning?"

She jerked her shoulder. "He called me. To tell me that

you were downplaying our relationship in the press," she added in a charge. "Not even wanting to acknowledge we ever had anything between us—" She kneaded the place between her eyebrows, making her eyes sting.

"Clair, I was doing everything I could think of to protect you. Giving you an easy way out. You know what my life was like then."

"No, actually, I don't," she railed, lifting her glossy eyes to him, vision too blurred to see the way his expression contracted with pain. "You barely told me anything. Never looked to me for comfort or... You hardly looked at me at all!" She snatched up a tissue with a shaking hand, mortified she was falling apart like this. "Not that we had that sort of relationship," she reminded herself. "But I would have listened. I was trying to be there—"

"You were." He was suddenly close, far too close, big warm hands covering hers as she tried to dab at her eyes. "You have no idea what it meant to me that you were there. The only bright spot I had. Don't cry. Don't let me make you cry. I can't bear it."

She was shaking even worse, swimming in the scent of his aftershave. His heat and strength reached out to her, making her want to sway into him and hold on tight.

She swallowed, trying to brush away the solicitous hands wiping the tears off her cheeks. "Don't."

"Don't what?" He cradled her damp cheeks in his firm palms, making her entire body tremble. "Don't try to protect you from every possible thing that could hurt you, including myself?"

"Is that why you sent me back to London?" she asked, stretching to understand what had seemed impossibly cruel and was far beyond what she could accept as reality.

"You wanted to go, Clair. I'd already forced you into

an affair you didn't want. I couldn't keep you when you said you wanted to go."

"You didn't force me."

"Don't say that." He dropped his hands and took a step back. "I showed all the finesse of a Neanderthal, conking you in your tender heart for this place, threatening your reputation, practically throwing you over my shoulder to carry you to my cave."

"You really are your own worst critic. I know how to dial the police if I need them. I wouldn't have gone with you if I didn't want to."

"You really are naive," he countered with a feral glint in his eyes that made her pulse skip. The way he sobered and watched her so closely made her heart beat even faster. "Did you want to go when you left Russia?"

The question backed her into a corner. Her feet tingled with a need to retreat while hot-cold shivers raced over her. She crushed the damp tissue she still held, knuckles going white.

"Please don't ask me to be your mistress again," she managed to say.

"I won't."

The backs of her eyes filled with a hot sting. What a stupid thing to ask, she berated herself.

"Don't," he groaned, and suddenly she was yanked against his chest, off balance and caged by hard arms that held her in a gentle grip when she reacted and began to struggle. "Listen, Clair. Please listen for just one minute," he whispered against her hair.

The movement of his lips on her skin stilled her more than the words, plucking at her heartstrings as she recalled all the tender ways he'd touched her. Need stirred in her, liquid heat settling low, preparing her for the pleasure they gave each other.

"You came into my life when I thought I had only one thing to offer a woman. I made you my mistress because that's all I was capable of. I couldn't offer myself. I was a shell. A robot programmed for revenge. And you were the last woman I should have had anything to do with. I didn't even understand why I had to have you, I just did."

"It was a temporary need for human closeness. I understand. I felt the same." She pressed for escape.

"No! That's not what it was. You were like the sun coming back after the longest Arctic winter. I was bitter and frozen and suddenly I was thawing. Feeling. Do you know how much it hurts when feeling starts to come back into a numb limb?" His fingers wove into her hair and stroked the nape of her neck.

"Oh, Aleksy," she murmured, hating to hear of his suffering. Drawing back, she reached to cup her hand against his scarred cheek, feeling the muscles tense beneath her touch. She almost pulled away, but he covered her hand and closed his eyes. Turning his mouth into her palm, he pressed a kiss into her hand before letting her touch settle against the jagged line again.

"Are you really able to accept all that this scar means?" he asked with a mixture of anguish and hope.

"It means you're a man who would fight to protect the people he loves. That's not something to be ashamed of."

"I am. That's what I came here to tell you. I would die protecting you."

His image blurred as her eyes filled with tears, afraid to believe what she was hearing.

He moved his hands over her with fervent possession. She couldn't seem to catch her breath, especially when he looked at her with uncertainty edging the blaze in his eyes.

"Can you imagine for a minute how difficult it has been for me to know that you deserve every type of happiness and be completely convinced I'm the last man who can give it to you?"

"About the same as it feels for me?" she suggested, feeling something crazy and optimistic battering at the thinning shell she'd always held tightly around her heart.

He shook his head. "All you had to do was stay and I would have been the happiest man alive."

The feeling inside her became massive, too big to be contained. "How could I stay when you didn't seem to w—" Her chin crumpled and she bit her bottom lip, vision blurring again.

When she would have drawn back, he hugged her close, his thickly accented words breaking her open. "I want you, Clair. Of course I want you. I love you with all my heart."

She shuddered at the cataclysm of hearing him say that, at feeling love all around her as he held her tightly and pressed hot kisses to her wet face. Her hands sought to grasp all of him, sliding up his chest, over his flexing shoulders, following the line of his tense neck, smoothing over his hair…. Their mouths met in damp, sweet, poignant ecstasy. Clair's heart was so full it was going to explode.

In a move of agile, male strength, he hitched her to sit on her desk, sending files skating to the floor. Bracing his hands next to her hips and his forehead sternly against hers, he said, "Tell me you're not just reacting to the first man to tell you that. I don't have it in me to be noble and give you up again, Clair. A man like me loves for life, and this is it."

Life. She smoothed his bottom lip with the pad of her trembling fingertip. "Just because I'd never had sex before doesn't mean I didn't know what it was or ache deep down to experience it. It's the same with love. I don't need a hundred men to compare to in order to be sure what I feel for you is the real thing."

"Good, because you're not getting a hundred. You're not even getting one other man," he muttered with a self-deprecating curl of his lip. He tilted her chin up, his gaze so tender it warmed her to her soul. "Are you too shy to say it properly?"

She smiled, stunned by how easily the words formed on her tongue. "I love you."

The expansive emotion seemed to fill the room. The adoring smile he gave her as he stroked her cheek made fresh tears spring to her eyes, happy ones. His kiss was reverent and full of longing.

"Aleksy," she said, reluctantly breaking a kiss that so easily could have spun into something very compromising. "This is my work. There are children here. We have to take this off-site if we're going to keep this up."

He sobered. "Can you leave? In the long term, I mean. Can you—will you—work from Russia or must you stay here? We can come back whenever you're needed," he promised.

She melted, thrilled but at the same time incredibly touched by his understanding. "Thank you for seeing how important the foundation is to me."

His ironic expression made her chuckle.

"I didn't sleep with you *just* for the foundation," she insisted.

"I'll choose to believe that," he said with disgruntlement. "But you'll marry me for no other reason than that you want to."

Not a question. A demand. Wounded he might be, but never weak. Her grin widened. "Of course I will. But I'm given to understand I have to anyway. A woman's virginity belongs to her husband, doesn't it?"

He didn't betray one iota of compunction, only smiled with wolfish satisfaction. "True. But I don't just miss you in my bed," he added with deep sincerity. "I miss you in my life." With utmost tenderness, he asked, "I mean it, Clair—will you come home with me? Be my wife and make a family with me?"

All the details flitting through her mind scattered, completely eclipsed by the momentous wish that had just come true for her. She couldn't even speak she was so overcome.

Aleksy tensed as a shadow passed across Clair's face, but when he tilted up her chin, her blue eyes gleamed. Her joy was so tangible he could taste it like spun sugar on his tongue.

"I always wanted someone to come here and say that to me," she managed to husk. "It was worth the wait."

Aleksy's heart expanded beyond what he could contain. Pressing his mouth to her crooked, trembling smile, he drew her into his arms.

"No more waiting. I'm here now."

* * * * *

A DEAL BEFORE
THE ALTAR

BY
RACHAEL THOMAS

Rachael Thomas was born in Cheltenham, but grew up in Worcester. As a young child she loved to read and make up stories. For as long as she can remember she's wanted to be a writer. As a teenager she became an avid reader of Mills & Boon, borrowing endless copies from her local library—a place she loved to be.

In her early twenties she moved to Wales, where she met and married her own hero—which meant embarking on the biggest learning curve of her life as she settled in to her new role as a farmer's wife. When her two children were in primary school she decided it was time to rekindle her dreams of being a writer.

It took almost seven years to realise those dreams, but along the way she's met some wonderful people, travelled to amazing places and had a fabulous time. When she entered her story into Harlequin's *So You Think You Can Write* contest she never for one moment imagined a publishing contract would be the result. Now she's thrilled to have achieved her dream, and to be writing for her favourite Mills & Boon line is the icing on the cake.

She loves to contrast her daily life on the farm by spending time creating irresistible heroes and determined heroines whose love affairs play out in glamorous settings. You can visit her website at www.rachaelthomas.co.uk.

To my family and friends, who have supported me always as I've pursued my dream, and to the wonderful friendships I've made along the way.

CHAPTER ONE

GEORGINA ENTERED THE sleek luxury of the office and knew she was being watched. Her every step scrutinised by a man who was revered and feared by businessmen and women alike.

'Ms Henshaw.' His deep voice, with a hint of accent, was firm and commanding. 'I don't think I need to ask why you are here.'

He leant against his desk, arms folded across his broad chest, as if he'd already decided he didn't want to hear what she had to say. His black hair gleamed, but the intensity in his eyes nearly robbed her of the ability to speak.

'I'm sure you don't, Mr Ramirez.' She injected as much firmness into her voice as she could, determined she wouldn't be dismissed before she'd said all she had to say. 'You are, after all, the cause of the problem.'

'Am I indeed?' Santos Lopez Ramirez locked his gaze with hers and for a moment she almost lost her nerve. Almost.

She studied his face, looking for a hint of compassion, but there was nothing. His mouth was set in a firm line that highlighted the harsh angles of his cheekbones, softened only slightly by his tanned complexion. His jaw was cleanshaven, but she didn't miss the way he clenched it, as if biting back his words.

'You know you are.' She paused briefly before continuing. 'You are the one person who is preventing Emma and Carlo from doing what they want.'

'So what are you going to do about it, Ms Henshaw?'

As he raised his brows in question a flutter of nerves took flight in her stomach. But now was the time to be the woman the world thought she was—the cold and manipulative woman who took exactly what she wanted in life and discarded what she didn't.

'I will do whatever it takes to make it happen, Mr Ramirez.'

The butterflies dissipated as she thought of Emma, of all the dreams of a fairytale wedding her younger sister so often spoke about. Her own ideas of love and happiness had long since been shattered, but she wanted her sister to find that dream.

'That's a very bold statement.'

Bold. Stupid. It didn't matter what he thought. All she cared about was Emma's happiness—happiness was something neither of them had experienced much of in recent years.

'I'm a very bold woman, Mr Ramirez.'

He smiled. An indolent smile that tugged at the corners of his mouth. Her breath caught in her throat and nerves almost swarmed over her as he unfolded his arms and took a purposeful step towards her.

'I admire that in a woman.'

Tall and unyielding, he stood before her. And despite the spacious office, the wall of windows and the sparse furnishings, he dominated the room.

She stood her ground, refusing to move, to be intimidated. 'Your admiration is not the reason I'm here.'

'I don't have time for games, Ms Henshaw.'

'I have a deal to put to you, Mr Ramirez.' He couldn't

dismiss her yet. It had been hard enough getting past his secretary, and she didn't intend to waste the opportunity.

'A deal?'

'I meant what I said.' She spoke firmly, determined he should never know just how anxious she was, how desperate to achieve her aim. 'I will do whatever it takes.'

Santos took in the determined jut of the brunette's chin. She looked so arrogantly sure of herself that he wondered if she was going to start the Paso Doble right there in his office.

Lust hurtled through his body at the images such thoughts brought to mind.

'And why would you want to do that?'

Santos returned to his chair and sat down, his gaze running over her body. The charcoal skirt and jacket, although professional and businesslike, did little to disguise her womanly figure. The tantalising hint of a lace camisole beneath the jacket caught his eye, but it was the heels she wore that stole the show. Her designer leopard print heels not only spoke volumes about the real woman, but showcased the most fantastic pair of legs he'd seen in ages. He was entranced, but it was the attitude radiating from her glorious body that really intrigued him.

'Emma is my sister and I want her to be happy.'

The intensity of her gaze as she spoke only aroused his interest further.

'I'll do anything to achieve that.'

He rose from his chair, his body suddenly restless, to stand in front of the floor-to-ceiling windows of his office. He surveyed the view of London glinting in the autumn sunshine, recalling all he'd discovered about the sister of quiet and demure Emma, the woman his half-brother Carlo was currently dating. A situation that had thrown everything into turmoil.

This woman certainly had a reputation. Widowed at twenty-three, and having been left a substantial fortune, she now led a socialite lifestyle and was never short of male company. A mercenary woman, if the circumstances of her marriage were to be believed.

'And just how far are you prepared to go in the name of sisterly love?'

Behind him he heard her intake of breath and knew he'd touched a nerve. A stab of desire shot through him as he imagined her sighing in pleasure as he kissed her. Quickly he regained control. Now was not a good time to find himself attracted to a woman—especially one with such a tarnished and scandalous reputation. He had a business to run. One that was a contentious issue between himself and Carlo. One he had to find a solution to quickly. Time was running out.

'As I have already said, Mr Ramirez, I will do whatever it takes.' Her voice had a slightly husky quality to it, which threatened to undo his control, so he remained focused on the view of London a moment longer.

Finally he turned to face her, strode across the thick carpet until he stood at her side, his right arm almost touching her shoulder. He looked sideways down at her, catching her light floral scent as he did so. Not the sort usually favoured by a woman of her reputation—it was soft and very feminine.

'So you agree with their plans to marry…your sister and my brother?'

She stood firm, like a soldier on parade being inspected by a commanding officer. He walked slowly round behind her, admiration building. She didn't flinch, didn't move. His gaze was drawn to the streaks of fiery red which entwined in her hair and again he thought of her in his bed, hair wildly fanned out across the pillow.

'Why shouldn't they get married?'

Her words drew him sharply back. 'They are young,' he said quietly, and walked away from her. Being close distracted him, took his mind from the current problem to more primal matters. 'Too young.'

'They are in love.' The words flew at him across the room with such passion that he stopped to look at her, wondering if she was as indifferent and in control as she wanted him to think. He looked at her beautiful face, the firm set of her full lips and the haughty rise of her brows. Had he just imagined that spark of passion? Conjured it up because of the direction his thoughts had gone? He must have done. As she stood before him she was not only sculpted from ice but frozen to the core.

A challenge indeed.

'And you believe in love, do you?' All through his younger years he'd been introduced to an endless stream of his father's girlfriends. Then as a teenager he'd watched from the sidelines as his father had fallen under the spell of a younger woman. The love they'd shared and later bestowed on Carlo, his new brother, had been incomprehensible to him. It had done little to instil ideas of love and happiness in him.

'About as much as you do.'

Her gaze met his, stubbornly holding it, provoking him to deny it.

'Very perceptive, Ms Henshaw. We are, then, kindred spirits, able to enjoy the opposite sex without the drama of emotional attachment.'

This was always the attitude he'd adopted, and one that had begun to feel less and less favourable. But the idea of being so captivated by a woman, so completely under her spell it would make a man turn his back on his son, was even less appealing.

'Put like that, then, yes, I suppose we are.'

Georgina cringed inwardly, knowing exactly what he was referring to. Was he really going to drag up her past, use it as a reason to stop his brother from marrying Emma? She wouldn't let him—not when she now knew the real reason he didn't want them to marry. She had to change his mind.

For a moment her nerves almost got the better of her. There was only one option she could think of to secure her sister's happiness, and although it didn't sit well with her she had to persuade him it was possible.

'What exactly is it you want, Ms Henshaw?'

A distanced, almost bored tone had entered his voice and she watched him stalk back to the windows, looking more like a caged animal than a businessman.

'I want to put a business proposition to you.'

He turned instantly, his interest piqued, and she stifled a smile of triumph. She was now talking his language. Business was what made this man tick. That was obvious.

'A proposition? You?'

He moved back to his desk and gestured her to sit, the muscles of his arm rippling beneath his white shirt snagging her attention. Mentally she shook herself. Getting distracted by his good looks would not help her through this. And hadn't she told herself months ago that relationships were not what she needed?

'I'd prefer to stand,' she said firmly, not missing the quirk of his dark brows.

'As you wish.'

He sat behind his desk, his dark eyes watching her. She wouldn't let him intimidate her. She had to remain as calm and detached as possible. So much was riding on her being able to deliver her proposition in an efficient, businesslike manner.

'I want my sister to be happy, and Carlo makes her happy.' She tried to keep her voice steady and devoid of emotion. This hard businessman obviously believed all that was written about her in the press. He believed she was cast from the same mould as him. 'From my understanding of the situation, there is only one solution.'

He didn't say a word, waiting for her to continue. His silence unnerved her, but she had to stay strong, remain focused.

Quickly she pressed on. 'I know about the condition in your father's will.'

'You are very well informed of my affairs, Ms Henshaw, but I fail to see what business of yours that is.'

His hard expression gave her a glimpse of the formidable businessman he was. She'd done her research on him. 'I know you have built your business up to the international concern it is today since your father passed away, and that once either you or Carlo marry the business will pass solely to that brother.' She paused, almost wanting to give up as she looked at him, his dark eyes as bleak as a starless night.

'Full marks for research,' he said, his voice as emotionless as she hoped hers was.

It had been Emma who had told her about the condition of the will. She'd sobbed for the loss of her dreams of marrying the man she loved, dreams of living happily ever after with Carlo, just because of the greed of his elder brother.

'I also know Carlo doesn't share your appetite for success. He has little or no interest in the business, wanting only to live a normal life married to my sister.'

'A *normal* life?'

She knew he was stalling, being evasive. Wouldn't she hate it if he picked apart her private affairs? But she had to carry on before she lost all confidence in her plan. For Emma she had to do it, just as she'd had to five years ago.

'A life that isn't centred on a business but one that is centred on a happy family home.' The words flowed from her with practised ease.

'And an example of that would be your own family, would it?'

She felt her eyes widen, shocked he'd brought it up. 'I see you have done your own research, Mr Ramirez, but my parents' marriage has nothing to do with Emma and Carlo.'

'I have no wish for my family name to be joined by marriage to a woman's whose mother is an alcoholic and whose father has been absent so long nobody knows where he is.'

'So it has nothing to do with your power-hungry need to take the business from Carlo by preventing this marriage?' Her heartbeat was rising and her emotions were beginning to take over. She had to remain composed.

'They have sent you here to plead their case, have they?'

He glowered at her. But her last words seemed only to have bounced off his tough exterior. She took a deep breath, wanting to appear poised before she spoke again.

He laced his long tanned fingers together in front of him on the desk in a relaxed fashion, but Georgina knew he was anything but relaxed. The firm set of his broad shoulders gave that away. He was confident, self-assured and powerful.

'On the contrary, Mr Ramirez, they have no idea I'm here and I want it to stay that way.'

One dark brow quirked up, but he said nothing.

'I can see only one way to secure their happiness…' She paused, refusing to be drawn. 'And to satisfy your insatiable need for business success.'

He leant forward at his desk. 'And that is?'

'You get married first, inherit the business, and leave them to enjoy a happy married life together.'

As he looked at her his handsome face set in a mask so emotionless she blinked in shock. Did this man not have any compassion in his heart?

'As you seem to have it all worked out, who do you suggest I marry?' The question came out slowly, as if he was sure he'd foiled her plan.

She took a deep breath and looked directly into his eyes. She mustn't show any nerves, any fear. He was like a predatory lion and she knew he'd smell it.

'Me.'

There—she'd said it. And now she had she wanted to bolt like a frightened animal. He didn't say a word. Not a trace of emotion could be seen on his face. Silence hung between them, and a tension so taut she thought it was going to snap with a crack at any moment.

Shock rocked through Santos as he listened to her ridiculous proposition. It was the last thing he'd expected to hear, but then her reputation should have given him forewarning. She already had one marriage behind her—one that had made her a very wealthy woman indeed. And if rumour was to be believed it had not been a love-match.

'Why, exactly, would I wish to get married? And to you, of all women?'

His voice was hard, his accent suddenly more pronounced. He sounded dangerous.

Briefly Santos saw pain flash across her face, saw the

curling of her manicured fingers and wished the words unsaid. Marriage was the one thing he wanted to avoid at all costs, but even though his legal team were working on a solution he had to consider the option. If he wanted to save his business, and the last five years of hard work since his father had first become ill, he might actually have to take a wife. So wouldn't this woman, who had so willingly walked into the lion's den, be the perfect choice? Costly, maybe, if her track record was anything to go by, but he could deal with that.

'It wouldn't be a marriage in the true sense of the word.'

Her words, spoken with conviction, dragged his attention back to her face.

'And what is that?'

'A marriage for love, of course—like the one your brother and my sister wish to make. A commitment for life.' Her words flowed freely, and once again he thought he heard a spark of passion.

Suspiciously he looked at her as he sat back again in his chair. 'You are not looking for love, Ms Henshaw?'

'Not at all, Mr Ramirez. I only want my sister's happiness. I will do anything to achieve that. Once they are married we can annul our marriage and go separate ways.

Santos considered this wild suggestion more seriously. Would it hurt to go along with it for now—to have another option if his legal team were unable to sort out an alternative?

'And you would want what, exactly, from this *marriage*?' His mind raced. On a business level it made perfect sense. He would finally have the security of inheriting the business he'd built up and would have done his duty by his brother, freeing Carlo of obligations he had little or no interest in.

'I want nothing from you other than our names on a marriage certificate. Once that is done we need not see each other. We just apply for an annulment.'

Her voice had hardened and his past rushed back at him. He saw the teenager who had hardly grieved for his controlling mother. Felt the pain as his father eventually remarried and moved on with a loving and kind woman whom Santos had resented. A woman who had changed his father, almost taking him away from his firstborn with the power of her love.

'I find that hard to believe. You must want something.' Experience had taught him that. Everyone wanted something. Everyone had a price.

'Nothing more than I've already stated.'

Her cool, calm words sounded believable.

Santos thought of the conditions of the will and gritted his teeth against the memory of the day he'd realised what his manipulative father had done. It seemed this attractive woman knew a lot about the will, but she didn't know it all. She hadn't mentioned the other conditions that he would have to meet before finally inheriting. It wasn't as simple as marriage.

'I require more than that. My wife, when I take one, will be a wife in every sense of the word.'

Did she really think he was going to accept her proposition meekly, without attaching his own conditions? If he had to get married he'd rather do it for business than become as vulnerable as his father had after his second marriage. There was also the matter that he was a hot-blooded male and this woman had stirred his blood the second she'd walked proudly into his office.

Santos watched as realisation dawned on her pretty face, followed by defeat. But he said nothing more. To do so now would be to show his hand. He would never give away the fact that he actually saw her proposition as a serious option—his back-up plan.

'I can't do that.' She gasped the words out, her face whitening before his eyes.

'Then your very first words to me were lies.'

Part of him felt relieved. She hadn't really been serious. But another part of him, the deal-chaser, wanted this—but on his terms. Marriage would not only secure the business but would put a stop to the endless rounds of parties. It would enhance his image in the business world, giving him what appeared to be a happy marriage, and it would mean he didn't have to get emotionally involved. Something he avoided at all costs.

She still hadn't spoken so he carried on, pushing forward his conditions, turning it completely to his advantage. 'That is the only deal I'm prepared to make.'

Georgina's heart sank. Was he seriously suggesting a real marriage—one that would entail her being at his side publicly *and* sleeping in his bed at night?

'We know nothing of each other.' She grabbed at the first thing that came to mind.

'On the contrary, Georgina. I think we both know enough.'

The use of her name sent a warm tingle down her spine. His gaze fixed on hers so intently she felt as if he was physically holding her captive. Her pulse-rate leapt, then beat hard as she thought of spending the night in his bed, of being his wife in every sense of the word.

She couldn't banish the image of him with one of his model-like women hanging on his arm. Would such a man as Santos Ramirez even want to be seen publicly with her? Worse still, would he find her lacking as a lover? No, *lover* wasn't the right word. Would he find her lacking as a sexual partner?

'I know that the world would never be fooled into thinking we had married for any other reason than convenience.' She clutched awkwardly at excuses as she still struggled to take in what he wanted.

'And that would be because you have already been married and widowed purely for financial gain.'

Pain lanced through her as she thought of Richard Henshaw—the man she'd married because she had been genuinely fond of him. The same man who had given her stability and security in her life for the first time ever. In that moment she hated Santos more than any other man for bringing Richard into it.

'No.' Her voice filled with entreaty. 'Because I am nothing like the type of woman you date.'

He raised a brow, and a slight smile teased at the corners of his lips. 'As far as people would know I'd have become besotted with you exactly *because* you are not like any woman I have ever dated.'

'Would you really want people to think that instead of thinking we were married in name only to keep your business?'

'I have no intention of anyone ever thinking I have married for business gain only.' He looked steadily at her. 'Especially Carlo.'

Georgina couldn't take it in. Her whole plan had been turned upside down. He'd taken complete and utter control of the situation and turned it into something she just couldn't think of doing.

'How is that achievable?'

She struggled to comprehend how Emma would ever believe she had married such a man simply because she wanted to. Not now Emma knew all about her first marriage and the reasons behind it.

'You said that nobody knows you are here—is that not true?'

'No, nobody,' she replied, trying to grasp where this was leading.

'Good,' he said, and stood up, making her feel small and insignificant as he moved around his desk to stand before her once more. 'I will host a party tomorrow evening, to which you and Emma are invited.'

'How is that going to help?' Georgina couldn't figure out where he was going with this.

He smiled. A lazy smile that did nothing to hide his amusement at the situation. 'We won't be able to leave each other alone; the attraction will be obvious to all there. Then we will spend the entire weekend together, maybe longer, after which we shall make the announcement.'

The tone of his voice had changed, giving it a warm depth, and she had the distinct impression that if he was really attracted to her she would be unable to resist. A tingle shimmied down her spine, causing her pulse-rate to leap—which had nothing to do with anxiety and everything to do with the dark and possibly dangerous man who watched her intently.

'Okay,' she said quickly, aware that her voice had become a husky whisper. She wanted to push on with her plans but hoped she could change his mind later. A real marriage surely wasn't necessary. 'We'll do it your way.'

'There was never any doubt about that, *querida*.'

CHAPTER TWO

GEORGINA'S ANXIETY LEVELS had risen tenfold since entering the hotel where Santos was having his impromptu party. Her sister, who was so excited, believing a party meant there was hope for her and Carlo to be married, had vanished from her side the moment they arrived. Georgina now felt conspicuous as she stood just inside the doorway of the hotel room.

'*Buenas noches*, Ms Henshaw.'

She looked up at Santos, her breath catching as he moved closer to her. He was immaculately dressed in a dark suit and tie, the white of his shirt enhancing his attractive tan. The smile on his lips was warm and welcoming. That same warmth reached his eyes as he took her hand. The touch of his fingers as he lightly held hers made her shiver, as if a feather had been trailed down her spine.

Speak, she told herself firmly. *Don't let his act of attraction distract you.*

'Good evening, Mr Ramirez,' she said, injecting firmness into her voice as she remembered they were not yet supposed to have met. She certainly didn't want Emma to discover what she was about to do. 'It is a pleasure to meet you at last.'

He quirked a brow, and she wondered if she'd gone too far, but around her they were already drawing speculative gazes. It seemed to Georgina that the elite of London society were here—and all at his request.

'Please, call me Santos,' he said as he lifted her hand to his lips.

Her stomach did a strange flutter as those lips brushed sensuously over the back of her hand. Stunned into silence, she was mesmerised by his dark hair as he lowered his head. The barely controlled waves of shiny black hair looked so inviting she wondered what it would feel like to run her fingers through it. Then he straightened, towering over her once more, his gaze locking with hers.

Don't go there, she warned herself, and tried to pull back her hand, but his fingers tightened on hers. A sexy smile spread across his lips and she dragged in a ragged breath, then swallowed hard. What was she doing, allowing this man to get to her?

'The pleasure is mine.' His words were deep and uneven. He didn't let her hand go, instead forcing her to stay, so that she could do nothing other than stand there. She looked into the ever darkening depths of his eyes and felt a sizzle of awareness slide over her like the slow thaw of mountain snow. Shy and flustered was something she'd never felt—but, far worse, she knew she was already out of her depth. How was she ever going to get through the evening when he turned on charm like this?

She would because she had to. She was doing this for Emma's happiness. She clutched her bag, thinking of the few essentials she'd slipped into it, knowing she wasn't going to be returning home that night.

She smiled, more to herself than anyone else, determined not to let this man's charisma knock her off balance. It was all for show, and if he could do it then so could she.

'Something is amusing you?' His fingers traced a slow,

teasing circle on the palm of her hand, making tingles race along her arm. She wanted to pull away, wanted to break the contact, yet couldn't. Somewhere deep inside her something stirred—an emotion long since locked away.

'I was merely admiring your charm.' She smiled up at him, pulling herself closer against him. It felt flirty. Dangerous. 'I'm sure women just drop at your feet.'

He laughed. A soft rumble that made her tremble. Instinctively she tried to pull her hand free. Again his fingers tightened and his eyes darkened, and for a moment her eyes locked with his. She drew in a quick breath as she saw the sparks of desire within those dark depths. Her body responded to the primal call of his as heady heat thundered around her.

'That is always my intention, *querida*.'

He smiled down at her, letting her hand go so that she felt suddenly bereft of his contact—like a ship torn from its anchor to drift in the harbour.

'Champagne?'

She blinked, not quite able to keep up with his train of thought. Glancing around her, she caught her sister's eye as she chatted with other guests, Carlo at her side. Emma looked radiant and happy, and Georgina knew there was no going back now. Just as she had done five years ago, she had to put Emma first. She'd done it once, and she could do it again, but Emma must never know.

'Champagne would be lovely,' she purred, being as flirtatious as she possibly could. Maybe a little champagne was just what she needed to boost her confidence.

With his hand in the small of her back she moved into the room, aware of the curious glances being directed their way. Santos handed her a flute of champagne, but her head was becoming light, as if she'd already had several glasses of the bubbly liquid. She couldn't quite believe how this handsome and powerful businessman was able to make her feel so special, so fresh and alive. His charm offensive was potent, making her feel unique and, worse than that, desired. If this was how he was going to play out their planned public scene of attraction she would have to be careful, remind herself it was all an act. Because right now it felt very real. And she liked it.

Santos couldn't help but watch Georgina as she sipped her champagne. The need to act as if he were attracted to her had gone out of the window the moment she'd entered the room. He'd heard the hush, felt the ripple of interest, and had been as mesmerised by her as every other man in the room.

Still looking as proud and defiant as she had yesterday in his office, she'd stood framed in the doorway. The jade silk of her dress skimmed over her body, neither revealing nor concealing her curves. A black wrap hung loosely off her shoulders, and he'd been unable to take his eyes off the creamy expanse of her skin, broken only by the thin jade straps. Her neck was bare of any jewellery—something many of the women he knew couldn't carry off.

Even if he hadn't had to go up to her and start the charade of attraction he would have wanted to. The same kick of lust he'd felt yesterday had stirred in his veins once again, propelling him towards her. As he'd taken her hand, enjoying the softness of her skin, he had known he wanted her.

'Your plan is working.' He leant down and whispered against her hair, the fresh scent of it invading his senses, making his pulse throb with unquenched desire.

She pulled back from him, confusion filling her eyes, her fingers clutching tightly to her glass. 'It is?'

He heard the uncertainty in her voice and had the strangest desire to stroke his fingers down her cheek. An affectionate gesture he'd never normally think of making. Just what was it about this woman that stirred something unknown deep within him?

'With your dedication to the role, how could anyone question what they are seeing?' She turned away, exchanging her empty glass for another bubble-filled one.

The brittleness of her words reminded him just who he was dealing with. Georgina Henshaw was an avaricious woman who, with one marriage already behind her, could play his game with as much detachment as he employed.

He watched her beautiful yet emotionless face as she scanned the room, her eyes finally resting on her sister. With a sternness that would have become any teacher her gaze followed Emma as she moved across the room, until she nestled herself against his brother.

Unable to stop himself from watching the loving moment, he saw how his brother looked down at Emma. Saw the open adoration in the young woman's eyes. Even as Carlo dipped his head and kissed her he couldn't avert his gaze. Whatever it was between them was so powerful he felt it from the other side of the room. Just as he had done as a youth, when Carlo's mother had first met his father, he felt excluded. It was almost as if he'd gone back in time, watching Carlo grow strong from his mother's love while he could only look on.

'They make a good couple, don't they?'

Georgina's words dragged him back from a past he rarely visited. For a moment he was disorientated.

'They don't have to marry to prove that.'

He couldn't keep the harshness from his words. Beside him Georgina stiffened, as if she was taking a step back from him. He forced his mind to more pleasant thoughts—like the way the woman at his side stirred his desires like no other.

'I hope you aren't going back on our deal, Mr Ramirez?'

He deflected her sharp-toned words with a smile. 'Santos,' he said softly, placing his arm across her shoulders and pulling her body against his, relishing the warmth of it. 'I think you should call me Santos. If you want this to work.'

He looked down into her upturned face. Her eyes darkened until they reminded him of the depths of a forest. Her full lips parted slightly and he felt the heavy tug of desire.

He wanted her.

Slowly he lowered his head and brushed his lips over hers. Her breath mingled with his, warming his mouth, and he imagined the sensation of her sighing in pleasure. This was going to be a *very* interesting night.

Briefly her lips responded. Softening beneath his. And his whole body suddenly ached for hers. It was stronger than the heady lust that usually coursed through his blood when he kissed a woman. This was potent. Vibrant and alive. It was more powerful than anything he'd known before.

Georgina's body heated as his lips touched hers, the contact so light it almost didn't happen. Involuntarily she closed her eyes as the liquid warmth of desire slid over her. She swayed closer to him, felt his arm, strong and firm, draw her closer.

She knew there and then that he had power over her. He had the ability to stir emotions she never again wanted to explore, and she would have to be on her guard.

Her fingers clutched the stem of the glass in her hand as she hardened herself against what she was feeling. This wasn't for real. This was all an act. And if she didn't keep that in mind she'd make a fool of herself, because at this moment in time she wanted nothing more than to be kissed by Santos.

Not this light, lingering kiss. After several years without experiencing the intimacy of any kiss she knew he'd awakened something deep within her. She wanted more. Her body hungered for passion. To her horror, she realised her body hungered for *him*.

But she couldn't let that happen. She had to stay in control—not just of herself, but of the situation. Never could she allow herself to become a woman so desperate for love that she'd beg a man to stay, as her mother had done to her father. In Santos she recognised the same inability to commit to a relationship her father had possessed. He would be the worst man for her to give her heart to.

No, to allow Santos to know just how easily he could stir her hidden and unexplored desires would be fatal.

She pulled away from him and looked into his smouldering eyes. He was good. Nobody could question what he was thinking right now. He looked as if he wanted to ravish her right there in the middle of the party.

A tingle raced around her at the thought and her breathing deepened. It was as if her body was working in opposition to her heart and her head, and it was winning.

She flirted back at him, ignoring the heavy ache of her limbs and the throb of desire deep inside her. 'Santos, that was…' She paused and looked beyond him into the throng of partygoers who mingled around them, looked to her sister. 'Amazing,' she finished, hoping he'd think the husky note in her voice was part of her act and not something she had little or no control over—a reaction to him.

'Amazing, huh?'

His voice was deeper and his accent, which had only been a hint before, much stronger. He sounded sexy. *Too* sexy.

'Definitely. Emma looks so shocked. I'm certain she'll believe there is something between us.' She moved against him as she spoke, felt the firmness of his body and tried to ignore the sizzle of electricity zipping around hers.

'And what about you, *querida*? Do you believe it?'

He smiled down at her, pulling her just a little closer, so that she could feel her breasts pressing against his chest. Her breath caught in her throat and for a moment she couldn't say a word.

Focus, she reminded herself. *Focus on why you're even here with him.*

'I believe we look convincing.' She hated the way her voice stammered, and to hide it lifted her chin and raised a brow at him.

He laughed. A soft sound she felt rumbling against her. It was all too close, too personal. She tried to step back from him but he pressed his hand firmly into the small of her back, bringing her hip close against him.

She gasped as she felt the hardness of his arousal, and nerves made her heart beat wildly—so hard she could feel the pulse in her neck throbbing. His dark eyes, smouldering with desire, met hers.

'I too am convinced.'

His voice was a harsh whisper as he spoke against her ear, his breath blowing on her neck, making it tingle.

'I am also convinced that now would be a good time to leave this damned party.'

She turned her head towards him, intending to speak, to try and douse the fire that had ignited between them. A fire she could never allow to burn. Her cheek touched his as he lowered his head and, following some kind of instinct she'd never before experienced, she moved until his lips were against hers.

Briefly her gaze locked with his, then her eyelids fluttered closed as the pressure of his lips met hers. The kiss was hard, demanding much more. She wound her arms around his neck, one hand still clutching her empty champagne flute, and gave herself up to the mastery of this man's kiss. Her lips and her body asked for more and he responded, making her heart thump hard.

His tongue slid into her mouth, entwining with hers. He tasted wild and untamed. She sighed, making him deepen the kiss, and he began to invade every cell of her body with a heady desire she'd never known before.

Heaven help her, she wanted this man. Wanted him in a way she hadn't known was possible.

Just when she thought she couldn't remain standing against him any longer he broke the kiss. She slid her arms down slowly from his neck and he took the glass from her hand, putting it on a nearby table. Cool air rushed around her as their bodies parted and she felt exposed, naked, as if everyone in the room would be able to see just how much her body wanted his.

Santos's gaze slid over her, just as it had done when she'd entered the room, but this time her skin sizzled. When it lingered on her breasts her knees weakened and breathing was suddenly the hardest thing to do. She was transfixed, unable to move, unable to hide from his open desire.

Around them the noise of the party slowly came back

to her and she was thankful that they were not alone. What would she have done if they were?

She'd have made a big mistake, that was what. She would have allowed passion and champagne to take over, allowed them to destroy everything, exposing emotions and leaving her vulnerable. She'd seen it with her mother, knew the consequences, and had promised herself she'd never allow that to happen to her.

'We leave now.'

His voice, though still deep and throaty, radiated total command and, afraid hers would sound weak and trembling, she nodded in agreement.

With his hand possessively in the small of her back he propelled her towards the door. Partygoers stepped aside for them. Envious glances from women came her way. The cool façade she lived behind slipped firmly back into place. She lifted her chin, smiled, and walked proudly at Santos's side.

What would they think if they knew the truth? Would they gasp in shock at the calculated plan she was acting out?

'Georgie?' Emma's voice filtered through the defensive wall she'd quickly rebuilt, despite the hum of her body.

She looked into her sister's face and saw genuine happiness. It shone from her eyes so brightly that she knew she was doing the right thing. She touched Emma's arm and gave her a secretive smile. The smile of a woman who was being swept away by the most magnetic man she'd ever met.

'I'll call you in the morning.'

Emma's smile widened and she looked from her to Santos and back again. 'Okay.' She grinned and turned to leave, obviously in a hurry to tell Carlo.

'Let's go,' Georgina said, without looking at Santos. The taste of deception was strong in her mouth.

'I like it.'

His voice purred like a big cat content to take it easy for a while. He led her out of the noise of the party into the hotel foyer. The lights were brighter—too bright—as if she was now under his spotlight. His gaze slid down her again, desire still sparking in his eyes despite the latent control in his voice.

'*What* do you like?' she questioned sharply as he began to lead her out onto the streets. She shivered against the cold autumn air.

'Georgie.'

Emma's pet name for her sounded so exotic on his lips—sexy, even. Her body heated despite the wind, which blew her hair quickly into disarray. She combed her fingers through it, gathering it at her neck, trying to prevent herself from becoming a totally dishevelled mess.

'I prefer Georgina,' she said, trying to ignore the way her body hummed as he took her hand and pulled her close against him. Was this what it was like to be protected?

Minutes later she was in the back of his chauffeur-driven car. The light from the streetlamps cast a glow around the interior and she glanced at Santos, startled to find he was watching her intently.

She looked down at her hands clasped in her lap, unable to look into the heat of his eyes.

'You are a very beautiful woman.'

Georgina tensed. This wasn't supposed to be happening. 'You can drop the act now.' Her words were stiff and she looked up at his face. The angles of his cheekbones were severe in the ever-changing light.

'I'm enjoying the role.' His deep voice seemed to ripple around the car, sending pinpricks of heat rushing over her. 'And you never know who may be listening or watching.'

Georgina glanced at the chauffeur, who appeared to be concentrating on driving. She heard Santos laugh softly and her gaze flew to meet his once more. He really was charming—but on a lethal level. Somewhere deep inside her she recognised him as the kind of man who could hurt her or, worse, destroy her. He was the same type of devil-may-care man her mother had fallen for time and time again, and exactly like her father.

'You don't really think I'll buy that, do you?' She raised a brow at him, infusing indifference into her body with each syllable.

Cool and aloof. That was the protection she needed.

'My staff are nothing but discreet,' he replied as the car came to a stop outside some very exclusive riverside apartments.

'That is a relief—but then I suppose I'm just another on a very long list as far as they are concerned.' The haughty demeanour she routinely hid behind sounded in her voice, and from the look on his face, the frown that furrowed his brow, she knew she'd scored a direct hit.

With one final look at her he got out of the car, almost instantly appearing at her door. He held out his hand for her, but the look on his face suggested he was far from happy. For a moment she was worried. Had she pushed things just a little too far, taunting him like that? A man like him was used to people pandering to his ego.

She had the sudden urge to bolt past him and run away. Reason followed swiftly. She wouldn't help her sister like that, and the shoes she was wearing certainly hadn't been created for running.

'If you want to drop this charade you can go home

now.' His voice was rough, edged with exasperation. 'But just remember, *querida,* it was your idea.'

He was right. She had started this and she would finish it—but only when she knew her sister could marry the man she loved without any implications from this power-hungry man who now stood waiting for her, looking devastatingly sexy. Did he really mean to keep this up, even in private?

For a moment she wondered if she'd already done enough. They'd been seen leaving the party together. Then she remembered Emma's smile, the hope that had shone from her eyes. Georgina realised that it didn't matter what anyone else thought, whether they believed their whirlwind romance was real. It only mattered what Emma thought. There was no way she could let her sister think that yet again she was marrying to secure her future. Emma was all she cared about.

She could do this—even if it meant continuing with the charade of attraction.

Taking his hand, she stepped out of the car and looked up at the tall modern building. She'd never given any thought to where he might live, but the clean, precise lines of this apartment block didn't surprise her.

'I suppose you have the top floor, complete with river views?'

'Very perceptive of you.'

His voice had lowered to a steely tone, interwoven with charm, and her stomach fluttered irrationally.

'It seems you *do* know something about me after all.'

Yes, I do. I know too much. I know you have an abundance of charm and the ability to break a woman's heart.

'It was merely an observation.' Georgina kept the words light as he gestured her towards the entrance of the building. She was beginning to feel disorientated by him, by his seductive tone and sexy smiles. She couldn't allow that to happen. As far as she was concerned once his name was on their marriage certificate and her sister was married all contact would be severed. She had no intention of becoming a *real* wife. Whatever motivation was behind that absurd request she would find a way out of it. She had to.

The lift doors closed on them with expensive silence and as they were taken upwards she kept her eyes straight ahead, watching the doors, not daring to look at him or at their reflection, which seemed to mock her from all sides. She could feel the intensity of his gaze, but refused to meet it. She didn't dare. He was still acting the part of an attracted and attentive man and it was beginning to stir emotions she'd long since locked away.

She almost let out a sigh of relief as the lift doors opened. The opulence of the corridor wasn't lost on her. He wrapped his arm around her, so her elbow nestled in the palm of his hand, and she moved towards the door of his apartment, a sense of dread filling her.

'Do we really need to take it this far?' The words left her in a rush, before she'd had time to consider them.

He stopped outside the white double doors to his apartment, his arm still around her, keeping her close. She looked up at him, desperate to keep calm. He mustn't know just how unnerved he made her feel.

'Yes—if you want authenticity you need to be seen leaving here tomorrow morning.' Amusement lightened his eyes before he turned to open the doors.

'We could have just stayed at the hotel...' She clutched at the idea, not daring to cross the threshold, not wanting to be alone with him—especially on his territory.

'On the contrary.' He smiled that heart-stopping smile that could very easily make her think she was the only woman he saw, the only woman he wanted. 'To bring you here gives a clear message to everyone who knows me—including my brother.'

With his arm firmly around her, he walked into the apartment. She had no choice but to go too. Her heels clicked on a marble floor and the low lighting hinted at a very sparse and masculine living space.

'I don't understand...' The words rushed out on an unsteady breath as he finally moved away from her. At least she could breathe properly, now he wasn't so close.

Dropping his keys onto a table, he took off his jacket and tossed it over the back of a large black leather sofa. Unable to keep her eyes off him, she watched as he loosened his tie and unbuttoned the top of his shirt. Dark tanned skin drew her eyes and she had to force herself to look away.

'I *never* bring a woman back to my apartment.'

The implication of his words sank in. He was giving a very clear message—not just to Carlo, but to her. He wanted the business so badly he was prepared not only to accept her proposal of marriage, but to do everything to make it look real. Even appear to cast aside his womanising reputation and ways and take her as his wife.

'I should be honoured, then,' she replied flippantly, in an attempt to hide her thoughts.

He might be able to discard the way he lived for the sake of his business, but she couldn't quite let slip the distant demeanour *she* hid behind. After all, it wasn't a business she was doing it for, but the love of her sister.

'The first woman to spend a night here with you?'

Santos flicked on a light, wanting to see Georgina's face better. In fact he wanted to see more than just her face. All evening her soft skin had teased his senses—so much so that he'd done the one thing he never did with any woman. He'd kissed her publicly. Not just a light brush of lips on lips either, but a desire-laden kiss that held a promise of passion and satisfaction.

'More champagne?'

He should just be showing her to her room, as he'd intended when he'd formed this bizarre back-up plan yesterday. But even then, as she'd stood so proudly in his office, he'd found the cocktail of icy control laced with underlying passion tempting. Too tempting. And challenging. What man could refuse such a challenge?

'No, thanks.'

Her frosty tone made it clear the ice maiden was back. He watched as she walked across the room to look down on the Thames, at the city's lights reflected in the dark water.

Ordinarily, if he'd taken a woman back to a hotel suite, he wouldn't be thinking of any kind of drink. He would be enjoying holding her, kissing her, and thinking only of satisfying their sexual needs. But this was different.

It unnerved him, but he quickly pushed the notion to the back of his mind. It was different simply because of the deal they'd struck. Never before had he spent time with a woman for any other reason than that he wanted to.

'Coffee?'

'No, thanks.' She turned to face him. 'We both know this isn't for real, and there isn't anyone here to witness anything more, so can we just say goodnight and go to bed—separately?'

He raised his brows at that last word and was rewarded with a light flush to her cheeks, giving her an air of innocence. Their eyes met and for a moment it was as if everything hung in the balance. Boldly she held his gaze.

Did she have any idea how magnificent she looked? A glacial beauty with barely concealed simmering passion.

'I'll show you to your room.'

He turned and broke the contact, but could feel her gaze following him. A sizzle of desire zipped through him and he gripped his hands into fists. If she could be so coldly in control, then so could he.

Her heels tapped rhythmically as she walked behind him, out of the vast open space of the living area and into a long corridor. He stopped outside a door, opened it, and reached in to flick on the light. 'I trust this will be comfortable for you?'

Then he looked at her face, saw a moment of hesitancy in eyes which now sparkled like rich mahogany.

'If you need anything I'll be in here.'

He pushed open the door to the master bedroom, where the lights of the city were visible for miles through large windows.

'I won't need anything,' she said, lifting her chin defiantly, and he fought hard the urge to lower his head and capture those full lips beneath his. He wanted to taste her again, to feel her mould to his body as if she were meant to be there.

'I'll see you in the morning, then,' he said, and stepped away from her—away from the temptation of her body, away from the sweet seductive scent that wrapped itself around him.

In that moment he realised he was no better than his father if he couldn't allow this woman to sleep alone. But she fired something deep within him. Something so powerful he didn't want to ignore it.

'Goodnight,' she whispered. and moved into the room, using the door to shield her glorious body from his view, apprehension clear in her eyes.

Anger simmered in his blood, mixing with unquenched desire. He was worse than his father, moving from one woman to the next. Memories from childhood, of watching an endless stream of woman enter his home, surfaced like a tidal wave. Was he now just as bad, if he couldn't walk away from Georgina?

'Goodnight.' His voice was harsh as he battled with emotions long since packed away.

Damn it all—this was a business arrangement, a means to an end. If he couldn't get out of that clause in the will legally, then he would damn well take her up on her proposition. Keeping the business was his priority. Nothing else mattered. And if Georgina had offered herself as a sacrificial lamb, so be it. Soon she would be his wife, and he had no intention of saying goodnight then.

CHAPTER THREE

GEORGINA WOKE WITH a start. Her heart thumped in her chest like a hammer as she tried to blink away the images that had haunted her sleep. Images of Santos kissing her, wanting her. Images that had heated her body as surely as if he had spent the night next to her.

She dragged in a sharp breath and looked around the room, different now the calm light of dawn was casting its glow. Her jade dress was draped over a chair, just where she'd left it, and she pulled the sheet tighter against her, feeling suddenly naked in her underwear.

Waking up in a man's bed, even if it was only the guest bed, was something she wasn't used to. She groaned at the thought of the field-day the press would have if they ever found out.

She hadn't given a thought to the morning as she'd left the party last night. Her mind had been elsewhere, thanks to Santos's charm attack.

In that moment she knew she couldn't face him. There was only one option. She had to leave now.

Could she make a quick getaway? The thought raced into her head and quickly she flung back the sheet and grabbed her dress. The silk was cool against her skin as she stepped into it and embarrassment washed over her as she thought of all those who'd know about this walk of shame.

She would be able to slip away without seeing Santos, she reassured herself, especially at this early hour.

She washed her face in the en-suite bathroom, trying hard to remove the traces of last night's make-up before applying fresh mascara and lipstick—all she'd been able to fit into her evening bag.

At the bedroom door she paused, took a deep breath, forcing her racing heart to calm before slowly opening it. Silence greeted her and she smiled, sure she was going to be able to slip away. With her bag in her hand and sandals dangling from her fingers she closed the door and padded softly along the wooden floor of the hallway, but as she entered the vast open living space the smell of strong coffee greeted her.

Her heart sank.

Someone was up.

Did Santos have a housekeeper who prepared breakfast for him? Yes, that must be it. Could she slip out without whoever it was in the kitchen noticing her? Quietly she walked across the huge room, feeling more like an intruder with every step.

'Going somewhere?'

The deep, seductive tones of Santos's voice halted her in her tracks. She turned to look at him and tried not to react to the sexy image he created in denims and a shirt. Casual suited him. But she didn't want to dwell on that now.

'Home, of course.' She kept her voice bright, as if this scenario was one she was familiar with, and met his gaze. Lifting her chin, she made every effort to appear totally indifferent to him—which was hard when he stood before her, cool and powerful, just like the man who had haunted her through her dreams last night.

'This early?' He pushed back the cuff of his shirt and looked at his watch, a small smile lingering on his lips. 'I think you have time for a coffee first. Even the most hardened shoppers aren't about *this* early on a Saturday.'

'It's not the shoppers I'm worried about,' she said with a huff of exasperation. 'Emma will be wondering where I am.'

'Precisely.'

The curt word made her blink, and despite her need to get away she walked towards him. As she did so Santos turned and headed back into the kitchen, its sleek design as contemporary as the rest of the apartment.

'How do you take your coffee?'

'This is a game to you, isn't it?' She really wasn't in the mood for pleasantries. 'We were seen leaving the party together and your housekeeper will know I've spent the night. I think that is enough, don't you?'

Santos didn't answer, and she found herself mesmerised as he poured the coffee. In her chest her heart was pounding, and a whole stream of butterflies had taken flight in her stomach.

It's not him, she told herself firmly. *It's just that you haven't been in this situation for years.* It was exactly this kind of awkward morning-after she had witnessed her mother and her lovers enduring, and exactly what she'd then gone and done herself as a naive young woman. But she'd changed, and repeating her past wasn't something she wanted to do.

'Try this.' He took her sandals and bag from her and replaced them with a steaming mug of black coffee. 'And even if my housekeeper *had* seen you—assuming she was working, that is—I would expect nothing other than her discretion.'

He smiled at her, and the butterflies in her stomach fluttered ever more wildly, but before she could respond he continued, 'At least no one will know you didn't sleep in my bed. That would really upset our plans.'

Georgina's fingers burned, and she was sure it wasn't just the mug of hot liquid in her hands. His touch, brief as it was, had jolted her with a voltage more powerful than any coffee. She took a sip—anything other than stand and look at him, fearing that if she did he would see just what an effect he was having on her.

'We left the party together. It will have to be enough.' She instilled as much courage into her voice as she could muster, which was difficult given the way her body now tingled.

Purposefully he moved past her, to place her shoes beneath a small ornamental table and drop her bag onto its glossy surface. His expression when he turned back to her was one of guarded control.

'I'm not a man to do things by half, Georgina. If I do something, I do it properly.' He stepped closer to her, the fresh scent of pine and his dark hair still slightly damp evidence that he'd recently showered.

She thought of his kiss last night at the party. The feel of his lips on hers, the way she hadn't been able to do anything other than sway towards him, and knew he was right. He didn't do anything by halves.

'I'm sure you don't, Mr Ramirez—'

'Santos,' he interrupted, his voice firm as he moved towards her.

He was coming so near she had to brace herself against the urge to move closer to him. The desire to experience his kiss just once more was almost overwhelming. She clung to her cup of coffee as if it were a lifeline.

Distance was what she needed. Distance was the safest option. She stepped back, out of the shadow of his power. She didn't know what was the matter with her—she'd never experienced this before. It was insane. Of all the men to find herself attracted to, why did it have to be *this* man? She furrowed her brow.

'If you don't use my name, who is going to believe this charade of yours?'

He raised his brow in question at her. Did he really think he could get the better of her so easily?

'You appear to be taking this far more seriously than me,' she goaded, and took another sip of her coffee before placing it on the table. Then, turning to look directly at him, she added for good measure, 'Santos.'

'You can be assured of that, *querida*.'

His lips—the ones that had set light to a trail of heady need as he'd kissed her last night—spread into a smile of the kind that made his dark eyes sparkle, full of triumph.

'I have as much to gain from this deal as you do.'

'More, if your commitment to it is anything to go by.' The words flew from her before she'd had time to think. She had to remember her goal—the sole reason she'd even approached this man in the first place. Antagonising him could put it all in jeopardy.

He didn't respond with words, but she saw his expression change. The smile still lingered, but granite hardness blazed from his eyes and he folded his arms across his chest, highlighting the breadth of his shoulders.

'Which is why I have made plans for us to go to Spain.'

Shock coursed through her body, leaving her almost gasping for air, as if she'd been plunged into a cold sea. 'Why Spain? We can stay in London. Spend the weekend here together quite easily.' She almost spluttered the last words. 'Why do we need to go to Spain?'

Santos watched as her brown eyes widened in shock and decided he preferred her with less make-up. Her soft skin looked fresh, and he fought hard against that unfamiliar urge to reach out and brush his finger against it, feel its softness.

Mentally he shook himself. The morning after was always a time to be brief—a quick goodbye had never failed him before. So why did he want to keep her here? Was it because this morning wasn't a normal morning-after? His body still fizzed with need, despite the cold shower he'd forced himself to stand under after he'd woken alone, knowing she was there, in his apartment, as untouchable as if she was the other side of the world.

'My home is in Spain, and if we are to be married I can cut through the red tape far more easily there.'

He heard her sharp intake of breath, saw her shoulders stiffen. His gaze was drawn to the way the jade silk clung to her body. She was as desirable in the morning light as she'd looked in the subdued lights of the party last night.

He wanted her more than he'd ever wanted a woman. She wasn't simpering and needy, looking for something that he couldn't give. She was strong and as in control as he was. But underneath all that he sensed a passion that would engulf him, rendering him helpless, and that was a position he would never put himself in.

He would never be as weak as his father had been.

'I still have to go home.'

She reached past him to grab her bag and sandals, her shoulder brushing his arm. He braced himself against the urge to pull her into his arms and kiss her as he had done at the party.

'A girl can't flit off for a weekend with nothing more than her Friday evening outfit.'

Her voice was light, almost lyrical. She was obviously used to loving and leaving. She also appeared used to coping in situations like this, and he'd do well to remember that. He watched as she placed her hand on the table, leaning against it as she lifted one shapely leg and slipped on a sandal. Mesmerised, he watched her fiddle with the straps, her brunette hair cascading over her shoulder, shielding her face from his view.

She straightened, taller now. His gaze locked with hers and a sizzle of something undefinable zipped between them. She blinked, long lashes breaking the connection, and bent to put on her other sandal.

'Okay,' she said softly. 'What do I need for this wedding in Spain?'

He smiled. He hadn't ever thought he would be getting married, and never in his wildest dreams had he imagined such a reluctant bride. Women usually fell over themselves to please him, and he knew if he'd asked the magic question to any one of the glamorous models he'd recently dated they would have been dragging him away.

'Your passport and birth certificate is all you need to bring. I have everything else sorted.'

'To perfection, by the sound of it. I suppose you have organised a pre-nuptial agreement?' She pushed her thick hair behind her ear and looked straight at him, her eyebrows raised in question.

Of *course* he'd arranged a pre-nuptial agreement. Any man in his position would. He'd had his legal team on it since she'd left his office on Thursday—just as they'd been finding out if it would be quicker and easier for them to marry in Spain. Her track record showed an ability to marry for financial gain and, no matter how passionately

she declared sisterly love as the reason behind her proposition, he'd decided to safeguard everything.

'It would be foolish not to, *querida*.'

Her eyes sparked with burnished gold and he knew
he'd hit a raw nerve. It was well known that she'd become
a wealthy woman after her husband died.

'Fine.'

The word crackled between them, and her lips were
firmly pressed together, as if she was holding back what
she really wanted to say.

He looked at her lovely face, her lips set in a firm line
of discontent, and he couldn't help himself. He reached
out and brushed his fingers down her cheek. She didn't
move, didn't pull away from him, just looked at him with
such wide-eyed innocence he wondered if it was the same
woman he'd met a few days ago.

'It will protect us both.' Her skin was so soft he wanted
more. He stepped closer, the urge to kiss her stronger than
anything he'd known.

'I have packing to do.'

Georgina's heart was pounding in her chest so hard she
was sure he would be able to hear it. She couldn't do
this. Why ever had she thought it was a good idea? Had
it *really* been her only option? Offering herself to a man
renowned for his ruthless business tactics.

For a moment his gaze locked with hers, the dark
depths of his eyes seeming to search hers as if looking
into her soul. Just when she thought she couldn't take it
any more he dropped his hand and moved away from her.
As he'd done a few days ago in his office he walked to
the windows and stood looking out over London.

She needed to go home and think. Once she was
away from him she could think of other options, but she

couldn't do any of that if he was around. Just one smouldering look from his eyes made her pulse leap. She wasn't supposed to feel anything for him, but the attraction that simmered like an undercurrent waiting to snare the unsuspecting unnerved her more than anything else.

'My car will take you to your apartment and wait while you pack.'

'Wait while I pack?' She laughed. 'Have you any idea how long it takes a woman to pack for a trip abroad?' Not that she would count herself among one of those women, but she needed time alone.

'Yes.' He turned to face her. 'As a matter of fact I do—which is why you will find just about anything you need waiting for you in Spain.'

'You've thought of everything, haven't you?' She couldn't believe the calculated way he'd planned all this. From the party where they would first be seen together to the trip away to get married.

'As I said, I do things properly. I cover every eventuality. Which is why my car will wait for you.'

'I made a deal with you, Santos.' Did he actually think she was going to run away? She was made of stronger stuff than that. 'I have no intention of going back on that deal, despite the fact that you have manipulated the situation to your advantage.'

'The "situation", as you call it, will be to the advantage of both of us.'

He smiled and his eyes darkened with the promise of something she didn't want to think of.

'Of that you can be sure.'

CHAPTER FOUR

GEORGINA HAD THOUGHT the private jet was luxurious, but the villa, with its stunning sea view, was beyond anything she could have imagined. White curtains stirred in the breeze, making the sunlight dance across the marble floor. The fashionable furnishings offered every comfort possible, giving the villa the feel of a home.

She stood and looked out of the open doors, which led onto the terrace. The heat of the afternoon sun must be having an effect on her. She'd been here for several hours and still she couldn't get over the world of opulence she'd entered. But, determined that Santos shouldn't know how out of her depth she felt, she kept her awe of her new surroundings hidden.

'We'll eat out tonight.'

Santos's voice brought her thoughts back to the present as he came to stand next to her. Each time he was near, her skin sizzled and anticipation zinged down her spine, but she couldn't and wouldn't go there. This was a business deal and nothing more. She could never allow it to be more.

She dragged her gaze from the sparkling sea and turned to face him. He too had changed. He'd washed away the hours spent travelling and stood before her looking more relaxed then she'd seen him before. She couldn't help herself and allowed her gaze to linger, to take in the latent strength of his body as he walked across the room to the doors of the terrace. The commanding strength he exuded excited her and terrified her at the same time.

'Would that be to keep up the pretence of an affair?' The words slipped from her mouth with practised ease, the facetious tone one she regularly used. 'It's obvious now why we are here.'

'Is it?'

Damn him, he appeared to be laughing at her. His new, relaxed mood made him smile at her prickly demeanour. It was as if he was genuinely flirting with her, teasing her as he might one of his lovers.

'Of course it is. This area is a playground for the rich and famous, and with them come photographers and journalists, all waiting to catch the next big story. I saw them taking photos as we arrived.'

She took a deep breath and forced herself to stop talking. Allowing Santos to see how he unnerved her wasn't going to do any good at all. If he wanted to parade her around as part of the pretence then so be it.

'For a woman who dreamt up this whole idea you're very touchy about it.'

He walked out onto the terrace, where he leant his strong arms on the balustrade. Briefly she remembered how it had felt to be held in their strength, but immediately she dragged her wandering mind back. She had to keep focused. It was almost as if he knew he was distracting her. She was convinced he was using it to his advantage.

'I didn't *dream* this up.' She flung her hands wide, gesturing around them, and pushed to the back of her mind the terms he'd agreed on, hoping it would never have to go that far. 'It's you who took the idea from marriage in name only to this—this pretend love affair.'

He turned back to face her and folded his arms across his chest, the sun behind him making it difficult to read his expression. 'This is the best way.'

'Best for who?'

She realised she'd never questioned his motivation for changing things. She'd been so desperate to achieve her aims she hadn't given it a thought. Yes, she knew he wanted the business—that much Emma had told her—but why would such a wealthy and successful man, who had women falling at his feet, agree so easily to her proposition of marriage?

'It doesn't matter who it's best for. Once we are married your sister can marry Carlo and you will have got what you wanted.'

'Not forgetting what *you* want. You will inherit the business, then we can both get on with our lives. As if this had never happened.' She kept her words firm, as if she believed wholeheartedly in what she was doing. One thing she would never do was let him know her doubts.

The clinking of ice in glasses halted further conversation as drinks were brought out to them. She watched as a petite Spanish girl placed the tray on the table before she slipped away, seeming to melt into the background.

'*Exactamente, querida.*'

He turned to face her as he spoke and a shiver of apprehension slipped over her.

'It all seems too easy, Santos,' she said, realising she'd used his name without having to force herself. 'I can't believe a man like you would agree to my deal so easily. There must be something more in it for you.'

He moved away from the balustrade and came close to her. Too close. Her first reaction was to step back, but she stood her ground and met his gaze head-on, despite the pounding of her heart and the race of her pulse. Something in his expression had changed. He looked more intense, his eyes darker. She couldn't help but look into them and momentarily floundered.

'Yes, there is, *querida*.'

He stepped closer and the air seemed alive with something she'd never experienced before.

'And that is?' She feigned bravado, her words short and sharp.

'I want what we agreed in my office. A wife.'

He was serious, and from the resolute set of his mouth she knew he wasn't going to change his mind any time soon. 'We don't need to make this marriage any more difficult to get out of than need be,' she said

'I have no intention of *getting out* of it, Georgina. I want a real wife—not someone joined to me just because we signed the same bit of paper.'

His gaze dropped from her eyes and lingered on her lips and she realised she was biting her bottom lip. The tension of waiting to hear what he really wanted was too much. As was his proximity. Her stomach fluttered wildly and she had to concentrate hard just to breathe.

'But why me?' She moved backwards, but still the sizzle was there. She could feel it with every pore of her skin. *He's just trying to throw you off balance*, she assured herself, and asked again. 'Why me, Santos? Why now?'

'Because you're the only woman who's asked me to marry them at a time when I need to be married.'

When I need to be married.

Those words rang inside her head like a cathedral choir. He didn't want to be married either, and she clung to the hope that she could persuade him later that separation was the best option.

Images of being with Santos, of spending days and nights with him, filled her mind. She became dizzy at the thought of what the nights would entail. Why did he want her in that way when he could have any one of the glamorous women who always seemed to be in his life?

Santos watched as an array of emotions flashed across her beautiful face. She might well have asked him to marry her, but he could see the idea of a real marriage unsettled her as much as it did him. Marriage was something he'd never wanted to enter into. He hated that he was being forced to marry by his father's ridiculous clause in his will. As a child he'd witnessed the destructive side of marriage—a side he knew lurked beneath every claim of love.

Love. He knew it didn't exist. It was a false and misleading emotion that could destroy any man, woman or child. It was open for exploitation. Never would he allow any woman close enough to manipulate him. Marrying Georgina was a necessity, nothing more.

'Lucky I asked when I did,' she said, and flashed a smile at him. But sadness clouded her eyes.

Was she thinking of her first husband? Had she loved him? Had he been manipulated just as easily? *Fool,* he told himself, fighting back irrational emotions that were completely alien to him. *Don't even go there.*

'Lucky for who, *querida*?' He couldn't resist the urge to provoke her, wanting to see those soft brown eyes spark with passionate fire, as they had done the very first time he'd seen her in his office.

She raised her brows at him. 'For you. I could have just encouraged Emma and Carlo to slip off and get married without anyone knowing. So I suppose you have the most to lose, Santos, and you have the most at stake.'

His name sounded hard on her lips, fierce. He wanted to go over to her and kiss them until they softened, until every last drop of restraint disappeared. Instead he focused his mind, because if one thing was true it was the fact that he *did* have the most to lose.

But he'd never admit that.

'We both have things at stake, Georgina.' Impatience crept into his voice. 'So I have had a mutually beneficial agreement drawn up.'

'Ah, the pre-nup.' She picked up her drink, ice clinking, and took a sip, all the while maintaining eye contact with him. 'I'll sign whatever is needed. I made that clear when I first put the proposition to you.'

'In that case, now would be a good time to do it.'

He saw the colour drain from her face, watched as she took a deep breath and met his gaze.

'Okay.'

That one word shook with fierce determination.

'We can finalise the formalities of our arrangement so that we can enjoy a relaxed evening out.' His business mind took over, insisting he secure everything before going any further with this deal—because a deal was all it was. One struck for the mutual benefit of both parties.

A flicker of guilt flashed into his mind. A moment ago she'd looked vulnerable, outside her comfort zone, but now she was as dignified and collected as she could be. Was she trying to throw him off balance in a bid to secure more for herself out of the marriage?

'Let's just get it done, Santos.' Her shoulders straightened and the spark of fire flared in her eyes, leaving him in no doubt that she meant every word.

He nodded his approval and admired her undaunted tone. 'The agreement is on my desk.'

He led the way to his study. For the first time in his life he was anxious about the outcome of a deal. Normally he would be in total control, able to steer deals his way, manoeuvring people like pieces on a chessboard.

But not with Georgina.

It wasn't her rigid sense of purpose or her defiance that left him second-guessing where their conversations would lead, but the woman herself. The soft curves of her delicious body, the passion in her eyes in those rare unguarded moments, always left him feeling distracted.

He wanted her.

But she was unlike any woman he'd wanted before. He sensed she was different, sensed that he had to play it cool. He knew she was like a proud lioness, knew that she would show her strength, her courage, but if she needed to she'd turn and flee, leaving him in the dust. And if she did that all would be lost. She was, after all, his last hope—his legal team had made that clear—but, like a card player, he'd keep his hand close to his chest and certainly wouldn't be revealing the full extent of the will just yet…not when he was still trying to get his head around it himself.

He clenched his hands and drew in a deep breath. Damn Carlo. His rush to marry had forced him to contemplate things he never would have entertained before.

He gestured to a chair on one side of his desk, taking in the graceful way she sat and noting the guarded expression on her face. He had to handle this as he would with any deal—ruthlessly. It was the only way. Otherwise he risked being weakened by her smile or, worse, by the undercurrent of something passionate that always seemed to surround them. How much of that was an act on her part he wasn't sure, but he had to fight hard against the way his body responded to her.

'My legal team have drawn up an agreement in Spanish and English. I think it will be beneficial to us both.' He kept his voice controlled as he took his seat opposite her, then he turned the document round and slid it across the desk towards her.

Their eyes met and a simmer of tension passed between them. She lowered her lashes and with slender fingers drew the document closer to her. He watched as she read the conditions, certain she'd be happy with his generous terms.

'It looks very comprehensive.'

She glanced up, but he wasn't sure if he was relieved or not to see a teasing smile on her lips.

'You obviously feel the need to protect yourself from my scheming ways.'

'It protects us both.'

He tried unsuccessfully to keep the irritation from his voice. Did she *have* to remind him of her past right at this moment? Was she proud of all the men she'd dated within weeks of her husband passing away? He pushed to the back of his mind all he'd learnt about her after that first visit to his office.

She raised her brows at him suggestively. Damn, was the woman deliberately trying to provoke him?

He stood and walked round the desk and leant down, one hand flat on the hard polished surface, bracing his arm. With pen in hand he pointed at the contract. 'As my wife you will be entitled to a substantial allowance to do with as you please.' Her perfume invaded his senses and he realised his mistake in coming close. 'Any children the marriage produces I will stand by and support, regardless of the outcome of our marriage.'

At least he'd touched on the subject of children. It was hard to believe that he, a man who'd never wanted to be married and certainly hadn't wanted to father a child, now sought both. Or at least was being forced to.

'Children?'

There was no doubting the shock in her voice. He looked down into her eyes, bright and wide. 'Yes. Children.'

He watched her slender throat as she swallowed and guilt sliced at him. He should tell her that a child might well become essential to secure the business, but something kept him silent. He wasn't sure if it was the fear of spooking her or the still raw anger at his father for creating such a clause. He had mentioned he wanted a *real* wife—surely that left her in no doubt.

He hoped he'd never have to go that far. It went against everything he believed in. As a *mistake* himself, he did not want to bring a child into the world unless he could give it love and security. The latter wouldn't be a problem, but love…?

'Do you want children?'

Her hesitant question made him clench his jaw and he saw her gaze dart to the movement, then quickly back to his eyes.

Georgina had asked the question lightly, despite the way her stomach had flipped over and was now churning. Did he really anticipate children? From a short-term marriage contract? She hoped not. Having a child was the one thing she'd never wanted to do. It was simply out of the question.

She looked down at the contract, the words blurring on the page as she fought back memories of her childhood. A childhood that had left her scarred and certain she didn't ever want to be a mother.

'As I said, I have covered all eventualities—to protect both of us.'

She swallowed hard and looked again up into his eyes. Their dark magnetic depths almost made her lose her nerve. For one tiny second she imagined a child with eyes the same colour, but quashed the image before it could manifest itself into anything bigger.

She had to have breathing space. His closeness, the fresh scent of his aftershave and the heat of his body so close to hers, was undoing her last remnants of self-control. She needed space and she needed it now.

'You have covered everything concisely, just as I would have expected from you.' She picked up the pen and with a flowing movement of her wrist signed the contract. The pen dropped to the desk as she pushed back the chair and moved away from him—away from the power he had over her every time he came close. 'There. All signed.'

'You don't have any questions?' He looked startled by her bravado and stood straight, towering over her, leaving her no option but to stand and face him.

'Just one.'

'And that is?'

'When are we going to finalise this deal and get married?'

That isn't the question, her mind screamed as she watched a sexy smile spread across his lips. *You should have asked when you can call Emma*, she scolded herself. She wanted to tell her sister that she could start making plans for her own wedding.

'Tuesday.'

'What?' All the air seemed to have left her lungs, as

if she'd run into a brick wall, and her heart was pounding madly. 'But that is only three days away.'

'Is there a problem with that?' His voice resonated with control and his expression hardened in challenge, the smile of moments before gone.

'No…no,' she stammered, hating herself for doing so. 'I just hadn't expected it to be so soon.'

'I see no reason to delay.'

His eyes hardened and his voice was firm as he spoke and she knew deep down that he was right. The sooner they were married the better. But Tuesday felt all too soon. She hardly knew him. *You don't need to*, a nagging voice inside her chided.

'I'll need to get something to wear. I'm sure you don't want your bride turning up in jeans.' She tried at humour, but her voice sounded brisk even to her ears.

He looked at his watch. 'That wouldn't be the image I was planning—which is why I've arranged for outfits to be brought here this afternoon. Select whichever one you want, and also something suitable for this evening.'

The velvet-edged strength of his voice and sexy accent caused her to drag in a ragged breath.

'What exactly *is* this evening?' In a bid to quell the nauseous tremor in her stomach she lifted her chin, dropped her shoulders and met his gaze.

'Our engagement.'

The words were curt and she watched as he walked back around to his side of the desk. He picked up the pen, pulled the papers towards him and signed next to her signature on the contract before looking back up at her.

'I fully intend for us to be seen out this evening as if we are a couple madly in love.'

'It's only Emma who needs to think we actually *want* to get married. It doesn't matter to me what anyone else

thinks—not now.' She couldn't believe he wanted to put
on a public engagement.

'I don't want doubt in anyone's mind,' he said as he sat
back and looked up at her. 'Least of all people I've known
for many years. I want them to think that we are in love.'

'There will be people you *know* there tonight? Not
family, surely?'

It was all getting too much. Everything was happening
so fast—much faster than she'd ever planned. She was
getting deeper and deeper all the time into something she
obviously hadn't given enough thought to.

'*Sí,* my cousin.'

Amusement shone from his eyes. Was he enjoying
her discomfort?

'Other than that, just friends—but they will talk. I
want the right things said.'

Further conversation was halted as the maid Georgina
had seen earlier knocked on the door. Spanish words
flowed melodiously between her and Santos, and Georgina felt strangely excluded. Her grasp of the language
was basic to say the least.

'I shall leave you now to select your wedding gown.
Señora Santana is well known in Spain for her gowns.' He
turned his attention back to her, the smile that the maid
had been treated to still lingering on his lips.

She felt a nervous panic at the thought of being left
alone, hardly able to communicate with his staff, let alone
whoever was here with wedding outfits. Santos laughed.
A soft throaty chuckle that was maddeningly sexy.

'Don't panic. I shall be in here. I have plenty of work
to do.'

'I'm not panicking,' she flung at him, and smiled at
the maid, who was waiting to show her where to go. How
did he always manage to know what she was thinking?

'I'll wait for you on the balcony at seven,' he said as she left the room.

She stopped on the threshold and turned to look at him. His tall frame dominated the study so that he seemed almost dangerous. And he was, if the way she reacted to him was anything to go by.

Georgina was taken to yet another bedroom, as big and airy as the one she'd been shown to on arrival. The only difference was the rail of white and cream silk almost mockingly awaiting her approval. One glance at the dresses and Georgina knew that most of them weren't suitable.

'*Buenas tardes, señora.*' An immaculately dressed woman in her forties all but glided across the marble floor. 'A little too romantic maybe?' Her accent was heavy and she stroked the dresses lovingly and smiled at Georgina.

'I have already been married....' Georgina began, resenting the need to explain anything, but Señora Santana put up her hand as if to tell her to stop.

'Not a problem. Señor Ramirez has explained,' she said, and walked behind the rail of dresses to another which Georgina hadn't noticed.

Just what had Santos explained? Curiosity piqued, she followed and drew in a breath of awe. These dresses were beautiful. Bold colours of red, green and midnight-blue had been added to frills or even completely forming a bodice.

Georgina couldn't help but smile. These were more like it. A sweet, innocent bride was not the image she was going for. She trailed her fingers over the silk and chiffon. But one dress in particular caught her attention. She took the dress from the rail and held it against her. It was perfect. It was everything, and more, that she could want this dress to be.

'*Perfecto.*' Señora Santana smiled and urged Georgina to try it on.

Caught up in the moment, she relished the feel of silk and chiffon against her skin and looked at her image in the mirror. The dress fitted perfectly. As if it had been made for her. She slipped her foot into a dainty strappy sandal, feeling more and more like Cinderella every moment.

'You will need a veil.'

'No,' Georgina replied quickly, and glanced in the mirror at the other lady. 'No veil,' she said more gently, and smiled. She hadn't had a veil for her first wedding—hadn't even had a dress—so she saw no need to go over the top now. Especially as it was, once more, a marriage of convenience.

Señora Santana shrugged. 'Ah, I have the perfect alternative. You will see. But now we choose a dress for dinner. No?'

No was just what Georgina wanted to say. She'd gone along with the wedding dress, knowing it was part of the whole plan and necessary. Photos would almost certainly end up in the glossy magazines, whether she wanted them there or not. But a dress for this evening wasn't necessary. At least not one of this quality.

'No, the wedding dress is enough.'

The woman's eyes widened. 'But Señor Ramirez insisted. You *must* choose one.'

Finally Señora Santana's insistence had worn Georgina down and she'd selected a classic black dress, which now lay on her bed. The hours had just disappeared whilst she was trying dresses on, leaving very little time before she was to meet Santos. Now, after a quick shower, she dried her hair and applied make-up.

Why was she feeling nervous about seeing Santos again? She looked at her watch. Five minutes to seven. He would be waiting on the terrace very soon. She looked again at the dress, feeling almost like a sacrificial lamb.

But wasn't that exactly what she was?

For her sister's happiness she'd once again taken on a role she didn't want. Marrying Richard had been to put Emma through school and a roof over their heads. It had been his suggestion, and even to this day she couldn't believe a man had done that for her. She'd been on tenterhooks during all the three years they were married, just waiting for him to leave her. But she'd never expected him to leave her the way he had. As a widow. She'd known he was ill—but not that ill.

With a heavy heart she picked up the dress, stepped into it. For a moment the zip eluded her and it took several minutes of contortions to pull it up. Flustered by her efforts, she slipped on the new pair of shoes insisted upon by Señora Santana and left the bedroom, her heels sounding loud on the marble.

CHAPTER FIVE

Santos was looking out at the sea, dressed in a dark suit, as she approached the balcony. When he turned and his gaze met hers her breath caught in her throat. It wasn't right that a man could be so sexy. The cloth of his suit had been cut with precision, emphasising his broad shoulders and strong thighs to perfection.

She swallowed hard, desperate to calm her racing heartbeat. If she carried on like this there wouldn't be any need for pretence. Her attraction to him was becoming stronger, and if he turned on the charm as he had at the party she'd be lost. Worse still, if he kissed her again she didn't think she'd be able to resist him.

'You look beautiful,' he said, his voice deep, with a husky edge to it. 'Exactly what I had in mind.'

Well, if that didn't serve as a reminder that it was all an act, then nothing would.

'I'm glad it meets with your approval,' she said tartly and, desperate to hide her confusion, walked past him to the table, selecting a drink from those prepared. Anger fizzed in her veins at the thought of the way he made her feel: light-headed and soft one minute, then short and sharp the next. In a bid to rein in her rising and very mixed emotions she all but downed her drink in one go.

'Steady, *querida*.' He smiled. A mocking smile. As if he knew her turmoil. 'That drink is pretty potent.'

She looked at the almost empty glass. The remains of the liquid looked more like a soft drink, but its effect on her head was already clear. Whatever was she trying to do to herself? She put the glass down and turned to look at him, holding her hair back as the sea breeze toyed with it just as he was toying with her.

'If you are ready shall we go?'

He didn't wait for her to answer, but placed his hand in the small of her back, its heat scorching through the silk of her dress, and all but propelled her towards the door. Outside, a sleek, gleaming sports car waited, fiery red. Exactly what she'd imagined him driving.

'Suits you,' she said in a cavalier tone, and dropped down into the low seat as he stood by the open door.

He raised his brows and smiled at her. '*Gracias*.'

When Santos climbed in beside her she became all too aware of just how close she was to him. His tanned fingers pulled the gearstick backwards as the car growled into life. She couldn't help but notice that the space beneath the steering wheel seemed almost too compact for his powerful thighs.

A small but insistent fire sparked to life deep inside her as she watched him drive. Each move he made sent a shiver of awareness over her and she bit down hard on her lip against the new wave of emotions that assailed her. She couldn't be falling for him—she *couldn't*.

'Is it far?' Nerves made her voice quiver as she finally acknowledged the attraction she felt for him, and he glanced across at her before returning his attention to the road ahead.

'No, but arriving in style will attract the attention we need.'

'Attention?' Her mind was scrambled as she looked at his profile. The shadow of stubble only added to the sexy appeal he emanated.

'How else is the world going to know we are engaged?' He glanced across at her again, his gaze meeting hers briefly before returning to the task of driving. 'This is what you wanted. Puerto Banus is a renowned favourite of the rich and famous, and with them come the press photographers, hungry for gossip.'

Now she understood his insistence on dressing for dinner. This was Act Two. The next part of their public courtship, played out to perfection. It was time to retreat behind her public persona.

'And tonight, *querida*, we shall give them something to gossip about.'

His voice was laden with promise and as the fire rose higher inside her she looked away.

The car growled into the small harbour town and Georgina couldn't help but take it all in. Cars as sleek and powerful as Santos's lined the narrow streets, parked outside global designer shops. Yachts that looked more like floating palaces were moored all around the harbour, many with lights glinting and parties in full swing on board.

This was most definitely a playground for the wealthy.

Santos parked the car, expertly manoeuvring it into a space in front of one of the bigger yachts. He switched off the engine and silence seemed to cloak them. The leather seat crunched as he turned to face her.

'You look absolutely stunning tonight.' He reached up and pushed her hair back from her face and she trembled.

She didn't say anything. She couldn't. All she could do was look into the mesmerising depths of his eyes.

'You are playing your part well—so well even I'm convinced.'

His voice was a husky whisper and she wished he wouldn't slide his fingers through her hair like that.

'Convinced of what?' She forced the words out, alarmed at the throaty sound of her voice.

'The attraction between us…'

He moved a little closer and she wondered if he was going to kiss her. She wanted him to, but knew it would be her undoing. Then, before she even had a chance to think, his lips claimed hers. Try as she might she couldn't stop her eyes from closing, couldn't help reaching up to touch his cheek, feeling the slight stubble against her fingertips. She was attracted to him, despite all she'd promised herself, and he must never know. That would be to show her weakness. Give him all the power. She'd seen it before.

She pulled back a little from him, her lips still very close to his, and opened her eyes. 'I'm a brilliant actress,' she whispered as her fingers smoothed once more across his face.

The sound that came from him resembled a growl as his hand caught and held hers. 'Don't take your role too far, *querida*. I might just go past the need to act.'

For a moment she sat transfixed by the tension that hung between them. The promised threat of his words was not lost on her. Did her really want her? Did he find himself struggling against the same raw need she was fighting right now?

'It's showtime, Georgina.' His words were firm and sharp as he pulled away from her and got out of the car.

She watched him walk around the front of it, relaxed but masterful. Obviously she didn't have the same effect on him—didn't scramble his emotions until he couldn't think straight.

Okay, showtime it is, she thought as she got out of the

car and walked with him towards the busy street lined with restaurants. She could do this—even if it meant putting on the biggest show of her life.

Suddenly a man's shouts caught her attention and a waiter from one restaurant came out to greet him, hugging Santos and then stepping back to cast an enquiring look her way.

'Georgina, this is my cousin Raul—owner of this restaurant and at our bidding for this evening.'

She felt suddenly shy beneath the man's gaze. He took her hand and with the same charm Santos possessed kissed it. 'I can see why my cousin is so entranced.'

To her horror she blushed, but managed to smile back at him. 'What more could a girl ask for?' She raised her brows, made her voice light and melodious, even a little flirty.

Raul laughed and after a brief look of shock Santos did too. Then he smiled at Georgina, a dangerous light in his eyes.

'Raul, do you have the table I requested?'

'Sí,' Raul replied, and continued in Spanish.

Santos put his arm around her shoulders, pulling her close as he followed his cousin to their table. It was private, and candles fluttered in the evening breeze. The sea could be heard lapping gently onto the shore close by.

It was perfectly romantic.

The whole meal was. Each course was divine and all the while Santos exuded what she was fast becoming aware was his lethal charm. She smiled, played her part all through dinner, but reality was beginning to blur. She sipped her wine and looked out at the sea, where the setting sun cast an orange glow across the rippling surface.

'Georgie?'

Her attention swung back to Santos when she heard her

name on his lips. His voice sounded hoarse, as if he was choked with emotion. Oh, he was good at this, she thought, and smiled at him. He'd never used her pet name before.

'Will you marry me?'

'What?' she gasped as he slid a small velvet box across the table. *Calm down. It's probably for his cousin's benefit.*

'Will you make me the happiest man alive and marry me?'

His dark eyes were watching her intently. When she looked into them she thought she saw the same desire she'd seen at the party, the same simmering passion. Just as she'd thought she'd seen it earlier, when they were in the car. But that couldn't be, could it?

She reached for the box, aware of the role she had to play, but he caught her hand in his. The heat of his touch was almost too much.

'Marry me?'

'Yes.' Her whole body quivered, but she couldn't lower her gaze, couldn't break that tenuous connection. 'Yes, I'll marry you.'

Slowly he let her hand go, opened the box and pulled out a glittering diamond ring. As he slid it onto her finger the candlelight made it sparkle, bringing it to life. He lifted her hand to his lips, his gaze holding hers captive, and kissed her fingers.

This was what it would really feel like, she thought as she looked into his dark eyes. This was be the closest she'd ever come to having a real proposal.

Applause erupted around them, making her jump. She hadn't realised they were being watched, and neither had Santos. Even he looked taken aback. She laughed, unable to help herself, and the tension of the moment slipped away as the other diners returned their attention to their meals.

'Let's go,' he said in a throaty growl, sounding as if he really couldn't wait to get her home. Something indefinable skittered over her, making her tummy somersault and her breath tighten in her chest.

Don't do this to yourself. You are just a means to an end. He doesn't really want you.

It was dark as they walked back along the street. Yachts were lit up, giving everything a magical appeal. The warm breeze on her skin felt wonderful, but not as wonderful as Santos's arm about her waist, pulling her against his magnificent body. She savoured the moment, stored it for later. The champagne she'd drunk was making it easier to enjoy being with him like this and easier to let go of her usual anxiety. This wonderful feeling was going to have to last her a lifetime.

By the car Santos stopped. Instinctively she looked up at him, then couldn't help herself as she reached up and kissed his lips. His response was gentle at first, setting her body alight. The fire was fuelled further by his hands sliding down her back, pulling her so very close to him. Whatever it was that had simmered between them at the party was now well and truly alight. As her hips pressed against his aroused body she knew he wanted her. Was it so wrong to give in to it? To enjoy it for what it was? A passing attraction.

'Santos,' she murmured against his lips.

It was all the encouragement he needed and he deepened the kiss, plunging his tongue into her mouth as she sighed in pleasure.

Need rocketed through her body and she almost became incapable of thought as he stepped closer, forcing her back against the side of his car, pressing hard against her and stoking the fire deep within her body. Unleashing an insatiable need for him.

His hand slid down her side, over her hip and down to her bottom. He pulled her hard against him and raw desire tore through her, leaving her gasping against his lips as her arms clung around his neck. It was mind-blowing. She'd never known anything like it.

A flash lit up the world for a second—or so it seemed to Georgina. But in that second she regained her breath, and the control she'd so very nearly lost. She turned her face to the opportunist photographer, knowing he was just what she needed to bring her feet firmly back to the ground.

Beside her Santos spoke in Spanish, his voice thick and hoarse as the photographer snapped another photo. Quickly Santos put some distance between them and opened the car door for her, but she didn't miss the raw desire in his eyes.

Once they were inside she asked, 'What did you tell him?'

'That we'd just got engaged and needed private time.' His voice was husky and heavily accented.

Of course he'd say that. But she couldn't help feeling humiliated. His kiss—which had been part of the act, the charade—had nearly been her undoing. She'd wanted more…wanted him to take her home. More than anything she'd wanted him to take her to his bed. But that could never happen.

Never.

To allow him to know how much her feelings towards him had changed would be the worst possible scenario. With that in mind she retreated to her room as soon as they arrived back at his villa.

The next morning Georgina used the excuse of it being Sunday and stayed in her room. Eventually she ventured out, hoping the quietness of the villa meant Santos was ensconced in his study.

As she strolled through the living area movement in the pool caught her eye. Santos was powering through the water, his strokes effortless. She shouldn't be watching but couldn't help herself, almost unaware of each step towards the pool she took. The afternoon sun shone brightly and she put on her sunglasses, watching as his muscles flexed.

Abruptly he stopped and looked at her, his dark eyes gleaming with amusement. 'Are you coming in?'

The husky depths of his voice made her stomach flutter and she was glad of the sunglasses she could hide behind. 'I'll give it a miss,' she said as she sat down on the edge of a sun lounger, even more drawn to him.

'Pity,' he replied, and swam over to her. His hair was flat against his head and rivulets of water ran down his face. 'It's very relaxing.'

Hardly. The thought of being in the water with him made her pulse race, and inwardly she cursed the attraction she felt for him. It was making things complicated.

'Maybe a walk along the beach?'

'That would be nice,' she said, and stood up, aware that at any moment he would haul his bronzed body from the water. And she wasn't ready for that. 'I'll go and change.'

Not trusting herself to look back at him, she hurried to her room and changed into a cool dress and flat sandals. Regaining her composure, she returned to the terrace and waited.

She knew when he was there as if her body was completely tuned in to his. She turned to face him and that spark of attraction zipped instantly between them.

'Shall we?'

He took her hand and for a moment their eyes met,

his darkening instantly. She remembered his touch last night, his kiss, and could hardly draw breath.

Right now, with his hand holding hers she felt safe. Cherished.

As if he could read her thoughts he held her hand just a little tighter. She smiled a genuine smile, one she couldn't hold back, as he stepped closer and brushed his lips over hers.

Everything around her ceased to exist. It was just the two of them. No deal—nothing. When he pulled back she looked up into his eyes. Was this what she'd been searching for? This strange warm feeling of contentment?

'We won't get very far like this,' she teased lightly, her heart almost melting as he laughed softly.

'*Sí*, you are right. We will walk.'

Sand, warm from the afternoon sun, poured into her sandals, but she didn't care. She just wanted to savour this moment. Because this was what it must be like, that glowing feeling of a new relationship. The first tender stirrings of love. Was it even possible?

'You're smiling,' he said as he pulled her to a stop, his hand not relinquishing its hold on hers. 'For the first time since we met you look happy.'

'I am.' And she meant it. Right now all she wanted was to be herself, to bask in the warmth of this new sensation. Santos made her feel things she'd never thought possible, and knowing those feelings wouldn't last for ever she wanted to relax and enjoy them. 'What about you?'

'In the company of a woman as beautiful as you, how could I not be happy?'

She searched his eyes, looking for a hint of mockery, but found only a heart-rending tenderness. He stroked his fingers down her cheek, lifting her chin as he bent and lightly kissed her lips.

Her heart pounded erratically and a tingle of excitement raced around her. Light-headed and almost giddy, she kissed him back, tentatively at first. This wasn't the needy kiss of last night—this was giving and caressing. It was loving.

She pulled back from him a little, shyness making her look up from under her lashes as heat infused her cheeks. 'You don't have to say and do these things—not now, anyway.'

'What I say is true.'

His voice was husky and raw as he brushed her hair back from her face, sending waves of delicious sensation all over her.

'And I only do what I want.'

It was as if a bond was forming with each gentle caress of his hands and each soft word. He was pulling her towards him. This man was so far removed from the compelling man she'd first felt a spark of attraction for she was lost for words.

Without another word he pulled her against him, holding her so close she could hear his heart thumping as wildly as hers. Was he aware of what was happening? Did he also feel as if he was wading out to sea, getting deeper and deeper, unable to turn back to the safety of shore?

The next morning Santos planned to work, but all he wanted was to be with Georgina. It was as if magic had been in the air last night on the beach and had weaved around them, bringing them closer in a way he'd never been with a woman before.

Was it because she still hadn't shared his bed? Was that one fact making him delusional? Like a man lost in the desert?

A bit of distance, that was what they needed, he decided, and for the best part of the day he shut himself in his study. He tortured himself when he heard her in the pool, but it was more than desire that raced around his blood. Something new, something undefinable, now simmered there too.

Finally, as the sun was setting, he could stand it no longer and went in search of the woman who would tomorrow be his wife. She was curled on the sofa, her phone in her hand. She looked up at him as he stood in front of her.

'I can't get Emma on the phone.' Her words were rushed.

Guilt shot through him, he'd completely forgotten her need to phone her sister.

'I sent a text instead.'

He didn't know how to respond to the obvious anxiety in her voice. Worrying about siblings was not something he'd ever done. Distraction was what she needed, he decided. 'Would you care to join me for a walk?'

'Another walk? Tonight?' She put her phone on a nearby table and smiled at him, the same warm smile she'd given him the night before. 'It's supposed to be bad luck for the bride to see the groom on the eve of her wedding.'

'I won't tell if you don't,' he teased, and held out his hand to her. She hesitated, then laughed softly. It was such a sexy sound he had to brace himself against the onslaught of thudding desire which rushed over him.

'In that case, how can I refuse?' She seemed different, as if all pretence had been abandoned, and he knew this was the real Georgina. The fiery, demanding woman who had burst into his office last week no longer existed.

The sea was calmer than he'd ever known it, with the waves hardly making any sound. They walked along the sand hand in hand, as they had done the previous afternoon. The sky was dark and the stars were shining brightly as he stopped and turned to her.

'I've enjoyed your company,' he said awkwardly. 'It's hard to believe it's only been a few days since we arrived.'

Georgina looked up at him. Was it possible he felt it too? He was so different now, so relaxed, and she knew she was in danger of falling in love with him.

'Don't say any more,' she whispered, putting her finger on his lips. She didn't want him to give her hope if he didn't mean it.

He kissed her fingers and before she knew how she was in his arms, her body pressed close to his. Fire tore through her as she kissed him, giving way to all the new emotions she was battling with. She wanted him with a fierceness that shocked her.

He deepened the kiss, his arms pressing her close against him, leaving her in no doubt that she needed to stop things now. She pulled back from him, her heart racing, and her breathing fast.

'I can't, Santos.'

'Can't what?' His voice was hoarse and he tried to kiss her again.

'This,' she said, moving back from him. 'We shouldn't even be seeing one another tonight. It's bad luck.'

CHAPTER SIX

SANTOS'S PULSE POUNDED in his head and a fire coursed through his veins which had little to do with the punishing early-morning run he'd just completed. After yet another night of trying to douse his need for Georgina he'd given up and, despite it being the morning of his wedding, had gone out to find some kind of release. He wasn't sure how much more he could take.

How could one woman drive him to such distraction?

Refusing to explore the answer to that question, he returned to his villa. As he did so he heard female voices and knew that Señora Santana had arrived, along with the others, to do the bridal hair and make-up. He clenched his hands into fists, fighting hard against the urge to go to Georgina's room, send everyone out and continue what she'd started last night—because start it she most definitely had.

Patience, he reminded himself, and headed for a cold shower instead. His run had not had the desired effect. Heady lust still throbbed through his veins and he knew of only one antidote for that—other than taking Georgina to his bed right now. *Work*. Once he'd showered he would shut himself in his office and work until lunchtime, when he would escort Georgina to the beach to become his wife.

An hour later he admitted it was impossible. The figures blurred before him and all he could think about was that kiss last night. At first so innocent and tender, then passion had taken over. Santos realised he'd been so consumed by need he'd behaved like a teenager, raging hormones taking control of his senses, rendering him completely under her spell.

Just as his father had been with Carlo's mother.

That thought alone had the sobering effect he needed on his body. He could never allow himself to be at the mercy of a woman—wanting her so much that nothing else mattered. Not even his inheritance. He'd never wanted a serious relationship, and certainly didn't want to get married, but his father's interfering had changed that.

In a bid to divert his mind he turned to his laptop, scanning the business pages and the headlines from Spain and England before looking at the celebrity gossip columns. Sure enough, just as he'd expected, he and Georgina were featured leaving the party together. Speculation as to what would happen next had filled the columns for the last two days.

At least now nobody would think him grasping enough to marry purely for financial gain. That sort of reputation wouldn't go down well when making business deals in the future. But if his business rivals thought he had a human side, one touched by love—whatever that was—they would be less guarded with him, giving him the edge he always sought.

He looked up at the clock on the wall. Eleven-thirty. Almost time to seal the hardest deal of his life. He turned off the laptop, put away his papers and headed back to his room to put on his suit.

As he fixed his cufflinks he looked in the mirror. Was he doing the right thing? He thought of the clause in the will, the need for an heir, and knew in that moment he should have told Georgina exactly what might be expected of her unless his legal team could find another way out. So why hadn't he? Because he didn't seriously think it would come to that when he was paying to find a solution. But then he hadn't thought he'd ever have to marry either.

A knock at the door drew his attention and he strode over to open it, knowing he was to be given the message that she was ready. It was time to make Georgina his wife. Guilt shot through him. She didn't know exactly what she'd signed up for. He had to tell her as soon as they were alone. Tell her that his mention of children in the prenuptial agreement might prove vital in the deal she'd come up with. Even *he* wasn't that harsh. Despite everything, he still clung to the hope that it wouldn't be necessary.

She was waiting for him on the terrace, but nothing could have prepared him for that moment if he'd spent several years organising it, instead of several days.

Georgina looked amazing.

Cream chiffon and silk encased her slender figure, but the slit in the floor-length dress drew his eye to her leg as she moved towards him. Her dark hair had been pulled back into a chignon and lace was attached to it, giving her a very Spanish air. The bodice of her dress clung to her breasts lovingly and on the single strap diamonds sparkled.

'I trust this meets your requirements?'

Her chin lifted defiantly, and her voice was as sharp as a razor, but her eyes still blazed with the same desire he'd seen in them last night. Gone was the woman he'd held in his arms as the stars sparkled above them.

'Every bride should look stunning on her wedding

day,' he said firmly, admiring the confidence that radiated from her. 'And you do.'

He fought to stop his mind envisaging removing the gown later as he truly made her his. Because if the attraction that existed between them—the one they had both been trying to deny—finally got the better of them when they were alone, there would be no doubt about consummating their marriage.

'You look very handsome too,' she said, a small blush creeping across her cheeks, her words softer.

'I'm pleased you didn't choose one of those fussy, frilly gowns I saw being brought in.' He tried to lighten the mood with small talk, but each step she took towards him showcased her slender legs and it was having a powerful effect on him. 'Such a daring dress was made for you.'

'Having been married before, I didn't think the usual fairytale image was appropriate.' She followed his lead and kept her voice light.

'It is far better than what you wore the first time,' he said slowly, his gaze holding hers. 'A business suit at a registry office? Hardly the stuff of fairytales.'

'You know that?' Her beautiful dark eyes widened slightly and she drew in a sharp breath.

'I always research my business deals, Georgina, and this one is no exception.' His words sounded firmer than he'd intended as he remembered exactly why they were doing this. The effort of not reaching for her, taking her in his arms and kissing her as he had last night, was almost too much. 'Ready?'

She looked at him for a moment, her brown eyes cool and emotionless, then she swallowed hard, giving away the fact that she wasn't as composed as she wanted him to think.

'I'm ready.' Still her voice was hard, full of determination.

He took her hand and led her from the terrace, down the steps towards the beach, where his cousin and a friend waited to witness their marriage. He glanced at her, smiling at her continued air of defiance.

Pride unexpectedly swelled in his chest as he realised just what was about to happen. He was about to take this gorgeous woman as his wife—a woman any man would be proud to be seen with. She was clever, witty, and incredibly sexy. Her hand in his was small and he clutched it tighter, enjoying the warmth of her.

Georgina's step almost faltered, and it was nothing to do with the grains of sand sliding through her sandals as she made her way across the beach. It was everything to do with the proud and arrogant man at her side.

His hand was warm as it held hers and she risked a quick look at him. He looked as if he'd stepped from her long-ago abandoned dream of a happy-ever-after. He was exactly the image of the man she'd used to dream of marrying: tall, dark, and devastatingly handsome. But this man was also dangerous. The way he could send her senses into overdrive meant she had to guard herself well or risk being hurt.

The waves rolled onto the sand before rushing back to sea and Georgina wished she could slip away with them. Doubts… Surely they were natural for a bride, but they clouded her mind, making her homesick. She wanted to see Emma, to tell her what was happening. This morning she'd nearly called her, but as she'd looked at her sister's number she'd known she didn't have enough strength to conceal the truth.

She wished she had someone here she knew. Someone for *her*. Someone who could reassure her she was doing the right thing.

When Santos stopped, not far from Raul and two others, she knew it was too late.

'I'm sorry there wasn't time to find one of your friends to witness this.'

Santos spoke softly next to her ear, almost making her jump and dragging her from her melancholy. It was as if he knew her thoughts.

She smiled brightly at him—maybe a little too brightly. 'It might have given the game away if you'd started flying my friends out here.'

'If you're sure?'

'I'm sure,' she replied quickly, injecting as much bravado into her voice as possible. 'Let's just get this over and done with.'

He looked shocked, but time for any further discussion was lost as the minister greeted them.

Everything seemed to spin. The minister's words, first in English, then Spanish, blended with the rush of the waves. Santos continued to hold her hand tightly and the heat of his body beside her was matched only by the sun.

She couldn't think—couldn't even grasp the concept of the words that were being said. When she'd walked into Santos's office last week she hadn't envisaged this—a beach ceremony with a man she was finding ever harder to resist. A man who wanted to be married to her about as much as she wanted to be to him.

'Georgie?'

She looked slowly up at him, remembering the need to act like a real bride, and smiled. He smiled back. A smile that reached into the dark depths of his eyes, melting her from the inside out.

He took her hands in his and spoke in Spanish to her.

She had no idea what he was saying, what he was doing. Everything seemed unreal. Then he slid a gold ring on her finger, repeating the words in English, and she realised he was doing exactly what she should be. Acting.

Panic raced through her. She didn't have a ring for him. Should she have got one? A polite cough at her side caught her attention and Raul handed her a ring, his smile full of charm. She smiled and turned back to Santos, slid the ring onto his finger and repeated the words that bound them legally in a marriage neither wanted.

Moments later Santos covered her lips with his, almost knocking the air from her as his arms wrapped around her, pulling her closer. She should resist, but sparks took off inside her like New Year's Eve fireworks and she wound her arms about his neck. It was as if the desire of last night still simmered.

Just as suddenly as the kiss had begun it ended, and Santos pulled away from her, but he kept her hand in his as he thanked Raul, his friend and the minster. Spanish flowed around her and all she could do was stand and wait, trying to come to terms with what she'd done.

It's for Emma. Just as it was last time.

'Now it is time for us.' Santos returned his attention back to her, his dark eyes sparking with fire.

'Us?' she asked as she watched the three people who'd witnessed her marriage walk back across the beach.

'*Sí.*' He dropped a kiss lightly on her nose and she blinked in shock at the affectionate gesture. 'We have to have at least a few days for our honeymoon before we return to London.'

Honeymoon.

Had he gone mad?

'Is that really necessary?' She couldn't believe he was serious. 'We're married now. You've got your business.

Can't we just go back and tell Emma and Carlo they can get married?'

'This was your idea, Georgina. You wanted to make it look as real as possible.' He frowned and looked down at her, his hand still clasping hers.

'I only wanted our names on a marriage certificate. I didn't want all this *acting*.' She should never have hoped to change things so late in the day. Not when she was dealing with a man like Santos.

His dark eyes narrowed in suspicion. 'You wanted authenticity and you've damn well got it.'

He let go of her hand and stepped back from her, then turned and walked back to the villa. She watched him go, just as she'd watched her father go all those years ago.

What was she doing? She couldn't stay on the beach—an abandoned bride for all to see. Propelled into action, she kicked off her sandals, picked them up and marched after him. They'd been married for only a matter of minutes and were already arguing. Surely that would make him see they needed to go their separate ways?

'Okay,' she said as she caught up with him, injecting as much ferocity as she could into her voice. 'We'll have the honeymoon. But once Emma and Carlo get married this farce ends.'

'Farce?'

He stopped and turned to face her. The fury in his face served only to increase her need to keep what she really felt for him concealed.

Without warning he pulled her into his arms, his lips claiming hers in a demanding and hungry kiss, weakening her body so that she could barely stand. She wanted to respond, wanted to take the pleasure his lips promised, but instead she reminded herself it wasn't real. None of it was. At least not for him.

His hands pressed her ever closer to him, until she had no doubt that although the marriage wasn't real his desire for her was. Her lips parted and his tongue plundered her mouth, entwining with hers in an erotic dance, making her sigh with pleasure.

Heaven help her, she wanted more. She wanted this man in a way she'd never wanted a man before.

He pulled back from her, his breathing deep and ragged. 'Now, deny that, Mrs Ramirez. Deny that you want me. Deny what your body tells me.'

'This wasn't supposed to happen.' Her lips were bruised and her body trembled with unquenched desire as she looked into his eyes, seeing sparks of passion within their depths.

'Come,' he demanded as he took her hand, and the gentleness of yesterday was gone.

Was he about to drag her to his room, take her to his bed? Excitement fizzed in her veins, only to be replaced by disappointment as he walked straight through the villa and out to his car.

'Where are we going?'

He opened the door of the car for her and she got in, hampered by the silk and chiffon of her dress. Mesmerised, she watched his hands expertly gather the silk skirt and bundle it into the car, his fingers brushing against her bare leg where the gown so daringly parted. She shivered as their eyes met. Their gazes remained locked; his hand rested on her leg.

'To my yacht.'

His voice was deep and incredibly seductive. Her heart jolted and her pulse raced as his fingers trailed over her thigh, moving teasingly higher.

'For our honeymoon.'

The smouldering flames she saw in his eyes should

have been warning enough, but she didn't want to listen to sense any more. This man wanted her, desired her, and she wanted him too. All sensible reasoning slipped away as he bent and kissed her thigh, where his fingers had made a blazing trail.

'Santos.' She placed her hands either side of his face, forcing him to look up at her. 'Please don't. At least not here.'

He smiled and stretched up to press his lips to hers, breathing Spanish words against them. She had no idea what he said and neither did she care. She watched, anticipation throbbing in her blood, as he shut the car door and strode around the front to the driver's side. He looked at her as the engine growled to life, his gaze so hot it seemed to melt the chiffon from her body and dissolve the silk of her skirt. And when those dark and dangerous eyes met hers she knew it was already too late. She'd lost. His expert charm and arrogant confidence had won.

She was as good as his.

She sat silently contemplating what had just happened between them as Santos drove. The car sped along the coast road, but she didn't doubt his ability to handle it. The sea glistened in the afternoon sun and she realised that very soon they'd be alone out there.

Tyres screeched as he came to an abrupt halt next to what was probably the biggest yacht in the harbour. She wasn't sure if she felt relieved or disappointed that they weren't going to be alone after all. A yacht this size must have at least a dozen crew members.

As they boarded he fired off rapid instructions in Spanish and everything seemed to come to life around them. A maid stepped forward, offering a glass of champagne, and Georgina took it, grateful to have something to hold other than Santos's hand.

She looked at him and he raised his glass to her. 'To my beautiful wife.'

His gaze openly devoured her and her body tingled.

'To my handsome husband,' she flirted.

Just one sip of champagne was making her braver than she really was. She had to play the game well, so she smiled as he smiled. But her words weren't lies. He was more handsome than she could ever have dreamed of, standing on deck in his designer suit, glass of champagne in hand, passion for her sparking in his eyes. He was everything and more from her abandoned dream of the perfect man.

'As we sail we shall have our wedding breakfast.'

He sipped his champagne and she watched him swallow, mesmerised by the movement of his throat. Food was the last thing she wanted right now, but maybe it would bring her back to her senses, dull the thud of desire in her veins and enable her to think rationally.

Whilst they'd been talking the yacht had slipped away from the harbour and was now sailing past the long stone wall and out into the sea. The small but affluent town of Puerto Banus looked picturesque, nestled below the looming mountains, and Georgina was transfixed by the view.

'So beautiful,' she whispered, unable to drag her eyes from it.

'Beautiful indeed.' Santos's voice was firm and strong as he stood next to her. 'But it is outshone by the beauty of my bride.'

Georgina took another sip of champagne—anything to calm her nerves—and then turned to face him. 'Surely we don't need to keep up the pretence here?'

His hand reached out, his fingers lifting her chin so that she had no option but to look at him. Her legs became unsteady and she wondered if it wasn't more to do with the man next to her than the motion of the yacht.

'Tonight I ask only one thing of you, Georgina.'

Her heart accelerated and pounded in her chest like a drum. Her gaze locked with his, held there by only the smallest touch of his fingers to her chin. Her breathing deepened and she wondered if she'd be able to stand for much longer so close to him.

'And that is...?' She maintained control of her voice, but control of her body was much harder. Heat was building low down in her stomach, spreading slowly and re-lighting the fire that had so nearly consumed her last night.

'No pretence. Not tonight, at least.'

Santos saw her eyes widen, watched as the soft brown of her irises turned darker until they were as black as the night sky. Her full lips, the ones that had kissed him almost into oblivion last night, parted and he fought hard against the urge to crush them beneath his.

'Not even a little bit?' She smiled up at him, and a hint of mischief danced in her eyes.

She was still hiding herself from him.

'No.' He lifted her chin a little higher and brushed his lips against hers, feeling her body tremble as it so nearly touched his. She smelt good, her perfume sweet and light. 'No pretence at all, Georgie.'

He liked calling her that. It made her seem more real—warmer, somehow. Like the woman he'd glimpsed last night. And tonight he was determined to find her again. It was *that* woman he wanted—the woman who'd filled his dreams and every waking moment since.

He took the glass from her hand and without taking his eyes from hers dropped it onto a nearby seat. The yacht lurched as they headed out to sea, pitching her against him, and instinctively he wrapped his arms around her, keeping her close.

'You can let me go now,' she said firmly, her breath feathering against his chin as she looked up at him. 'I wouldn't want you to think I'm throwing myself at you.'

He laughed and let her go. 'I wouldn't ever think that of you.'

She was so vibrant, so beautiful, and she was his wife.

As he faced her he saw shyness spread over her face—an emotion he would never have associated with the demanding woman who'd all but barged into his office last week.

Her fingers brushed his and his pulse raced in anticipation, just as it had been doing every time she came near him. It was almost torture, wanting a woman and not being able to have her. But tonight would be different. Tonight she would be his.

He watched as she walked away from him, the sandals she'd struggled with on the beach long since abandoned. The wind whipped at her dress, lifting the silk around her, allowing him more than a glimpse of long slender legs as she moved inside the yacht.

Pushing back the carnal thoughts that filled his mind, he followed her—and almost stopped in his stride when he saw the sadness on her face as she stood and looked out of the window. Was she thinking of her sister? Missing her?

'I'm sorry there wasn't anyone at the wedding for you.' Uneasy guilt compelled him to say it again, despite her earlier assurances.

She turned and looked at him, blinking her lashes rapidly over her eyes. 'It's not as if it was a real wedding—if it was I'd have insisted on Emma being there.'

She shrugged and looked back out at the retreating coast-line. 'Besides, you only had your cousin.'

'Raul *is* my family.'

'I've never heard Emma or Carlo mention him before.' She rubbed her hands on her arms as if cold.

'He's my mother's brother's son, so not a blood rela-tion to Carlo.' His clipped words caught her attention.

'You make it sound as if having a stepmother and half-brother is a bad thing.'

This was the first window into his life he'd allowed her to see through, and it made him feel vulnerable, but he was strangely compelled to talk and continued.

'My father and I were happy enough after my mother left, but when she died in an accident a few years later my father went to pieces. It was as if he'd been waiting for her to come back to him.'

He'd never told anyone that before. Talking of his childhood was something he just didn't do. But memories rushed back at him now like a sea wind, keen and sharp.

'I'm sorry,' she said softly, touching his arm. 'It hurts when a parent leaves. As a child you feel...' She paused and his heart constricted. 'Responsible, somehow.'

He looked down at her upturned face, at her soft skin glowing in the late afternoon sun, her eyes full of genu-ine concern. When was the last time anyone had been concerned about him? He wanted to talk to her, share his memories with her. After all she knew something of his pain—his research on her had proved that.

'My father had a second youth—dating women as if they were going out of fashion. So when he met the woman who would later be my stepmother it was a re-lief. He settled down again. I just hadn't expected to be excluded from the family when Carlo was born.'

She frowned slightly but said nothing, her steady gaze encouraging him to talk.

'As time went by Carlo became the centre of everything and I stood on the outside, looking in. I refused to compete for my father's attention. When I left university I began to take over the running of the investment business and my father spent more and more time with his *new* family.'

'But surely they loved you?'

He could see pity in her eyes, the image he'd painted for her, and anger surfaced. He did not need her pity. Just as he hadn't needed his father's love as a boy.

'*Love*, Georgina? What is *that*?'

His words were sharper than he'd wanted. He sensed her draw back from him, both physically and emotionally, and was thankful when she didn't say anything else.

'You're cold,' he said when she shivered. 'We will go inside and eat.'

As far as he was concerned the discussion was now closed.

He led her inside and even he was stunned at the intimacy of the small feast that had been prepared for them. The large table was set at one end, just for two, candles glowed and rose petals were scattered across the cream tablecloth. He heard her stifled gasp of shock and smiled.

'Your staff have excelled themselves,' she said softly as she came to stand beside him. 'It looks divine.'

The intimacy only increased once he was seated at the table with her, the soft glow of candlelight casting her face into partial shadow. Her shoulders were bare apart from the one strap of the dress. They looked creamy, soft, and he wanted to touch her skin, to kiss it, taste it.

Food was the last thing he wanted.

* * *

Determined not to be put off by Santos's sudden change of subject, and desperate to keep her traitorous body under control, Georgina spoke. 'I can remember my father walking away late one summer's evening. It was dark and hot, and later there was such a storm I worried all night about him. It sounds like it was tough for you too after your mother died.'

He'd almost opened up to her—almost let her in.

His face hardened and she knew she'd touched on a nerve.

'It was. But I'm not going to talk about such things now.'

He offered her some of the delicacies on the table, his fingers brushing hers, causing her to look up into his eyes.

'There are far better things to talk of on our wedding day.'

Our wedding day.

The words hung in the air between them as his dark eyes held hers. She should say something—anything. But she couldn't. The intensity of the attraction sparking between them was too much.

'You're not eating.'

He glanced quickly at her untouched plate and her pulse-rate leapt as once again his gaze held hers.

'It's looks delicious, but—'

'You're just not hungry?' He cut across her words, then took her hand, his own tanned one covering hers easily, sending shock waves of heat up her arm, and she was glad he'd forgotten the talk of his family.

'No,' she answered boldly, and wondered what he would say if she told him just what she *did* want now. Would he laugh at her if she told him that all she could think of was kissing him, feeling his arms tight around her? She just couldn't fight the attraction any longer.

'So what *does* my sweet bride want?' He raised her fingers to his lips, dropping lingering kisses to each finger, and all the while he watched her, his eyes darkening with desire. 'Remember,' he teased, his voice deep and heavily accented. 'No pretence—not tonight.'

'I want…' She paused and smiled coyly at him as he waited. 'You.'

Shock laced with excitement fizzed in her veins as he raised his brows, slowly and suggestively. Once more he kissed her fingers, each time lingering longer, until she couldn't stand the anticipation any more.

He stood up from the table, keeping a tight hold on her hand, and pulled her up against him, holding her close.

Music began to drift around the room, reminding her that they were far from alone, that the crew and staff were lingering in the background to do his bidding. The disappointment she felt at not being totally alone with him shocked her. She wanted what they'd shared over the last few days.

'It is a tradition, is it not, for the bride and groom to dance together?'

He was so close now she could smell fresh pine mixed with the musky scent of pure male. It was intoxicating.

'In England it is, yes.' Her voice was little more than a husky whisper.

'Then we dance.'

He walked away from the table, guiding her to the middle of the room as the gentle rhythm of the music continued. When he held her close once more her knees threatened to give way, so intense was the attraction between them. It was an attraction that had been stamped out several times already, but Georgina knew this time it was going to be different—because this time she wanted him with a fever that engulfed her whole body. He was her husband now, and despite trying not to she had feelings for him.

This was how a bride *should* feel, and she pushed back memories of the clinical registry office service when she'd married Richard. It might only be for this one night, but she knew she had to live for the moment—had to surrender herself to it completely. This could be her one chance of sampling such heady romance.

As those thoughts flickered to life in her mind Santos kissed her—a soft, lingering kiss that held the promise of passion, one that awakened every nerve in her body. She deepened the kiss, closing her eyes against the onslaught of pleasure which crashed over her like waves onto the beach as she pressed close against him, feeling the evidence of his desire.

Breaking the kiss, he began to move her slowly around the room to the sound of the music. How could a dance be so erotic, so loaded with sexual tension and the promise of passion? The intensity of it was so much that she longed to give in and rest her head against his shoulder, close her eyes.

No pretence...not tonight.

His deep, husky words replayed in her mind.

Should she allow herself to taste what it might be like to love a man? To feel what it would be like to be loved back? Santos certainly seemed to be playing the part of devoted lover today. She didn't think for one moment it wasn't part of the charade they had created, but right now, as his arms held her close, the idea of happy-ever-after seemed tangibly close.

She laid her cheek against his shoulder, a soft sigh

escaping her as she closed her eyes. He tensed, and she knew he hadn't been able to abandon the idea of pretence completely. He was as on edge as she was, which made her a little less vulnerable—because together they could abandon the carefully constructed façades they each lived behind.

His arms tightened around her body, pulling her closer to him, and heat raced through her. As he pressed his lips into her hair she closed her eyes again, the sensation too much, and focused all her attention on the music instead of the feel of his strong body.

As she moved with him she realised the movement of the yacht had changed and glanced at the shoreline.

'Have we stopped?' Her words were husky. She'd never heard her voice like that.

'*Sí, querida.*'

He brushed his lips over hers as she looked up at him, sending another flurry of tingles skittering over her.

'We are to anchor here tonight. The crew and staff are leaving. They will be back in the morning.'

'So we will be completely alone out here?'

'Very much so.'

He stroked a hand down her face and she fought the urge to turn and kiss it.

'Does that worry you, *querida*?'

It should worry her, but it didn't. She wanted to be with him like this, to feel his body against hers, to taste his kisses. How could she pretend otherwise?

She searched the dark depths of his eyes, dropping her gaze to his lips briefly before looking back into his eyes. 'Should I be worried?' A flirty edge had slipped back into her voice as she struggled to keep her emotions under control and stay behind the safety of the barrier she'd erected long ago.

His voice was deep and incredibly sexy as he rubbed the pad of his thumb over her lips, making her lose those last doubts.

'Only if you don't want me to sweep you up into my arms and carry you to the bedroom.'

CHAPTER SEVEN

RIGHT NOW THAT was all Georgina wanted. It was all she could think about. It was as if the gently lapping sea beyond the yacht and the warm breeze had conspired against her. The luxury of everything was feeding the romantic dream she'd long ago abandoned.

But for tonight at least she could live it. Tonight she *would* live it—would allow herself to taste what she'd never thought possible.

'What more could a girl ask for from her groom?'

Her heart thumped in her chest and her breathing deepened, so that she had to drag every breath in, but still she couldn't quite let go of the bravado she always hid behind even as her body yearned for his.

In one swift movement he swept her feet from the floor to hold her firmly in his arms. The silk of her skirt fell apart at the slit and the heat of his fingers on her thigh scorched her skin, bringing a blush to her cheeks.

He swung round so that the tiny spotlights in the yacht's ceiling blurred behind him as she watched his face. It was set firm, as if his jaw was clenched.

'Then we will waste no more time.'

The depth of his voice, so sensual, laden with intent, sent a ripple of awareness cascading over her.

She felt every step he took as he marched through

the living area. A harsh Spanish curse left his lips as he reached the curving stairs which she guessed led to the bedrooms. Only vaguely aware of her surroundings, she remained focused on his face, but when he looked down at her the intensity of desire burning in his dark eyes made her smile.

He didn't smile back. His face remained set in firm lines. 'Damn stairs,' he growled, and turned his body slightly as he carried her upwards.

She reached up and touched his face, a small sense of triumph shooting through her as he dragged in a ragged breath. His skin was smooth, despite the darkness hinting at fresh stubble growth as her fingers slid down to his neck.

'You can put me down.' Her voice was barely above a whisper.

'Not until I have you where I want you.'

The strength of his words made her shiver with excitement.

As he reached the top of the stairs she looked around her and saw open double doors through which was the most magnificent bedroom she'd ever seen. Briefly she took in the dark mahogany furnishings and the big bed, its cream covers scattered with pink rose petals, as Santos walked briskly towards it.

Gently he placed her on the bed, and she leant back on her arms as he stood like a magnificent bullfighter at the side. She trembled as he looked down at her, his eyes as dark as the depths of the ocean.

Nervousness suddenly washed over her. It had been a long time since she'd been in a situation like this, with a man openly desiring her, his intentions clear. Would he be expecting the practised lover that society thought she was? The temptress she willingly portrayed herself to be?

'And this is exactly where I want you, *querida*.'

As the slow, purposeful words came huskily from his lips she watched him undo his tie and drop it to the floor, his jacket soon following.

Hungry for him, she let her gaze devour the strength in his arms as his white shirt pulled tight across his biceps. She bit her lip as he undid the top buttons, exposing dark chest hair and tanned skin. All the while he watched her with such intensity she knew she would be powerless to resist him.

Keeping her gaze locked with his, she reached up to her chignon, but something in his expression stilled her hand. The smouldering passion she saw in his eyes sent a dizzying current through her.

'Don't.'

His voice was harsh, and the arrogance that surrounded him maddened and excited her at the same time.

'But…' she whispered as he stepped closer to the bed, towering over her, dominating the very air she breathed.

'I've wanted to free your hair all day.'

He knelt on the bed beside her, his weight making her sway towards him as the mattress dipped. Within seconds he'd released the pins that secured her hair and she felt it slide over her shoulders.

'I've wanted to see it around your shoulders in all its glory.'

She closed her eyes against the sensation of his body so close to her, inhaling the intoxicating male scent that was uniquely Santos. When his lips pressed briefly against her shoulder she gasped softly in pleasure.

She opened her eyes and turned to face him, momentarily shocked at how close he was. His handsome face was only inches from hers. 'Santos…' she whispered as he kissed her cheek, her forehead, her nose, stoking the ever growing heat deep inside her.

'I want you, Georgie,' he husked out between each kiss. 'I want to make you mine.'

'I want that too.' And she did. Nothing else seemed to matter now except the two of them.

He silenced her with a long, lingering kiss that drew every ounce of reservation from her body, replacing it with unadulterated need. A small sound of pleasure escaped her lips as he broke the kiss, only to be smothered as his lips claimed hers in another greedy kiss that rocked her to the core.

Santos shook with need as he deepened the kiss. Never before had he felt as if he was on the edge of control with a woman—but then never before had a woman played so hard to get.

Her hand touched the side of his face, her palm pressing his cheek as she kissed him back, need for need, her tongue teasing his. He broke free of the kiss and looked at her full lips, already bruised from his kisses, then to her eyes, darker than he'd ever seen them.

She moved back from him, further up the bed, and a hot stab of lust grabbed him as her slender legs were exposed yet again. Teasing and testing him. He took hold of her foot and slowly undid one sandal, pulling it from her before tossing it to the floor.

She smiled and for a moment he thought he saw shyness in her eyes, but then it was gone as she lifted her other foot. He took it, and again slowly removed the sandal, but this time he didn't let go of her ankle. Unable to help himself, he smoothed his palm up her leg, past her knee, until it slid underneath the silk of her dress. A dress he desperately wanted to remove from her.

She closed her eyes and dropped her head back against the bed, a look of total abandon on her face as his hand slid higher. The warmth of her skin was almost too much for him. *Patience*, he urged himself. This was a night to take it slowly. This was a woman to savour.

He reluctantly moved his hand down her thigh, past her knee and back to her shapely ankle.

'How does a man get his wife out of her wedding gown?'

His voice was uneven and ragged. He was using every last bit of control just to stop himself from taking her right now.

'At the back.'

The words were a tremulous whisper, serving only to excite him further. He was used to his lovers being bold, but he liked this air of innocence she'd adopted.

She sat forward, waiting for him to unzip the gown. Sitting back on his heels, he steadied himself as he reached behind her and undid a clasp, then slid the zip down her back. His anticipation almost boiled over with every breath she breathed against his naked chest. Her scent invaded his senses and he dragged in a deep breath, tasting her.

At last the bodice of the gown sagged around her and he moved back, catching a glimpse of creamy soft breasts as it slipped lower. Part of him wanted to rip the gown from her, but a more disciplined part of him wanted to savour the moment, to make it special for both of them. It was, after all, their wedding night.

He kissed her, pushing her back against the pillows as his tongue delved deeper into her mouth. She tasted of champagne and his senses fizzed like a shaken bottle. Her arms wound their way around his neck, pulling him down to her, pressing against her.

He spread his hand over her bare shoulder, enjoying the feel of her skin, then slowly slid it downwards—until he met the resistance of the gown's bodice and wished he *had* ripped it from her.

She moved beneath him, thrusting her breasts upwards, inviting him to touch them—an invitation he had no trouble in accepting. His hand pushed aside the bodice, cupping her breast, his thumb and finger rubbing over the hardened nipple.

'Oh, Santos,' she whispered against his lips as her body arched even more. Need rocked through him.

Words failed him as he kissed down her throat, over her collarbone and down to her breast, finally taking her nipple in his mouth as her fingers ploughed through his hair. But still it wasn't enough. He wanted more—much more.

He pulled himself away from her, smiling at the disappointment on her face as he did so. 'This has to go.' He took hold of the bodice of her gown and pulled. Her breasts were slowly revealed, and then, almost erotically, her flat stomach and her beautifully shaped hips were laid bare to his hungry gaze. 'So beautiful, *mi esposa*.'

She smiled at him. And again that shyness he'd glimpsed earlier was in her face as she lay partially naked before him.

He kissed her stomach, revelling in his mastery as her body arched towards him again, begging him for more even if the words didn't come from her lips. Still lower his kisses went, until he found the silk of her panties. She bucked wildly beneath him then, almost undoing the control he was desperately hanging on to.

He looked up at her, at her dark hair spread about her on the pillow in sexy disarray, eyes closed as she enjoyed his touch. No sign of shyness now.

Agilely he rose from the bed, amused at the expression on her face as she looked at him, questions in her gorgeous eyes. As he pulled the wedding gown down she lifted her bottom, enabling him to pull it away in one go, leaving her dressed in only cream silk panties.

She looked divine.

And she was his.

'It's not very fair if you remain dressed, is it?' Her smile was coy and teasing as she looked up at him, completely at ease with her near nakedness. An accomplished temptress.

He undid the remainder of his shirt buttons with deft fingers and pulled it from his body. Her gaze roved hungrily over his body before finally meeting his eyes, and passion charged around him as his heart thundered like a herd of wild horses.

The air was electrified and he pulled off the remainder of his clothes without breaking eye contact. Her eyes were sending him a secret message of desire and need. How had he ever thought this woman cold?

Georgina couldn't help but look at him. Arrogantly naked before her, confidence in every move he made. She knew he'd achieved his aim. He'd made her desire him, want him completely. Every nerve in her body ached for his touch and being naked to his gaze excited her. Never before had she wanted a man as she wanted Santos.

Shyness took over once more, but she tried to act as if being naked in front of a man—a man as naked as she was, who so obviously desired her—was something she was more than used to. She watched as he sat back on the bed, his legs astride hers, rendering movement almost impossible. His aroused body was magnificent, and so very tantalisingly close to her, intensifying the rush of need, of raw desire she'd never known before.

He hooked a finger in the top of her panties, his gaze locking with hers. 'These too.'

Before she could say or do anything he'd pulled them down. The silk slid from her effortlessly and, in what she could only guess was a well-practised manoeuvre, he pulled them from her legs and threw them to the floor without moving from her at all.

She was exposed, naked and vulnerable, but for the first time in her life she didn't care. All she cared about right at this moment was satisfying the burning need she had for this man.

Her husband.

Her body ached for the fulfilment of his body. She wanted him in a way she'd never dreamt possible, and sparks of excitement at the prospect of being his shot round her.

He bent low over her and kissed her stomach before moving down further, his breath warm, sending fire gushing through her. She closed her eyes to the pleasure of his exploration. When she thought she couldn't take it any more his kisses moved back up her stomach to her breasts. In turn he kissed each hardened nipple. He pushed first one knee between her legs, then the other and, giving herself up to an instinct as old as time itself, she opened her legs, wanting to feel him deep inside her, desperate to be at one with him.

Her fingers gripped his shoulders as his erection nudged her moistness. He lowered himself onto her, kissing her as his body shook with the effort of holding back. She felt his heated hardness teasing her, and then, just when she thought she couldn't take one more second of it, he thrust deep inside her. She gasped at the pleasure of his possession, her fingers gripping ever tighter to his shoulders as she moved with him. Her legs wrapped around him, pulling him deeper into her, and he groaned in Spanish and thrust harder, deeper.

Their rhythm increased until she couldn't help but cry out in joy. A new and exciting sensation washed over her and she opened her eyes to look out of the sloping windows above the bed, feeling as if she too were flying among the stars that now sparkled above her in the night sky.

Santos's body shook and he cried out before burying his head in her hair, his body pressing hers into the bed. She wrapped her arms tightly around his back, keeping him there, wanting to feel him deep within her.

Finally her heart-rate began to slow and her breathing returned to normal. Santos lifted his head and looked into her eyes. 'Now you're truly my wife, Georgie.'

She didn't know what to say—what to do, even—so she just smiled back, her body still too sluggish with the aftermath of passion.

Santos rolled off and away from her and the cool evening air shocked her naked body, making her shiver. He reached down, grabbed a throw from the bottom of the bed, pulled it up over them and, to her total amazement, pulled her close.

She hadn't expected this. She'd thought he would disappear to the bathroom and come back partially clothed, ready to move on from what they'd just shared. Was this relaxed closeness part of his idea of no pretence? Was this the real man he didn't want the world to see?

'I should have asked this sooner,' he said, his voice sounding strangely unsure, and she wondered what was coming next. 'But we didn't use any contraception.'

'It's okay,' she whispered softly, and trailed her fingers down his arm, feeling a thrill of excitement when he groaned and pulled her close against him. Her mind quickly raced, wondering where her handbag was. Thankfully she'd put her contraceptive pills in there when she'd hurriedly packed for Spain. Not that she'd thought she'd actually need their protection. 'It's sorted.'

He stiffened slightly. 'Even so, I should have at least asked, but—'

'Don't worry. There won't be any repercussion from tonight. Just sleep.' She kissed him lingeringly on the lips, feeling the tension slip from him. Finding herself pregnant was not an option she relished, and she was certain he'd feel the same. 'Relax, Santos, try and sleep.'

He kissed her, pulling her close against his nakedness, stirring slumbering desire again. 'How can I sleep with you naked next to me?'

'At least for a while,' she teased as he kissed her again, his hands smoothing over her back.

She closed her eyes against the rising need for him, determined to play it cool. He must never know just how much she wanted him at this moment.

As he slept his breathing became deeper and steadier, and in the dim light of the bedroom she could see his naked back. Her fingers were desperate to touch him again, to create a trail over his tanned skin. The temptation became too much and she moved, but as soon as she did his relaxed hold on her tightened and he mumbled something in Spanish. It was enough to stop her.

Instead she lay and looked up at the night sky through the sloping windows just above the bed. The motion of the yacht was soothing and finally she relaxed, after what felt like days of being on edge, waiting for Santos to pull out of their agreement. They were married. The deal was well and truly sealed.

Tomorrow she'd call Emma, tell her to make plans for her own wedding. She smiled, remembering the morning she'd first met Santos. His arrogance and undeniable air of authority had almost made her turn and run from his office. Never in her wildest dreams had she thought that the man she'd proposed to as part of a business deal would end up being the first man she'd ever wanted— *really* wanted. The first man to show her just how good loving could be. The first man she could love, if only she let herself.

He didn't love her and had gone to extreme lengths to tell her he couldn't love anyone. He might have discarded pretence for the night, but would tomorrow be different?

Santos murmured again, pulling her against him and kissing her hair, sending a rush of heat through her body. Firmly she closed her eyes against the new wave of desire that was washing over her—because surely tomorrow it would be different.

Tomorrow she had to focus on Emma, on making sure Santos kept his side of the deal.

Santos woke in the early hours of dawn, his body heavy and relaxed in a way he'd never felt before. Georgina's scent lingered on the pillow next to him, reawakening the desire that had coursed like an overflowing river through him last night.

From the other side of the room he heard movement and he propped himself up on his elbow. With amusement he watched as Georgina, sexily naked, appeared to be looking for something to put on. He took in her slender waist, shapely hips and long legs as she stood, her back to him, looking around the room.

'*Buenos dias, mi esposa.*' My wife—that was something he'd never thought he'd call a woman.

She turned to face him and despite her nakedness looked as in control as she always did. For him, last night had changed something, softened the way he felt about her, but apparently it was not the same for her. She looked as if finding herself naked in a man's room was perfectly normal. A situation she was well used to.

'Morning,' she replied huskily, a smile playing about her kissable lips. 'I was looking for something to put on.'

'Your bag is in the wardrobe, but you will also find everything else you need in there too.'

Transfixed, he watched as she walked across the room, the swell of her breasts causing the blood to pound in his veins. If she didn't put something on very quickly she'd find herself back in his bed.

'Very convenient.'

The hint of sarcasm in her words was not lost on him. Keeping an array of women's clothes in his villa or on his yacht was not something he'd done before—but then catering for a future wife was not something he'd had to do either.

'I was merely trying to think of your convenience, *querida*.'

She opened the door of the wardrobe, assessed the contents, then opted for a cream silk dressing gown. She slipped it on and pulled it tight around her, knotting the belt at her stomach. The garment should have doused the fire now raging in his body, but it didn't. The outline of her body, still clearly visible, was more teasing than seeing her naked.

'Come here.' His voice was gruff and husky as desire pumped through him.

Instantly she looked shy, a blush creeping over her face, and he wondered which was the act. The bravado he saw more often or the innocent shyness she now displayed.

Slowly she walked towards the bed, her eyes darkening, remaining locked with his. He reached towards her, grabbed her hand and pulled her down to the bed.

'Santos!' she gasped in shock. 'What are you doing?'

'I would have thought that was obvious, *querida*.' As she lay beside him on the bed, her breathing faster, her breasts rising and falling in the most erotic way, he pulled the belt undone and pushed aside the silk, exposing her delicious body. 'I'm going to make love to my wife.'

Those words lit a raging fire inside him.

Unable to analyse those feelings now, he silenced her with a kiss so hard and deep he almost couldn't breathe. His need for her was far greater than last night—as if now he'd tasted her he needed more, like some kind of addict. Her hands explored his body, pushing aside the sheet and touching him until he couldn't stand it any longer. Urgently he pushed her back against the bed, covering her body with his as he thrust hard and deep within her delicious warmth.

It was as if his whole world rocked as he climaxed, relishing the feeling of being deep inside her. She cried out, her body arching towards him as she too found release. As his heartrate slowed and his mind regained the ability to think he realised he'd done the one thing he'd never done before. Early-morning sex. It gave women the wrong message. Made them think he wanted more.

But Georgina was already his wife. What more could she want from him?

He lay back, exhausted and exhilarated at the same time, his breathing and heart-rate finally returning to normal, and contemplated what had happened. Because something had changed, but he just couldn't understand what.

* * *

'I'll just go and shower.' More vulnerable than ever, Georgina wanted to put a little distance between herself and this man's magnetism.

'Don't be too long, *querida*.' He smiled at her, sending her senses into a spin as her heart flipped over.

Instead of answering him, she slipped from the bed with a bold teasing smile, grabbed her abandoned dressing gown and headed for the bathroom.

How on earth was she going to cope with today after what they'd shared last night? Would his rule of no pretence continue into the first day of their married life, or would he return to being the arrogant and controlling man she knew he was?

The hot water of the shower did little to ease her worries and she knew she had to talk to Emma. Just to hear her sister's voice would reaffirm why she'd married Santos.

With a towel wrapped round her body she emerged from the bathroom to find the bedroom empty. Quickly she reached into the wardrobe for her bag and pulled out her phone to see Emma had sent her a message.

OMG Georgie! You and Santos!

As she read the text from her sister she could almost hear her voice, the laughter in it—relief, even—and quickly she called Emma.

'Georgie!' Emma's excited voice was so vibrant it was as if it was on loudspeaker.

'Emma, I *so* wish you could be here, but…' Georgina swallowed. The first lie was about to leave her lips. 'We just had to get away and be alone.'

'You're really happy?'

'Do you think I'd jet off to Spain if not? After all that I've been through?' Thoughts of Richard mixed with the lies she was telling, the web of deceit she was spinning. *It's for Emma*, she reassured herself.

'Then I'm happy for you—but can you do one thing for me?'

'Anything for you, Emma.' That at least was true.

'Don't come back just yet. Carlo and I… Well, we're going to arrange our wedding, and if Santos finds out he's sure to put a stop to it. He's so against us getting married.'

Georgina swallowed hard. She should tell Emma. Instead she lightened her voice. 'We're enjoying our time together.' Was that a lie? she wondered as her body warmed at the memory of last night—her wedding night. 'Do you really think we're going to rush back to London?'

As she ended the call she let out a big sigh—relief that her sister and Carlo were now actually able to plan their wedding. She wished she'd been able to tell Emma that Santos was now her brother-in-law, but that was the kind of news to tell her face to face, when they got back to London.

Anxiety rose up. Just how was she going to convince Santos that heading back to reality was *not* what he wanted to do?

CHAPTER EIGHT

THE SUN WAS hot by the time Georgina came up on deck, to find Santos relaxing, an empty coffee cup on the table. She hadn't yet seen him look quite this relaxed before, so at ease with life.

As if aware of her presence he turned to face her, and she wanted to hug her arms about her body, to shield herself from his appraising gaze. Instead she fought the urge, and when the wind blew the sheer kaftan against her like a second skin, revealing the tiny blue bikini she'd reluctantly put on, she walked towards him. As confident as any of the top models he'd dated, she smiled.

'It's so wonderful out here, away from everybody. I'd love to stay a bit longer.' She slid seductively into the seat opposite him, nerves tingling all over her body.

Anxiety, she told herself, refusing to acknowledge the fact that it was Santos who did that to her.

He looked past her briefly and she wondered if she'd gone too far. But a moment later a tray of breakfast and fresh coffee arrived. The crew were obviously back on board. Once they were alone again he turned his attention to her, his dark eyes sparkling like the sea in the morning sun.

'There would be one condition.' He poured coffee, the aroma reminding her of how little she'd eaten last night.

'And that would be…?' Her voice was flirty—the exact opposite of how she felt.

'The same as last night.'

'Last night…' she breathed, in a husky echo of his words as her body responded to the memory of his touch, his kisses.

He smiled, a dangerously seductive smile, and she all but melted. 'No pretence.'

'None at all?' She teased him with a coy smile, her fingers twining in her hair.

'I like the real Georgie.' He leant forward in his seat, his brows lifting suggestively. 'The Georgina you don't let the world see.'

She laughed a nervous laugh that made him smile even more, which in turn sent her heart thumping erratically. 'You make me sound fake—as if I'm a total fraud.'

'Not fake,' he said, and passed her a coffee.

She sipped it, thankful for something to do other than look into his handsome face.

'Just scared to let anyone know the real you.'

His words hit her with the precision of a marksman. Not letting the world see the real Georgina was just what she'd tried to do for the last five years. For so long that sometimes she forgot who she really was—forgot the woman with dreams of happiness. No, going there wasn't an option.

'Well, I guess we'll just have to spend time together—get to know one another a bit better.' She sipped her coffee and looked out at the sea, its ever-moving waves sparkling like diamonds, before turning her attention back to him.

'Exactamente.'

His gaze held hers, dark and passionate, sending shivers down her spine, and she wondered if she could do this. But if Emma was to stand any chance of making her wedding arrangements in peace she had to ensure they stayed in Spain.

'Thank you,' she said, alarmed at how husky her voice had suddenly become, how easily she could slip into the role of seductress.

'We'll sail further along the coast. There is a secluded cove we can stop at—a good place to swim in the sea.'

He smiled at her again. Her heart flipped over and butterflies took flight in her stomach. Perhaps it wouldn't be hard, keeping him occupied, because she really did want to. He was so very different from the man she'd first met in his office, the man her sister had talked of. This man consumed her very soul—made her want him and the dreams she'd long since forgotten.

'I'd like that.' A blush crept over her cheeks as she met his gaze before it slid down over her body, taking in all that the bikini did very little to hide.

'For my beautiful bride—anything.' He stood and leant down over her, his lips hovering tantalisingly close to hers as she looked up at him.

His breath was warm on her face and she resisted the need to close her eyes, wanting to see his. With excruciating slowness he brought his lips down onto hers, the sensation sending sparks of awareness all over her until she could only close her eyes, give in to the pleasure of his lips as they brushed gently over hers.

The kiss ended and he stood upright, dominating the sheltered outside area of the yacht. 'I will go and make arrangements while you enjoy breakfast.'

She watched him stride away, his casual jeans hugging his long legs to perfection. She shook her head briefly, trying to stop the images of last night, memories of his tanned body against her pale skin.

In a bid to quell her rising desire she turned her attention to the breakfast, not sure if she could eat anything. But the array of fresh fruit and the lure of warm croissants soon won her appetite over.

She became aware of the coastline receding, the yacht moving smoothly through gently rolling waves. Excitement fizzed inside her. It was like being young again.

She'd been happy before life had plunged her into a situation she really hadn't wanted. Her whole outlook on life had been carefree and full of adventure until the night her father had left. Now those memories were the reason she'd promised herself she'd never have children—because what would happen if she became like her mother? What would happen if she too went from one man to the next, looking endlessly for something that didn't exist, ignoring her children to the point of neglect?

'Why so sad, *querida*?'

Santos's accented voice shattered her thoughts as surely as if she'd been viewing them through a mirror.

'I was just remembering.' Quickly she tried to hide her emotions, recreate the impenetrable wall she hid behind, because right now her defences were low. Too low. And Santos was watching her with such unexpected sympathy she almost couldn't look at him.

'We all have things we shouldn't remember, but sometimes it helps to talk.'

His tone was soothing and reassuring. He sat next to her, taking her hand, his thumb stroking over the back of it gently. His concern as genuine as a lover's. She wanted to pull away, to distance herself from him. She felt utterly exposed, as if every emotion was completely visible to him.

'It was just my excitement as I realised the yacht was

moving,' she said, aware of the hoarseness in her voice. 'It's like being young again.'

He nodded once, his eyes full of understanding. 'What happened?'

'My mother found solace in the bottle after my father left.' Her heart thumped hard as pent-up anger flowed through her like a tidal wave—one that couldn't be halted now as it roared towards the shore. 'I had no choice but to care for Emma, try and shield her from it all. I had to grow up very quickly.'

'Shield her from what, Georgie?'

She looked up at him. His voice was now hard and controlled, his eyes narrowed and his brows pulling together in concentration.

She shouldn't be telling him this. It had nothing to do with him, and would serve no purpose whatsoever, but it was liberating to finally share it with someone.

'What was it, Georgina?' he urged as her silence lengthened.

He reached out and pushed back the hair from her face and she dropped her gaze, not wanting to see the sympathy in his eyes. How could a man as ruthless and in control as Santos possibly understand?

'Tell me, Georgie.'

One hand stroked her hair whilst the other held firmly onto her hand. She had no means of escape, no way out.

What would he think of her if she told him?

'At first she was just incapable of looking after us—that was unless she was in the throes of a new affair—but soon it was down to me to get Emma to school, to put a meal on the table.'

He stopped stroking her hair, his hand resting on her shoulder, warm and comforting. 'Go on.'

Those first words had unleashed all her hurt and she

knew she should stop. She shrugged, not wanting to allow him any closer emotionally.

'So I got out as soon as an opportunity presented itself. I had to. It was the only way of keeping a roof over our heads and food on the table. Any money my mother had was spent on what she considered important—not on what actually *was*, like food and rent.'

He sat back from her, his hands falling to his thighs, silent for a moment as he took in what she'd said. 'That opportunity being your marriage to Richard Henshaw?' His voice was hard, a slight growl in his throat.

She looked up at him. He really did think she'd married purely for the money and status Richard had given her. Words of defence were on the tip of her tongue, but something stopped her, froze them as if the warm sea breeze had changed to a bitter winter wind. Instead she wanted to tell him—wanted him to know.

'He offered me everything I wanted—and more.'

She sat taller in her seat and looked him in the eye. For a moment she'd almost told him the truth—told him how Richard had literally rescued her, offering her security for Emma and asking for nothing other than that she took his name. But sense had prevailed. If he wanted to think of her as a gold-digging socialite then he could.

'And, yes,' she added, with the haughty tone she knew made her sound so like the woman he thought she was resounding in her voice, 'I married him for his money and his status. But you can't accuse me of hiding that from you. Not when it is common knowledge.'

Santos's stomach hardened as his breath came fast. He clenched his teeth against an attack of jealousy as he imagined Georgina with another man—one she'd just admitted she'd had no feelings for. She hadn't attempted to hide the fact that she'd used a man who must have known he was ill when he married her.

She'd used Richard and she sat there now with the innocence of a child and waited for his reaction. He was angry with himself—angry at the irrational jealousy that raged inside him just thinking of her with another man. She was his wife, and what he felt for her now surpassed anything he'd felt for previous lovers.

'We all have a past, *querida*.' He kept his tone as nonchalant as possible, regretting having started the conversation. He'd known of her reputation when he'd agreed to their ludicrous deal, so why did it matter so much?

Control, he reminded himself. Whatever happened he had to be in control, and for a moment there he'd almost lost it—almost given in to the temptations of the devil. This whole episode was about getting what he wanted, not about emotions. Never emotions.

He stood up and walked to the side of the yacht, checking their location, almost relieved to see they had arrived at his chosen bay. He breathed deeply, enjoying the salty tang in his mouth, trying to revitalise himself before he turned back to look at the woman who was now his wife.

'Yes, we do. Including you.'

The accusation in her voice was clear and he couldn't help but smile at her pretence at fury. Her expression was severe, but her eyes were telling a different story.

'It's called life, Georgie.' He put out a hand and stepped towards her. 'And right now ours is for living. What about a swim in the sea? Wash all your troubles away?'

For a moment he thought she was going to refuse. Confusion furrowed her brow, then she regained her composure, took his hand and smiled up at him, openly flirting.

'A swim sounds delicious.'

Delicious. She was delicious, with the wind wrapping the almost see-through kaftan close to her glorious body, the blue bikini showcasing just what a figure she had. Lust thudded in his veins and he cursed his wayward thoughts.

'Something wrong?' A hint of a playful smile tugged her full lips up at the corners.

She knew exactly what was wrong, damn her.

'No. Unless it's wrong for a man to want to drag his wife back to bed instead of going swimming?' His voice was deep and guttural with the effort of reining in his libido.

She blushed and, as he had many times in the last few days, he wondered how she managed that little trick—how she managed to appear so innocent. 'I think we should swim first. It's not even midday yet.'

First.

She wanted him as much as he wanted her. Her darkening eyes were smouldering, giving him the message, setting fire to the embers of desire that had scorched his body last night. Never before had a woman affected him so much, made him want her so badly—but then never before had he had to wait so long to get a woman into his bed. And he certainly hadn't had to marry her to do so.

The irony of it wasn't lost on him as he felt her hand in his. It felt surprisingly good, as if it was right. 'I'll hold you to that,' he managed, despite the heat that raged within him. A swim in cold water was exactly what he needed.

He led her to the platform that had been lowered once the yacht was anchored and slipped off his deck shoes. Her gaze heated his blood as he pulled off his shirt, the sun instantly warm on his skin.

'Not joining me?' he teased, tugging off his jeans, amused by the blush that crept over her cheeks as her gaze slid down his body, resting on the evidence of just how aroused he had become at her loaded promise of what was to follow their swim.

The air crackled around them, their attraction as overpowering as if he hadn't touched her, hadn't tasted her skin or made her his. It was like the first time all over again, with anticipation raging in him like a bull.

He dived into the blue waters, and the rush of cold over his body was just what he needed. As he broke the surface he wiped water from his face and looked back up at Georgina, now sitting on the edge, feet dangling in the water, wearing only that very sexy blue bikini.

'It's cold!'

She laughed, her face lighting up, giving her an air of playful innocence, tugging at something deep within him.

'Only at first. Come on—you'll never know how good it is until you try it.' He trod water as he spoke, energised by the exercise and cold water.

Georgina watched, mesmerised, as his strong arms kept him exactly where he wanted to be. His strength and power were undeniable. She was behaving like a lovestruck teenager. Her heart was still pounding after that moment when he'd stood before her in his trunks, his tanned skin gleaming in the sun, the hardness of his arousal obvious. She wanted him with a ferocious need so alien that her breath had caught in her throat, and she'd been relieved when he'd expertly dived into the clear water. Relieved he had taken the temptation from her.

Cautiously she slipped into the water, gasping and laughing at the same time. 'It's so cold!' She tried hard to be sophisticated and serene, but all she managed was a fumbling splash.

'Only for a while,' Santos said, and in one stroke he moved towards her, encircling her body with his arm, keeping her safe and close. 'Like *you* were the day you propositioned me in my office.'

Shocked that he'd brought that up, she stopped moving her arms and immediately sank below the surface. His arm around her body pulled her back up, spluttering like a child.

'How dare you?' She tried to move away from him, back to the platform.

'Oh, I dare, *querida*—because it's true. You want everyone to think you are carved from ice, but you're not, are you?

She clutched the platform, gained a foothold on the ladder and pulled herself out of the water, then turned to face him as he looked up at her from the blue waves. 'Neither are you.'

'Can you blame me when you stand there like a sea goddess, water dripping from you in a most inviting way?'

'You're impossible.' The words rushed out, her frustration making her want to march away, but she couldn't tear her gaze from Santos as in one swift movement that made the muscles in his arms flex he hauled himself out of the sea.

Water ran down his tanned chest, trickling among his dark hair, heading downwards. She knew she shouldn't be looking, but she couldn't help herself. His thighs were strong and more dark hair lay flat against his wet skin, creating patterns all the way to his ankles. He was magnificent as he stood, sunlight gleaming on his skin.

He grabbed her hand and without a word headed back inside the yacht, leaving her little option but to follow. She couldn't say anything. The same sexual tension that had last night completely robbed her of the ability to think, let alone speak, raged around them.

In seconds they were alone in their suite, and only then did he let go of her hand. For a moment they looked at one another, gazes locked in some sort of primal dance. His chest rose and fell with the effort of breathing, just as hers did, and she knew instantly where this was going to end—and, worse, where she wanted it to end. He was an addiction.

With a muttered Spanish curse he turned and opened the door to the bathroom, and she watched through the doorway as he turned on the shower. She swallowed hard as he turned back to her, his expression almost fierce with control.

'Santos...' She managed a croaky whisper as he held out his hand to her. She took it and he pulled her hard against his wet body. Only then did she realise she was trembling.

'You're cold,' he said quietly, but she didn't miss the intensity in his voice.

She wasn't cold—not enough to tremble like this. It was him, and the electrified air that seemed to surround them.

'Come on.' He led her into the steam-filled bathroom and into the shower—one that had definitely been designed for two.

His hands slowly untied the bikini where it fastened at her neck, and each time his fingers touched her she had to suppress a shiver of pleasure. He let the thin straps go and peeled the wet material slowly away from her breasts, his gaze lingering enticingly on them.

He made a signal with his hands for her to turn around and slowly she did so, meeting the jets of warm water. Behind her she felt his hands as he released the final clasp of the bikini top and it dropped to the shower floor. Seconds later it was joined by his black trunks and her knees nearly buckled beneath her. Desire flooded her as he pressed his naked body against her back.

Instinctively her chin tilted up and she leant her head back against his shoulder, turning her face towards his. Hot, urgent lips claimed hers with such force she staggered forward, taking them both under the hot jets of water. His hands cupped her breasts and fire engulfed her, making her cry out with pleasure.

'You are the most desirable woman ever, *mi esposa*.'

He kissed down her neck, uttering words she didn't understand. But she did understand the desire and passion entwined with each one. A desire and passion that raged as wildly inside her.

'Santos, I want you.' Her voice was husky as his hands slid down her stomach, his fingers tugging at the ties on the side of the bikini briefs. As the material fell away his fingers moved towards the heated centre of her need for him and she arched away from him, trying to fight the ripple of pleasure from his touch.

With a suddenness that knocked all the breath from her body he turned her around, grasped her thighs, lifting her against him.

'Santos, it's never been like this before,' she gasped between ragged breaths as he lowered her onto him, plunging deeply and urgently inside her. She didn't care that she was telling him too much, giving away just how inexperienced she really was and how she was falling in love with him.

'Never?' The question rasped from him, halting her thoughts, as his fingers dug into her thighs, holding her where he wanted her.

She moved with him, encouraging him in this hot,

hard and primal dance. 'Never,' she gasped out as stars shattered around her so that instead of water coursing all over her it was stardust. 'Never. *Never.*'

As he found his release she clung to his body, trembling more now than she had when she'd stood before him in the bedroom just moments ago. He was breathing hard, his chest heaving against her tender breasts, one arm braced against the shower wall.

'At least we agree on something.' His voice, heavily accented, was a ragged whisper.

He released his vice-like grip on her thighs and she slid down, her legs so weak she wondered if she'd be able to stand. She couldn't. Her knees crumpled, but his arms were about her and in seconds he'd swept her up off her feet and left the shower.

Pausing briefly to grab a towel, he made his way to the bed. As if she were the most precious thing in the world he let her down to stand in front of him and then wrapped the white towel around her, heedless of his own wet body. Then he bent and kissed her lips so tenderly she thought she might actually cry. This was exactly what she'd abandoned all hope of ever finding, this warm, loving feeling.

Except this wasn't for real. This was just part of a deal, satisfying the attraction that had been arcing between them since that very first meeting. It was also the only way she knew of keeping Santos from heading back to the villa and maybe London.

'You're still wet,' she whispered, not wanting to analyse her motives or question her dreams now.

He stepped back from her and started rubbing his hands over the towel to dry her. This was getting too intense, too close to being like a proper romance, so great was the attraction she felt for him. Her breath shuddered as he pulled the towel from her and dried himself off.

And all the while his gaze held hers, the passion and desire still flowing between them evident in the depths of his eyes.

He picked her dressing gown off the bed, now remade after their night of passion, and handed it to her. 'You must care for your sister very much.'

Instantly her senses were on high alert. What was he suggesting? 'She's all I have.'

He handed her the cream silk garment. 'But to marry just so that your sister can marry for love?' His voice rose with incredulity as he took fresh clothes from the wardrobe and hastily got dressed.

'Maybe I love my sister as much as you hate your brother.' Was he referring to their marriage or her first one? It made no difference; both had been made out of love for her sister.

Tension filled the room and his eyes sparked with anger as he stood in front of her, all the passion and desire of moments ago forgotten.

'Half-brother.' The words were harsh and staccato.

She pulled on the dressing gown, no longer wanting him to see her naked now he was clothed, as if it somehow weakened her. He turned and paced across the room towards the door, but she couldn't let him go, couldn't let him walk out now, even if it meant killing the loving moments they'd shared.

'Coward.' The word rushed from her lips, provoking him.

Instantly he whirled round and fixed her with a fierce glare, his face a hardened and angry mask. 'I don't do emotions, Georgina. Hate or love. I don't do them.'

'And because of that two people who love one another are suffering.'

'How?' He strode back across the room, but she stood

her ground. 'And how do you know they are in love? How do they even know?'

'You must have loved someone, Santos, despite what you just said.'

'Love is for weak-willed fools.' His voice was like granite and his eyes glittered dangerously as he looked at her.

'You don't really believe that?' she whispered in disbelief.

She'd vowed she'd never love anyone other than Emma, never give her heart to a man as her mother had time and time again. But somehow she'd become dangerously close to loving Santos.

'Isn't that why you made this damn deal, Georgina, because you don't believe in love?' He was like an angry lion, caged up and looking for a way out as he strode across the room to glance out of the window. He turned and looked at her, waiting for her reply.

'I did it *for* love.' She rallied against his contempt. 'I did it for the love of my sister.'

'Ha!' He laughed, so arrogantly she almost cringed. 'You did it for money, for all you could get from it—just as you did the first time around.'

How dared he bring Richard into this? The man who had seen she needed a lifeline and offered one without expecting anything in return? Well, if that was what he thought of her, so be it. Attack was the best form of defence.

'Yes, just as I did the first time.'

For a moment he looked at her in stunned silence, his jaw grinding hard. He looked for all the world as if he was jealous of Richard. How could a powerful man like Santos be jealous of anything or anyone?

He glared at her. 'Get dressed,' he snapped after what seemed like an eternity. 'We're going back to the villa.'

Panic tore at her. She'd promised Emma she'd keep him out of the way, and here on the yacht was the perfect place.

'So soon?' She hated the nervous edge to her voice, but knew any attempts at flattering him would be futile.

His eyes narrowed. 'I have work to do. Playing at this newlywed game has gone on for long enough.'

With that he strode from the room and she sank onto the bed. Last night they had made love for the first time, been given pleasure so intense it still lingered in her body. Only minutes ago they had been consumed by desire and need for one another. How could the man who kissed her so passionately be the same man who'd just left the room?

She dragged in a deep breath, pressing her fingertips to her lips, bruised from his hard kisses in the shower. How could she, a woman who'd renounced love, feel such desolation as the man she'd given herself to last night with total completeness walked out on her?

CHAPTER NINE

SANTOS'S MOOD WAS as dark as the storm clouds rolling down from the mountains. He'd thought Georgina was different, thought she could keep emotions out of things. Instead she'd proved beyond doubt that she was as clingy as any woman, unable to resist the urge to delve into his past.

He'd thought he'd met his match—a woman who could share his passion without the need for anything more.

But he'd been wrong, damn it, very wrong.

'I have business matters to attend to.'

Unable to keep the frustration from reverberating in his voice as they arrived back at the villa, he swung the car in through the gates without giving the photographers loitering there a second glance and powered up the driveway.

Georgina was silent next to him, but he could feel her watching him. He couldn't look at her now. She'd already proved just what an effect she had on him, proved how easily she could distract him.

'I'll get ready to go back to London.' Her voice was quiet, but firm.

'London?' The car halted abruptly as he fought for control. His fingers curled hard around the leather of the steering wheel as he gripped it even harder. One thing was for certain: she was not going back to London. Not yet.

'It's what I'd planned once the world knew we were married.' Her voice still had a husky edge to it, but strength and determination echoed there too.

That unsettled him even more. She seemed able to shut off and return to icy control much more easily than he was able to do. The carefree hours they'd spent on the yacht meant his usual detached approach to relationships was eluding him. And he didn't like it.

Santos looked at her lips, full and still very kissable. Fire leapt to life deep within him—a ferocious burning need to take her straight to his bed once more. It was more than lust, this need to be with her. He gritted his teeth; he had to be as collected as she was right now.

'That is what you *originally* planned, Georgina.' He tossed the words carelessly at her, trying to appear as unaffected by her as possible as he turned off the engine and got out of the car. 'But it is not what we finally agreed on.'

She got out of the car, all elegance and poise, then faced him across the shiny red roof. She looked stunning, sexy, and very different from the woman he'd brought here just a few days ago. Her eyes were bright, her skin lightly tanned and her hair looked tousled, as if she'd just got out of his bed.

'I'm going home, Santos.' Her words were clipped as she slammed the car door shut.

'You *are* home. You agreed to live as my wife, to be by my side, and right now I'm here.'

Not wanting to discuss it further, he locked the car and marched into the house, heading straight for his study. The sound of her footsteps on the marble floor would have told him she was following even if his body hadn't tingled so wildly, alerting him to her presence.

'Look, Santos…' She practically purred as she followed him into the sanctuary of his study. Hell, she was
good at this—good at putting on a show of whatever
she wanted people to see. Anger, gentleness or hot desire, it didn't matter—she was an accomplished actress
through and through. 'Is there really a need to keep up
this pretence?'

He thought of the clause of his father's will, the way it
had pushed him into not only marrying but considering
having a child, an heir. Frustration mixed with his anger
and he pushed the thought roughly aside.

'It was in the agreement.' He kept his words firm as
he headed to the filing cabinet and the file containing
copies of their pre-nuptial agreement.

'I did not sign anything to say I would stay by your
side like a faithful puppy dog. You must be mistaken,
Santos.' Her eyes sparked fury at him, their colour light-
ening to a brilliant bronze, and her voice had a sharp
edge to it, but she still looked sexy, still made his body
ache for her.

If she continued to stand there like that, her hand on
her hip, her lips almost pouting, he'd have to kiss her. And
if he did that he'd never stop. She was like an addiction.

He turned his back on her, opened the cabinet drawer
and pulled out the folder, tossing it on the desk so that
the contents slipped from it, spreading across the table
like a pack of cards. 'Take a look.'

Her gaze dropped from his face to the documents, then
back to his. 'I know what I signed.' Her voice wavered
slightly. 'But we've done what we set out to do. If I have
to stay here then at least let me ring Emma, tell her she
and Carlo can set a date.'

He inhaled deeply. He had to tell her just what else he
needed from the marriage.

Her phone rang and she delved into her bag and pulled it out. For a moment she looked at it, then at him. 'It's Emma,' she said as the ringing ceased. 'What do I tell her? That we are happily married so they can be the same?'

He cursed harshly and paced to his window, taking in the view of the mountains almost obscured by dark clouds laden with the promise of a storm. The air was heavy and he knew that at any moment it would break.

He cursed again and dragged his fingers through his hair with an unaccustomed feeling of tumultuous emotions. What the hell had happened to him to make him feel so out of control?

He'd got married. One of the two things in the world he'd never wanted to do. The second was to become a father, and now it seemed his hand was to be forced there too unless he could find another way.

Again he raked his hands through his hair. He couldn't think straight. The air was becoming heavier and more oppressive by the minute and he could feel Georgina's gaze fully on him, expectantly waiting for an answer.

'Tell her to arrange their wedding.' His words were sharp, and it was an effort to keep his frustration at the situation he now found himself in from showing. Damn it, he still couldn't tell her why she had to stay.

Her gaze locked with his, the soft brown eyes that had almost melted his soul as he'd made her his now burnished like copper, angry and glittering. He clenched his hands and met her challenging gaze.

'This is what you wanted all along, isn't it?' What was she waiting for now? His blessing for the marriage?

'You know it is…'

A *but* seemed to linger in the air with as much threat as the storm he could feel waiting to erupt.

He raised a brow at her, finally slipping back into his professional mode. 'Anything else?'

She shook her head, a look of disappointment crossing her face and he bit down hard on the sudden urge to go to her, to hold her and make everything right. Because he couldn't. He would never be able to make this right— for Georgina or himself.

She stood tall and resolute for a few more seconds, her gaze fixed to his, then she left, taking with her some of the pressure that dominated the room.

He needed to contact his legal team. There just had to be a way out of that final clause. Satisfied he'd sorted the situation for now, he turned on his laptop. He had far too many emails to answer, but the first one snared his attention with such ferocity he dropped down into his chair.

It was offering him congratulations on his marriage. Just what they had planned. But it was the last line that almost made his heart stop. He and Georgina weren't the only couple to have got married.

Blood pounded in his ears, the sound so loud it almost masked the first rumble of thunder as the storm finally broke.

It couldn't be true.

Quickly he scanned the headlines and within minutes found confirmation that, yes, it was true. He'd been tricked, manipulated, and totally played for a fool. He wanted to rage and shout, but one thing life had taught him was that rushing in without first knowing all the facts could leave him in a weak position.

No, this had to be approached with caution. He had to know what part Georgina had played in this. Instinct told him it was a very big part. He was angry he'd lowered his defences enough for her to see the man he really was. For the first time ever he'd felt the stirrings of something he'd shut out of his life long ago and had almost been fooled into opening that door.

Georgina slipped outside to the pool. The clouds were dark and heavy. It looked as if a storm was brewing, and she hated storms—she'd never shaken off her childhood fear of them. Despite the dark clouds that hung low in the sky she settled on a lounger by the pool, her need to speak with Emma greater than her desire to hide from the storm. She could hardly wait to hear her sister's squeal of delight when she told her they could set a date.

'Georgie.' Emma sounded different somehow as she answered the phone. 'Where are you?'

'I'm still in Spain, and you can get set a date for your wedding.' She took a breath, putting on an air of jubilation—one she was far from feeling. 'Santos and I— we're married.'

Emma hesitated, and a shiver of apprehension slipped down Georgina's spine as the silence lengthened down the phone connection.

Finally Emma spoke, sounding oddly far away. 'I know. It's all over town.'

At least her plan had worked, Georgina consoled herself. All she could hope for now was that Emma would believe that she and Santos had married because of the attraction they had for one another, after the whirlwind romance that had started at the party.

'Georgie…'

Emma's voice sounded nervous, and as the silence lengthened still further Georgina heard the first rumble of thunder. 'Georgie, Carlo and I…we got married a few days ago.'

Georgina almost dropped the phone with shock. Her

quiet, biddable sister had gone against everyone and married in secret, without even telling *her*. Hurt lanced through her as she thought of the day she'd always imagined for Emma—a day when she would be there to see her married, not on a yacht off the coast of Spain.

A flash of lightning made Georgina's heart-rate accelerate wildly, but she tried to keep it under control. She didn't want Emma to worry—didn't want her to know of the ramifications her actions.

'Georgie, are you still there?'

She could hear the unease in her sister's voice and tried to focus her mind. How could Emma have betrayed her?

'I have to go, Emma, there's a storm coming. I'll call you later.'

She cut the connection as the full implications of what this meant hit home.

And Santos. What would *he* think?

A low rumble of thunder followed by the first heavy drops of rain made her retreat to the safety of the villa. Her fear of the storm outweighed the fact that Santos was himself like a brewing storm—one she didn't want to be around when it broke. From the doorway she watched the raindrops falling into the pool, disturbing its smooth surface. Deep down she knew she had more than a storm to fear.

The temperature dropped and a cool wind picked up. The white curtains billowed into the room where she stood, watching the increasingly heavy rain. Lightning lit up the darkening sky and she shuddered in a breath, as tense as the air around her. The clap of thunder was so loud she had to suppress a scream as she beat a hasty retreat further into the villa, feeling as shaken by Emma's revelation as by the storm itself. The trembling of her hands was very real.

'Scared of the storm?' Santos's voice was clipped and hard. 'Or is this another of your wonderful acting roles?'

She frowned, blinking in confusion as he came to stand before her. His dark eyes were full of fury and as he folded his arms across his chest and looked down at her she saw visible tension in his neck and shoulders.

'A little,' she lied, and rubbed her hands up and down her arms as if she were cold, refusing to rise to the bait of his last comment.

His gaze darted to the movement, watching through narrowed eyes, then moved back to her face. She fought the way her body responded to him, despite her apprehension about telling him what she'd just found out. She took a deep breath and tried to focus herself, curb her fear of the storm and deny the need to be held by him, to feel safe in his arms.

He marched past her and closed the doors to the terrace. The curtains ceased their wild dance but the tension of the storm remained, wrapping itself around them, drawing them towards each other. His dark gaze met hers and defiantly she lifted her chin, straightened her back, determined not to show him her fear.

There were two storms raging, she realised with a sinking feeling. Two storms she was going to have to ride out, no matter what. There wasn't any escape from either now.

'Your plan worked,' he said as he stood with his back to the doors and the lashing rain.

The dark clouds behind him only intensified the image of anger he projected.

'My plan was for Emma to think we were lovers so she wouldn't question our marriage.' Her voice didn't sound as firm as she wanted, and anxiety made her stomach flutter. She had to regain her composure.

'And why was that so important, Georgina?'

The use of her full name hurt, somehow, and the light sarcasm in his voice was unmistakable.

'You openly admit to marrying for financial security once already—why would she question *our* marriage?'

She watched his jaw tighten as he took in a deep breath, as if he was holding back what he really wanted to say. 'She never knew I married Richard so that I could fund her education and give her a secure home. My first marriage isn't part of this, Santos.'

Thunder cracked overhead, the villa seeming to shake with the force of it. Georgina glanced anxiously around the room, thankful that she was no longer out at sea.

'It damn well is when your reputation precedes you.' His voice was hard and echoed the aggression of the storm. The expression on his face was as dark and brooding as the sky.

'My reputation?' Lightning lit the room and her heart thudded almost as loudly as the thunder. 'If by that you mean that I married Richard, an older and unwell man, because he offered me lifelong security in return for a few years of companionship, then, yes, my reputation does precede me.'

She glared at him, hardly able to believe they were discussing her first marriage when it was the marriage of his brother to her sister that should take precedence. That was the one that affected them both, whether they liked it or not.

She had to tell him, but anxiously kept the conversation on its current course. As the next crack of thunder threatened to shake the foundations of the villa she stood her ground, glaring at Santos.

'A companionship so loving that you were dating other

men just weeks after his funeral.' He practically snarled the words at her, so intense was his anger.

'It was what he wanted,' she said, softly but firmly, remembering how insistent Richard had been that she should move on in life, find herself a man she could love.

She'd dated a few men just to do as Richard had wanted, to honour the memory of the man who'd given her a future. But she hadn't enjoyed their company and very quickly gossip had started.

After the initial shock of being at the centre of everyone's speculation she'd soon realised it provided a wall to hide behind.

'I found out very quickly that seeing a man once or twice only was the best way.' Let him think the worst of her. She had other worries right now. Besides, if he believed that of her it would keep him at arm's length— something she had to do now no matter what. She couldn't dwell on the closeness they'd shared.

Santos's brow furrowed. 'Best way for what?' The words snapped from him.

'For doing what *you* do,' she flung at him as another rumble of thunder, just as intense, reverberated around the room. 'For keeping the world at bay, keeping the gossips with something to get their teeth into, because ultimately it meant I could be on my own. I never wanted to be married the first time and I certainly don't want to be married now.'

She flopped down onto the sofa, unable to fight any longer. Remaining indifferent to what was being said about her and the shock of what Emma had done was finally too much.

How could her sister have said nothing? How could she have sneaked away the moment she'd left for Spain? It was a complete and utter betrayal. Emma had as good as thrown everything she'd ever done for her back in her face.

Santos walked across the marble floor. A hint of softness entered his tone as he crouched before her, forcing her to look into his eyes. 'Then why offer yourself to me?'

She swallowed down the urge to cry, to collapse into an emotional heap, and looked into his eyes. Their dark depths were almost unreadable. He was so close, and the spark of attraction passing between them was as strong as ever, but she mustn't let that cloud her mind and muddle her judgement.

'Why, Georgina?' he prompted, his voice a little firmer, and she realised the anger she'd seen in him earlier was still simmering beneath the surface.

She took a breath to tell him what she'd just learnt, but couldn't. The look in his glittering eyes halted those words

'For Emma,' she began, trying to put off the moment just a little longer. 'She believes in the dream of love, the happy-ever-after, and it's Carlo—your brother—who is that dream for her. When she told me about the will it seemed the most obvious deal to make. I'd married for convenience for Emma's benefit once before. I could do it again.'

Georgina was emotionally wrung out, but she had to tell him. She didn't want to—didn't want to rouse his anger—but she knew she had to. She couldn't keep it from him. He had a right to know.

'They are already married.'

The words were out before he had a chance to say anything.

He studied her for a moment, crouching in front of her as if he was talking to a child, making her think he'd be good with children. An image of her holding a baby with Santos's dark eyes and complexion rushed into her mind, not for the first time in recent days, but she pushed it harshly away. Marrying him was one thing, but she'd never have his child. She could never have a child, full-stop. She didn't want to risk being as useless as her own mother.

'When did you know?' His words, although cajoling, still reverberated with anger.

She looked down at the phone she still clutched in her hand and sighed. 'Minutes ago.'

Betrayal ripped through her again at the thought of what Emma and Carlo had done, but she knew Emma would never have done it alone—never.

'I can't believe it,' she whispered, more to herself than Santos.

'They married on Saturday.'

He stood up and looked down on her, his height making her feel small, his words like hailstones raining down on her. Another rumble of thunder followed, echoing his anger.

'Saturday?' She blinked back tears as she thought of Emma getting married whilst she'd been flying out to Spain. Then it hit her. 'That means Carlo married first.'

He nodded, folding his arms across his chest once more.

'So our marriage was for nothing. Carlo inherits the business and I miss the biggest day of my sister's life.' She wanted to jump up, to stand and face him, but her knees were too weak so she just buried her face in her hands.

What was she going to do now? Santos probably thought she'd conspired with them to outsmart him. There was only one thing she could do. Go home. Get far away from Santos.

'I'll go and pack,' she said, finally finding the strength to stand as another rumble filled the room, this time sounding as if it was finally receding.

'No.'

Santos grabbed her arm as she made to leave and she looked up into his face. A small part of her wanted to see the gentleness she'd seen on their wedding night. She wanted to feel as special as he'd made her feel that night. But instead his eyes were brittle with hardness.

'You are my wife. You will stay here.'

She shook her head. 'No, Santos, I can't. Their marriage changes everything.'

'Your scheming, meaning that Carlo married first, has changed nothing. We are still married.'

He held her arm tight, pulling her against his body. She could feel the heat of it and, despite the anger and tension in the air, her body responded traitorously to his.

'It's all about the business for you, isn't it?' Accusation rang in her voice as she lifted her chin, finding her defiant streak once more, denying the burning need that raged inside her. 'You can't bear it that you've lost it.'

He shook his head and his voice was hard. 'I haven't lost it. Not yet. And we will remain married.'

'Why?' Her breath was heaving in her chest.

His eyes darkened, the brittleness of earlier replaced with hot desire.

'Because of this.'

Before she could question him further his mouth claimed hers in a hot, searing kiss. She gasped in a mixture of annoyance and pleasure as his hand cupped her breast, making her arch against him, only being held upright by the firm grasp of his hand on her arm. She had no escape. Neither did she want an escape. She wanted his touch, his kiss. Damn it, she wanted *him*. She wanted him because she loved him—and that was exactly why she had to go.

She could hardly think straight, let alone put coherent words together, as he broke the kiss and looked down at her.

'This undeniable attraction that exists between us. We can't fight it for ever.'

'No,' she managed in a croaky voice. 'But it can't last for ever.'

He shrugged, relinquishing his grip on her arm to hold her hand instead. 'True, but we can explore it while it lasts.'

'Why would I want to do that?' Indignation at his knowing glance leapt through her.

'Because we are man and wife,' he said in a smooth tone that rippled over her heightened senses like velvet. 'Truly man and wife.'

She shook her head. 'Not really, we aren't. It was just a deal. Just a marriage of convenience.'

'Was our wedding night on the yacht just part of the deal?'

His self-satisfied smile made her blush at the memory of just how abandoned she'd been. He kissed her—a brief but intense one.

'I thought not.'

'No, Santos.' She pushed at his chest, needing space to think. 'This isn't what I wanted. Neither of us did. And now Emma and Carlo have married there is no need for us to be together.'

'That's where you are wrong, because Carlo hasn't yet inherited the business.'

'Of course he has. He's married—before you.' She almost froze with shock. Some of his earlier words were now making sense, like his accusation of her acting. He'd been playing with her.

'Yes, they are married.' The smile didn't reach his eyes this time. 'But, *querida*, that doesn't change anything.'

'What do you mean?' Confused, she stopped pushing him away. She didn't understand. Emma and Carlo had got married before she and Santos had even arrived in Spain, making Carlo the first son to marry. 'Why doesn't it change anything?'

Santos struggled with his conscience. Her act of being the wounded party was very convincing, just as her act of fear of the storm had been, but he didn't believe she'd known nothing of their plans. Why else would she have asked so seductively to stay on the yacht longer, or even agreed to leave London with him, if not to make it as difficult as possible for him to contact the outside world? She'd practically thrown herself at him, used all that a woman could to snare his interest and keep him from going back to the villa. She'd made him want her, teased and dallied with his desire since that first kiss at the party, and there was only one reason as far as he was concerned.

She'd planned it all along.

True, she'd wanted him as much as he'd wanted her. He'd have to be blind and stupid not to see how her body responded to his slightest touch. And each time he'd kissed her the attraction between them had intensified, until they couldn't ignore it any longer.

She'd deceived him, duped him, like all females did, with her body. And just like his father he'd ignored everything to be with her, to make her his. He'd been like a man possessed, unable to think of anything else other than Georgina. Thoughts of her had been all-consuming.

He enjoyed being with women, but never had he been so completely under a woman's spell.

Even now, when her kisses tasted of deceit, he wanted her. Passion burned in her eyes as she stood and glared at him. How dared she look so wounded? There could only be one winner in this game of passion and deceit she'd started. And that would be him.

'It isn't the first son to marry who inherits.' The words slipped out effortlessly. Finally he'd got her attention. 'But the first married son to produce an heir.'

He watched as his words slowly filtered through, like water permeating through limestone, until finally the expression on her face told him she understood the full implications.

She shook her head, backing away from him as if he was evil itself, her beautiful face ashen white, her eyes wide with disbelief. Oh, but she was a good actress. He almost believed it. Almost.

CHAPTER TEN

THE FIRST MARRIED son to produce an heir.

No, she screamed in her head, whilst outwardly the shutters came down, cocooning her behind a safe barrier.

'How long have you known this?' How could he stand there so calmly and tell her that? He might as well say her whole plan had been a waste of time. He'd lied all this time, but she couldn't see a trace of remorse.

'Long enough.'

His words sent a shiver down her spine.

'So what were you hoping for? A honeymoon baby?' She wanted to close her eyes against the pain of shattered dreams as they splintered around her. For just one night she'd thought she could sample that dream. She hadn't expected her attraction for him to turn into something deeper. Now it was spoilt by his admissions. His deceit. 'No wonder you were so—what was it?—unusually *relaxed* about contraception.'

'That's absurd.'

His eyes looked dark and hostile but she stood tall, remaining as defiant as she could manage.

A ray of sunlight speared the gloom and she glanced out at the clearing sky, glad that at least one storm was over.

'Not absurd, Santos.' She looked directly at him, something akin to anger and disappointment flitting through her. 'Not when you consider the clause of the will and that you knew Carlo wanted to get married. He loves my sister. Just by marrying he was a threat to you—because not only would he be the first married son, but probably the first married son to have the required heir.'

It was like a puzzle, and finally she was putting it together. She still had a few pieces to find, but it was all beginning to make sense now.

'Why are you so against Carlo?' She felt frustrated by those missing pieces. 'When you could have married any one of the women you've dated in the past and inherited everything you believe is yours.'

She watched as he paced the room—long, lean strides that drew her attention. As if needing escape, he opened the doors to the terrace and strode out. The fresh smell of dampness after the rain rushed into the room as he left. For a moment she stood and watched him, saw his pain, his frustration, with every move he made, and something deep inside her tugged at her emotions.

She knew that kind of pain, that kind of emptiness.

She walked to the door. Santos stood looking out to sea, his broad shoulders tense and the muscles in his arms taut as he leant on the balustrade. She longed to go to him, to touch him and soothe his pain. But sense prevailed. This was all of his making. She couldn't let him know how she felt—not when he'd used everyone as pawns in his power game.

It rushed at her so hard she almost stumbled. All her breath momentarily left her body and her heart raced like a wild horse fleeing captivity.

It couldn't be true—it just couldn't.

She loved him. Completely and utterly.

She pressed her fingertips to her lips to stifle a cry of distress. She didn't want to love anyone. She *couldn't* love anyone. And certainly not Santos Ramirez. Since the day her father had turned his back on them she'd watched her mother take a path of self-destruction. Her parents' actions proved beyond doubt that love was all-consuming, but also that it hurt, left you alone and killed all joy in life when it went wrong. It was a gamble she'd never wanted to take, so how had it happened? How had she fallen in love with Santos?

'I'm not against Carlo.'

His harsh words dragged her mind back from the pain of her past.

'Just the marriage.'

She sensed his vulnerability as he remained with his back to her, looking out to sea, at the sky clearing and brightening after the storm. Knowing she shouldn't, but unable to stop herself, she crossed the terrace and stood by him, her shoulder almost touching his arm as she stood surveying the view.

'Why did your father put such a clause in his will, forcing you to marry?' This was something that had niggled at her since Emma had first mentioned it. She'd imagined two young boys vying for their father's attention. A man who didn't deserve any from either of them as far as she was concerned.

'It's a family business, started by my grandfather— my mother's father. I suppose he assumed that as I was older by nine years I'd marry and have a family a long time before Carlo did.'

He sounded resigned and it tugged at her heart to hear him, almost as if he was admitting defeat.

'He must have thought he was being fair to us both, putting that clause in his will.'

'So why didn't you marry?' The question just had to

be asked. He'd never been short of female company. She'd very quickly learnt that.

He turned to face her and she held her breath as he looked down at her. His eyes searched her face as if looking for answers to questions he didn't even know. She watched as his face set into hard lines, shutting her out.

'To avoid the mess we are in now.' The angry words all but barked out at her.

She shivered despite the sun. 'It's easy to sort out.' Her words were curt as she lifted her chin in defiance and challenge, the softer emotions quashed by his frozen expression. 'I leave and you file for divorce.'

In one swift stride he came towards her, his hand holding her arm firmly. 'You are not going anywhere unless I do—and as for a divorce…'

He spoke with a voice so stern and disapproving she blinked in shock.

'There will not be a divorce. Your meddling has made sure of that.'

'But—' she began, wondering what she wanted to try and tell him, even what she didn't. 'There isn't any reason to remain married—not now.'

'You are forgetting, *mi esposa*, that an heir may yet still be needed.' He let go of her, keeping her where she stood with just the fixed glare of his dark eyes.

'No,' she snapped, and backed away from him, bumping against the chair she'd sat in to call her sister earlier. 'Even you're not so cold and callous that you'd bring a child into the world just to inherit a business.'

'I had hoped not even to marry to inherit. When you so kindly offered yourself I believed it would be enough, that I could find a way out of the clause long before Carlo married. But your meddling has changed everything.'

His eyes glittered furiously at her but she held her

ground, squared her shoulders and met his accusation head on.

Her *meddling*? 'What do you mean?'

'Don't play the innocent with me.'

His eyes glittered dangerously but she refused to be intimidated, refused to back down.

'Not when you've led me on, driven me wild with need for you since the night of the party.'

'I did not lead you on.' Indignation flared to life in her and she almost stamped her foot in frustration.

Santos knew he was losing his patience, reaching the boiling point that very few people managed to push him to. All he wanted was to prevent her from leaving. He needed her, yes, but he wanted her more.

'So what was our wedding night if not to divert my attention and keep me out of the way?'

She gasped at him, a blush creeping over her cheeks, and she looked as if she was struggling for words.

'You must have been delighted when I took you to the yacht. What better place to keep me out of the way?' Humiliation burned through him like a forest fire. He'd been used, played for a fool, and it wounded him even more to think that he'd relaxed. He'd wanted to open up to her, wanted to be who he really was, when all along she'd been as fake as snow in the desert. 'You flirted yourself at me in an attempt to stay longer on the yacht.'

Her brow furrowed and pain and confusion swirled in her eyes. For a moment he wanted to reach for her, wanted to kiss it all away. But kissing had got him into this mess. Kissing and much more had left him emotionally exposed and vulnerable.

'If that's what you think, Santos, it would be much better if you just let me go home. Alone.' Her words were firm and devoid of any emotion.

'That,' he snapped, instantly reining himself back, 'is not negotiable. You will stay here with me now I know where Carlo and Emma are.'

'Where they are?' She spoke rapidly, shock sounding in her tone. 'You mean they're not in London?'

Was it possible he'd got it all wrong? That she'd known nothing of their marriage plans?

He moved away from her—away from the intensity of her eyes and the questions deep within them. Maybe sending her back to London alone would be for the best, enable him to think clearly. Because his need for her had increased since they'd spent the night together and each time she came close his body remembered, even if his mind refused to acknowledge what he was beginning to feel for her.

'Perhaps you can tell me.' He tossed the words across the terrace as he made his way back inside the villa. 'You can explain everything to me on our way out this evening.'

'There's only one place I'm going this evening and that's the airport—with or without your help.' He knew she had followed him inside. He could feel her, sense her.

He sat down on the sofa, stretching his arm along the back of the black leather, and watched as she stood, fury blazing from her, in the centre of the room. A smile twitched the corners of his lips despite the bitter taste of humiliation. She looked stunningly sexy, a little fireball of passion.

'Tonight we are expected at a party my cousin has arranged for us and I have no intention of arriving without my bride.'

'Well, I'm sorry to disappoint you, Santos, but your bride is leaving. Right now.'

He clenched his jaw as his mind raced. 'You can't. You signed the agreement. You have legally agreed to live as my wife for twelve months.'

Her eyes widened in shock. 'I don't believe you actually put that in. You're barbaric.'

'I need an heir, Georgina.'

Right there in front of him she seemed to deflate. All the fire and fury drained from her and he sat forward, his elbows on his knees. Was she actually going to faint?

'I can't give you what you want.'

The anguish in her voice alarmed him and he leapt up and stood before her.

'I can't have a baby—I can't.'

Can't have a baby.

He hadn't considered this. He'd assumed that, like almost every woman, she'd want to become a mother.

'Why not?'

This threw everything into turmoil. If Carlo and Emma returned from Vegas as parents-to-be he would have lost everything—exactly what he'd promised his mother he'd never do the last time he saw her. Although he still didn't know what kind of misguided loyalty made him want to keep that promise.

Large tears welled up in Georgina's eyes. One broke free and ran down her cheek. Santos didn't know what to do. He hadn't considered the possibility that she couldn't have children. She'd been so adamant that she'd do anything to enable her sister to marry. He'd seen her as a viable back-up plan—a marriage of convenience to a woman who would be the mother of his child, should that drastic step be needed.

'I can't…I just can't,' she croaked in a whisper, tugging at something deep inside him so much that he wanted to hold her close, to soothe her.

Instead he clenched his hands into fists and marched away from her. 'This changes nothing. You are my wife. You agreed to it for one year and I'm not going to allow you to publicly humiliate me any further. I don't need my wife deserting me within days of our supposed whirlwind romance. It's bad enough that Carlo and Emma have run off to Vegas…'

'Vegas?' Incredulity made her tear-laden eyes widen and he steeled himself against the need to hold her.

'As if you didn't know.'

Attack was the only way he could control the myriad of strange new emotions running riot inside him. He wanted her with him, yet he didn't. Above all he wanted to punish her for her part in deceiving him, but even *he* wasn't so callous that in the face of what she'd just told him he'd actually do that.

Vegas. Emma had gone to Las Vegas to get married.

'I didn't know,' Georgina whispered, betrayal rushing through her.

They must have planned it for weeks. Why hadn't Emma said something? Taken her into her confidence?

He took her hand, his mood softened. 'It seems we are both victims of their deception.'

His deep voice sent shivers of awareness down her spine, but she remained firm and resolute, not trusting him.

'Have you spoken to Carlo?' She pulled back, watching his face as she asked the question.

'No, but the gossip columns are full of it. When we left for Spain they must have gone straight to Vegas. They must have left as soon as we'd left the party. Damn it, they knew all along.'

He let go of her as his frustration built again and she felt strangely alone. The touch of his hand had been grounding, somehow. He blamed her for what Emma and Carlo had done, that much was obvious, yet still she wanted his comfort, wanted to feel his arms around her.

If she was going to survive the next few days she had to push her emotions right to the back of her mind—had to ignore them before they exposed her to the biggest pain of all. One thing she was sure of: she couldn't remain his wife for a year—not if it meant living with him.

Twice in her life she had trusted and loved a man and twice he had let her down. Her father, whom she'd adored, had walked away one stormy night without a backward glance, leaving her in tears, clinging to the front door. Then Richard, whom she'd loved in a gentle, appreciative way, had left her alone in the world—more alone than she cared to admit.

Now Santos.

She'd fallen in love with him so passionately and deeply she couldn't even think properly any more. Her usual unemotional demeanour was smashed into icy crumbs.

'Emma would never have done it if she'd thought it would end like this.' She tried to think back to all they'd spoken off when they'd been getting ready for the party Santos had thrown. She shook her head in disbelief. 'She just wouldn't.'

'It would seem your sister isn't as loyal to you as you are to her.' Santos's voice was hard as he paced the room. 'Whatever possessed them to run off and get married?'

'Love,' Georgina whispered.

Santos rounded on her. 'Love is for fools. It destroys lives.'

'How can you say that?' Her frustration matched his fury and she glared at him, daring him to answer. 'You must have loved once.'

An echo of a previous conversation filled her mind.

He closed the distance between them in long strides, dominating the room with his volatile mood. 'Your father walked out on you, no?' His accent was stronger than ever as he battled with his emotions.

Her breath caught in her throat as he brought up her past, made the memories of that night—already too fresh after the storm—rush back. 'My father has nothing to do with it.'

'If he'd loved you he wouldn't have left. That's what you think, no?'

His eyes locked with hers, holding her prisoner, forcing her to face things she didn't want to face.

Before she could answer his harsh words came at her again, as if he no longer cared what he was saying. 'It's the same for me. Love will never be a part of how I think of my mother, or she of me.' He whirled around and marched back outside, as if needing more space to vent his anger.

Cautiously she followed him outside. 'What happened with your mother?' Her words were a whisper as she watched him drag in a deep breath.

He turned to look at her once more, his face set in firm lines.

'I was a mistake.' He swallowed as if the words tasted bitter and her heart tugged for him. 'A mistake that forced her to marry my father. A mistake she always made me pay for.'

'But your father loved her, didn't he?' She scanned her

mind for the little snippets of his life he'd told her about, trying to piece things together.

'And that love was rewarded with my being ignored as a young boy.' Pain resounded in his voice and he sighed and turned to look out to sea.

He was turning his back not only on her but on the conversation. It was what he always did, she realised. Right from that first time in his office when he'd looked out over London. It seemed a lifetime ago instead of less than a week.

'But your father moved on and you have a brother now.'

She heard him inhale deeply, saw his shoulders lift and then fall. She'd said the wrong thing again.

'Half-brother.' The words were grated out, and still he kept his back resolutely turned. 'One who has just proved how little he thinks of me. Just as always, he's got what he wants.'

Georgina thought again of all Emma had told her about Carlo. 'I'm sure it's not like that. In fact I'd go as far as to say he doesn't want to inherit the business. He wants to do his own thing, make his own way in life.'

Santos turned round to face her, questions in his dark eyes. 'You're wrong. How could any man not want to inherit his father's business?'

'Not everyone is as motivated by power as you are, Santos. Carlo and Emma just want to make a life together—a normal life.' Without thinking she reached out and touched his arm, her fingers heating as they felt the firmness of his muscles.

'What is that, Georgina?' He sounded drained and tired.

'They want to be together. They're in love, Santos. Is that so hard to accept?' She moved closer to him, trying to quash the surge of love she felt for him as he opened up and let her see his pain.

He looked down into her eyes, his darkening. She thought he might kiss her as he moved closer, with his head dropping lower. But then he stopped, the abruptness of it sending a chill through her.

'No, Georgina, no.' He moved away from her and for the first time ever he looked at a loss for what to say.

This powerful all-controlling man that she'd fallen in love with couldn't and wouldn't accept that love even existed. If that didn't staunch the love that was rapidly growing for him, then nothing would.

'No to what, Santos? Can't you just accept that they love one another and there aren't any ulterior motives at work?'

He changed as he stepped away, as if the distance was enabling him to regain his power, his authority. 'You engineered this whole thing—encouraged them to fly off to Vegas, kept me busy in the way only a woman of your reputation can, and secured a big financial settlement for yourself along the way.'

Hurt raced through her, stinging like a thousand bees. 'You can keep your money, tear up the agreement—anything.' She rounded on him, angry at herself for feeling for him, for wanting to reach out to him, for wanting to love him. 'I don't even know why you haven't just bought Carlo out. It would have been much less complicated than getting married.'

'Don't insult my business management. You know nothing about it—about the way Carlo has refused my generous offer, not once but twice, holding out for the ultimate prize.'

His voice was fierce but she didn't pay any heed to it

at all. Her emotions were running so high she no longer cared what happened.

'No, I *don't* know anything about it. All I know is that I should never have got involved.' She hissed the words at him as his dark eyes accused her. 'I should have just helped them get married.'

'You did.'

'No!' Exasperation made her voice sharp.

He really believed she'd done this for money, for her own gain as well as Emma's. Enraged beyond comprehension, she marched to his study. Her thoughts were beyond rational as she barged into the room, and when she saw the file holding their agreement on his desk she picked it up.

Santos entered the study just as she took hold of the agreement they'd both signed such a short time ago, his face as dark as the thunderclouds had been earlier. She looked at him, smiled sarcastically. Challenging him. Then she tore up the agreement into as many tiny pieces as her shaking hands could manage.

'You can do what you like, *mi esposa*, but you will still be my wife.'

'I'm leaving, Santos, as your wife or not. I don't care, but I'm going back to London.'

She pushed past him and almost ran to her room. Without pausing she grabbed her handbag, checked for her passport and spun on her heel, not wanting anything from him.

She'd get a taxi to the airport and sit there all night if she had to, but one thing was for sure: she'd be on the next flight back to London. With that plan of action in mind she headed for the front door of the villa, glad Santos was nowhere to be seen.

Anger and frustration still raced in her veins as she pulled open the heavy ornate door—but Santos stood there, hands folded across his powerful body.

CHAPTER ELEVEN

'I HAVE TO go, Santos,' she fired at him, her heart thudding so loudly she thought he might hear it. 'We should never have married. I was stupid to think it could work.'

'Stupid to try and deceive me—that's what you mean, is it not, *querida*?' His words were slow and very deliberate.

The setting sun cast an orange glow around him as he stood firm and resolute before her. Despite the pain in her heart, her body responded to the image of him—the man she loved. The man she must never think of again once she'd got back to London. Perhaps she'd move away, get a small place in the country, live simply and quietly. Anything not to have to see him again.

'I'm not even going to deny it.' Her temper flared. 'You're determined to think the worst so you can go ahead and do it, just like you have with your brother and his mother. Even your father.'

He inhaled deeply, his handsome face becoming sharper than she'd ever seen. His eyes hardened until they resembled polished obsidian, with glittering hints of the lava that formed it hidden in their depths.

'Get in the car, Georgina.' His tone brooked no rebuke and she stiffened at the challenge. There was no way she was going to let him stop her. She had to get away—as far away as possible.

'No,' she said vehemently, and tried to move past him, but his reactions were fast and he instantly blocked her, his dominating body filling the doorway.

'I'm going to the airport.'

'Then I shall take you.' His tone was as overpowering as his body.

She looked from his face to the car behind him and noticed for the first time that the passenger door was open and the engine running. Her heart raced at the thought of being with him for just a little while longer, because despite everything that was where she wanted to be. But he would never want her as his wife now—not when he believed her capable of such deception. A deception she was innocent of.

'Why?' She couldn't help herself asking, as if in just a few seconds he would have changed his mind about her.

'You are my wife, and as such I will drive you to the airport.'

He left her in no doubt that there wouldn't be any further discussion on the subject and she dropped down into the low sports car, nerves taking flight in her stomach as he climbed into the driver's seat.

She glanced across at him as the air inside the car filled with his raw masculine scent—one that would haunt her for ever—only to find he was looking at her. Furiously she glared at him, then looked away. She wasn't going to be a victim of his charm this time. The sooner she got to the airport the better.

The drive along the busy roads was fast and painfully silent. Each time she looked at him his stern profile hinted at the anger he held in check. Each passing second became tenser than the last, the air more laden and heavy, and she breathed a sigh of relief as the airport came into view.

He passed the entrance and she panicked. 'Where are we going?'

'My plane is waiting on the Tarmac.'

'You don't need to do that. I'll book on the next flight.' She tried hard to keep her desperation from him, but it wasn't just him she was annoyed with. She'd almost hoped he was coming to London too and that he did want her.

'We shall be in London by midnight.'

'We?' She silently cursed that last thought—that last futile wish.

'Did you really think you could walk out so easily?' He turned to look at her briefly as he manoeuvred the car into the airport and headed for the plane. Within seconds of them stopping he was out of the car and at her door, and once their passports were checked he took her hand and led her up the steps of the plane.

The door closed and a strange stillness settled inside the cabin. Santos sat in one of the white leather chairs, his long legs stretched out before him, looking relaxed, but she knew from the tension in his face he was anything but.

Georgina resigned herself to the situation and sat down, fixing her attention on the darkening skyline rather than look at the man who'd turned everything in her life upside down, including her heart. She consoled herself with the fact that at least she was going back to London. Once there she could so much more easily walk away from Santos. But that thought didn't make her feel as she'd wanted it to. It made her heart ache. Pain lanced through it, shattering it into pieces. But she couldn't let him know.

* * *

If Santos had thought the flight to London was tense, then the drive through London's streets was worse. Georgina sat at his side, irresistibly close, yet undeniably far from him. He knew she was trapped in her deceit. The evidence was stacked against her. She'd deceived him, tricked him into marrying her so her sister and his brother could take all he'd worked so hard for over recent years. This time Georgina's gamble wasn't going to pay off.

'I can't stay here.'

Georgina's words drew him up sharp. She'd realised where they were. The storm, it seemed, raged on.

'Take me back to my own apartment, please.'

He didn't say anything, just shook his head once as she looked across at him, her face partially lit by street lamps.

'Santos, please, don't prolong the agony.'

The anguish in her voice was so acute it was almost physical. But what did she mean, agony? Had their time together been so awful?

'Agony? What agony?' he snapped at her recklessly, instantly furious with himself for allowing her to see even a moment's loss of control.

She looked taken aback, as if she hadn't meant to say those words. 'Just admit it's time we went our separate ways, Santos. Things haven't worked out.' She hesitated for a moment as the car pulled up outside his apartment. 'We've both been deceived—let's leave it at that.' She sounded tired, as if struggling with defeat.

'You are my wife, Georgina, and as such I want you with me when Carlo and Emma return. I want us to present a united front.' He couldn't admit it yet—not even to himself—but he seemed to be clutching at every possible reason for her to stay, as if he didn't want her to go.

The chauffeur opened the car door and he stepped out

into the cold autumn night. Light rain had fallen and the small amount of traffic that passed swished by on the wet road. He walked round to the other side of the car and opened Georgina's door, marvelling at how suddenly she seemed at ease. Was he even now falling into line with one of her devious plans?

She stepped out onto the pavement and looked at him. 'I don't see why we should keep up the pretence any longer.'

'No?' He walked towards the entrance doors, glancing back and hoping she would follow. He wasn't in the mood for any more in-depth discussions. 'Do you not want to continue until Emma comes back? It would be better if she thought you were happy, would it not?'

He watched as her expression changed from defiance to realisation that he spoke the truth. He certainly didn't want Carlo to think he'd married Georgina in a bid to secure the business; it was an ongoing issue between them. One that now threatened everything he'd ever cared about.

'You're right.' She sighed and smiled sweetly at him—a little too sweetly, convincing him that even now she played the game, using him as she had from the very beginning. 'It wouldn't do if they found out what we'd done—for reasons other than love, of course.'

Opening the door, he walked towards the lift, pressed the button and turned to her. Did she *have* to keep brandishing that word about? As if it was the very centre of everything that had happened?

Irritated, he looked above the lift doors, anxious to see if it was coming. 'It will be for the best,' he said tersely.

'That's debatable,' she tossed at him as the lift doors opened and she walked in. 'I've yet to decide just who it will be best for, but tonight, at least, I'm prepared to stay here.'

He didn't know what to say to that—his usual quick thinking had totally deserted him—so he remained silent as the lift took them up to his apartment, acutely aware of her so very close to him. He could smell her sweet floral scent and clenched his hands into fists in a bid to stamp out the threatening fire.

Santos unlocked the door and Georgina couldn't believe she was back at his apartment. Everything she'd planned had gone wrong and, worse, had been for nothing. She'd told Santos she could have just encouraged Emma and Carlo to run off and get married and now she wished she had. At least then she wouldn't have tasted something she could never have. She wouldn't have fallen in love with a man who openly admitted he wasn't capable of love in any form.

She sighed wearily. The last few days had been emotionally challenging for all the wrong reasons and she just wanted to be on her own.

'It's late,' she said softly as he flicked on the lights in the kitchen. 'I'm going straight to bed.'

She looked across at him, wanting to add that she was going alone, that she would spend the night in the same room she'd occupied before, but something in his expression held her back. Her heart began to race as the intensity of his gaze rested on her, as if he too couldn't bring himself to suggest she sleep alone.

He walked towards her, his footsteps echoing on the wooden floor, and like an animal caught in car headlights she just stood there and watched, mesmerised by him. Nerves made her bite gently on her bottom lip as he stopped in front of her, so close and yet so far.

'Where are you going to sleep, *mi esposa*? With your husband or alone?'

His accent had become more defined, sending shivers of awareness all over her. When his gaze rested on her lips she stopped biting them and smiled, almost tasting the saccharine of it.

'Alone.'

With you, her mind screamed as that one word left her lips. She wanted to sleep beside the man she loved, feel the warmth of his body next to her. But she reminded herself the man she loved didn't really exist. That man had been pretence and nothing more. This was the real Santos.

'Then I shall say *buenas noches, mi esposa.*'

He moved closer. Instinct told her he was going to kiss her, and heaven help her she wanted him to, but if he did…

She stepped back. 'Goodnight, Santos,' she said as firmly as possible, before retreating to the safety of the room she'd previously occupied.

Santos watched her go, confusion racing through him. Why was he trying to prevent her from leaving? Just what kind of power did she have over him? Perhaps it was better if they slept alone—although his body protested at the idea. He knew he needed time to think. He had to be sure of what to do next and at the moment he hadn't a clue.

With an exasperated sigh he tousled his hair and turned on his heel. Strong coffee was what he needed. And work. Going to an empty bed when Georgina slept in the next room was not going to be an option. Neither was going to her and trying to explain—to himself as well as her—why he didn't want her to go.

The aroma of fresh coffee lingered in the air, and

the taste of it invigorated his senses as he headed for his study. He had reports to catch up on and an aching need to deny.

A neatly stacked pile of post almost made him groan aloud. He wasn't in the mood. But as he sat at his desk the postmark on one letter caught his attention. A solicitor's name glared out at him from the large white envelope. Anxiously he tore it open, but was totally unprepared for what he saw.

So unprepared he had to read it again.

Carlo had renounced all claims to his father's estate in deference to him. Santos closed his eyes in relief, but that was short-lived as the implications of the letter hit home. What would this mean for him and Georgina?

He tried to get Carlo on his mobile, but it went straight to voicemail. Annoyed, he hung up. He wasn't about to leave a message. Instead he tried to focus on his work, but all sorts of jumbled thoughts raced through his mind. He'd never felt this disorientated or distracted before.

After several hours he gave up on trying to work or contacting Carlo. He picked up the letter again and headed for the kitchen, unable even to consider trying to sleep. More coffee was required. As it brewed he read the letter again, trying to understand why his brother had felt the need to do this when he'd offered to buy him out several times. What point was he making?

Exasperated, he tossed it on the kitchen table and walked over to the windows. The faint light of dawn crept across the sky, and with it he hoped would come answers and solutions.

It was still very early, but Georgina knew that Santos was likely to be up and about, so she quickly scanned the living room, relieved to see it empty, and headed for the kitchen. She flicked on the kettle and searched for a mug, needing as much caffeine as she could get after her sleepless night. She noticed the partly drunk cups of cold coffee—evidence that either Santos had been entertaining or he too had had a bad night.

The coffee's aroma revived her and she leant back against one of the kitchen units to sip her drink, wrapping her hands comfortingly around her mug. It was then that she noticed the letter. It looked official, and at first she turned the other way, but as she did so a name caught her attention.

She looked more closely and nearly gasped at what she saw. The letter very clearly stated that Carlo had renounced his claim on his father's estate.

Guilt rushed through her for even thinking of looking at Santos's mail, but that was hotly followed by anger and disappointment. This letter changed everything. Santos would inherit his father's business without the need for a wife—or an heir. He didn't need her any more. So why was he tormenting her like this? Insisting she stay with him? To punish her?

She should feel relieved. At least she could walk away from him and try and piece together her life. Emma had Carlo and didn't need her any more, so she could get that longed-for peaceful cottage in the country.

The coffee turned bitter in her mouth and she put the nearly full mug down on the side, turning her back on the letter and all it meant. She felt sick when she should be relieved that she could at last walk away from this sham of a marriage. She should be heading out of the door right now and not giving the man she'd married a second thought. But she couldn't.

She couldn't just walk away.

She loved him.

'They're back.'

Santos's voice broke through her rambling thoughts. His hair was still damp from the shower. The last time she'd seen his hair wet they had just shared the most amazing moment in the shower. Did he remember that? She looked at him, as immaculate as ever in his designer suit, and found it hard to believe he would.

'Are they all right?' She pushed aside her memories and worries as she watched him walk past her into the kitchen. She was mesmerised by him, by the powerful aura he exuded, and found all she could do was watch as he organised fresh coffee.

'Of course they are. We'll have dinner with them tonight. Sort everything out.'

He sounded cheerful, not at all weighed down by the problems of the last few days. That letter had obviously made everything right for *him*, but when was he going to tell *her*? Then it hit her. How long had he known?

'No.'

The word rang out in the kitchen and he stopped and looked at her, a frown creasing his brow.

'I can't.'

'Don't you want to see Emma? I thought it would be what you wanted?' He looked puzzled. He flicked the switch on the coffee machine and walked over to her. 'What's the matter, Georgina?'

The concern that should have been in such words was missing, replaced by suspicion.

She bit down hard on her tongue. She wanted to tell him she knew about the letter, wanted to demand to know when he'd known about it. But as she looked up into his face, searched his eyes, all she could do was shake her head.

He reached out to her, holding her arms loosely, and

looked at her. 'What's wrong?' And this time he did sound concerned—but not for her, surely?

Wrong? *Everything* was wrong. And suddenly she knew she couldn't walk away from him without telling him why.

'You wouldn't understand.' She dropped her gaze, not able to bear his scrutiny any longer. And if he turned on the charm she'd never resist, never be able to explain anything.

'I could try.' His voice wasn't as firm as usual, and a waver of doubt lingered in it.

'No, Santos, you couldn't. You don't do love. You don't know how it feels to love someone so much you'd do anything for them, only to find they've deceived you.' The floodgates had opened and the words tumbled out as she looked up at him again, her eyes begging him to understand.

He let go of her arms and stepped back a pace, his tall, athletic body dominating her, as big a hurdle for her to overcome as the shock of seeing the letter.

'Don't do this to yourself, Georgina.'

'What do you want me to do? Shut myself away from love just like you have?'

He stood, immovable and silent as she waited for him to say something. Finally he spoke. 'You're right. I don't understand.'

She closed her eyes for a second against the pain of his admission, then opened them and looked at him, injecting as much firmness into her voice as possible. 'There's no reason for us to be together any more, Santos.' She hesitated as she saw the firm set of his shoulders. 'I'm going home.'

'Leaving, you mean?'

She watched his jaw clench as he stood, all but blocking her way out of the room.

'Yes, leaving.' She walked past him into the living area, her arm brushing his as she did so. The shock of that contact made her take in a sharp breath.

Santos clenched his hands into tight fists and bit down hard. He wanted to tell her to stay, but he didn't know how to—let alone why. Was it because not only was she the first woman who hadn't succumbed to his charm immediately, but the first woman to walk out on him?

But she *wasn't* the first woman to walk out on him. His mother had done the same. He'd stood and watched her leave, not understanding why. He'd felt helpless then too.

'Georgina.'

Her name snapped from his lips and for a moment he wondered if he'd actually spoken, then he heard her footsteps stop. Ominous silence filled the apartment.

He took in a deep breath and left the kitchen. She stood by the front door. Last time she'd tried to walk out on him he'd gone with her, but this time he couldn't. This time all he could do was watch her go. He couldn't risk opening his heart to her.

She raised her brows at him in question. She wouldn't even speak to him. Should he ask her to stay? Tell her he wanted to understand? That somewhere deep inside he was beginning to understand that elusive emotion love?

But still he couldn't.

'My solicitor will contact you with regard to the divorce.'

CHAPTER TWELVE

GEORGINA HELD THE letter in shaking hands. Santos hadn't wasted any time. He must have instructed his solicitor to file for divorce the moment she'd left his apartment. But what had she expected? That he would miss her? Come after her and declare his undying love?

He'd admitted that he didn't understand. They'd been almost his last words to her that morning.

Well, if he thought she'd hide away and meekly sign the papers then he had another thought coming. She would show him she could be as strong as he was. She would go down fighting. Fighting for the love she couldn't deny herself but had to.

With that in mind she tapped in to the same fiery determination that had given her the courage to march into his office and suggest they marry in the first place.

She put on her charcoal suit, her high heels and applied make-up. Then she pulled out her rarely used briefcase, put the letter inside and left, slamming the front door behind her. The few persistent photographers waiting intently outside her flat almost fazed her—they'd been camping out since the details of their marriage had hit the headlines, desperate for a story—but she passed through them, refusing to answer their questions or make a comment, quickly hailing a taxi.

By the time the taxi pulled up outside the Ramirez International offices it had started to rain, but she refused to rush in, head down against the rain. With her head held high she walked determinedly in, hardly giving the rain a second thought. Alone inside the lift she had time to check her appearance. It was vital she looked as sleek and sophisticated as possible. He must never know how devastated she was by the last two weeks, how little sleep she'd had recently.

She smoothed her hands down her skirt, took a deep breath and walked proudly out of the lift as soon as the doors opened. His secretary looked up as she pushed open the heavy glass door, but Georgina wasn't about to stop and ask permission to see her husband. He was going to listen to what she had say whether he liked it or not.

'Excuse me, Miss…' the shocked woman said as she made her way straight towards Santos's office.

Georgina stopped and turned to face her. 'It's Mrs,' she said firmly. 'Mrs Ramirez. And I'm here to see my husband.'

With that she turned and walked down the wide corridor that led to his office. Nothing was going to stop her now.

She paused briefly outside the door, her hand poised above the handle. Last time she'd stood there full of nerves, hardly able to believe she was about to propose to a man she'd never met.

Not for one minute had she thought she would find him so devastatingly attractive. And if she'd known that from the very first moment their eyes met a sizzle of desire would weave a spell so strong about them she would have turned and run, regardless of her motives.

She'd never expected to fall in love with him so quickly and so completely.

It had taken the letter instigating their divorce this morning for her to realise what she had to do—that she couldn't run any more. She'd stood by and watched two men she'd loved in very different ways from the way she loved Santos leave her. This time she was determined it would be different. This time she wouldn't shrink from the pain. This time she'd face it head-on.

She took a deep breath, gathered all her nerve and opened the door.

He was sitting at his desk, looking cool and composed. Her heart lurched just at seeing him, but she couldn't let that get the better of her now.

'To what do I owe this pleasure?'

His words were as cool and clear as a mountain stream but she couldn't falter now.

She put her briefcase on his desk, looked him in the eye and flicked it open. The dark depths of his eyes glittered as he watched every slow, purposeful movement. Taking out the letter, she placed it on the desk and then closed her briefcase.

'Don't play games, Santos. You know why I'm here. To put an end to our marriage.'

But not until he knew how she felt—knew she loved him. But telling someone who hated even to hear the word, let alone acknowledge the emotion, wasn't going to be easy.

He stood up, his height as intimidating as the breadth of his shoulders, but she held his gaze, trying hard to ignore the lurching of her heart.

'A marriage *you* instigated, Georgina. Here, in this very room.'

Santos moved from behind his desk and came closer to her, even now unable to resist the challenge her eyes fired at him. The first time she'd stood in his office, with fire and determination burning in her eyes, he'd wanted her.

He still wanted her. The force of the attraction hadn't lessened after spending the night with her. It had increased.

'One you willingly went along with. You changed it to suit your needs simply to get a business. You didn't think I was worthy of an explanation about the heir you needed to inherit everything.'

Her angry accusation had found its mark but he wouldn't let her see that.

'You make it sound calculated when it wasn't.'

He leant against the edge of his desk, folded his arms across his chest, fighting the urge to tell her everything. Then he remembered the pain in her voice when she'd told him she couldn't have children.

'I had no idea then that you couldn't have children.' His voice sounded unsteady even to him, and she closed her eyes, her long lashes shutting him out. He reached out to her, his hand touching her arm in a gesture of concern. She jumped back from him, her eyes now blazing. 'I'm sorry.'

She remained silent, her steady gaze holding his, and he wished she'd let him close. He'd never meant to hurt her. She had made him feel things he'd never thought he would. He still found it hard to comprehend the aching void in his life, an ache born out of love. But now she hated him.

'It's not that I *can't* have children, Santos.'

She spoke in a harsh, raw tone, her words snagging his conscience.

'I just couldn't bring a child into the world for that reason. I would have thought you of all people would understand that.'

His mind roared as the pain of his childhood rushed back at him. He'd been a mistake. One that had forced his mother into marriage with a man she couldn't love. With dreadful clarity he realised Georgina was right. If he'd had to he would have resorted to fathering a child just to get the business—a child that he didn't want. But wasn't that why he'd never married? To avoid such a decision?

Guilt slashed at him, making his next words harsh and serrated.

'If I could have avoided that I would have done.'

'The same as you could have avoided all this.' She pointed fiercely at the letter which lay on her briefcase. 'If you'd just talked to Carlo he wouldn't have had to go to the extremes he did. You denied Emma her big day.' She paused for a moment, her dark eyes flecked with gold sparks of determination. 'You should still talk to Carlo.'

Again she was right, and he gritted his teeth angrily. Talking to Carlo hadn't been an option before, but he could put that right. With an exasperated sigh he thrust himself away from the desk and strode towards the windows. Raindrops ran down them, diluting the view of London.

'Don't hide from it, Santos. You used me to score points on your own brother.'

The accusation flew at him but he kept his back resolutely to her. She made him feel exposed, vulnerable. Damn it, she made him feel emotions he didn't want— emotions he didn't need.

He turned to face her, and despite the hardness of her expression he saw the pain on her face, felt it radiating out.

'I was caught up in battle started by my mother. On her deathbed she made me promise never to let go of what was rightfully mine. When you so calmly offered marriage I never meant it to go any further.'

She made a sound that was a mixture of a gasp and a whimper—a sound full of pain. 'So seducing me, getting me into your bed, was a mistake too?'

He watched the rapid rise and fall of her chest and realised she wasn't nearly as rational as she wanted him to believe. 'No, Georgina,' he said as he moved towards her, his tone lower and huskier just from his memories of that night. 'I wanted you then as much as you wanted me.'

She blushed, and it shocked him to realise how he'd missed that innocent blush.

'I hate you for that.'

She hated him.

The venom in her voice left him in no doubt that she meant it and something changed inside him—as if somewhere a key had turned, unlocking something, some sort of emotion he wasn't yet ready for.

'Don't play the wounded party with me when you already have one very convenient marriage behind you.' Anger was the best line of defence. It would supress whatever it was she'd unlocked, because right now was not the time to analyse it.

'Richard never forced me into his bed. He didn't seduce me and I love him for that.'

Her words rang loud and clear in his head, as if she were at the top of a bell tower.

Santos gritted his teeth against those words. She'd loved Richard. It was as if he'd stepped back a few decades— as if he was witnessing the love his father and stepmother had shared, a love that had excluded him. But that exclusion hadn't made him feel raw with the pain he now felt.

'So you openly admit you married him for money?' He maintained his angry defence—anything other than accept what the raging pain inside him might mean.

'Yes, I did!' She flung the words at him. 'He asked

me, he saw I needed help and offered it, but I had no idea then just how ill he was. That's why he insisted I marry him—because he knew it was the only way to be sure he could provide for me into the future.'

He didn't want to hear it, yet at the same time he did.

Her face softened. 'He loved me, and for the chance he gave me I loved him.'

Santos was consumed with jealousy. He couldn't hear anything else other than that she'd loved Richard.

Georgina watched as Santos's face hardened. He couldn't even stand to hear the word *love*—couldn't contemplate such an emotion existed. He'd been denied it as a child and now, as an adult, he was determined to continue to deny himself.

She knew she was taunting him, using that word again, but she pressed on, hoping he'd see how she felt. 'I loved him in a compassionate way. There wasn't even a flicker of a spark of passion. It was a comfortable love. A safe love. Not the way I love you.'

Silence stretched between them. She remained tall and straight, even though she wanted to crumple on the floor right in front of him. The silence lengthened.

She shouldn't have said anything—shouldn't have opened her heart to his ridicule. Not when she knew how he scorned love. A lump gathered in her throat, almost choking her. This was no different from watching her father walk away. No different from having to say goodbye to Richard. As if her love had made them leave. She knew it wasn't true, but the pain of it had made it feel that way.

Fear of going through that again was what drove her now. It was why she'd come here—why she was exposing herself so utterly to Santos's contempt. If she was yet again to lose a man she loved, she was going to make her feelings clear.

'Do you really expect me to believe that when these last weeks have been nothing but a big lie, an act for you?' His words were sharp, heightening the tension between them.

'It wasn't a lie. There were times…' She paused, feeling heat spread across her cheeks as she remembered their wedding night, the passion they'd shared. That night there hadn't been any pretence, any acting on her part. She swallowed hard and continued. 'There were times when it was real.'

'Would that be the moment you kissed me at the party, or the morning you all but seduced me into staying on the yacht? Or the times when all your acting skills were called upon so that you could cover for Emma and Carlo running off to get married?'

The cynicism in his voice lashed at her like hail, each word stinging. How could he still believe she had had any part in it?

'I had no part whatsoever in their marriage,' she fumed at him, frustration rising like a spring tide. 'They deceived me too, Santos.' She stood facing him across the office, the expanse of soft cream carpet seeming to grow bigger between them with every passing second. 'They were desperate.'

'Back to that again, are we?'

Each word was like a bullet in her heart, each one wounding her further.

'I can see that whatever I say won't make any difference to you, Santos. You're incapable of love.'

'I made that perfectly clear from our very first meeting.'

In exasperation she covered her face with her hands

briefly, dropped her head and took in a long, shuddering breath. She couldn't take it any more, and gave vent to her frustration. 'You're so cold, so proud, and so damned stubborn. It was a mistake coming here.'

She pulled her jacket tighter about her body, as if it would deflect the hurt. For a moment his gaze lowered, caught by the movement. He took a step closer to her, his eyes meeting hers once more. She stepped back instinctively, needing space to be able to think.

'So why *did* you come, *mi esposa*? Tell me. Why?'

His accent became heavy and to her dismay he moved closer still, rendering thought almost impossible.

She whirled round and grabbed the papers from his desk, knocking her briefcase to the floor in the process. 'To sign these.' She waved the papers at him furiously. 'To put an end to something that should never have been started.'

'You could have sent them via your solicitor.' His calm voice irritated her further.

'And I wish I had. But I was taking a chance—a gamble.' She watched as he frowned, his dark eyes narrowing. 'I had to know.'

He said nothing, as if he was trying to take in what she said, so she dropped the papers on the desk purposefully, picked up a pen and signed, tossing the pen back onto the polished surface next to the papers.

'And now I do.'

Santos watched her sign the papers, listened as the pen crashed to the table. Each breath was hard to take, as if he was being suffocated. He hurt. Pain raced through him.

Even as she walked across the office he couldn't say a word, couldn't move, as if he'd been frozen in time. What the hell was the matter with him?

Something snapped, as if chains had broken. He inhaled deeply. The noise caught her attention and she turned to look at him. Her face was pale.

'I know I was a fool.' She threw the words at him as if he was nothing more than dirt at the edge of the road. 'I gambled and I lost.'

He tried to make sense of her words. What was she trying to tell him?

Not the way I love you.

His mind replayed what she'd said moments before. Purposefully he moved towards her, and when she turned again panic tore through him. If she left now he'd never see her again. He couldn't let her go. Not yet. He loved her; he'd just refused to admit it.

'I gambled too.'

The words hurried out and he clenched his hands, trying to keep himself from reaching for her, from preventing her from leaving.

She spun round and faced him again, her eyes sparkling with molten gold. 'Not with emotions, you didn't.'

She moved towards the door so suddenly he was taken off guard.

'You gambled with your brother's happiness, your greed. You won, Santos, and I hope you're happy.'

Happy? He was the furthest thing from happy. He hadn't felt like this since the day his mother had calmly left, saying goodbye as if she was just going shopping.

'Georgina.'

He tried to form the words, tried to tell her he hadn't gambled with Carlo's happiness—at least not intentionally. He wanted to tell her he'd gambled his own—and hers. Something he hadn't even realised until just a few seconds ago.

'Don't, Santos. I don't want to hear how you're driven by power and the need to control everything.'

'That may have been true once.' The words rushed out and for the first time in his adult life he knew he was losing.

'And it still is.' Her words were softer now, as if she'd given up fighting.

Mutely he watched as she opened the office door and paused in the doorway.

'Goodbye, Santos.'

His reaction was so swift he didn't have time to think. All he wanted to do was stop her from leaving, from walking out of his life for good. A life that wouldn't be the same once she'd gone.

He reached out and took hold of her arm, propelling her back into the room, and kicked the door shut on the enquiring glances of passing staff. She looked up at him, her brown eyes wide, darkening rapidly, her breathing hard and fast. But it was the current of pure electricity between them that told him he was doing the right thing.

He didn't want her to go. It wasn't possession. It wasn't power. It was more than that.

It was love.

He loved her.

This passionate woman had unlocked his heart, healed his wounds and shown him how love could be. He'd just been too stubborn to realise.

Georgina stepped back as he let her go, watching the show of emotions cross his handsome face. His pain and confusion were palpable, and she wanted to reach out to him—but to do so would be her undoing. Again she stepped back, but he moved closer until she had nowhere to go, the wall against her back.

'This is what you do to me.' His voice was hoarse with emotion. 'I can't think around you. I can't sleep without you by my side. I can't let you go.'

Her heart fluttered wildly and she dragged in a ragged breath. 'Santos…?' His name was barely a whisper from her lips.

He placed his palm on the wall above her shoulder, his face coming closer to hers, bringing him irresistibly close. Too close.

'I want you, Georgina,' he said huskily as he lowered his head to kiss her.

She moved sideways, away from temptation, but instantly he placed his other hand above her shoulder. Trapping her.

'I want you with a passion so raw it almost hurts. In fact it does.'

She looked up into his dark eyes, so close now she could see how enlarged his pupils were, see the desire swirling there.

Say it, her mind urged him, but she refused to utter the words aloud. The blood rushed in her ears as her heart thumped and she bit her bottom lip hard. She would never beg anyone to say it. If he loved her he had to tell her.

'I've never known this before, Georgina.'

'What?' she asked in a timid whisper, hardly daring to hear the answer.

'Love.'

Her heart sang as he rubbed the pad of his thumb over her lips, easing the pain where she'd bitten into them hard.

'I've never met a woman like you. From the moment you walked in here my fate was sealed. I just didn't know it then. I couldn't admit it—not even to myself.'

'Can you now?' she said in a cracked whisper.

He took her in his arms, pulled her close against him. 'I love you, Georgina. My heart belongs to you and I never want it back.'

Her knees weakened and his arms tightened around her as he brushed his lips over hers. She pushed against his chest so she could look into his eyes. 'I love you, Santos.'

With that he claimed her lips in a kiss so passionate it took all her breath away, leaving her light-headed.

'Can we start again? Begin our marriage now, with honesty and love?'

As she looked up into the handsome face of the man she loved sunbeams lit up the office, casting a glow all around them. Once again the storm was over—and this time it was for good.

'Only if it means we get another wedding night,' she teased.

He laughed gently. 'Now, *that* I can promise you, *mi esposa.*'

EPILOGUE

THE LEAVES WERE turning all shades of gold and brown as Georgina looked around the country cottage garden. Autumn sun cast its last lazy glow as it slid slowly behind the hill.

'Happy anniversary,' Santos said softly as he came to stand behind her.

He wrapped his arms around her. She leant back against him, happier than she'd ever been.

'You've brought me to the country for our anniversary weekend?' She hadn't doubted he'd remember their first anniversary—she just hadn't expected him to help her realise one of her dreams, even if it was only for a weekend. It would be a wonderful place to give him her gift.

'I've done more than that, Georgie.' He nuzzled her hair and then kissed her head. 'I've bought you this piece of the English countryside. This place is yours.'

Georgina swivelled round in his arms and looked up at him, excitement almost exploding inside her. 'This place? You've bought it?'

'I most certainly have, and now is your chance to show me just what is so wonderful about living in the countryside.'

'Oh, Santos, it's perfect.'

She couldn't believe that this cottage, with roses rambling around the front door, was all hers. He opened the door and led her inside. It had been furnished and decorated to the highest standard, just as she would have expected from Santos, but it still maintained that country charm she'd always longed for.

'In fact it's more than perfect.'

'There's more, *mi esposa*.'

'What more could there be than this?'

'Emma and Carlo will be joining us.'

'They will?'

'It's their anniversary too, and I thought it would be nice to be together, but we still have a few hours before they arrive. Carlo has become a workaholic since he opened his own hotel, and he wouldn't leave until he'd sorted everything out for the weekend.'

Georgina laughed at the image of her brother-in-law putting the business before a weekend with Emma. 'Perhaps there is more of you in him than you realise?' she teased, and reached up to brush a kiss on his lips.

'Well, you should know what we Ramirez men are like by now.'

He kissed her and passion sparked to life, zipping between them.

She pulled back from him and looked into his eyes, which were darkening by the second. 'I have a gift for you too.'

He put her at arm's length and smiled. 'Can you beat this?' he asked as he took her into the living room, which looked cosy and inviting.

'You're going to be a father.'

'Are you serious?' He looked deep into her eyes, studying her reaction.

She nodded, unable say anything. After years of telling herself she'd be the worst mother a child could have, she was still apprehensive.

'When?' His words seemed choked and hard to come by.

'You're impatient, aren't you?' she teased gently.

'Not impatient. Overjoyed. And very much in love with you.' He kissed her softly and with so much love she fought back the tears of happiness that threatened.

'April,' she said as his lips left hers. 'Our baby will be born in April.'

'That,' he said huskily as he smiled down at her, 'is a cause for celebration.'

She laughed and snuggled against him, relishing the strength of his arms around her. 'I love you so much, Santos,' she said as she heard his heartbeat.

He swept her off her feet and, looking down at her, smiled. 'I'm the happiest man alive and it's all thanks to you. How did I ever manage to exist before you arrived in my life?'

He edged his way out of the living room towards the stairs, a stream of Spanish rushing from his lips as he looked at the narrow staircase.

Georgina laughed.

'Put me down.' She placed her hand on his cheek and kissed him briefly. 'This is one flight of stairs you *won't* be able to carry me up.'

* * * * *

A DEAL
WITH DEMAKIS

BY
TARA PAMMI

Tara Pammi can't remember a moment when she wasn't lost in a book—especially a Mills & Boon romance, which provided so much more excitement to a teenager than a mathematics textbook. It was only years later, while struggling with her two-hundred-page thesis in a basement lab, that Tara realised what she really wanted to do: write a romance novel. She already had the requirements—a wild imagination and a love for the written word.

Tara lives in Colorado, with the most co-operative man on the planet and two daughters. Her husband and daughters are the only things that stand between Tara and a full-blown hermit life with only books for company.

Tara would love to hear from readers. She can be reached at tara.pammi@gmail.com or via her website: www.tarapammi.com.

For the strongest woman I know-my mother.

CHAPTER ONE

"Ms. NELSON IS here, Nikos."

Nikos Demakis checked his Rolex and smiled. His little lie had worked, not that he had doubted it. Not an hour had passed since he had had his secretary place the call.

"Instruct security to bring her up," he said, and turned back to his guests.

Another man might have felt a twinge of regret for having manipulated the situation to serve his purpose so well. Nikos didn't.

Christos, it was getting more unbearable by the minute to see his sister trail after her boyfriend, trying to make Tyler remember, and playing the role of the tragic lover to the hilt. Only instead of the usual volatility, Nikos was beginning to see something else in her gaze. Obviously he had underestimated how much power Tyler had gained over her. The announcement that they were engaged had stirred even his grandfather's attention.

Just as Nikos had expected, Savas had laid down the ultimatum. Another excuse for the old tyrant to postpone declaring Nikos the CEO for Demakis International.

Sort out Venetia and the company's yours, Nikos. Take away her bank account, her expensive car and her clothes.

Lock her up. She will forget that boy soon enough once she starts remembering what it feels like to go hungry again.

Nikos's gut roiled, just remembering Savas's words.

It *was* time to get the charming, manipulative Tyler out of her life. However, he had no intention of starving his sister to achieve that end. Nikos had done, and would do, anything for survival but hurt Venetia in any way. But the fact that Savas had not only considered it but dangled it like an option in front of Nikos, expected Nikos to put it into action, was unsettling in the least.

His expression must have reflected his distaste, because Nina, the leggy brunette he usually got together with when he was in New York, slipped to the other corner of the lounge.

"Ms. Nelson would like to meet you in the café across the street," his assistant whispered in his ear.

Nikos scowled. "No."

Bad enough that he would have to deal with not one but two emotionally volatile, out-of-control women in the coming days. He wanted to get this meeting done with as soon as possible and get back to Athens. He couldn't wait to see Savas's reaction when he told him of his triumph.

He grabbed a drink from a passing waiter and took a sip of the champagne. It slid like liquid gold against his tongue, richer and better tasting for his sweet victory. Against Savas's dire predictions that Nikos wouldn't find an investor, Nikos had just signed a billion-dollar contract with Nathan Ramirez, an up-and-coming entrepreneur, by granting exclusive rights to a strip of undeveloped land on one of the two islands owned by the Demakis family for almost three centuries.

It was a much-needed injection of cash for Demakis International without losing anything, and a long-fought chance that Nikos had been waiting for. This was one victory Savas couldn't overlook anymore. His goal was so close that he was thrumming with the energy of it.

But a month of intense negotiations meant he was at the tail end of the high. And his body was downright starved for sex. Swallowing the last sip of his champagne, he nodded at Nina. Ms. Nelson would wait.

Just as they reached the door to his personal suite, the sound of a laugh from the corridor stalled him.

He ordered Nina back into the lounge and walked into the corridor. The question for his security guard froze on his lips as he took in the scene in front of him.

Clutching her abdomen, the sounds of her harsh breathing filling the silence around her, a woman knelt, bent over, on the thickly carpeted floor. His six-foot-two security guard, Kane, hulked over her, his leathery face wreathed in concern. The overhead ceiling lights picked out the hints of burnished copper in her hair.

Nikos stepped closer, curiosity overpowering everything else. "Kane?"

"Sorry, Mr. Demakis," Kane replied, patting the woman's slender back with his huge palm. A strange familiarity with a woman he'd just met. "Lexi took one look at the elevator and refused to use it."

Lexi Nelson.

Nikos stared at the woman's bowed head. She was still doubled over, slender shoulders falling and rising. "She did what?"

Kane didn't raise his head. "She said no one was forcing her into the elevator. That's why she had me call you back asking you to meet her at the cafe."

Nikos tilted his head and studied the state-of-the-art elevator system on his right side. One sentence from her file popped into his head.

Trapped in an elevator once for seventeen hours.

Of course she could have turned around and left. His irritation only grew, a perverse reaction because her leaving wouldn't serve his purpose at all. "She walked up nineteen floors?"

Kane nodded, and Nikos noticed that even his breathing was a little irregular. "And you walked up the stairs with her?"

"Yep. I told her she was going to collapse halfway through. I mean, look at her." His gaze swept over her, a curious warmth in it. "And she challenged me." He shoved her playfully with a shoulder, and Nikos watched, strangely fascinated. The woman unfolded from her bent-over stance and nudged Kane back with a surprising display of strength for someone so...tiny.

"I almost beat you, too, didn't I?" she said, still sounding breathless.

Kane laughed and tugged her up, again his touch overtly familiar for a woman he met a mere twenty minutes ago. As she straightened her clothes, Nikos understood the reason for Kane's surprise at her challenge.

With her head hardly reaching his shoulder, Lexi Nelson was small. Maybe five feet one or two at best, and most of that was legs. The strip of exposed flesh between her pleated short skirt and knee-high leather boots was... distracting, to say the least.

Her shoulders were slim to the point of delicate, her small breasts only visible because of her exertion. Wide-set eyes in her perfectly oval face, a dazzling light blue, were the only feature worth a second look. A mouth too wide for her small face, tilted up at the corners, still smiling at Kane.

Honey-gold hair cut short to her nape, in addition to her

slim body, made her look like a teenage boy rather than an adult woman. Except for the fragility of her face.

The image of an Amazonian woman on her crinkled T-shirt—long-legged, big-breasted, clad in a leather outfit with a gun in her hand—invited a second look, and not only because of the exquisite detail of it but also because the woman in the sketch was a direct contrast to the woman wearing it.

"Please escort Ms. Nelson into my office, Kane," Nikos said. Her blue gaze landed on him and widened. "You are causing too much distraction here." Her smile slipped, a tiny frown tying her brows. "Wait in my office and I will see you in half an hour."

He didn't turn around when he heard her gasp.

Lexi Nelson snapped her mouth shut as Nikos Demakis turned around and left. He was rude, terse and had a spectacular behind—the errant thought flashed through her mind. Surprised by her own observation, she pulled her gaze upward, her breath still not back to normal. Powerfully wide shoulders moved with arrogant confidence.

She hadn't even got a good look at the man, yet she had the feeling that she had somehow angered him. She trembled as the elevator doors opened with a ping on her side. Ignoring Kane's call, she marched down the path his rude boss had taken, wondering what she had done to put him out of sorts.

She had walked up nineteen floors and had almost given herself a heart attack in the process. But she couldn't risk leaving without seeing him, not until she knew how Tyler was. She had planned to dog his New York base the whole week, determined to get answers, until she had received a call from his secretary summoning her here. The moment she had introduced herself at the security desk and asked to see Mr. Demakis, she had been herded to the elevator which she had promptly escaped from.

Lexi came to an abrupt stop after stepping into a dimly lit lounge that screamed understated elegance. High ceilings, pristine white carpets and floor-to-ceiling glass windows that offered a fantastic view of Manhattan's darkening skyline. A glittering open bar stood on one side.

It was as if she had stepped into a different world.

She worked her jaw closed, the eerie silence that befell the room penetrating her awe. While she had been busy gaping at the lush interior of the lounge, about ten men and women stared back at her, varying levels of shock reflected in their gazes. It was as though she were an alien that had beamed down from outer space via transporter right in front of their eyes.

She offered them a wide smile, her hands clutching the leather strap of her bag.

Having realized that she had followed him, Nikos Demakis uncoupled himself from a gorgeous brunette he was leading out of the lounge.

Lexi clutched the strap tighter, fighting the flight response her brain was urging her into.

"I asked you to wait in my office, Ms. Nelson."

Her mushy brain was a little slow processing his words when presented with such a gorgeous man. Dark brown eyes fringed by the thickest lashes held hers, challenging her to drop her gaze. The Italian suit, she would bet her last dollar that it was handmade, lovingly draped the breadth of his wide shoulders, tapering to a narrow waist. A strange fluttering started in her belly as she raised her gaze back to his arresting face.

Nikos Demakis was, without exaggeration, the most stunning man she had ever laid eyes on. Easily two inches over six feet, and with enough lean muscle to fill out his wide frame, he was everything she had been feverishly dreaming about for the past few months; her space pirate, the villainous captain who had kidnapped her heroine, Ms. Havisham, intent on opening the time portal.

Her heart racing, her fingers itched to open the flap of her bag and reach for the charcoal pencil she always kept with her. She had done so many sketches of him but she hadn't been satisfied.

A real-life version of Spike, marauding space pirate extraordinaire.

"Excuse me? Are you drunk, Ms. Nelson?"

Blushing, Lexi realized she had said those words out loud. There was a sly look in his eyes that sent a shiver down her spine. As if he could see through her skin into the strange sensation in her gut and understood it better than she. "Of course not. I just…"

"Just what?"

She pasted on a smile. "You reminded me of someone."

"If you are done daydreaming, we can talk," he said, pointing toward a door behind her.

"There's no need to walk away from your…party," she said, cutting her gaze away from him. *What had she done wrong?* "I just want to know how Tyler is."

He flicked his head to the side in an economic movement, and his guests moved inward into the lounge, or rather retreated from her. Even their conversations restarted, their apparent curiosity swept away by his imperious command. Her spine locked at the casual display of power. "Not here," he said, and whispered something in the brunette's ear, while his gaze never moved from her. "Let's go into my office."

Lexi licked her lips and took a step to the side as he passed her. Now that she had his complete attention, a sliver of apprehension streaked through her. She looked around the lounge. Safety in numbers. Really, what could he do to her with his guests outside the door? But the sheer size of the man, coupled with that unexplained contempt in his gaze, brought out her worst fears. "There's nothing to talk about, Mr. Demakis. I just want to know where Tyler is."

He didn't break his stride as he spoke over his shoulder. "It was not a request."

Hints of steel coated the velvety words. Realizing that she was staring at his retreating back again, she followed him. Within minutes, they reached his state-of-the-art office, this one with an even better view of Manhattan. She wondered if she would be able to see the tiny apartment she shared with her friends in Brooklyn from here.

A massive mahogany desk dominated the center of the room. A sitting area with its back to a spectacular view of the Manhattan skyline lay off to one side and on the other was a computer, a shredder and a printer.

He shrugged his jacket off and threw it carelessly onto the leather chair. The pristine white shirt made him look even more somber, bigger, broader, the dark shadow of his olive skin under it drawing her gaze.

He undid the cuffs and folded the sleeves back, the silver Rolex on his wrist glinting in the muted light.

Leaning against the table, he stretched his long legs in front of him. Whatever material those trousers were made of, it hugged his muscular thighs. "I asked you to wait."

Coloring, Lexi tugged her gaze up. What was she doing, blatantly staring at the man's thighs? "I walked up nineteen floors for a few minutes of your time," she finally said, feeling intensely awkward under his scrutiny. He just seemed so big and coordinated and thrumming with power that for the first time in her life, she wished she had been tall and graceful. A more nonsensical thought she had never had. "Tell me how Tyler is and I'll be on my way."

He pushed off from the table and she tried not to scuttle sideways like a frightened bird. Hands tucked into the pockets of his trousers, he towered over her, cramming his huge body into her personal space. His gaze swept over her, somehow invasive and dismissive at the same time. The urge to smooth out her hair, straighten her T-shirt, attacked again.

"Did you just roll out of bed, Ms. Nelson?"

Her mouth dropped open; she stared at him for several seconds. The man was a mannerless pig. "As a matter of fact, yes. I was sleeping after an all-nighter when the call came in. So please forgive me if my attire doesn't match your million-dollar decor." For some reason, he clearly disliked her. It made her crabby and unusually offensive. "FYI, you might have nothing better to do with your time than loll around with your girlfriend, but I have a job. Some of us actually have to work for a living."

Amusement inched into his gaze. "You think I don't work?"

"Then why the sneering attitude as if your time is more precious than mine? You obviously make more money per minute than I do, but mine pays for my food," she said, shocked at how angry she was getting. Which was really strange. "Now, the sooner you answer my question, the sooner I'll be out of your hair."

He shifted closer, unblinking and Lexi's heart pounded faster. A hint of woodsy cologne settled tantalizingly over her skin. She stood her ground, loath to betray how unsettling she found his proximity. "You're here for your precious Tyler. No one's forcing you. You can turn around and walk down the stairs the same way you came up."

Lexi wanted to do exactly that, but she couldn't. He had no idea how much it had cost her to come here to his office. "I had a phone call from someone who refused to identify himself that Tyler has been in a car accident along with your sister." Maybe this was Nikos Demakis's response to his worry over his sister? Maybe usually, he was a much more human and less-heartless alien? "How is he? Was your sister hurt, too? Are they okay?"

His brows locked together into a formidable frown, he stared down at her. "You're asking after the woman who, for all intents and purposes, stole your boyfriend of—" he turned and picked up a file from the desk behind him in a casual movement and thumbed through it "—let me see, eleven years?"

There was no winning with the infuriating man. "I thought maybe there was a reason you were being a grouchy, arrogant prig—you know, like worry about your sister. But obviously you're a natural ass…" Her words stuttered to a halt, the bold letters *N-E-L-S-O-N* written in red on the flap of the file ramming home what she had missed.

She moved quickly, a lifetime of ducking and evading bred into her muscles, and snatched the file out of his hands. She found little satisfaction that she had surprised him.

Cold dread in her chest, she thumbed through the file. There were pages and pages of information about her and Tyler, their whole lives laid out in cold bare facts, complete with mug shots of both of them.

Spent a year in juvenile detention center at sixteen for a household robbery.

Those words below her picture felt as if they could crawl out of the paper and burn her skin. Sweat trickled down between her shoulder blades even though the office was crisply cool. She dropped the file from her hands. "Those are supposed to be sealed records," she said, struggling through the waves of shame. She marched right up to him and shoved him with her hands, the crushing unfairness of it all scouring through her. "What's going on? Why would you collect information on me? I mean, we've never even laid eyes on each other until now."

"Calm down, Ms. Nelson," he said, his voice gratingly silky, as he held her wrists with a firm grip.

The sight of her small, pale hands in his big brown ones sent a kick to her brain. She jerked her hands back. *How dare he toy with her?*

"I'll lose my job if that information gets out." She clutched her stomach, fear running through her veins. "Do you know what it feels like to live on mere specks of food, Mr. Demakis? To feel as though your stomach will eat itself if you don't have something to eat soon? To live on the streets, not knowing if you will have a safe place to sleep in? That's where I will be again." She looked around herself, at the thick cream carpet, at the million-dollar view out the window, at his designer Italian suit and laughed. The bitter sound pulsed around them. "Of course you don't. I bet you don't even know what hunger feels like."

His mouth tightened, throwing the cruel, severe lines of his face into sharp focus. For an instant, his gaze glowed with a savage intensity as though there was something very primitive beneath the sophistication. "Don't be so sure of that, Ms. Nelson. You'll be surprised at how well I understand the urge to survive." He bent and picked up the file. "I don't care if you robbed one house or a whole street to feed yourself. Nothing in the file has any relevance to me except your relationship with Tyler."

His smooth mask was back on as he handed the file to her. "Do what you want with it."

Nikos smiled as the slip of a woman snatched the file from him. Clutching the file to her body, she moved to the high-

end shredder, ripped the pages with barely controlled vehemence and pushed them in.

With his photographic memory, he didn't need to refer
to the file, though. She was twenty-three years old, grew
up in foster care, had little to no education, worked as a
bartender at Vibe, a high-end club in Manhattan and had
had one boyfriend, the charming Tyler.

Based on the personal history between her and Tyler,
and the codependent relationship between them, Nikos had
expected someone meek, plain, biddable, easily led, someone with no self-esteem.

The woman standing in front of the shredder, while
small and not really a beauty, didn't fall into any of those
categories. The tight set of her shoulders, the straight spine,
even her stance, with her legs apart and hands on her hips,
brought a smile to his face. The fact that she wasn't exactly what he had been expecting—really, though, what
kind of a woman would be concerned about her lover's new
girlfriend?—meant he would have to alter his strategy.

She turned around, dark satisfaction glittering in her
gaze. The hum of the shredder died down leaving the air
thick with tension.

He ran his thumb over his jaw. "Are you satisfied now?"

"No," she said, her mouth set into a straight, uncompro-
mising line. "Whatever you might have read in that file,
it should tell you I'm not an idiot. It was one paper copy I
shredded. You and your P.I. still have the soft copy."

He raised a brow as she picked up the paperweight from
his desk and tossed it into the air and then caught it. "Then
what was the point in shredding it?"

Up went the paperweight again, her blue gaze, alight
with defiance, never wavering from him. "A symbolic act,
an outlet because as much as I wish it—" she nodded at the

shredder behind her and caught the paperweight in a deft movement "—I can't do that to you."

Nikos reached her in a single step and caught the paperweight midair this time, his hand grazing hers. She jumped back like a nervous kitten. "I mean you no harm, Ms. Nelson."

"Yeah, right. And I'm a Victoria's Secret model."

Laughter barreled out of him. Her blue eyes wide, she stared at him.

She was no model with her boyish body and nonexistent curves. Yet there was something curiously appealing about her even to his refined tastes. "I think you're a foot shorter—" he let his gaze rove over her small breasts, and her hands tightened around her waist "—and severely lacking in several strategic places."

Crimson slashed her cheeks. She lifted her chin, her gaze assessing him, and despite himself, he was impressed. "Why the power play? You didn't open that file in front of me to double-check your facts. You wanted me to know that you had all that information on me. Is that how you get your kicks? By collecting people's weaknesses and using them to serve your purpose?"

"Yes," he replied, and the color leached from her face. He has no delusions about himself. He was by no means above using any information in his hands to gain the upper edge in business or life. And especially now when it concerned his sister's well-being, he would do anything. If you didn't protect the ones who depended on you, what was the point of it all? "I need you to do something for me and I can't take no for an answer."

CHAPTER TWO

DISBELIEF PINCHING HER mouth, she stared at him. "It didn't occur to you to just ask nicely?"

He covered the distance between them, shaking his head. She stepped back instantly, but not before he caught her scent. And racked his brains trying to place it. "Nicely? Which planet are you from? Nothing in this world gets done with please and thank you. Hasn't your life already taught you that? If you want something, you have to take it, grab it with both hands or you'll be left behind with nothing. Isn't that why you robbed that house?"

"Just because life gets hard doesn't mean you lose sight of the good things." Her hands tightened around the strap of her bag, her skin tugged tight over her cheekbones. "I robbed the house because it was either that or starve for another day. It doesn't mean I'm proud of my actions, doesn't mean I don't wish to this day that I had found another way. Now, please tell me what happened to Tyler."

Her words struck Nikos hard, delaying his response. The woman was nothing short of an impossible paradox. "Venetia and he were in a car accident."

Her face pale, she flopped onto the leather couch behind her, her knees tucked together. "Physically, there's not a scratch on him," Nikos offered, the pregnant silence grating on his nerves.

She pushed off from the couch again. "The person who called me made it sound like it was much worse. I kept asking for more details but he wouldn't answer my questions."

She walked circles around him, running long fingers over her bare nape. Once again, the boyish cut only brought his attention to her delicate features. Bones jutted out from her neck, the juncture where it met her shoulders infinitely delicate.

Her knuckles white around her bag, she came to a stop in front of him. Shock danced in her face. "It was your doing. You had one of your minions call me and make it sound like that. Why?"

He shrugged. "I needed you to be here."

"So you manipulated the truth?"

"A little."

Her forehead tied into a delicate little frown, she cast him a sharp look.

"I don't have a conscience when it comes to what I want, even more so when it comes to my sister, Ms. Nelson. So if you are waiting for me to feel guilty, it's just a waste of time. Except for a hitch in his memory, your ex is fine."

"A hitch in his memory?"

"A short-term memory loss." He leaned against his desk. "To my sister's eternal distress, he doesn't remember anything of their meeting, or their plans to marry."

He paused, watching her closely, and right on cue, the color leached from her face.

Her teeth dug into her lower lip. "They are engaged?"

He nodded.

She ran a shaking hand over her nape again. "I don't understand why you are telling me this."

"All he remembers is you, and he keeps asking for you. It's driving Venetia up the wall."

He thought he would see triumph, pure female spite.

Because whatever else he might think, Venetia *had* stolen Tyler from this woman. He braced himself for a deluge of tears, OMGs and "why-did-this-happen-to-me?"s. At least, that's how Venetia had reacted, even though she had been pretty unscathed from the accident. But once the doctors had informed them about the memory loss, it had become worse as though she had taken on the leading role in a Shakespearean tragedy. And contrary to his expectations, that their relationship would lose its appeal, Venetia had only held on harder to Tyler.

Seconds ticked by. Ms. Nelson stared out through the glass windows, but the tears didn't fall. She took a deep breath, pressed her fingers to her forehead and turned toward him. "Where is he now, Mr. Demakis?"

The glimmer of stark pain in her eyes rendered his thought process still. Much as he would detest it, he wanted her to throw a tantrum. That he could handle. This quiet pain of hers, the depth of emotion in her eyes, however, he wanted no part of it.

It reminded him of another's pain, another's grief so much that a chill swept through him. He had worked very hard to keep his father's face neatly tucked away. And he wanted to leave it that way. "On our island in Greece."

"Of course, it is not enough that your sister and you are gorgeous. You have to own an island, too."

He smiled at the caustic comment, at the glimpse of anger.

"All the lengths you have gone to get me here, I'm assuming it's not for the pleasure of giving me bad news. No more games. What is it that you want me to do?"

"Come with me to Greece…take care of him. Venetia won't stop turning everyone's life into a circus until he remembers her."

"You're kidding, right?" Her gaze flew to him, shock

dancing in its blue depths. "Did I miss the memo on amnesia that says there's a switch to turn it on and off? An ex's kiss, maybe? What makes you so sure that I can just make him remember her?"

"Your ex wants to come back to New York so that he can see you," he said, joining her in the small sitting area. "Venetia won't let him out of her sight until he remembers their great love. His confusion and her ongoing drama are driving me insane."

"And I care about this why?"

Her tone was so irreverent that it was like seeing a different woman. "You don't. That's why the little twisting of the truth."

The moment he stepped into the sitting area, she tensed. Nikos could almost feel her suspended breath as she wondered if he would sit too close. Stifling a curse, he settled onto the coffee table instead. Instantly, her breathing evened out. Never had a woman irritated him so well and so easily.

"I want her future settled. More than anything else in the world. Which means, the only thing to do is for you to join them. With the long history between you two and your unwavering support now, Tyler will mend soon. He will remember his undying love for Venetia, and they can ride off into the sunset together," he said, struggling to keep the mockery out of his tone.

She settled back onto the couch, and crossed her legs. "You've got balls asking me to help you."

Nikos grinned. There was such a change in her demeanor, in the way she met his gaze head-on from the woman who had timidly followed him in. Because she knew now that he needed her, and she was adjusting her attitude based on that just as he had done. And to his surprise, he liked this gutsy version of her so much better.

"My…*manhood* has nothing to do with the matter at hand. It's something I need to do for my sister, and I'm doing it."

Pink flooded her cheeks and she averted her gaze from him as though she had just realized what she had blurted out. He had a feeling she did that at lot—spoke without thinking it through.

Scooting to the edge of the couch, she pointed a finger in his direction, her little body shaking. "Just a month ago, you had two giant brutes pick me up like I was a sack of garbage and had them throw me out, and I mean, they *literally* dropped me on that concrete road outside your estate in the Hamptons."

She had no idea how much he regretted that decision. By the time Venetia had dropped her bombshell at that very party, announcing that she and Tyler were engaged, Lexi Nelson had already been thrown out.

"You somehow bypassed security, broke into my estate and almost ruined the party, Ms. Nelson. It seems your colorful past is not as completely behind you as you would believe," he said lazily, and her color rose again. "You're lucky I didn't have you arrested for trespassing."

Her chin tilted up stubbornly. "I meant no harm. All I wanted was to see Tyler, even then."

"Ah, yes. The wonderful Tyler. For whom you will risk anything, it seems." He bent forward, leaning his elbows on his knees. "The fact that he didn't answer your million calls on his cell phone didn't alert you that he wanted to have nothing to do with you? Because you don't strike me as the particularly stupid kind," he added, more than a whisper of curiosity niggling him.

A shadow darkened her blue gaze, and he knew she was remembering her conversation with Tyler. "He was angry with me, yes. But I didn't want him to make a mistake."

"You don't really believe that even now, do you? Because that would make you the most pathetic woman on the planet."

Her blue gaze widened. "Wow, you really don't believe in pulling your punches."

"Because hearing the actual truth instead of your own romantic version sticks in your throat?" he said, a burst of caustic anger filling him. He ran a shaking hand through his hair, annoyed by the strength of his own reaction. Telling this woman that her love for that boy had turned her into a fool was not his responsibility. But making sure his sister didn't fall into the same mold was. "You're right. I don't care why you went to see him. All I care about now is that you take care of him."

"Why go there? Why not just bring him back here, back to New York? As you've already learned from that file, Tyler and I have lived here our whole lives. I'm sure being in a new country amidst strangers doesn't help."

"The answer to that question is one word, Ms. Nelson. *Venetia*. Believe me when I say that it's better for all parties involved if we do this there."

She nodded and stood up.

He studied her, her calm demeanor not sitting well with him. She was ready to abandon the sense she was born with for the man she loved, even if he had kicked her to the curb. *Was all that fire he had spied in her just a sham? And why did he care when that's what he needed to happen?* "I have already arranged for you to leave immediately with your boss at Vibe."

She met his gaze then, a quick flash of anger in hers. "Of course you have." She pulled her bag over her head and adjusted it over her breasts.

Coming to a halt at the door, she tugged it open, and leveled that steady gaze at him again. "I find it really curious. Why would you think you needed all that information on me?"

Nikos shrugged. "Let's just say I wanted to make sure you accepted my…proposal."

She didn't even blink. "And yet you were also very confident that I would come. Please tell me."

If she wanted to hear what he found so distasteful about her coming here, so be it. "I was standing in the corridor with Venetia when you managed to sneak into the party that night. I heard what he said to you."

She flinched, her tight grip on the doorknob turning her knuckles white. He couldn't contain the disdain that crept into his words nor did he want to. And the way she stared at him, focused, every muscle in her face stiff and tense, she heard it, too. "He called me a selfish bitch who couldn't stand the fact that he had found love with someone else and moved on, that I couldn't be happy for him," she recited, as though she was reading lines from a play.

"He conveniently turned his head and walked away while you were thrown on the street," he continued, refusing to lay off.

"And you thought no self-respecting woman would agree to help him after that."

He nodded. "I thought I would need some additional… *leverage* to persuade you. Obviously I don't."

She raised an eyebrow, her chin tilting up. "No?"

"You're here, aren't you?" he said, standing up. Lexi Nelson was the epitome of everything that had gone wrong in his life in the name of love. He felt a tight churning in his stomach, a memory of the grief and rage that he had propelled into the need to survive, for his sister's and his sake. "One call and barely an hour later, you come running back for him, your heart in your throat, and you walked up nineteen floors. Why ask so many questions, Ms. Nelson?

Why pretend as though there's even a doubt as to whether you will drop everything to take care of him?"

Lexi struggled to remind herself that Nikos Demakis didn't know her, that his opinion didn't matter. But the incredible arrogance in his words that she had fallen into his plans exactly as he had intended chafed her raw.

How she wished she could turn around, throw his disdain back in his face.

But this wasn't about the infuriating man in front of her. This was about her friend, her family, the one person in the entire world who had always cared about her. After Tyler's caustic words, after this last fight, she had finally accepted that whatever had been between them had never stood a chance. And she had no idea why.

It would hurt to see Venetia Demakis with him for sure. The young heiress was everything Lexi wasn't. Rich, sophisticated and exceptionally beautiful.

But what if she was being given another chance to right things between her and Tyler, to have her friend back? He had been there every time she had needed him. Now it was her turn.

The scorn of the man in front of her, however, was a bitter pill to swallow. She was going to say yes, but it didn't mean she had to do it on his conditions.

She leveled her gaze at him, stubbornly reminding herself that Nikos Demakis needed her just as much as she needed to see Tyler. And she couldn't let him forget that, couldn't let him think for one moment that he had the upper hand. "You have made a miscalculation, Mr. Demakis. I have no wish to help you or your sister."

His dark brown gaze gleaming, he neared her before she could blink.

She stood her ground, but she was too much of a chicken

to wait and hear what he would threaten her with. "Not without a price."

"What is it that you want, Ms. Nelson?"

"Money," she said, satisfaction pouring through her at the surprise in his eyes. She smiled for the first time in more than a month. Her heart thundering inside her chest, she closed the door and leaned back against it. "You have oodles of it and I have none."

The dark browns of his eyes flared with something akin to admiration. Lexi frowned. She had meant to anger him, needle him, at least. She had uttered the first thing that had come to her mind. Instead, the edge of his contempt, which had been a tangible thing until now, was blunted.

"Quite the little opportunist, aren't you?" he said, gazing at her with intense interest.

There was no rancor in his words. Struggling to keep her confusion out of her face, she smiled with as much fake confidence as she could muster. "I have to protect my interests, don't I? You're asking me to put my life here on hold and place my trust in someone like you."

He laughed. "Someone like me?"

"Yes, by your own admission, you don't have a conscience when it comes to what you want. What if things don't go your way, what if something happens that you don't like? You'll blame me…"

"Like what?"

"Like Tyler regaining his memory and deciding he didn't want to be with Venetia anymore."

A feral light gleamed in his gaze. "That would not do."

"I have no older brother to rescue me, no family to watch out for my welfare," she said, swallowing the painful truth. "For all I know, you and your sister could do untold harm to me, so I'm being prepared."

"Believe me, Ms. Nelson. Family is highly overrated.

You grew up in foster care—doesn't that tell you something?"

The vehemence in his tone gave her pause. She had wondered a million times why her parents might have given her up, wondered in the lowest times if there was anyone who thought of her, who wondered about her, too. Except for excruciating sadness and uncertainty, it had brought her nothing. "But you're here, aren't you? Taking every step to ensure Tyler remembers your sister, setting her world to rights. Making sure no one deprives her of her happily ever after."

"What if I don't agree to your condition?" He moved in that economic way of his and locked her in place against the door. His scent teased her nostrils, his size, the quiet hum of power packed into his large body, directed toward her making her tremble from head to toe. He had neatly sidestepped her question. "What if, instead, I alert your boss about your colorful teenage years?"

It took everything within her to stay unmoving, to meet his gaze when all she wanted was to skittle away from him. *Don't betray your fear,* she reminded herself, even though she had no idea if it was his threatening words or his nearness that was causing it. "You will ruin me and it will be pointless, but it won't go like that. Are you that heartless that you would wreck a perfect stranger's life because she won't suit your plans?"

"Yes, I will," he whispered, moving even closer. His palm landed on the door, near her face, his breath feathering over her. The heat of his body coated her with an awareness she didn't want. Every inch of her froze, and she struggled to pull air into her lungs. "Make no mistake about me. To ensure my sister's happiness, I will do anything that is required of me, and not feel a moment's regret about it."

Her stomach tight, she forced herself to speak. She had

no doubt that he was speaking the truth. "But it doesn't really serve your purpose, does it? Ruining me won't set your sister's world right. You need me, and you don't like it." His mouth tightened an infinitesimal amount and she knew she had it right. "That's why you collected all that information. Because you needed at least an illusion that you have the upper hand in the situation, to make sure you're the one with control."

Something dawned in his gaze and she knew she had hit the nail on its head. Her pulse jumped beneath her skin. "You have twisted something very straightforward into a game. I would have dropped everything to take care of Tyler. But now, I'll only come if you agree to my condition," she finished, every nerve ending in her stretched tight.

She was playing a dangerous game. But she would do this only on her terms, refused to let herself be bullied again. Even for Tyler.

His gaze swept over her. "Fine. Just remember one thing. I'm agreeing because this suits me. This way, you're my employee. You do what I say. You can't cry foul, can't say I manipulated you."

"Even if I did, it's not like you'll lose any sleep over it."

His teeth bared in a surprisingly warm smile. "Good, you're a fast learner. I'm the one who will be paying you. I'll even have my lawyers draw a contract to that effect."

"Isn't that a little over-the-top? I'm there to help Tyler, not for any other reason." His continued silence sent a shiver of warning through her. "Am I?"

He didn't answer her question and his expression was hidden by the thick sweep of his lashes. A knock sounded on an interconnecting door she hadn't noticed. The brunette she had spied earlier walked in, her mouth set into a charming pout. Her long-legged gait brought her to the sitting area in mere seconds while her expertly made-up gaze took in Nikos and her with a frown.

She pulled him toward her, nothing subtle or ambiguous in her intentions. "I thought you wanted to celebrate, Nikos. Are you ever going to be free?"

Her mouth dry, Lexi watched, her thin T-shirt too warm.

His gaze didn't waver from Lexi. A sly smile curved his mouth as he obviously noticed the heat she could feel flush her cheeks. He wrapped his hand around the woman's waist, his long fingers splayed against the cream silk of her dress. "I believe Ms. Nelson and I have concluded our business to mutual satisfaction. So, yes, I'm free to celebrate, Nina."

CHAPTER THREE

NIKOS CURSED LOUDLY and violently. The words swallowed up by the crowd around him didn't relieve his temper one bit.

It had been three days since Lexi Nelson had come to see him and yet the sneaky minx had avoided his assistant's phone calls. Exasperated, Nikos had been reduced to having Kane discover her shift times at the club. Thoroughly disgusted by his minions'—a word he couldn't stop using ever since she had—failure to persuade the woman to leave for Greece, he had flown back to New York.

He had arrived at three in the morning, forced himself to stay awake and arrived at Vibe five minutes after five. Only to find her gone. So he had his chauffeur drive him to her apartment in Brooklyn.

But even after a ten-hour shift, the irritating woman still hadn't returned. He had been ready to call the cops and report her missing. In the end, he had entered her apartment, barged into a bedroom and forced the naked couple in the bed to tell him where Ms. Nelson was. Her eyes eating him up, the redhead had finally informed him that Lexi had gone straight to another shift at a coffee shop around the corner.

So here he was standing on the sidewalk at nine in the

morning outside the bustling café amidst jostling New Yorkers. He was tired, sleep-deprived and furious.

He understood the need for money. He was the epitome of hunger for wealth and power, but this woman was something else.

Ordering his chauffeur to come back in a few minutes, he entered the café. The strong smell of coffee made his head pound harder. With the hustle and bustle behind the busy counter, it took him a few moments to spot her behind the cash register.

His heartbeat slowed to a normal pace.

A brown paper bag in hand, she was smiling at a customer.

Her hair was combed back from her forehead in that poufy way. The three silver earrings on her left ear glinted in the morning sunlight as she turned this way and that. A green apron hung loosely on her slender frame.

She thanked the customer and ran her hands over her face. He could see the pink marks her fingers left on her skin even from the distance. And that was when Nikos noticed it—the tremble in her fingers, the slight sway of her body as she turned.

He tugged his gaze to her face and took in the dark shadows under her stunning blue eyes. She blinked slowly, as though struggling to keep her eyes open and smiled that dazzling smile at the next customer.

Memories pounded through him, a fierce knot clawing his gut tight. He didn't want to remember, yet the sight of her, tired and ready to drop on her feet, punched him, knocking the breath out of him.

He hadn't felt that bone-deep desolation in a long time, because as hard as Savas had made him work for the past fourteen years, Nikos had known there would be food at the end of it. But before Savas had plucked them both from their old house, every day after his mother had died had been a lesson in survival.

The memory of it—the smell of grease at the garage, combined with the clawing hunger in his gut while the lack of sleep threatened to knuckle him down—was as potent as though it was just yesterday.

The bitter memory on top of his present exhaustion tipped him over the edge.

A red haze descending on him, he stormed through the crowd and navigated around the counter.

With a gasp, Lexi stepped back, blinking furiously. "Mr. Demakis," she said, sounding squeaky, "you can't be back—"

He didn't give her a chance to finish. Ignoring the gasps and audible whispers of the busy crowd, he moved closer, picked her up and walked out of the café.

Crimson rushed into her pale cheeks, and her mouth fell open. "What are you doing?"

She wriggled in his hold and he tightened his grip. "Seeing dots and shapes, Ms. Nelson? I'm carrying you out."

Weighing next to nothing, she squirmed again. The nonexistent curves he had mocked her about rubbed against his chest, teasing shocking arousal out of his tired body.

For the first time in his life, he clamped down the sensation. It wasn't easy. "Stop wiggling around, Lexi, or I will drop you." To match his words, he slackened his hold on her.

With a gasp, she wrapped herself tighter around him. Her breath teased his neck. He let fly a curse. As rigid as a tightly tuned chassis in his arms, she glared at him. "Put me down, Nikos."

His limo appeared at the curb and he waited while the chauffeur opened the door. Bending slightly, he rolled her onto the leather seat. She scrambled on her knees for a few seconds, giving him a perfect view of her pert bottom in denim shorts before scooting to the far side of the opposite seat.

He got into the limo, settled back into the seat and stretched his legs. Perverse anger flew hotly in his veins. He shouldn't care but he couldn't control it. "A bartender at night, a barista by day. *Christos,* are you trying to kill yourself?"

Lexi had never been more shocked in her entire life. And that was big, seeing that she had run away from a foster home when she was fifteen, had stolen by sixteen and had been working at a high-class bar in Manhattan, where shocking was the norm rather than the exception, since she had been nineteen.

She clumsily sat up from the leather seat. The jitteriness in her limbs intensified just as the limo pulled away from the curb. "I can't just leave," she said loudly, her words echoing around them. The arrogant man beside her didn't even bat an eyelid. "Order your minion to turn around. Faith will lose her job and I can't—"

He leaned forward and extended his arm. Her words froze on her lips and she pressed back into her seat. The scent of the leather and him morphed into something that teased her ragged senses. The intensity of his presence tugged at her as if he were extending a force field on some fundamental level. Outside the limo, the world was bustling with crazy New York energy, and inside…inside it felt as if time and space had come to a standstill.

He reached behind her neck and undid the knot of her apron. She dug her nails into the denim of her shorts, her heart stuck in her throat. The pad of his fingers dragged against her skin and she fought to remain still. The long sweep of his lashes hid his expression but that thrumming energy of his pervaded the interior. Bunching the apron in his hands, he threw it aside with a casual flick of his wrist.

Even in the semicomatose state she was functioning in, unfamiliar sensations skittered over her. She had never been more aware of her skin, her body than when he was near. Noting every little movement of hers, he handed her a bottle of water. "Who is Faith?"

The question rang with suppressed fury. Lexi undid the cap and took a sip. She was stalling, and he knew it.

"Why are you so angry?" she blurted out, unable to stop herself.

He pushed back the cuffs of his black dress shirt. The sight of those hair-roughened tanned arms sent her stomach into a dive. "Who is Faith?" he said again, his words spoken through gritted teeth.

She sighed. "My roommate, for whom I was covering the shift. She's been sick a few times recently, and if she misses any more shifts, she'll lose her job. Which she will today, because of you."

He leaned back, watching her like a hawk. His anger still simmered in the air but with exhaustion creeping back in, she didn't care anymore. She let out a breath, and snuggled farther back into the plush leather. She was so tired. If only she could close her eyes for just a minute…

"What does this Faith look like?"

"Almost six feet tall, green eyes, blond."

"But she's a natural redhead, isn't she?"

Heat crept up her neck at the way he slightly emphasized the word *redhead*. "How would you know something like that?" Tension gripped her. "Nikos, you barge into my work, behave like a caveman and now you're asking me these strange questions without telling me what—"

"The last time I checked, which was an hour ago, your so-called 'sick' friend was lolling about in bed naked with a man, while you were killing yourself trying to do her job. From what I could see of her, which was a lot, she's perfectly fine."

Her cheeks heating, Lexi struggled to string a response. "Faith wouldn't just lie…"

Faith would. And it wasn't even the first time, either. Her chest tightened, her hands shook. But Faith was more than a mere roommate. She was her friend. If they didn't look out for each other, who would?

Struggling not to show how much it pained her, she tucked her hands in her lap. "Maybe it wasn't Faith," she offered, just to get him off her back.

"She has a tattoo of a red rose on her left buttock and a dragon on her right shoulder. When it was clear no one would answer, I opened the door and went right in. Your friend, by the way, is also a screamer, which was how I knew there was someone inside that bedroom."

Flushing, Lexi turned her gaze away from him. Even if she didn't know about the tattoos, which she did, the last bit was enough to confirm that he was talking about Faith. "All right, so she lied to me," she said, unable to fight the tidal wave of exhaustion that was coming at her fast. As long as she had felt that she was helping Faith, she'd been able to keep going. She pulled up her legs, uncaring of the expensive leather. "What I don't get is why you felt the need in the first place to barge into our apartment and confront her."

"You left that bar at five in the morning, and two hours later, you weren't at your apartment in Brooklyn. I've no idea how you've managed to not get yourself killed all these years."

Her breath lodged in her throat, painfully. Hugging her knees tight, she stared at him. Shock pulsed through the exhaustion. She lived in the liveliest city on the planet, and even with Tyler around, she'd felt the loneliness like a second skin most of her life. Nikos's matter-of-fact statement only rammed the hurtful truth closer.

"You don't have to worry about me. I take my safety very seriously." His anger was misplaced and misdirected. Yet it also held a dangerous allure.

His nostrils flared, his jaw tight as a concrete slab. "My sister's welfare depends on you," he said, enunciating every word as though he was talking to someone dimwitted. "I need you alive and kicking right now, not dead in some Dumpster."

"You don't like it that you felt a minute's concern for me? At least it makes you human."

"As opposed to what? Are you also a part-time shrink?"

The caustic comment was enough to cure her stupid thinking.

"As opposed to an alien with no heart. Why is this even relevant to you? Are you keeping tabs on all my friends so that you can manipulate me a little more?"

"She took advantage of you." He looked at her as though he was studying a curious insect, something that had crawled under his polished, handmade shoes. "Aren't you the least bit angry with her?"

"She doesn't mean to—"

"Hurt you? And yet it seems she has accomplished that very well."

Was she imagining the compassion in those brown depths? Or was her sleep-deprived mind playing tricks on her again? She scrunched back into the seat, feeling as stupid as he was calling her. "Faith's had a rough life."

"And you haven't?"

"It's not about who had the roughest life or who deserves kindness more, Nikos. Faith, for all her lies and manipulation, has no one. No one who cares about her, who would worry about her. And I know what that loneliness feels like. I don't expect you to—"

"I know enough," he said with a cutting edge to his words. "You haven't signed the contract yet. Now you have forced me to fly back to New York for the express purpose of accompanying you to Greece."

Way to go, Lexi, exactly what you wanted to avoid.

"I've been busy."

He leaned forward in a quick movement. For such a big man, he moved so quickly, so economically. But she must be getting used to him because she didn't flinch when he ran the pads of his thumbs gently under her eyes. The heat of his body stole into hers. "Are you having second thoughts about dear Tyler? Have you decided that he's not worth the money I'm paying?"

It almost sounded as if he wanted her to refuse to help him. Which couldn't be true.

She had been unable to sleep a wink ever since the horrid contract had arrived on her doorstep and she had taken a look at the exorbitant amount of money listed there. More than she had ever seen in her lifetime or probably ever would.

Just remembering it had her heart thumping in her chest again.

Money she could use to take art classes instead of having to save every cent, money she could use to, for once, buy some decent clothes instead of shopping the teenager section at the department store or thrift store.

Money she could use to take a break from her energy-draining bartending job and invest her time in developing her comic book script and develop a portfolio without having to worry over her next meal and keeping a roof over her head.

The possibilities were endless.

Yet she also knew that anything she bought with that money would also bring with it an ick factor. It would feel sullied.

But there had been something more than her discomfort that had held her back from signing that contract.

The man studying her intently had volunteered it happily enough. In fact, he had seemed *more* than happy to make her his paid employee.

Because it gave him unmitigated power over her. That was it.

She stilled in place, her stomach diving at the realization. That's what had given her the bad feeling.

If she had accompanied him without complaint, it meant she was doing him a favor. This way, she wasn't. It seemed he was either prepared to blackmail her into it or pay her an enormous amount of money so that she was obligated to do as he ordered.

Rather than simply ask her for help. The lengths he would go to just so that his position wasn't weak made her spine stiff with alarm.

"About that money," she began, feeling divided in half within. She couldn't even stop seeing the number in front of her, a bag with a dollar sign always hovering in her subconscious as though she was one of her own comic characters, "I was angry with you for manipulating me. I can't accept—"

His long, tanned finger landed on her mouth, short-circuiting her already-weak thought process. Her skin tingled at the barest contact. "In the week that I have had the misfortune to make your acquaintance," he said, leaning so close that she could smell his cologne along with the scent of his skin, "asking for money to look after Tyler was the one sensible, one clever thing you did."

Really, she had no idea what he would say next or what would suddenly send him into a spiral of anger.

"Don't embrace useless principles now and turn it down, Ms. Nelson. Think of something wild and reckless that you have always wanted but could never afford. Think of all the nice clothes you can buy." His gaze moved over her worn T-shirt, and she fought the impulse to cover her meager chest. "Maybe even something that will upstage Venetia in front of your ex?"

Her mouth falling open wordlessly, she stared at him. Apparently, her new, standard expression in his company. "I have no intention of competing with Venetia, not that I harbor any delusion that I even could."

Dark amusement glittered in his gaze. It was as if there was a one-way connection between them that let him see straight into her thoughts. Like Mr. Spock doing a Vulcan Mind Meld. If only it worked both ways. She had absolutely no knowledge about him, whereas he literally had a file on her.

He settled back into the seat and crossed his long legs. "You're a strange little woman, Ms. Nelson. Are you telling me you didn't think of using this opportunity to win him back? That the idea didn't even occur to you?"

"No," she repeated loudly, refusing to let him sully her motives. She would love to have her friend back, yes, but she wasn't going to engage in some bizarre girl war with Venetia to get Tyler back the way he assumed.

"Fine. My pilot's waiting. We leave in four hours."

"I can't leave in four hours," Lexi said, anxiety and the energy it took to talk to him beginning to give her a headache. "I have to find someone to sublet my room, have to get the plumber to fix the kitchen before I leave and I promised Mrs. Goldman next door that I would help her after her surgery in two days. I can't just up and leave because your sister can't bear the thought of not being the center of Tyler's universe for a few more days."

He shrugged—a careless, elegant movement of those broad shoulders. "I don't care how many things you had lined up to do for your parasitic friends or how much you were planning to bend over backward for the whole world, Ms. Nelson. I won't wait anymore."

She frowned. "I don't bend over back—"

His gaze sliced through her words. "You're the worst kind of pushover."

She slumped against the seat, bone-deep exhaustion taking away her ability to offer even token protest. She shouldn't be hurt by his clinical, disparaging words. But she was.

And the fact that his words could even affect her only proved him right.

How could she feel bad about what a stranger, someone as ruthless as Nikos Demakis thought about her?

"Your room at the apartment will go nowhere. If there's anything else you need help with—" his gaze lingered on her clothes again "—something that is solely *your* concern, *your* problem, I can have my assistant at your disposal."

"If I don't agree?"

He shrugged. "Your agreement or the lack of it doesn't play into it. The choice is whether you travel as my guest or my captive."

"That is kidnapping."

He plucked a couple of pages from his case and pushed it toward her along with a legal pad and a pen. "It's hard to admit, but I see that I did this all wrong."

"What?"

He leaned forward, resting his elbows on his knees. His gaze solemn, he blinked. Really, no single man should be allowed to be so gorgeous. "I should have appeared on your doorstep with my heart in my hands, pleaded my sister's case, begged you to help, tried to become your best friend. Maybe talk about my own horrible childhood, pretend to be on my death bed—"

"Okay, okay, fine. You've made your point," Lexi said loudly, cutting off his mocking words. She had always liked to help if she could. She would not let the manipulative man in front of her make her feel stupid about it.

Pulling her gaze away from him, she scanned the document again. She'd had the contract looked over by a paralegal friend, but there was no discounting the hollow fear in her gut.

She would be in his personal employ for two months and would be paid fifty thousand dollars for it, half now, and half when he deemed her job done, subject to his sole discretion.

She was being paid an exorbitant amount of money to spend time with Tyler on a Greek island, the likes of which she had no other hope of seeing in this lifetime.

Yet as the limo came to a stop on her street in the cheap neighborhood of her apartment complex, she couldn't shake off a feeling that there was an unwritten price that she would have to pay.

And she had no idea what that was.

CHAPTER FOUR

NIKOS CLOSED HIS laptop, and refused the stewardess's offer of a drink. He hadn't had a good night's sleep in four days now. He had finalized the deal with Nathan Ramirez; he finally had a solution for Venetia's problem. And yet he was restless with a weird kind of pent-up energy simmering just below his skin.

He itched to get back to his garage and get his hands dirty. He had been pushing himself this past month and he needed a break. Once everything was settled with Venetia, he would take her on a vacation. She had always wanted to see more of New York.

The passing mention of New York and his thoughts immediately shifted to Ms. Nelson. Not a peep sounded from the rear cabin. There was something about the woman that always left him on edge. Stepping into the cabin, he froze.

She lay on the very edge of the bed, half out, half in. Her knees tucked tight into her legs, her hands wrapped tight around herself, she slept hunched tight into a ball.

Her honey-gold hair glinted in the low lights, her wide mouth open like a fish.

Her white T-shirt couldn't hide the outline of her small breasts. A plastic watch with a big dial in the shape of a skull covered most of her wrist. A thoroughly distracting strip of her back was exposed by the scrunched-up top, above denim shorts. Delicate calves and even more delicate feet topped with toes painted black completed the picture.

Even while telling himself that he should just walk away, he stood rooted to the spot.

He usually paid very little attention to the women he slept with. What he wanted, he took and got the distraction out of the way. Because that's all anything a woman ever had been to him. Something to take the edge off the grueling hours, or the pace he had set himself to succeed.

Ms. Nelson, on the other hand, perplexed, irritated and downright annoyed him with her mere existence. There was such a mix of innocence and calculation about her that he found mesmerizing. He smiled, remembering her confusion, her beautiful blue eyes widened, her breath hitching in and out uncomfortably, when he had leaned toward her in the car.

Noticing a page peeking from under her arms, he leaned over her and pulled the rolled-up magazine.

His blood slowed in his veins to a sluggish pace as he breathed in that scent of her. Vanilla, that's what she smelled of. Simple yet fascinating, like her.

He straightened the magazine and looked at the article she had been reading. How To Use Sex to Get Your Man Back.

So the little minx did want that parasite back. Apparently, being called a selfish bitch wasn't enough of a deterrent for her. Displeasure and a relentless curiosity vied within him. What kind of a woman worried about an ex who turned his back on her, a friend who manipulated her and yet faced Nikos down when he had cornered her?

Shaking his head, he tried to stem the flow of resentment coursing through him. Because that's what it had to be. Ms. Nelson's effervescent outlook toward life and her sheer naïveté were beginning to grate on him. The sooner he got her out of his life and back to her I'm-all-that-is-love-manipulate-me-all-you-want existence, the better.

Muttering a curse, he turned around to leave when a sleepy moan rumbled from the bed. Still hunched tight, she scooted a little more over the edge. With a quick movement, Nikos caught her just as she would have toppled off the bed.

He ended up on his knees next to the bed, her slender body cradled on his forearms. Blue eyes flew open, terror cycling through them.

Before he could blink, she squirmed in his hold, throwing punches and kicking her legs. He turned his face just at the right time, and her punch landed on his jaw. His teeth rattled in his mouth. Grunting at the pain shooting up his jaw, he threw her onto the bed none too gently.

She rolled over to the other side, and stared up at him, her eyes wide and full of shock. "What are you doing?"

"What do you think?" he shouted back, running a hand over his jaw. "I should have let you fall. The bump would have given you some much-needed sense."

Theos, but the woman could throw a mean punch. If he hadn't turned he would have had a severely displaced nose.

She scooted to her knees on the other side, her movements wary and tight, her mouth pinched. "I'm sorry. I just acted on reflex."

Running a finger over his jaw, he looked at her and curbed his anger. "Would you like to explain, Ms. Nelson?"

Her hair stood up at awkward angles. Moving as though in slow motion, she got off the bed, walked around it and stopped at a good distance from him.

Her gaze was set on his jaw, her lips trembling. "I'm fine," he said, cringing at the thought that she might cry. He sat down on the bed and waved toward the empty spot. "Sit down."

Remaining silent, she slid down onto the edge of the

bed, leaving as much distance as possible between them. And it finally struck him. All the times she had scrunched tight when he came near. Even now her slender frame was coiled with tension. For some reason, the thought filled him with a cold anger.

"You're afraid of me."

Her silence rang around them.

He shoved away the questions and, of all the strangest things, the dent to his ego, aside. He might not like her but the fear in her eyes, it had been real. "I know that you think me a heartless bastard, and you are right, but I would never lay a finger on you."

She met his gaze finally. "I think I know that."

"Well, that's good, then." This time, he couldn't keep the sarcasm out.

She grimaced, and took a deep breath. "Sorry, that didn't come out right. I know that you won't harm me, Nikos, at least not physically," she added, just to annoy him, he was sure. "And it's not your intentions I'm scared of but…" Pink flooded her cheeks "But your… I mean…"

"*Theos,* Lexi! Just say it." Sitting here in the intimate confines of the luxurious cabin, he had never felt the strange energy that suddenly arced into life in the cabin.

Lexi sighed, fighting the urge to run away from the cabin. Even though the temperature was perfect, she still felt a line of sweat down her spine. And their sitting here on the same bed, even with the breadth of it separating them, it felt too intimate. Too many things, strange and unnerving, crowded in on her. But the man did deserve an explanation.

"Your size…I mean…you are a big man."

Amusement glittered in his gaze. "Yes. I'm six foot three. I am big, *everywhere.* And so far, you're the only woman who has not been spectacularly happy about it."

"What does your size have to do with women being

hap…" Heat rose up through her as she realized his meaning, tightening her cheeks, and there was nothing she could do about it. *"Oh."*

He laughed and she couldn't help but smile back. He looked gorgeous, down-to-earth and not at all like someone who should have scared her so much. "You gave me the perfect opening."

She nodded, and made a movement to stand up when he threw out his arm to stop her. He did it slowly, as if to not frighten her again. "Once again, you've made me extremely curious. And you owe me an explanation," he said, rubbing at his jaw.

Lexi pulled up her feet and hugged her knees. "This…it's nothing that is useful to you," she said, dragging her feet.

He didn't bat an eyelid at the insult. "Tell me anyway."

"I was transferred to a new foster home when I was twelve." She smiled, warmth filling her despite everything else that had happened. "I loved it immediately because the last one, they had always been kind to me but I was the only kid. The new home was perfect because there were six of us and it's where I met Tyler.

"But our foster parents had a son. Jason was almost seventeen, older than any of us, and was this huge, burly guy. From the day I walked in, he picked on me. Every month, it got worse. Sometimes he would just lift me up and throw me down, sometimes lock me in the closet. I got pretty smart about avoiding him for the most part. For two years, it went on but it was the place that I had been the happiest. Except for those moments with Jason. The worst was when…"

Nikos's hand clasped hers, his fingers strong and rough against hers. Holding back the urge to pull away, she took a breath. Her hand was tiny in his, but it felt good, strong, a spark of comfort filling her up. "You don't have to continue."

Lexi looked up, but didn't let go of his hand. She hated that the shadow of that fear that had been her constant companion in those years was still there with her. She swallowed the hot ache in her throat. "No…see, I thought I was over it. But I guess, the way I've been reacting around you…" Her fingers twitched in his grasp but he held on tight. "I…I refuse to give him any power over me."

She closed her eyes and instantly she was back in that room where she had slept again, on the metal-framed bed that had creaked with Jason's weight, the scent of his sweat, and she could feel his body pressing down on hers. "One night when I was fifteen—" her words came out in a ravaged whisper "—I was sleeping and I guess, I don't know… I don't know why he lay down next to me. I had no idea that he was even back in the house. One minute I'm sleeping peacefully, and the next, I wake up, and he is all over me." She shivered and her short nails dug into Nikos's palm. "He pinned me down with his huge body, locked my arms over my head. I can still feel his breath over my face. I don't know for how long. But I couldn't breathe, or move."

"Did he—"

The utter savagery in Nikos's words broke the hold of the memory. "No. I don't know what he intended. And thanks to Tyler, I never had to find out."

"Of course." The two words were laden with a vehemence that jerked her gaze to his face. "That's when you ran away?"

"Yes. I couldn't take it anymore. Except within a week, we realized how hard it was to feed ourselves. But Tyler refused to leave me." And she wouldn't leave him now.

"Didn't the parents believe what happened?"

She felt the intensity of Nikos's gaze bear down on her

and looked up. Bracing herself, she answered, instinctually knowing that he would not like it. "I never told them."

Shock widened his eyes, he clenched the muscles in his cheeks. "Why not?"

"I didn't want to hurt them."

"Hurt them?" His words were low, and yet brimming with a savage fury. "Their son attacked you while you were under their care. Protecting you was their duty."

He vibrated with an emotion that Lexi couldn't understand. The fact that a decision she had made years ago could affect him so much…she didn't know what to make of it. Only that she wanted to explain. "They were kind people, Nikos. They gave me a home for two years. It would have broken their hearts…"

He ran his fingers through his hair with palpable fury. "It was not your responsibility to worry about their feelings. It should never be a child's burden. Once you start taking that on, believe me, there is no turning back." He stood up from the bed, a latent energy pulsing under the controlled movement. His gaze filled with barely concealed scorn, he leveled a look at her. "Your kind of innocence and goodwill, it has no place in this world. Seeking to make a place for you in others' lives, it's…one thing. But to the point of undermining yourself… And before you imply so—" a softening glimmered in his gaze "—I have nothing to gain in this. This piece of advice is for your own benefit."

Lexi stared at his back as he strode out of the cabin without another glance toward her. He was once again the arrogant, condescending stranger from their first meeting, the one she didn't like, even a little bit. And not the least because he had a way of cutting right to the heart of uncomfortable truths she didn't want to hear, making her question her choices and even herself.

* * *

Lexi stepped out of the limo and for once, remembered not to grab her luggage. Hardly two days in Nikos's company, and she was already getting used to being served hand and foot.

Fascinated as she was with the sheer, majestic decadence of the hotel in front of her, it took her a minute to realize she was in Paris. Nikos had left the private airstrip in a different limo without a word. And she had been so glad to get a reprieve from him that she hadn't even realized where they had landed.

Shaking her head, she mounted the steps of the glitzy hotel. Stifling the urge to just hang around and look at everything around her, she walked to the reception desk.

Unease settled in her gut as she looked past the vast, marble-tiled foyer. Like a space portal waiting to swallow her whole, the glass elevator doors opened with a swish.

She forced a smile to her mouth and turned back toward the counter, her heart slowly but steadily crawling up her throat. She hated the hold her fear had on her, but neither could she shake it off. Stairs, it had to be again.

Stubbornly pushing her heart back into its place, she glanced through the upscale ground floor café first. She needed a high boost of carbs if she had to walk up twenty floors again.

"Mr. Demakis has a permanent suite with us on the forty-fifth floor," the receptionist said and Lexi's heart sank. "But we received an email to say you need a suite on the first floor."

Lexi could have kissed the woman. Feeling giddy with pleasure that she didn't have to chance a heart attack again, she followed the uniformed staff and clicked Nikos's number on her cell phone.

"What is it, Ms. Nelson?" His irritated voice came on

the other line. "I gave you my number in case of emergencies. Anything else you need, just ask the hotel reception and they will provide it for you."

The bubble of her excitement deflated with a tangible hiss. She licked her lips and forced herself to form the words. "The first floor suite...I... Thanks for remembering, Nikos."

Silence rumbled down the line, heavy, awkward and utterly embarrassing. "You're doing it again, Ms. Nelson. Thinking that everyone else in the world is like you. They're not. I need you alive right now. After that, climb fifty or a hundred floors, I don't care."

"Why are we lolling around here when you were in such a rush to leave New York then?" she said tartly.

"Because I have a meeting here which I had to postpone to come to get you."

And he disconnected the call.

Lexi stared at her phone, her mouth hanging open. Suddenly she felt like the stupidest woman on the planet for calling him. Especially when he had dumped her unceremoniously in a strange city without so much as an explanation.

She thumped her forehead with her phone, furious with herself. Fat good thanking him had done her. But neither did she believe him.

He might be an arrogant, infuriating pain in the butt, but he had a heart, whatever he might like to think.

Resolving to maintain a distance from him, she made her way toward the doorway that led to the stairs.

Pulling the edges of her robe together, Lexi stumbled out of the shower. Embarrassment, sheer fury, plain terror, cycled through her in a matter of seconds.

Her robe clinging to her wet skin, she followed the six-foot French woman, who was utterly naked, into the lounge of the suite.

"Where is Nikos?" the woman said in a delicious French accent.

So that's what this was about. "This is not Mr. Demakis's suite," Lexi managed, through the shock sputtering through her.

The woman's shoulders were thrown back, a perfectly manicured hand on her hip, not an inch of the confidence with which she had simply barged into the shower that Lexi had been occupying, had left Emmanuelle at realizing her mistake.

Blinking, Lexi shook her head, the utter perfection of the woman's body etched into her mind. She hurriedly looked around the lavish suite. The woman couldn't have walked through the street and into the foyer naked, could she? Though with a body like hers, no one would blame her.

Spotting a towel, Lexi threw it at her and continued her search again.

She breathed in relief as her gaze fell on a small, silken red heap on the cream leather couch.

She pulled it up just when the door to the suite opened and in walked the man she wanted to strangle. With a keycard in his hand as if he owned the hotel. "I don't believe this. Is the whole world just allowed to barge into my suite?"

His gaze moved from her face to the red silk dress in her hand and then toward Emmanuelle whose slender frame was hidden from the entrance.

The blasted man burst out laughing. The sound punched Lexi in the stomach, knocking the breath out of her.

Shaking with anger, she threw the dress at him with as much force as she could muster. The weightless garment fell silkily at his feet. "That woman barged into the shower, naked, and gave me the fright of my life."

"Calm down, Ms. Nelson," he said smoothly and picked up the dress.

Mumbling something Lexi couldn't hear in Emmanuelle's ear, he handed the dress to her.

Who, in turn, nodded and pulled her dress on. Next to Emmanuelle, who looked just as striking in her red dress as without it, Nikos was the very epitome of dangerous sophistication that Lexi might as well be from another galaxy.

Why she even cared she had no idea. Except that he was very good at turning her inside out.

"I'm assuming seeing Emmanuelle naked has sent your nervous system into shock?" With a look that took in everything from her wet hair to the thin silk robe that she had bought in the teen section of her local department store, he marched past her.

Knowing that he would just tease her mercilessly whatever she said, Lexi clamped her mouth shut. She stood there resolutely, refusing to hide.

Emmanuelle kissed his cheek, looked past him at Lexi, threw an air kiss at her and walked out of the suite.

Reaching her, he flicked a wet strand of her hair from her face. Lexi shivered, the hint of stubble on his jaw, the strong column of his throat, a feast to her senses. That sense of being tugged toward him came again. "Are you okay, or should I call for a doctor?"

She folded her arms. The prick of her nails into her skin was the only thing that helped her to focus on his words. "Am I in a bachelor-type reality show starring you?" Unwise curiosity gnawed at her. "Does the woman in New York know about this one?"

Wariness replaced the dark humor in his gaze. "Excuse me?"

"The brunette, your girlfriend in New York?"

He settled down onto the cream leather couch with a

sigh, his long legs extended in front of him. "Nina's not my girlfriend. I don't think she would even like the term. And neither is Emmanuelle."

"She walked in here, naked," she said, her line of thinking shocking her, "and left like a kitten when you asked her to." Mortification should have turned her into a red blob by now. "What was that whole…exchange?"

Clasping his hands behind his head, he slid lower into the couch and closed his eyes. "I told her I didn't want to see her anymore and she left."

"Then that was the end of your—" she scrunched her brow "—association?"

"Association, Ms. Nelson?" He leaned forward in the couch, something restless uncoiling in him. "Have I wandered into the sixteenth century? No wonder—"

"Affair then, okay?" she said hurriedly. She didn't want another taunt about Tyler. "That was ruthless. You say it's over and she leaves. Is that how—"

"How I conduct my *sexual associations?* Yes. And stop feeling sorry for her. If *she* had wanted to end it, I would have walked away, too."

"So wherever you go, you have a girlfri…a woman for sex?"

"Yes. I work hard and I play hard."

"And you or she have no expectations of each other?"

With slow movements, he unbuttoned the collar of his shirt. "This is sounding like an interview."

It took everything she had in her for Lexi to keep her gaze on his face. But even in the confusion, she couldn't stop asking the questions. "Do you spend time with any of them, eat together, go sightseeing? Would you call one of them a friend?"

"No." He stood up from the couch and reached her. The

hard knot in her chest didn't relent. "You're feeling sorry for me."

She raised her gaze to him and saw the detachment in his brown eyes. For all his wealth and jet-setting lifestyle, Nikos Demakis and she had something in common. He was as alone as she was. Except she had no doubt he had precisely tailored his life like that. *Why?* From the little she had gleaned about Venetia and Nikos Demakis, they came from a huge traditional Greek family. "It's a horrible life to lead."

He laughed and the sarcasm in it pricked her. "That's what I think of your life." Her gaze locked with his, and for once, there was no contempt or mockery there. Just plain truth. "In my life, there are no lasting relationships, no doing favors for friends who will take advantage of me. And when it comes to sex, the women I see want exactly what I want. Nothing more. You would understand that if you had—"

"If I weren't an unsophisticated idiot?"

Rubbing her eyes, Lexi flopped onto the couch he had just vacated. Because that's what Tyler had always said to her, too, hadn't he? That Lexi needed to live more, do more, just be…more.

That Lexi was living everyone else's life and not hers. She had always laughed it away, truly not understanding the vehemence in his words.

"I was going to say if you lived your life like a normal twenty-three-year-old instead of playing Junior Mother Teresa of your neighborhood." He took the seat next to her, and the heat of his body beckoned her. "If that's how you see yourself, change it."

This close, he was even more gorgeous, and his proximity unnerved her on the most fundamental level. The constant state of her heightened awareness of him combined with his continuous verbal assault made her flippant. "Is there a market here in Paris that sells sophistication by the pound?"

"You have a smart mouth, Ms. Nelson. I think we have already established that. Sophistication, or for that matter, anything else, can be bought with money. You spent enough time looking at the shops on Fifth Avenue in New York before we left. Why didn't you buy what you wanted?"

She blinked, once again struck by how far and how easily he wielded his power. "Did your assistant give you a minute-by-minute update on what I did?"

"I was in the limo stuck in traffic and saw you. You hung around long enough in each store. Apparently, you're as different from Venetia as I truly thought."

He had an uncanny way of giving voice to her most troublesome thoughts. "I hope you'll be so busy that I don't have to see you once we reach Greece."

"So that you can spend it all with your precious Tyler?"

The man was the most contrary man she had ever met. "Isn't that the reason you're paying me that exorbitant amount of money?"

"What did you do with the first half?"

"That's none of your business."

"If I find out that you have loaned it to some poor friend who *really* needs it—" his gaze filled with a dangerous gleam "—I will bend you over my knee and spank you."

Her cheeks stung with heat as a vivid image of what he said flashed in front of her eyes. The curse of being such a visual person. "I didn't give it to anyone nor will I spend it."

"Because of your stupid morals?"

"No. I...just want to save it, okay?" Realizing that she was shouting, she took a deep breath. "If I ever lose my job—and you have proved how easily anyone with a little money and inclination can find out my background—and if

I can't find a new one, I don't want to go hungry ever again. I don't ever want to be reduced to stealing or do something wrong again." The memories of those hunger pangs, the cold sweat of stealing, knowing it was wrong, were so vivid that her gut tightened. Feeling his gaze drilling into her side, she turned and laughed. A hollow laugh that sounded as pathetic as it felt. "You probably think I'm a fool."

His mouth, still closed, tilted at the corners. The flash of understanding in his gaze rooted her to the spot. "I do," he said, his hard words belying his expression. "But not for this."

A concession, spoken with that incisive contempt of his, and yet in that moment, she believed that he knew the powerless feeling, the fear that haunted her. "That day, you said you understood it. How?"

"I have been hungry before. And I was responsible for Venetia, too."

"But your family is rich. And *you're* rich. Nauseatingly so."

He smiled without warmth. "My father turned his back on all that nauseating wealth for my mother. When I was thirteen, they died within a few months of each other. And even before he died, he was usually drowning in alcohol and no use to us. My mother's treatment was expensive. For almost a year, I did everything and anything I could to bring in money, as much as I could. And I mean *anything*."

He delivered those words in a monotone, yet Lexi could feel the rage and powerlessness that radiated from him. She clasped his hand with hers, just like he had done. A jolt of sensation spiked through her, awakening every nerve ending.

Her touch pulled Nikos from the pit of memories he fell into. Even now, he remembered the stench of his desperation, his hunger. Still, he had rallied. Shaking it off, he met her gaze. The sympathy in her gaze, it made his throat raw.

"I'm sorry, Nikos. It was wrong of me to assume what I did."

He nodded, for once, unable to throw it back in her face. Because the slip of a woman next to him wasn't pitying him. She understood the pain of that thirteen-year-old boy. He had manipulated her and bullied her into coming with him, but she still had the capacity to feel sympathy for him.

How? How could anyone see so much hard life and still retain that kindness as she did, that boundless goodwill? What did she possess that he didn't?

Lexi Nelson, despite everything, was full of heart. Whereas he...the pain he had seen had somehow become a cold, hard part of him. He embraced it for it had driven him toward everything he had now. "Don't worry," he said, feeling an intense dislike of her stricken expression, "I survived. And I made sure that Venetia survived, too."

Curiosity flared in her gaze again, but she clamped her mouth with obvious effort. Standing up from the couch, she waited, with folded arms, for him to move.

He grinned, and didn't pull his legs back. Muttering something he couldn't quite hear, she stepped over him. The scent of her soap and skin combined wafted over him. His muscles tightened at the hard tug of want in his gut.

Why had he sent away Emmanuelle instead of taking up what she offered—easy, uncomplicated sex?

Leaning back against the couch, he slid lower and closed his eyes. Much as he tried, instead of Emmanuelle's sexy body and the pleasure she was so good at giving, his mind kept remembering stunning blue eyes and a slender body with barely there curves.

Lexi Nelson was definitely an interesting distraction. He gave her that. But nothing more.

Little Ms. Pushover, with her endless affection and her trusting heart, had no place in his life. With ruthlessness he had honed to perfection over the years, he shoved away the image.

CHAPTER FIVE

KNOWING THAT HIDING inside her bedroom was like inviting Nikos to mock and taunt her some more, Lexi dressed in denim shorts and a worn T-shirt that hung loose and ventured back to the sitting room.

She froze at the hubbub of activity. The sleek coffee table was gone and in its place stood a rack of clothes, designer if she was seeing the weightless fabric and the expensive cuts right. A tall woman, impeccably dressed in a silk pantsuit, stood next to it with a pad in hand, while another woman, probably assistant to the first, unwrapped a red dress from its tissue.

Even the sound of soft tissue sounded filthily expensive to Lexi's ears. Her heart raced in her chest, shameful and excited.

"You're practically drooling."

His lazy drawl pulled her gaze to Nikos. He was sitting in a leather recliner, his hands folded, his long legs extended in front of him. Latent energy rolled off him.

Sliding past the clothes with a longing glance, she reached him. "What's going on?"

"A little gift for you."

"A gift?" she said dully. One thing she had learned, and he had hammered it home, was that nothing he did was without calculation. "Like a 'give the poor little orphan a makeover' gift? Are my friends behind that glass waiting to jump up and down and shed tears at my transformation?"

He wrapped his fingers around her arm and tugged her close. "You've never seen your parents then?"

There was such an uncharacteristic gentling note in his tone that it took her a few seconds to respond. "No, I haven't."

"Do you think about them, wonder why—"

"I used to, endlessly." After all these years, she could talk about it almost normally, without crumpling into a heap of tears. "The first comic I ever had sketched had a little orphan who goes on a galactic journey and discovers that her parents are cosmic travelers trapped on the other side of the galaxy. One day I realized that as stories went it was fantastic. But reality, sadly, stayed the same." She jerked her hand away from him. "Now will you please tell me what's going on?"

His gaze stayed on her a few more seconds before he cleared his throat. "Venetia's life is a constant roller coaster of parties and clubs, and I'm providing you with armor so that she doesn't crush you. Think of me as your fairy godmother."

She burst out laughing. "Ple-e-e-ase. More like a rampaging space pirate."

"Like the one in the comic book you're working on now? That's what you called me that first day, didn't you?"

Shock reverberated through her at how clearly he remembered what she had uttered in a daze. He stood up and turned to the right, striking a pose with an imaginary pistol in hand. With his tall body, he should have looked awkward. Instead, he looked perfectly gorgeous.

"*Spike,* wasn't it? Did you model your hero after me, Ms. Nelson?"

She shook her head slowly from left to right, unable to

tear her gaze away from the perfection of his profile. Wishing she had a camera in hand, she studied him greedily. "Spike is the villain who kidnaps Ms. Havisham. You're not a hero, Nikos."

"Ahh…" His gaze moved over her face lazily, sliding past her chin to the shirt that hung loose on her, the vee of it, to her bare legs. "Is this Ms. Havisham a fragile little beauty that conquers his heart and teaches him how to love?"

Her heart came to a stuttering halt. Cursing herself for her runaway imagination, she smiled. There was nothing but mockery in his words. "Wrong again."

"Is the whole book done? Tell me what's involved."

A spurt of warmth filled her at his interest. "I am still doing the preliminary sketching and have written down the plot. Once I finalize the characters and the story, I'll do the model sheets for each character and the final step will be to begin inking."

"Hmm…so you do it all by hand, not software."

"Yes, mostly I'm a penciler. I like doing it by hand, getting all the expressions right and haven't really decided on an inking method for sure, mostly I'm just playing with all the techniques. Sometimes I will color, sometimes I…" She caught herself at his smile. "Sorry, I tend to get carried away on this topic."

"No explanation needed. Vintage cars give me a hard-on like that." He laughed as furious color rose through her cheeks. "It sounds really interesting. Do you have all the supplies you need?"

The small spurt grew into a gush of warmth. She nodded.

"When can I see them?"

"What?"

"Your sketches. I want to see them."

"Maybe when you learn to say please," she said, and he made a disappointed noise.

She almost liked him at that moment, *almost*. Which only proved how right he was in calling her a pushover.

He grinned in that sardonic way. "Now please, humor your boss and try that red dress on. I know you want to."

She took a couple of cocktail dresses from the woman and sneaked back to her bedroom. She wasn't going to accept any of it. But there was no harm in indulging herself, was there?

In her bedroom, she pulled off her shorts and T-shirt, and instead of the red one, pulled on a strapless sheath dress exactly the color of her eyes. It fit her as if it was made for her. Sliding the side zipper up, Lexi turned toward the full-length mirror.

Her breath lodged somewhere in her throat. Simply cut, the designer dress showed off her slender shoulders and slight build to maximum advantage, ending with a small flare just above her knees that contrasted with the severe cut.

She didn't look sophisticated as he had claimed. Maybe she never would. But better than that, for the first time since she had realized she was never going to have any curves, she looked like a woman.

A knock at the door meant she had to stop admiring herself. She stepped into the sitting area.

Nikos stood leaning against the open door, his dark gaze eating her up. A stillness came over him. The flash of purely male appraisal in his gaze knocked the breath out of her. That look…she had imagined Tyler looking at her like that so many times. It had never happened. But seeing that look in Nikos's eyes, it was as unwelcome as it was shocking.

She blinked as a sliver of tension suddenly arced between them.

"You look stunning, Ms. Nelson." He delivered those words with the same silky smoothness as when he insulted her. As if it had no effect on him. Had she imagined that look? "Your ex won't know what hit him when he sees you in it. If that doesn't bring him back to his senses…"

She didn't hear the rest of his sentence as something nauseating neatly slotted into place. The silky slide of the dress chafed her.

Her heart thumping in her chest, she followed him into the lounge and stood in front of him. "What is this really about, Nikos? Why do you care so much how Tyler sees me? Tell me the truth or I'll walk out right now."

With a nod of that arrogant head, he dismissed the stylist and her assistant. The prickly humor was gone. The man staring at her with a cold look in his eyes was pure predator. "Don't threaten me, Lexi."

Even his use of her name, given he usually patronized her with *Ms. Nelson,* was pure calculation to intimidate her. She was intimidated by everything about this man, but she refused to show it. Had she really thought him kind just because he had listened to her sob story, asked her about her little hobby? He had manipulated her from day one. "Don't lie to me, Nikos."

His silence was enough to convince Lexi of the truth that had been staring her in the face all this time. Her stomach felt as if it was falling through an abyss. "You mean to use me to separate Tyler from Venetia."

She reached for the zipper on the side, feeling as dirty as she had felt the day she had broken into that house. But her fingers shook, fumbled over the zipper. She grunted, impatient to get it off.

Nikos looked down at her, frowning. "Calm down."

"No, I won't calm down. And take this zipper off."

He did it. Silently and without fumbling like her, with his hands around her body, but not touching her. She felt enveloped by him, her heart skidding all over the place. This was wrong. Everything about this situation, everything about what he made her feel, everything about what he was using her for, they were all horribly wrong and quickly sliding out of her control. Cold sweat gathered over her skin.

The minute the zipper came down, she rushed into her bedroom, took the dress off and donned her usual shorts and T-shirt. Marching back into the room, she threw the dress at him.

"Drama, Ms. Nelson?" he said, bunching the expensive fabric in his hands and throwing it aside. "Finally, something Venetia and you have in common, other than Tyler."

"I'll scream if you call me Ms. Nelson again in that patronizing tone. You have manipulated me, lied to me and picked me up like I was a bag of potatoes. You *will* call me Lexi and tell me why you are doing this."

He took in her rant without so much as a flicker of his eyelid. "Tyler is a manipulative jerk who doesn't deserve Venetia. I want him out of her life."

"Tyler isn't—"

"Your opinion of him means nothing to me."

She flinched. "Why?"

"You're—" She had the distinct impression that he was choosing his words carefully, which was a surprise in itself. Because usually he didn't mince his words, cutting through her with his sharply acerbic opinions. "Blind when it comes to him."

Confusion spiraled through her, coated with a sharp fear. *What had she signed up for?* "Then why let her see him? Why pretend as though you support them?"

"Venetia, for all her outward drama, is very vulnerable and volatile. She never recovered from our parents' death. I'm the only one in the world who hasn't hurt her until now. I will not change that."

"So you're having me do the dirty work for you? And what do you think is going to happen to your precious sister if, heaven forbid, everything goes according to your plan?"

Distinct unease settled over his features. Granite would have more give than his jaw. "She will cry over him. I will explain it to her that you and he—" utter distaste coated his words now "—you always go back to each other, whatever transpires in between. Not unbelievable with your long history." He rubbed his jaw with his palm, his movements shaky. "I hate that I can't prevent this. But I will accept a few of her tears now than something more dangerous that she could do later when she realizes that Tyler never really loved her."

The emotion in his tone was unmistakable. His every word, his manipulations—everything had been to this end. And Lexi understood it, could almost admire him for it if it wasn't also highly misguided. "You can't protect her from everything in the world, Nikos."

"She saw my father shoot himself in the head. I failed long ago to protect her."

Lexi froze, her thoughts jumbling on top of each other. And she had thought she had been unfortunate. "Your father killed himself?"

"Because he couldn't bear to live without my mother." Ice coated his words. "Venetia was ten. She didn't even understand our mother's death. The worst part is she's exactly like him—emotional, volatile and prone to mood swings. With everything I know about your friend, I know he will walk out on my sister one day. I'm just expediting it so that the damage to her is limited."

His heart might be in the right place, but it was so twisted. Lexi walked back and forth, the gleaming marble floor dizzying her, her stomach churning with a viciousness she couldn't curb. "You can't just arrange her life to be without sorrow. It doesn't work that way. I won't do this."

"You will get your precious Tyler back. Don't tell me you haven't thought about that."

"Yes. That thought crossed my mind, but not like this." Disbelief rang in his eyes. "I don't care what it *might* mean for me. I'm out."

She turned around to do just that, but suddenly there he was, a terrifying prospect she couldn't escape. The tension in him was palpable, the rigid set of his mouth an unmistakable warning. "If something happens to my sister because of Tyler, I will hold you personally responsible. Knowing that you could have prevented it, can you handle that guilt, Lexi?"

She stilled as she saw that same guilt cast a dark shadow on his face.

There was nothing cold about Nikos. He was just incredibly good at pushing it all away, and tailoring his life to follow the same strategy. He'd put himself behind an invisible wall of will where nothing could touch him. And he wanted his sister next to him.

Her throat felt raw, her chest tight. So many people could be hurt by the path he was pushing her on. Tyler, Venetia, Lexi herself and Nikos, most of all. Nikos, whom she had thought impervious to any feeling, whom she had assumed ruthless to a fault. Only all he wanted was to protect his sister. *From what?* Another truth slammed into her. "Is this about getting Tyler out of Venetia's life or love out of it, Nikos?"

His head reared back in the tiniest of movements, his eyes cold and hard. A cold chill permeated her skin and she almost wished the words unsaid. "I'm not paying you to analyze me." His tone was low, thrumming with emotion he refused to give outlet. "I failed my sister once. And it broke her in so many ways. I will do whatever it takes to ensure it doesn't happen again.

"Call me a villain, like your space pirate. Tell yourself I'm forcing you into this if it helps you sleep better."

"My skin crawls to even think about manipulating him like that. But I just can't. If I could be some kind of *femme fatale* as you're plotting, Tyler and I would still have been together. But I'm not the kind of woman that men lose their minds over. So all this," she said, pointing to the designer clothes, "it's an utter waste. Because Tyler will never leave Venetia for me, of all people."

He looked at her with none of the resolve diminished. It was like banging her head against an invisible wall. "Don't underestimate yourself." A spark of something came alive in his gaze and was gone before she could blink. "I know how much you can mess with a man's head, and that's when you're not trying. Think of how easy your real job is now. All you have to do is convince Tyler that he belongs with you, as always."

He was not going to budge from this path.

Just thinking about what he suggested, the fact that he had paid for it, made her nauseous. But he would not rest until Tyler was out of Venetia's life. And she didn't doubt for a second the lengths he would go to. She had already seen proof of that. He would also do it in a way that caused his sister minimum pain. Which meant Tyler would suffer. And she just couldn't leave her friend at Nikos's mercy.

She would have to go with Nikos, play the part he wanted her to play. At least that way, she could find a way to protect Tyler in the meantime. Tucking her knees together, she kept her gaze studiously away from his. "Fine, I'll do it."

He stilled. She could almost hear the gears in his head turning. "You will?"

"You've left me no choice, have you?" she said, blustering through it. It was the only way to stop from going into full-on panic. "*You're* the manipulative jerk for doing this to them, but yes, I'll be your evil sidekick. And it's a NO to the sex clothes."

His gaze thoughtful, he walked away from her.

Lexi sagged into the couch, shivering. Lying had never been her strong suit. But she had pulled it off for now, managed to fool Nikos. A Machiavellian feat in itself.

She was playing a dangerous game, but she could see no way out of it.

CHAPTER SIX

LEXI WOKE UP with a start and jerked upright. The feel of the softest Egyptian cotton against her fingers, the high ceiling as her gaze flew open and the pleasant scent of roses, and curiously basil, only intensified her confusion.

Usually, all she could smell was old pizza and smoke.

The view through the French doors onto a vast island set her bearings straight. The water was an intense blue; the sand, burnished gold, a striking contrast against it. It stretched for miles, as far as she could see. And other than the lapping of the waves, silence reigned.

It was unsettling as she was used to the noisy din of her apartment complex.

Clutching the sheets to her, she took a deep breath and fell back against the bed.

She was in the Demakis mansion in her own room. On one of the two islands they owned in the Cyclades. Her heart had resumed its normal beat when the maid had said the Demakis family and the patriarch Savas Demakis lived on the other one.

She closed her eyes, but she knew she had slept for way too long already. Stretching her hand, she reached for her cell phone on the nightstand and checked the time. She jumped off the bed when she saw it was half past three.

They had arrived at the private airstrip at four in the morning.

By the time the limo had driven them through the islet, past the electronically manned estate gates, she'd had zero energy left. Nikos's curt "Tyler can survive a few more hours without you" had put paid to the thought before she uttered it.

Their flight from Paris had been filled with tense silence. She had been so wound up from everything Nikos had said, and her own impulsive decision to continue, she'd been on tenterhooks. Thankfully he had left her alone.

In fact, the chilling silence she had felt from him, the absence of those sarcastic undertones when he had spoken to her, which had been the barest minimum, had meant that she kept casting looks at him.

She had the most gut-twisting notion that he hadn't bought her easy agreement to his plan. But all she could do was to push on.

She padded barefoot to the bathroom and gasped at the sheer magnificence of it.

Done in gold-piped cream marble tiles, the bathroom was decadent luxury and could house both hers and Ms. Goldman's apartment next door. She rubbed her feet on the lush cream-colored rug, unwilling to leave dusty footprints on the marble.

The vanity on her left was a silver bowl, wide enough for her to sit in, with gold-edged lining in front of an oval mirror.

She rubbed the glinting metal just to be sure. Yep, pure silver. So everything she had heard about the Demakis wealth was true. And Nikos's father had walked away from it all.

Ruminating on the thought, she ventured farther. The silver-and-gold theme pervaded the bathroom. Having grown up in homes where shower time had been two minutes spray under cold water, the sheer beauty of the bath stole into her.

A shower stood to her right and the highlight of the bathroom was an oval-shaped, vast sunken tub, also made out of marble.

Laughing, she closed the door behind her and decided to take advantage of it. She was here, and she would do everything within her power to ensure Nikos didn't do something reckless. But she might as well get a luxurious bath out of it. Checking to see that there were towels aplenty, she stripped and got into the bath. Gold-edged silver taps and small handmade soaps in a variety of scents greeted her.

Turning on the jets, she immersed herself in the water.

She was sipping a mocktail on the glorious deck of a luxury yacht while a Greek heiress looked at her as though she wanted to reduce her to ash. If looks could throw her overboard, Lexi would have been kissing exotic seaweed on the floor of the sea an hour ago when she had stepped onto the deck by Nikos's side.

He had watched her with that inscrutable expression of his, accompanied her to the yacht and brought her to Tyler. Tyler had hugged her, his gaze curiously awkward while Venetia had been a sullen, disquieting figure behind him. Contrary to the dramatics Lexi had expected, the heiress had been all too composed, only the blazing emotion in her black gaze betraying her fury.

It hadn't been more than fifteen minutes before she had interrupted them and tugged Tyler away. Still, it was clear that Tyler had no intention of hurting Venetia by walking away, even if he had no memory of her.

Which was why he had asked for Lexi. Because he had wanted his best friend close by—to help him figure out what to do. Not the ex he had dumped for Venetia, as Nikos assumed. By the time Lexi had realized this, Nikos had disappeared.

She had been prepared to see them together, knew that whatever problems she and Tyler had, had begun before he had met Venetia. But even she, with her wishful thinking, couldn't miss that whatever Tyler and Venetia had shared was strong. Which was going to make one ruthless Greek very angry.

Lexi shivered even though the sea air was balmy. Tyler and Venetia stood on the far side of the deck surrounded by Venetia's friends. Venetia wasn't going to let Tyler even look at her tonight. Probably never, if Nikos wasn't there to persuade her.

Which made her want to find Nikos and give him a piece of her mind for dragging her into this mess.

Stepping off the deck without another glance, she refused the offer of a buggy from one of the security guards.

The warm breeze from the sea plastered her T-shirt and shorts against her. She clutched the worn-out cotton with her fingers, trying to root herself.

The wealth and the sophistication of the people partying behind her, it overwhelmed her. But that wasn't the reason for the heavy feeling in her gut.

She would not feel sorry for herself. It was a glorious island the likes of which she would never see again, and she would not let the loneliness inside her mar her enjoyment of it.

Nikos punched in the code and kicked the heavy garage door back, hot rage fueling his blood.

Once again, Savas had thwarted him. In the three years that Nikos had carved his way into the Demakis empire through sheer hard work and determination, he had brought

Savas's bitterest rival, Theo Katrakis, onto the Demakis board, despite Savas's vehement refusal, proving that it *was* time to bring new money and partnerships into the company.

And it had paid off. In two years of partnership with Theo, a shrewd businessman with a practical head, Demakis Exports had increased their revenue by almost forty percent. Nikos had no doubt he would succeed in the new real-estate venture, as well.

But Nikos's success, perversely, made Savas push him a little more.

Why else would he, again and again, deny Nikos what he wanted the most? Another board meeting, another refusal to elect him CEO.

Locking away the scream of rage that fought for outlet, Nikos stripped off his trousers and dress shirt and pulled on old jeans.

He walked back out into the hangar area of his garage and pulled the tarp off the Lamborghini Miura S that he was restoring. He was being tested, he was being punished, he was being denied his rightful place because he was his father's son.

Because Savas had still not forgiven his son, Nikos's father. The one thing Savas didn't understand was how much Nikos hated his father, too. He was nothing like his father and he never would be.

He had only two goals in life. He had hardened himself against everything else. He had driven himself to exhaustion and beyond, forgone any personal relationships, hadn't forged any bonds with his cousins, all in pursuit of being his own man, of doing what his father had failed to do.

Protecting Venetia and becoming the Demakis CEO. And he would do both at any cost.

Renewed determination pounded through his blood.

Switching on his mobile, he placed a call to his assistant and ordered him to arrange a meeting with Theo Katrakis.

"You will go blind drawing in the dark."

Lexi gasped and looked up, the growly rumble of Nikos's words pinged across her skin like sparks of fire. She did it so fast that that the pencil flew from her hand. Her legs ached under her, from their position on the hard concrete floor of the garage.

She had sneaked in, wondering what the structure was, and seeing Nikos, naked from the waist up, working with a furious energy on the car behind him, she had stopped still, feeling the familiar itch in her fingers to reach for her sketch pad. Every time he had crawled under the car, her breath had hitched in her throat.

Obviously, she hadn't realized how much time had passed.

Nikos's hand dangled in front of her. The veins in his forearm stood out thickly, his fingers shining with grease. "How long have you been here?"

With a sigh, she gave him her hand and let him tug her up. Her legs, sore from sitting in that position for so long, gave out from under her.

His arm going around her, he steadied her against his chest. Molten heat swathed Lexi inside and out. He smelled of sweat and grease, an incredibly strange combination that cut off her breath effortlessly. Sinuous muscle tightened under her fingers and she jerked back, the warmth of his skin singeing the pads of her fingers.

He looked nothing like the suave businessman that had mocked her that first day. This Nikos was more down-to-earth but no less intense.

Lean muscle covered up by glorious olive-toned skin. Tight, well-worn jeans hanging low on his hips. A chest that could have been carved from marble, despite the sprinkling of hair. Washboard abdomen and Dear God Of All Glorious Things, that line of hair that disappeared into those jeans.

Her breath came hard and fast, a permanent shiver on her skin.

His dark brown eyes glittered with unhidden amusement and something else. Something that sent hot little flares of need into every inch of her. "Would you like me to get completely naked?"

Yes, please...for my art, y'know...

Hot color rose to her cheeks and she looked away. She bent over and picked up the loose paper and pencil. A sharp knot in her right shoulder told her she had been sketching him for far longer than she had planned to. She clutched the spot with her left hand and turned back. "I didn't mean to disturb you."

His hands landed on her, gentle and light. He turned her around. And she went, without protest, her skin already singing to be in such close contact with him. "Here?" he whispered near her ear, his fingers tracing the tight knot in her right shoulder.

She nodded, her throat dry.

His warm breath caressed her skin as he rubbed at the sore spot with long, pulling strokes. He was like a furnace of heat behind her. Only it was the pull-you-into-it kind. The pressure was relieved by his fingers, only to flood the rest of her body.

"Relax, *agape mou*. Remember what we talked about?"

Lexi nodded. Because much as she puzzled about it, there was nothing sexual about the way he rubbed her shoulders. She'd seen him with the other women. He wore his sexuality like a second skin. His being sexy was like... her ability to draw. Only she had no idea how to handle the relentless assault. Her skin prickled with awareness, the rough grooves of his palm rasping against her skin.

She shivered at how much she wanted those fingers to move from her shoulders to the rest of her, how much she wanted to lean back into his body and feel the press of hard muscle.

He plucked the paper from her hand and let her go. Silence had never felt more unnerving. Slowly she turned around, every inch of her trembling.

Finally, he looked at her, turning the sheet in his hand so that she could see the sketch. "You're extremely talented. But you drew me, not your space pirate."

Lexi was incapable of muttering even a word. She glanced at the sketch and her gut flopped to her feet. Mortification beat a tattoo in her head. She had meant to draw Spike and yet…there was Nikos in all his glory.

There was physical hunger in his gaze, an elemental longing. The very thing she had imagined seeing.

"Are all your sketches so self-revelatory?"

He whispered the words, but the garage walls seemed to amplify them before sending them back. Unasked questions and unsaid answers pervaded the air.

Nooooo.

She stepped back, desperate to flee. "I shouldn't have come in here. I was…was just walking around—"

His fingers closed over her wrist. "Then stay," he said, cutting through all the confusion. "I won't bite, Lexi."

He tugged her gently and she followed, feeling divided within. She was pathetic enough to admit that she found him intensely interesting and yet…she was also scared.

Curiosity wiped the floor with her confusion.

"Did you sleep well?" he asked, wiping his large hands with a rag. "I informed the maids to not approach you when you are sleeping."

Lexi nodded, a hard lump in her throat making it hard to swallow. She wanted to be angry with him for manipulating her, for thinking so little of Tyler's feelings. And he crumbled it all with one kind thought. She understood his need to protect his sister. Just wished it didn't come at the cost of Tyler's happiness.

She followed him to where the vintage car stood and remembered his comments. "So this is like your Bat Cave?"

Turning around, he laughed. "You remembered."

She forced herself to hold his gaze, knowing that he was waiting for her to drop it, shy away like a blushing virgin. "I like you here."

He raised a brow.

"You seem nicer, calmer, less manipulative."

He stared at her without comment, a shadow dimming the amusement. Turning around, he grabbed a wrench. "Did Venetia say something to you?"

Mesmerized by the shift and play of the muscles in his back, she didn't answer.

He turned around and stepped closer. "Lexi?"

"What?" She colored and met his gaze. "Venetia… Venetia didn't say a word to me. Just glared at me, you know, like she wanted to reduce me into microparticles with her laser beam."

"Is that what Spike can do?"

"Naahhh… I think this is a new character—Spike's demon sister."

He threw his head back and laughed, the tendons in his neck stretching. "You're really tempting me, *thee mou*. So… you didn't get a chance to talk to Tyler then?"

"Not really. They left the deck. And I…I just didn't know what to do."

"You don't like parties?"

"Less than I like being amongst a sea of people who

don't even know I exist. I could fall into the ocean and no one would even know I was gone." She felt her face heat as he paused and looked at her. But she couldn't stop. "She's not going to let me near him, especially in front of her friends, Nikos. I'd rather not go to any more of these parties in the future unless you're there."

The echo of her words surrounded them followed by deafening silence. Of all the people in the world, she had to pour out her stupid fears to him? A man who had no place for emotions and the insecurities they brought.

"Go ahead. Call me a fool."

"Come here."

When she didn't move, he pulled her close to his side. He was all hard, lean, unforgiving muscle. Lexi exhaled on a whoosh, the aching lump in her throat mocking her and yet unable to resist settling against his side.

His arm long enough to wrap around her twice, was a heavy, comforting weight on her shoulders. Her skin tingled where it rasped against hers. She felt him exhale, his big body shuddering in the wake of it. "Fears are not always rational, I know that."

She pushed away from him and turned around, striving for composure. He didn't seem unfeeling right then. He sounded as though he had known fear and from everything he had told her, she believed he had.

"I thought you would be living it up at the party," she said, needing to clutter the silence.

"I'm not one for much partying, either. When I was younger, I didn't have the time, and now I don't have the interest. The party scene is nothing but a hunt for sex and I don't need it."

No, he didn't.

She tucked her legs into the couch as he settled down on the other side. He slid into the seat in slow, measured movements, and she knew it was for her. Feeling the silliest idiot ever, she unglued herself from the corner. Okay, so she didn't want to quite sit in his lap, but there was no reason to insult the man.

He noticed her effort with smiling eyes. "You're getting used to me."

The warmth in those eyes, the simple pleasure in his words lit a spark inside her. She sucked in a deep breath. "Why didn't you have time?"

He shrugged. "Until a few years ago, I worked every hour there was. I had no degree or work experience except the little I learned in my father's garage. The only way I moved up from being a line man on the manufacturing floor to a board member was by working hard."

"You didn't want to study?"

"I didn't have that choice. If I wanted security for Venetia and me, I had to do everything Savas asked me to do. Those were his conditions."

"Conditions?" she said, feeling sick to her stomach.

He stood up from the seat, as though he couldn't sit still. He wiped the immaculate surface of the hood with a rag. It was a comfort thing, Lexi realized with dawning awareness. There was something different about him today, and it was this place. He seemed comfortable here, almost at peace, a striking contrast to the man who had women in every city for sex.

"When Savas came to pick us up, he had specific conditions. If I was to live in his house, if I wanted Venetia to have everything she needed, I had to do anything and everything he asked of me."

"What did he ask you to do?" Her question was instantaneous.

He leaned against the car, his hands folded. "He told me to never expect anything that I hadn't earned. That I was his grandson meant nothing in the scheme of things. I was forbidden to mention my father or mother. Within a week, I started in his factory."

She shot up, his matter-of-fact tone riling her own anger. "But that was…unnecessarily cruel of him."

"He saved Venetia and me from a life of starvation and desperation. Only he refused to give it to us for free. It was not an unfair condition."

Holding his gaze took everything Lexi had when she was shaking with fury inside. "Yes, if he was only your employer. But this is your grandfather, your family we are talking about."

"Savas hated that my father walked out on all this. He wanted to ensure I didn't end up another fool like him."

Lexi wanted to argue some more, but the resolve etched into Nikos's face stopped her. Now she understood why he had been so ready to blackmail her or pay her, how everything was a transaction, how everything had a price in his mind.

How could he be any different when that's what he had been taught?

A thirteen-year-old boy, mourning his parents, dealing with his sister's shock, fighting for survival, and the price for it had been that he show no weakness. Could she blame him when she knew the depths to which the need for survival could push a person?

"He messed you up, Nikos." She said the words softly, slowly, burdened under a wave of sadness. Her childhood had been empty, her strongest memory was of craving for someone who would hold her, kiss her, hug her, love her unconditionally.

All she had ever wanted was to have a family.

Nikos, he had had one. And yet he had known less kindness than she had.

She heard Nikos's laugh through the filter of her own teetering emotions. It was fire in his eyes, curving that sinful mouth. It mocked her for feeling sorry for him. "Everything Savas has done has been to my advantage. Have you seen where I'm in my life right now? I will be the CEO of Demakis International in a few months, will have everything my father didn't have. Do you think I will ever be hungry again? We both know what that desperation feels like, *agape mou*. Admit it. Admit that any price is worth paying for it."

"I have seen your place in the world. I almost drowned in that glorious bathtub. Are you truly blind to what price you're paying for all this? Even sex is a transaction for you."

He hulked over her in an ever so gentle way. But his gentility, his concern, they were all lost on her. "You can dish it out, Lexi, but can you take it? Do you want to hear some truths, as well?"

Her stomach dipped and dived, her nerves pinging with a thrilling excitement that spread through her like a fever. Now she knew why she had drawn him with that look in his eyes. Being near Nikos, feeling everything she did in his presence, she couldn't spend another moment fooling herself.

She suddenly knew why her relationship with Tyler had failed on so many levels. Tyler and she had never meant to be more than friends. Ever. It was as if an invisible portal had been opened. Now she couldn't *un*believe its existence whatever she did. "You're right, I can't," she said, opting for cowardice. She wanted to run away before she betrayed herself, if he didn't know already. "I can, however, tell you that Venetia and Tyler...whatever they share is not so weak as you imagine. There's a fire between them. I've never..." She paused, the heat of his gaze lighting the very fire she had thought herself unaware of.

"You've never what?" His gaze widened with a dangerous curiosity that sent a pang of alarm through her. "With all your antiquated notions, did you refuse to put out, Lexi? Is that why he left you?"

Her gut flopped. She shivered, amazed at his razor-sharp mind. He was so close to the pathetic truth. "The P.I. couldn't figure out if I had already lost my V card?" She was attracted to Nikos, and it was nothing like she had ever felt before. It was intense, and it made her feel frayed, as if she was coming apart at the seams.

Why else would his amusement hurt so much?

He grabbed her wrist and tugged her closer. "Articles in *Cosmo* have nothing over practical experience."

"Are you volunteering then?" she said, before she could lock away the thought. "Will you help me practice so that I can then seduce Tyler away from your sister?"

A cavern of tension sucked them right in.

His dark gaze moved over her with lingering precision from the top of her hair to her feet clad in open-toed sandals. There was such a jaded look in those eyes that something within her rebelled and twisted.

He had no interest in her. She had seen his type and like every other man on the planet, it was boobs and legs. Neither of which she possessed enough to count, sadly.

For the first time in her life, she wished she had paid more attention to her clothes, had worn proper makeup. Because she wanted him to feel that hunger she felt for him, she wanted him to be mindless in his craving for her.

"I'm sure I can be persuaded," he finally answered.

The color leached from Lexi's face, leaving a pale mask behind.

Nikos instantly regretted his words.

She recovered fast, her mouth trembling with her fury. "I'm glad I'm such a source of amusement for you, but I'd rather be dumped by Tyler another hundred times than take you up on your *offer*. I'd rather sleep with one of the guys that frequent the club. You're unfeeling, manipulative and arrogant. You're toying with me just for the fun of it, and I don't need your pity sex."

She ran out of the garage as though the very devil was behind her. Stunned by how hard her words hit, Nikos forced himself to breathe, a storm of inexplicable emotion surging through him.

He had never meant to hurt her. He had only needled her, as he always did. His curiosity about every facet of her life, about her relationship with Tyler, it knew no bounds, shattering his usual reserve.

Had he hit the truth? Was there no end to her innocence? Why should it matter to him if she had slept with her blasted boyfriend or not? So he had covered his stunned reaction to it by needling her some more.

Are you volunteering?

Yes.

His body roared with its own answer. But he didn't want just sex, he wanted *her*. For the first time in his life, he wanted something that he didn't even understand.

He understood the pull he felt for her. It was more than just attraction; it was something as unique as the woman herself.

Her upbringing, her isolation even after the way she surrounded herself with people, her loneliness—it was like looking at an image of himself he didn't know existed. Only a better one, with compassion, affection, love.

And the fact that he was letting her burrow under his skin, blared like an alarm in his head.

Unfeeling, manipulative and arrogant.

He was all that and more.

Yet, right at that moment—with his body shuddering at

the very thought of kissing that mouth, his mind seething with hurt because she, Lexi Nelson, found him unsuitable— he was not the man he had forced himself to become. Old wounds and memories opened up, cloying through him, leaving him shaking.

The flash of pain, hot and shocking, that darted through him, forced him to focus like nothing else. He would not examine the whys or hows of it. There was nothing Lexi could offer him that wasn't easily available to him without complication.

Not her body, and definitely not her pitying, trusting, loving, heart.

It was good he had scared her off, good that he had hurt her, because he had nothing to offer her, either. Like Venetia's tears, the flashing hurt in her eyes was a price he would willingly pay.

Better she stay away from him, better she stopped analyzing him, better she stopped giving him glimpses of things he didn't even know were missing from his life.

CHAPTER SEVEN

LEXI RUBBED IN the sunscreen on her legs, loving the golden tan she had already acquired. The early-morning sun felt warm on her bare shoulders, while the cool waves tickled her toes.

A small whitewashed beach house, small compared to the enormous mansion, stood near the ocean while the Demakis residence lay almost two miles inland. Leaving Tyler to Venetia in the afternoons, she had taken to walking the two miles, enjoying the quiet.

Ten days had flown by since she had let herself be cornered by Nikos in the garage, since she had lost it in front of him like that. But instead of anger that he had toyed with her, it was the fact that he had no interest that bothered her more.

Which meant she really needed her head examined. Because with everything else going on, Nikos's lack of interest in her should be the high point of her life right now. Bad enough that she had to spend time with him in the morning, and evening, to feel his gaze on her, always a curious light in it.

Every morning brought a new facet of Venetia's wrath that Lexi was here, revealing her frustration that Tyler couldn't remember. Nikos hadn't been joking when he had warned her about his sister. But even with the elaborate schemes that Venetia hatched to help Tyler remember, Lexi only saw her gnawing fear, her love for him. Lexi understood the fear the dark emotion in Venetia's eyes caused Nikos.

Hearing Tyler's tread on the sand behind her, Lexi turned around with a smile.

Dark shadows swam under his eyes, his face drawn. She sat up straight, her stomach tight. "You remembered something?"

Sinking to his knees next to her, he shook his head. His mouth a bitter curve, he clasped her face. "How can you bear to even look at me, Lex?"

Cold fear swept through Lexi. "What are you talking about, Ty?"

"Venetia told me what I said to you when you came to see us that day."

"Why?"

"I guess to remind me how much I wanted you gone. Except, it didn't work like she wanted." He fisted his hands, his mouth tight. "I want to leave, Lex. There are so many things I have to apologize for. I don't want to be here another minute."

Stricken by the bitterness in his gaze, Lexi clasped his hand. Her throat stung with unshed tears, but she forced herself to say it, forced herself to see the truth she had been dancing around for so many days. "Listen, Ty. Yes, you hurt me. But I've no doubt that there was a reason behind it. This is you and me, Ty. We do this a lot. We fight, we yell and we make up. It's just that this time things are different."

He ran a hand through his hair, his gaze pained. "I... can't believe I said those hurtful things to you, Lex, on top of everything else..."

Lexi felt as though someone was sitting on her chest. "It's all forgiven, Ty. Truly."

His blue gaze shone with affection, his palms clasped her cheeks. The familiar smell of him settled in her gut, infinitely comforting.

"I messed up everything with us so badly. And now, I have to break Venetia's heart, too. I—"

Clasping his face in her palms, Lexi shook her head. "I have no idea what went wrong." Her breath faltered in her throat. It would never go back to what it had been. But her love for Tyler, it would never waver. Knowing that Nikos would roast her alive for it, she said the words. "You don't have to decide anything now, Tyler. About Venetia. Do you understand?"

His eyes glittering with the same pain, he shook his head. "I can't face myself right now much less Venetia. You're all I've ever had in the world, and I hurt you."

Lexi closed her eyes as he pulled her closer and pressed his mouth to hers. But the only thing she felt was a sense of comfort, and a growing desolation as an inescapable truth began to inch around her heart. It was the loss of a dream more than anything else. Had he felt this same desolation that day? Had he known that something was irrevocably wrong between them but hadn't known how to tell her?

He met her gaze, the same realization dawning in his. "We're going to be all right, Lex."

They were. Lexi curled into him and hugged him tight. He had always been there for her, had always made her feel as if she mattered to at least one person in the world, that she wasn't an unwanted orphan. They had no future together except as friends. The realization instead of hurting her only strengthened her.

She had her only friend in the world back, and she wanted nothing more.

Her skin prickled, the hair on her neck standing to attention. Without turning, Lexi knew it was not Venetia.

Nikos was close.

Bracing herself, she didn't know for what, especially because she was doing what he wanted her to do, she turned around.

And stared up at the open terrace of the beach house where Nikos and Venetia stood. They looked like a vengeful Greek goddess and god, come to cast a curse on them.

Focus on reality, Lexi.

She felt Tyler stiffen next to her and squeezed his hand. "Don't do this, Ty," she whispered in his ear, knowing that whatever her faults, Venetia did love him. "I'll always love you but there's nothing more between us. Don't ruin what you have with her."

Tyler turned toward her, a sad smile on his face. "If I really loved her enough to hurt *you,* it will come back, Lex. But no more of Venetia looking at you as if you were the cause of her problems, no more of her brother looking at you as if he wants to devour you."

Stunned, Lexi looked up.

His hand on his sister, and his gaze calculatingly blank, Nikos held Venetia there. Probably stopping her from running down the stairs to gouge Lexi's eyes out.

Lexi untangled herself from Tyler. Amnesia or not, heartbreaking realization that something between her and Tyler was right or not, she had kissed Venetia's fiancé.

Feeling as dirty as Nikos was paying her to be, she walked away.

Nikos stayed on the roof long after Venetia ran down the stairs after Tyler, tears streaming down her face.

The very tears he had wanted to stop her from shedding. He felt powerless, but he also knew that she needed to shed them now. Better she found the truth now than when it was too late, when her love had an even more powerful grip on her.

But the powerlessness he felt was nothing compared to the dark cavern of longing that rent him open at the sight of Tyler kissing Lexi.

Again, it was exactly what Nikos had wanted. He should be elated that, even now, Venetia was kicking Tyler out of her life. And yet all he could hear was the roaring in his ears, a possessive yearning to wipe the taste of that kiss from Lexi's mouth.

He wanted that hungry look in her eyes when she looked at him. He wanted to make her mewl with pleasure. He wanted to shower her with every possible decadent gift in the world. He wanted to possess her, he wanted to teach her to be selfish, he wanted to show her every pleasure there was to have in the world.

He wanted a part of her, that intangible element in her that made her *her*.

It took him a few minutes to get himself under control, to fight the urge to trace Tyler's steps and beat him down to a pulp, to shove the desire that thrummed in his blood into one corner.

The pleasure he had pursued had only ever been transient, and he had liked it that way. But now he wanted Lexi. And not just for a night. He wanted to understand what made her tick, he wanted to hold her when she cried, he wanted to show her the world.

And he would have her.

Stepping from under the lukewarm blast of the shower spray, Lexi grabbed a beach towel from the neatly folded stack and wrapped it around herself.

Wiping herself down in the deafening quiet of the beach

house, she pulled on her gym shorts and a pink tank top and threw her damp swimsuit into her bag. Venetia might have an army of servants to pick up after her, but she didn't feel comfortable leaving her dirty clothes for someone else. Even more so now that she was leaving.

A hollow pang went through her and she fought the silly sensation. She wasn't going to mope over a man who had nothing but mockery for her. And even if he did want her, taking on someone like Nikos Demakis, even for one night, wasn't something she wanted.

She had hardly handled the fallout with Tyler. Nikos would chew her up and spit her out, leaving her no place to hide, even from herself.

She pushed her feet into the flip-flops and tugged her beach bag onto her shoulder, looking around for a switch to turn off the lights around the small pool.

"Leave it on, Lexi," The words came from somewhere behind her, rendering her frozen for a few seconds.

She whirled around. "Nikos," she said stupidly, her heart still racing. "I thought you had left."

"And miss the chance to chat with you?"

In the low lights of the pool, she couldn't quite make out his features. Except for the rigid set of his mouth and the tension pouring out of him. "I really don't have the energy to argue with you, Nikos."

"You're not going anywhere until we have this discussion."

He was wearing a charcoal-gray dress shirt, the cuffs rolled back, and black trousers that hugged his hips. A couple of buttons were undone giving her a peek of golden-olive chest.

His sensuous mouth flattened into a thin line of displeasure, he leaned against the far wall, legs crossed at the ankles. But there was nothing casual in the way he looked at her.

"What happened with Tyler?"

"Venetia told him what he'd said to me that night at the party. He feels awful about it. Nikos, he—"

"Ahh...so everything is perfect in your little world again."

"What do you mean?"

"He's come back to you, just as I predicted."

Tension pulled at her nerves. He thought Tyler was done with Venetia. "You don't understand—"

"I do. Better than you think. I understand the crippling loneliness, the need to matter to someone, the need to be loved. But you are better than this, better than him. Tell me you're not going back to him."

"That's really none of your business, is it?" she said, pushing off the wall. She was goading him. But she couldn't stop. "You're not my pimp, or my boss."

And he took the bait.

He was in front of her before she could blink. His hands braced on the wall either side of her, he slanted his upper body just enough that she could smell the purely masculine scent of him, so that she could see the evening stubble on his jaw, so that she could feel the heat radiating off him and blanketing her in a sensuous swathe.

His mouth hovered inches from hers, and she wanted to close the distance between them with a raw ache that blinded her to everything else.

"Is there no end to your stupidity?"

She dragged her gaze to his, heat creeping up across her neck and into her cheeks. "Everything's going according to your sordid plan. Why do you care what I do?"

"I'm trying to protect you from yourself. Are you so infernally stupid to believe that's the real him or that he won't throw you away the moment he remembers everything? Or do you plan to sleep with him and seal the deal this time?"

"There's nothing to seal, okay?" She struggled to draw a breath, to form a coherent thought, cringing from the pain he could so easily inflict on her. "I've loved him since I was thirteen, and yes, I slept with him. But it was awful. Just as awful the next time too and then I just kept finding excuses to not do it. We had this horrible fight and he left me—he moved out. Are you satisfied? He's all I have in this world, but there's nothing left between him and me."

"You baited me." Instead of the anger she expected, a tight smile split his mouth. His gaze shone with a wicked fever. And Lexi regretted her behavior. Her attraction to him, it was frying her mind. "Why kiss him then?"

"Again. None of your business."

He tugged her close to him in a quick movement, with his hands on her hips, bringing her off the ground. With a gasp, she clutched his shirt, bunching the crisp fabric in her fingers.

His erection rubbed against her belly. It felt hard, and so unbearably, unbelievably good that she moaned loud. Arrows of pleasure sparked off every inch of her.

Her gaze flew to his, her skin on fire. "Nikos…"

"Yes, Lexi."

He was smiling, a wicked, buckle-your-knees smile. She was on fire and he was smiling. "This, you and I…I can't…this feels like…" She swallowed, barely catching the whimper of pleasure in her throat.

His hands spanning her tiny waist, he pressed an openmouthed kiss, wet and hot against the pulse in her neck. Nerve endings she hadn't known existed thundered into life. Her arms around his neck, she held on tight, every drag of her muscles against his sending a spasm through her.

His hands moved from her waist to capture her face, forcing her to look at him. Her mouth dried at the naked hunger dancing across those arresting features. There was a black, molten fire in his eyes and it was all for her. "What you do to me, it isn't amusing in the least."

The open, toe-curling want in his words set a low, pulsing ache in her lower belly. She closed her eyes and struggled to pull in air.

Nikos Demakis, the most gorgeous man she had ever seen, wanted her. That in itself had her shivering, and the storm of hunger he was holding back in his powerful body…it was as if every decadent fantasy of hers had come to life. And she…she was still just her…plain Lexi Nelson.

How was she supposed to say no to him?

Too tight in her own skin, she rubbed herself against him. Their mingled groans rent the air, the rasp of his body fully clothed against hers, pure torture. A shudder racked his powerful body, a string of Greek, curses she was sure, pervading the air.

She did it again, and he pushed her back against the wall, his hands spanning her tiny waist.

Lust stamped his features. "Don't do that, *thee mou.* Unless you want me to take you against the wall. Not that I won't oblige you if that's what you want."

"Wait." Panic bloomed in her stomach at the raw tingle that swept through her. She had to put a stop to this, now. While she still could. "Please, Nikos. Let me go."

He let her go instantly, his gaze devouring her. His silence screamed at her, his face a feral mask of control.

"I'm sorry. I didn't mean to lead… The fact that you want me, it's dangerous, it's gone to my head.…" She took a deep breath. This was not fair, to him or to her.

"I don't think there's a woman alive who could say no to you. But I…"

"Every time you look at me with those blue eyes, you're wondering how it would feel to kiss me. Your body, whether you don't know it, or you know it and don't want to accept it, is crying for my touch."

She wrapped her hands around herself. "It is, but I have control over it. I won't have sex with just anyone, without involving my heart."

His mouth curled into a sneer. "No, you will only have sex with a friend, for whom you're an emotional crutch and nothing else, to stop him from leaving you, even if you don't really want it, no? You're prepared to go to any lengths, give up anything to keep him in your life. Who's using sex now?"

Every word out of his mouth was the utter, inescapable truth. Only she hadn't seen it until now. It coated her mouth with distaste, twisted the biggest relationship of her life, the only one, to a painful, jagged mass.

Was that what everything between her and Tyler had been reduced to? Had she clung to him all these years knowing that things weren't right? She couldn't bear the desolate thought. "You don't know what you are talking about. You just can't understand what the big deal is, why Venetia and I are willing to go to any lengths for Tyler. Because you're incapable of understanding it, of feeling *anything,* and it's beginning to annoy the hell out of you."

His face could have been a mask poured out of concrete. Every muscle in his face froze in contrast to the blistering emotion in his gaze. It put paid to her stupid claim that he didn't feel anything. "You little hypocrite. I saw you when he kissed you. You couldn't wait to get away and yet you clung to him. You want to know how it feels when you feel the opposite, Lexi, when you can't wait to rip off someone's clothes?"

She could have said that she already knew—that it was all she wanted to do when she was near him. But he didn't give her the chance. Pressing his upper body into hers, he nudged a thigh between her legs and claimed her mouth.

Her shocked gasp was lost in his mouth. The stubble on his chin scratched her sensitive skin, the hard angles of his body imprinted on her and she shivered as he nipped at her mouth, knocking the breath out of her.

He didn't kiss her gently like Tyler had done. It was as if the storm had burst, as if he had been waiting forever to do it, as if his next breath depended on kissing her. His hands stole under her T-shirt until his hot palms were laid flat on her bare flesh.

His tongue licked the inside of her lower lip, sucked at her tongue, stroked her to a high that she had to climb.

It was a kiss with pure erotic intent, it was a kiss to possess her senses, it was a kiss to prove his point. But he didn't know that he didn't need to. She was already a slave to her body's wants and desires when she was near him.

A moan rose through her throat and misted into the darkness as he sank his teeth into her lower lip. An electric shiver tingled up her spine as a million nerve endings sprang into life, both pain and pleasure coalescing and shooting down between her legs.

The wetness at her sex shocked and aroused her even more.

She groaned loud, a whimper to stop and a plea to continue, all rolled into one. Her knees trembled and she rubbed against the hard thigh lodged against her throbbing core, mindless with aching need.

His hands gentled in her hair, his hard muscles pulled

back from her. He murmured something in Greek. She shivered as he blew a soft breath on her throbbing lower lip. Something almost like an apology reached her ears.

He claimed her lips again, but this time, he was exploring, teasing, and it was the unexpected gentleness that broke the spell for her.

With a grunt, she pushed him back from her, her chest rising and falling with the effort it took to pull air into her lungs. "No," she whispered into the darkness. And then repeated it louder for her sake more than his. "No, Nikos."

The dark intent in his eyes scared her, her own powerlessness in the face of the blazing fire between them scared her. If he touched her again, if he kissed her again, she wouldn't say no. She couldn't say no.

He was the first man to incite knee-buckling desire in her. Why did he have to be so out of her league, so different from who she was?

And look how things panned out with your best friend, an insidious voice whispered in her ear.

She ran the back of her hand over her trembling lips. The taste of him wasn't going to come off so easily. "I don't love you. I…"

He jerked back slowly, his gaze incredulous. "Have you still not learned the lesson? Your love for Tyler blinded you to everything, crippled you into not living your life. You still want that love?"

"I don't know what you're talking about."

"Tyler had an affair with Faith behind your back. He cheated on you with your friend."

She raised her head and looked at him, fury and self-disgust roiling through her. "You're making this up… you're…"

Her desperation had no end, it seemed. If Nikos had

been angry before, he was a seething cauldron of fury now. Taking her arms in a gentle grip that pricked through her, he set her away from him.

"I'm an unfeeling bastard, true. And I've no misconceptions about what or who I am. However, I don't settle for what people throw at me. I don't let them treat me like trash."

She closed his mouth with her hand, and sagged against him. "I had no idea about Tyler and Faith. That they even liked each other that way. I…"

There it was, the tiny truth that been evading her for so many months, the last piece in the puzzle that threatened to pull her under.

She had done all this.

She finally understood why Tyler had called her selfish. Because he had felt bound to her by his guilt, because even though there had been proof enough that they could never be more than friends, she hadn't wanted to let him go, because her refusal to move on had meant he couldn't move on, either.

Because she had been the one who had gone to juvie, even though both of them had been responsible for the robbery.

All because she had been scared to live her own life.

So many times, Tyler had asked her to apply to a college somewhere else, asked her to change her job, always encouraged her to reach for more, to take a risk and she… she had been scared to leave his side, scared to venture into an unknown life, amongst unknown people because she had been terrified of being alone.

Of having no one who loved her, of mattering to no one. And so she had continued on her little merry way, clinging to Tyler, clinging to Faith, ruining all their lives in the process. She had convinced herself that he loved her, that she loved him in a way she hadn't, forced herself and guilted him.

And that's what he was doing again. He was leaving Venetia, breaking her heart because he felt guilty about how he had treated Lexi. And Lexi couldn't let him do that anymore.

She couldn't be a coward anymore.

Straightening her shoulders, she looked at Nikos. Fear was a primal tattoo in her head that she had to mute long enough to speak. For the first time in her life, she wanted something. She wanted to be with Nikos, she wanted to revel in the desire she felt for him.

She had to do it now, before she lost her nerve, before she forgot how many lives she had ruined because she had been scared, before she crawled back into her safe little place and let life pass her by.

She had to let Tyler go, she had to set herself free. If she fell, he would be there to catch her. He always would. She knew that now. Which meant it was time to start living.

"You want me, Nikos? You got me," she said, knowing that there was no turning back now.

A blaze of fire leaped into life in his gaze. He took another step closer. Instinctively, she stepped back and the wall kissed her spine. Her breath came in ragged little whispers as he placed his palm on her midriff, right beneath her breast. It spanned most of her waist. Her pulse leaped at her throat, and immediately, she closed her eyes.

His fingers moved up, traced the shape of her breasts, and she arched into his touch. "Look at me, Lexi. You don't have to hide from this."

She did, and his gaze held hers. She took his mouth in a hard kiss that stoked the flames in his eyes a little more. "I won't hide anymore, Nikos, or hold back. I want everything you can give me."

His fingers kept moving over her body, over her breasts, her hips, until they came to rest on her butt. He cupped her and pulled her close. The heavy weight of his arousal pressing into her belly, it was the most sinful sensation ever.

Every muscle in her body turned into molten liquid, ready to be molded into whatever he wanted. She gripped his nape and wrapped her legs around his hips. His breath coated her skin, his fingers found the seam of her bra all the while he nibbled at her lips.

He was everywhere, in her breath, in her skin, in her every cell, and she wanted to do nothing but sink into him, to give herself over into his hands.

Suddenly, he wasn't kissing her anymore, and Lexi whimpered. Her heart slowly returning to its normal beat, she blinked and realized why he had stopped.

Nikos's head of security stood on the other side of the pool. His thumb running over her cheek, Nikos grinned. "We're not done."

Lexi nodded and tried not to sink back into the wall. Her breathing still choppy, she moved to stand behind Nikos, heat streaking her cheeks.

She watched Nikos talk to the other man with increasing agitation, until a curse flew from his mouth that reverberated in the silence. Her gut feeling heavy, Lexi reached him just as his head of security left. She clasped Nikos's arm, despite the angry energy pouring off of him. "Nikos, what happened?"

"Venetia and Tyler have been gone all afternoon." He clicked Call on his cell and waited. "And she's not picking up."

"I don't understand. What do you mean they've been—"

He ran a shaking hand through his hair, the color leaching from his skin. "The maids saw her pack a bag. Tyler's clothes are missing, too. And apparently one of her friends picked them up in a boat. They have left." She stilled as another curse fell from his mouth, ringing with his worry.

Without another word to her, he was gone.

CHAPTER EIGHT

WHAT HAPPENED WHEN Lexi Nelson, delusional coward extraordinaire, decided to finally live her life and throw herself at a six-foot-three-inch hunk of Greek alpha male who had a woman in every city?

Said Greek stud apparently lost all interest in sex because his sister ran away to God-knows-where with her lover, who happened to be Lexi's best friend, in tow.

So instead of living her fantasy, Lexi was getting a peek into Athens's nightlife with Nikos alternately cursing and glowering at her, apparently having easily dismissed any attraction he had felt for her in the first place.

This time, she was really pissed off with the Greek heiress.

Lexi had known Venetia had cared for Tyler, but she hadn't expected her to spirit Tyler away from under her brother's nose. All because Tyler had kissed Lexi.

If only Venetia knew the truth…

In her heart, Lexi was glad Venetia had refused to allow Tyler to simply bow out of her life. If only she could take away the guilt and worry shining in Nikos's eyes…that and the fact Nikos hadn't even looked at her, much less touched her again.

Every night for the past four days, Nikos, intent on interrogating every man or woman Venetia had ever spoken to,

or even looked at, had dragged her to a multitude of dazzling nightclubs and lavish penthouses, each more deca-
dently rich and sophisticated than the last.

This view into his sphere of life had her senses spinning. For the first two days, she had been awed, almost
enjoying the glimpse she was getting into a life she could
only imagine about.

Except each visit had steadily chipped away at her already frayed self-confidence. Everywhere they went
women—tall, beautiful and sexy—threw themselves at
Nikos. She might as well have been an alien existing in a
different galaxy.

Really, it was a testament to the man's focus, and his
love for his sister, that he hadn't spared any of them even
a second look.

She was beginning to believe Nikos might have been
delirious that evening four days ago. She would have easily called herself delirious, except she couldn't forget how
mind-bendingly good it had felt to be cradled against his
powerful body, how the simple caress of his mouth against
her neck had branded her.

Had his desire for her already cooled off? She'd braced
for that to happen *after,* not before he even kissed her again.
And it stung.

With a curt "stay here," he had dumped her in the private lounge of the nightclub almost forty-five minutes ago.

The nightclub was a glorious spectacle with live dancers
on raised platforms on either side of the dance floor. Soft
purple lights illuminated the crowd below. White couches,
white columns, white tables—all soaked up the light giving a sultry vibe to the club. And having noticed the lines
outside the entrance and the small crowd inside, she had
no doubt it was an exclusive type.

Judging however by the curious, almost-hungry looks

thrown up at the private lounge where she was sitting, she realized it was the private lounges that were the main attraction. And she could see why.

Separated and placed discreetly above the main party floor, the VIP lounge, enclosed by glass walls on all sides, offered a perfect view of the club. She sat on the edge of the provocative sofa bed, the leather luxuriously soft under her touch.

Amidst the crowd and music, she found Nikos as easily as if he was her honing beacon.

Leaning against the wall on the opposite side of the club, he was talking to a tall, curvy blonde. Her upper body was slanted toward him in an unmistakable invitation. Despite black envy scouring her, Lexi couldn't find fault with her.

Nikos Demakis would tempt any woman.

She was about to leave the private lounge when a bartender walked in to serve cocktails. The easy smile in the bartender's eyes boosted her flagging spirit. She took a sip of the cocktail as he left, placed it back on the table and started moving to the steamy number playing softly. She was not going to let Nikos's indifference to her ruin her evening any longer.

Refusing Venetia's friend's blatant invitation, which held zero interest for him, Nikos pushed his way through the crowd. His frustration must have been apparent because more than one group of people jumped out of his way.

He had severely underestimated Venetia's determination, her envy for Lexi. Before meeting her, he would have called Tyler and his fickle mind the root of Venetia's insecurity. There was no such doubt in his mind now.

Lexi might not be gorgeous, or sophisticated, or wealthy, yet there was something about her that made one look deep inside and come away wanting. He perfectly understood what his sister must have felt.

In four days of his security team and Nikos himself following several leads, there was no information about where she and Tyler had gone. He was beginning to believe his sister would return only when and if she wished it.

In the meantime, Savas was tightening the screws further, Theo Katrakis was ready to start discussions about the board and then there was Lexi, who with her mere existence was spinning his life out of control.

Four days of Lexi, waiting alongside him worried about what Venetia would do to her blasted friend, four days of Lexi looking at him with those big, blue eyes.

You want me, Nikos? You got me.

Never had a woman's acceptance to have sex with him, which put in those base terms felt like an insult to her, never had such simple words moved through him with such power.

He walked up the steps to the private lounge. He halted outside the entrance and pushed the door open.

She was moving in time to the music slowly, her short white skirt displaying her toned legs perfectly. Soft revolving lights from outside the lounge revealed her laughing mouth and warm eyes in strips and flashes. The delicate curve of her neck came into view next, the silver of her earrings glinted.

The sleeveless black leather vest hugged her, displaying the curves of her small breasts. With her hands up and behind her head, she moved so sensuously to the music that lust bolted through him. Every time she turned, that vest moved upward, flashing him with a strip of her midriff.

A lush smile played on her lips and she was totally lost in the moment. He closed the door behind him and she turned slowly.

Her eyes rounded in her delicate face. He waited for her to drop her gaze, shy away, but she held his gaze, even as a dusting of pink streaked her cheeks. She was different, and not just because of how she was dressed, but the tilt of her chin, the resolve in her eyes.

"Did she—" Lexi nodded toward the dance floor "—know anything about where Venetia could have taken Tyler?"

"We have no idea who's taken whom."

She frowned. "Tyler is unwell, has no money or connections, and the last I saw him, he was determined to not hurt Venetia. Are you the one with amnesia or him? Because you seem to have forgotten everything that happened four days ago completely."

She walked past him and the whisper of her scent had his gut tightening in a burst of need. His body was over-sensitized to her presence, wound tight in anticipation of wanting her, driven to the edge by having her near and not taking, or touching. And yet he had stopped himself.

He had spilled Tyler's indiscretion with Faith in a perverse moment of selfishness, acting directly against his own larger purpose of having her here.

It was a weak, impulsive, juvenile, completely uncharacteristic move.

And suddenly, his control over this thing between them, his control over his spiraling desire for her, over the maelstrom of emotions she released in him, was more important than anything else.

Because even his worry over Venetia hadn't blunted his awareness of this woman. "No, I haven't forgotten."

Her blue eyes held that same shimmering honesty that he had come to expect from her. "That woman, she wanted you. Wherever we go, there is always at least one woman who wants you."

Her statement was in reality a question. For the past four days, he had been only thinking of himself.

She had obviously taken his distance to mean that he didn't want her anymore.

His desire for her was a near-constant hum in his blood. And it was the very intensity of it that had shackled him. Lust had ever been only a function of his body until now, not his mind or heart. "I don't want her or any of them." He knew what she wanted to hear, yet some devil in him wanted her to ask, wanted to hear her admit it again.

Now, when she wasn't still reeling from the truth about Tyler; now, when it was only Nikos that she saw. And nothing else.

Her teeth clamped on her lower lip, she straightened her shoulders. And rose to the challenge. "Are you still interested in me?"

He laid his palm horizontally on her rib cage, felt her heart race under his fingers. "What do you think?"

She pushed herself into his touch, her gaze challenging him. "Then what are you waiting for?"

"You want this because you're angry with Tyler, hurt by what he did."

"I'm not hurt by what he did. If I didn't have to worry about you, I could actually be enjoying this glimpse into your filthy rich life right now."

Furious surprise rolled through him. "You are worried about me?" The question hurled out of him before he knew.

"Of course I am. Anyone with eyes can see how much you love Venetia, how worried you are about her. That night after they left, you spent the whole night looking for her. And I…" She took a deep breath, "I don't want *anyone* to be hurt at the end of this. Not Tyler, not Venetia and definitely not you. And I don't know how to tell you to not worry so much, how to make you see that she's far stronger than you give her credit for. She saw me kissing Tyler, Nikos, and she didn't crumble."

"You think that's the only sign of her weakness? She saw my father shoot himself. It has hurt her in ways I can't understand."

She clasped his hand with hers, willing him to look at her. A shaft of sensation traveled up his arm. She was so tiny, so delicate compared to him. "Tyler won't let her do anything, Nikos. What happened between him and me, it was just as much my fault. He would never do anything to hurt her."

"He was ready to walk out on her. That's what I said he would do."

"Yes, but because he wanted to do the right thing by her. Doesn't that tell you something? Or are you just too stubborn to see it?"

"I'm not discussing them with you."

"Don't. Believe me, I don't want to, either. Venetia's probably having the time of her life, and here I am, stuck with you. You hold me responsible for everything that's happening—"

"I don't hold you responsible for any of this. I just don't trust you to tell me if Tyler contacts you."

Lexi clamped her mouth shut. There was no point in even denying it. He knew her too well. "Okay, fine. But I don't have a phone and I don't think I can even sneeze on the island without you knowing, so can we stop with you dragging me around like unwanted baggage?"

"Unwanted baggage, *thee mou?*"

"You look at me as though you want to open a space portal and throw me through it. Do you understand what it took for me to say those words to you last week?"

He tugged her hands higher and tighter as his lower body pressed into hers. Lexi closed her eyes and fought for some much-needed oxygen. Her skin felt as if it was on fire, her limbs molten with longing. "Ever since I realized what a pathetic idiot I have been all these years, I have also realized that I'm not completely without appeal."

He grinned and she pressed on, growing bolder. When he smiled like that, she wanted to roll over in the warmth of it. She wanted to press her mouth to his and revel in it. "I might not be packing in the boob and leg department and probably hold little attraction to a man with refined tastes like you, but there are other fish in the sea. Cute, dimpled, down-to-earth fish like Piers, for example, who find me attractive and wouldn't dream of calling me any names in a million—"

His muscled thigh lodged between her legs and Lexi whimpered. For a man so big, he was so incredibly well-coordinated. Just the thought of all that finesse and power focused on her had her tingling in all kinds of places. "Who the hell is Piers?"

"Piers is the bartender who's been serving me cocktails."

"And he likes you?"

She nodded. "Yes."

His teeth clamped tight, he nodded. And she had the strangest notion that he hadn't liked what she had said. Intensely. "So help me understand, *thee mou*. Just any man with a working…" His gaze glimmered with a dark amusement. "Any man will do for this new risk-taking life of yours?"

She pushed at him, fighting the heat spreading up her neck. She was not going to back down from this. So she just evaded. "You're being purposely crude."

"Sex is all you want from me?"

"I… Yes, of course." She was getting good at lying. But then it was easy, because she didn't know what else she wanted from him. And she didn't want to know, either. She had never feared her feelings before or what they drove her to. But with everything she had learned about Tyler, with everything Nikos made her face, she preferred to not have any feelings right now. "You said it yourself. Sex should not be complicated." And she wanted it with the most complicated man she had ever met, whatever he thought of himself.

Nikos ran his thumb over her lower lip, his gaze drinking her in. Stepping back from her, he shrugged off his leather jacket. The V-necked gray shirt stretched tight across his muscled chest hugged his lean waist. "There should be a sign somewhere here. Find it."

Frowning, Lexi stared at the door. Shaking her head, she looked around the lounge. Tension pinged across her skin as she found it.

Do Not Disturb.

Her heart jumped to her throat. She held up the matte sign just as Nikos walked back in.

Meeting her gaze, he smiled. "Hang it on the doorknob and close the door."

The cardboard sign slipped from her fingers. Her skin tingled as his gaze stayed on her, challenging. Molten heat flared through her as she realized his intentions. Her knees shook, her entire body felt like a pool of liquid longing and anticipation.

She looked around the room to the huge glass to her right that gave a perfect view of the dance floor and the crowd below. She was not a virgin. Granted, the two times she had slept with Tyler had been almost painfully awkward. But with the tremble in her knees, the soft but persistent tug in her lower belly, she might as well have been one.

"Here? Now?"

Nikos came to a halt with an arm's length between them,

his gaze devouring her. He handed her the champagne glass. "Yes, here. Now. Is there a problem?"

Suddenly, Lexi felt hyperaware of everything around her. Her skin, the ratcheting beat of her heart, her breath rushing in and out, the din of the crowd below and Nikos—tall, gorgeous and within touching distance.

He moved to stand behind her. His hands landed on her waist, spanning it with his long fingers. She could feel every finger, every ridge of his palm on her skin.

"That glass is one-way."

His words rumbled over her skin. Lexi turned to look at him. "They can't see us?"

The heat from his mouth seared through her skin, his fingers slowly kneading her hips. "No."

She sucked in a much-needed breath. His hands moved to her rib cage and held her tight against him.

"They can't see us or hear us. This is what I want, Lexi. Are you ready for it?" Warm breath feathered over her ear, before he ran his tongue over the outer shell.

Lexi clutched his forearms, a shiver running through her.

She turned in his arms and looked up at him. His brown gaze dark, his aquiline nose flared. The liquid desire in his eyes, the feel of his rough palm over her bare arms, it was everything she wanted. Slipping from his grasp, she took the sign from the floor. She had no idea how she did it with her legs shaking beneath her, but she hung the sign and closed the door.

CHAPTER NINE

NIKOS STRUGGLED TO hold the lust rocketing through him in check and failed completely. She closed the door and stood there, the line of her back an inviting temptation. The strip of flesh exposed between the hem of her short skirt and her knee-high boots was the most erotic thing he had ever seen.

A shiver took root in his muscles. His nerves stretched taut, he felt as if he was the one taking a risk, as if he was the one who was new to sex.

He settled down into the luxurious sofa bed with his back against the wall. She turned around and leaned against the wall. Pink streaked her cheeks. Her mouth pursed and then opened.

"Come here, *agape mou.*"

Her shoulders tensed, and he thought she would flee in a streak of white and black.

Instead, she walked toward him, her gaze unmoving from his.

Doubts and questions pummeled through him with every step she took. They were as strange to him as the strength of his desire.

There was no shyness in her gaze, but there was no boldness, either. This was important to her, whatever lies she spouted. And that realization tempered his desire. She didn't know how to play by his rules.

He fought the protective urge that rose up inside him, shoved it away with a ruthlessness that had helped him survive, and win, against all odds.

He needed to stop making this moment more than it was. She wanted him. He wanted her. He wasn't going to change himself, wasn't going to start wondering about her feelings just because she was different.

That was the cause for his conscience ringing like a bell inside him.

She was different from the women he usually slept with. Not one of them had made an effort to know what was beneath his ambition or his drive. Or maybe there hadn't been anything worth knowing before. She was the first person who had looked beneath the surface, who had realized that a man, with fears and wishes no less, existed beneath it all. Even after everything he had done to manipulate her, made her face, she wished him well, she worried about him.

He took her hand in his and pulled her down to the sofa. He leaned back on the wide sofa bed so that she sat between his legs. His gut felt tight with want, every muscle in him poised for pleasure and possession. He wrapped his hands around her midriff, and kissed the crook of her neck. She tasted of lemon soap and vanilla. He closed his eyes, praying for control. She was so delicate under his touch, she felt breakable in his hands. And even through the anticipation coiling within every inch of him, lust heating through his blood, Nikos admitted one thing to himself.

He didn't want to hurt her. The sentiment was both strange and strong.

The soft flick of Nikos's tongue against her neck knocked the breath out of Lexi's lungs. He was like a tightly toned fortress of need. And yet he held her loosely, as if she would break.

Every press of hard muscle, every caress of his fingers, fueled her own need. She laced her fingers through his and held on tighter. Throwing her neck back, she gave him better access, liquid longing bursting into life inside her. "Kiss me, Nikos."

With agility she couldn't believe, he flipped her easily until she sat astride him. His hands remained on her knees. She moved to steady herself, and instantly, her aching sex rubbed against the hard ridge of his erection.

The sound of their mingled moans, desire and need, lust and want, reverberated in the room around them.

His mouth found hers in a fury of want; his hands on her thighs limited her movement severely. She struggled in his hold and moved over the hard ridge of his arousal.

"No, *thee mou*," he said, before capturing her mouth again.

He didn't kiss her like he had done at the pool. He kissed her softly, slowly, as though he had all the time in the world, as though there was no intensity to his need at all.

His tongue licked her lower lip and pressed for entry. Sinking her hands into his hair, Lexi let him in. Pleasure, unlike she had ever known before, bloomed in the pit of her stomach and arrowed downward.

Needing more than he was giving her, she clasped his jaw and forced him to look at her.

"More, Nikos," she whispered, her words falling over each other.

In response, he sucked her lower lip into his mouth with incredible gentleness. She sneaked her hands in under his shirt and found hot skin. The minute she touched his nipple, he jerked back and pulled her hands out.

Every time, she got closer to him, he held her off.

Lexi pressed a desperate kiss to his mouth and slipped out of his lap. She swayed on her feet before she found her bearings, her body thrumming with unfulfilled desire. Color streaking across his cheeks, Nikos looked up. A stamp of lust tightened his features, but it was just that. A shadow.

Because it was control that reigned over him.

Something snapped inside Lexi. She had wanted to start living her life; she wanted to take a risk. And going to bed with Nikos Demakis was one. On every level there was. He had a hundred lovers where she'd had one. But even more than that, Nikos was a risk because he refused to let her hide, because he refused to let her shrink away from the truth, he didn't coddle her.

And she didn't want that to change.

She hugged her arms, and forced the words out. "This isn't what I want."

He stood up from the couch like a coiled spring, his face a tight mask. She kept her gaze on his, amazed at how steady he looked. His jaw was granite. "We will leave immediately."

"I don't want to leave."

He covered the distance between them and smiled. With his hands on her shoulders, he tugged her closer, and smiled. "It's okay. I shouldn't have started this here. I know you are new to all this…" He pressed a furious kiss to her mouth, his lips clinging devouring, until she couldn't breathe. That's what she wanted—his passion. "It's not the end of it, either." He pulled back, and this time he didn't sound so steady.

She pushed his hands away, her heart stuttering to a halt. "Stop trying to protect me, Nikos. You're acting just like Tyler."

His gaze blazed with anger. "I don't know what you are talking about. But you should know this. No man wants to hear the ex's name and definitely not like that."

"Then stop acting like him."

A curse fell from his mouth. "Explain."

"You are doing what you *think* I want. You're not being yourself."

"That's the most ridiculous thing I have ever heard."

"I'm not going to break, Nikos. I want honesty between us, whether it is in the way you make love to me, or when it's time for you to say we're done. You are controlling yourself, wondering if I will break, wondering if you will hurt me."

He pushed his hair back, and Lexi noticed he was not as in control as she thought. This was not the Nikos that had pushed her into admitting how much she wanted him. Something had changed in him; something had changed between them, and she didn't know what.

"I won't be responsible for hurting you. Despite everything I proposed and did, I never intended to."

"Then tell me...no wait, show me what you like. Do this..." She moved her hand between them. "Make love to me the way you would do it with Nina, or Emmanuelle."

He jerked back from her as though she had polluted the air by speaking those names in this moment between them. "*Christos!* Stop comparing yourself to them. I cannot forget everything I know about who and what you are."

Lexi bit her lower lip. Warmth that had nothing to do with desire and lust flew through her veins. He was making concessions for her. She didn't want him to, but she couldn't help being affected by it, either. "You'll hurt me more if you are not yourself, Nikos. I believe that Tyler... He only slept with me because he thought it would make me happy. I can't bear the thought that you are doing the same..."

"*Theos!* I can't think straight with wanting you. I've never spent so much time thinking about it instead of just doing it."

Her heart stuttered and started. She couldn't speak for the breath caught in her throat.

She was terrified of what she was doing, of where she was going with him. But mixed in with that fear was also a sense of rightness. She covered the distance between them and pulled him down for a kiss.

His lips were soft and firm against hers, his hands on her waist lifting her off the ground. His tongue delved into her mouth, seeking and caressing, his hands on her buttocks tucking her tight against the V of his legs.

Pulling her hands up, he slowly guided her to the wall behind him. A slow smile curved his lips. "You want to know what I like?"

"Yes."

"I would like for you to tell me what you want me to do. You have to ask me for it, *thee mou.*"

Her gaze flew to him, heat streaking her cheeks. For some reason, he was pushing her, expecting her to back out of this. She had no idea why. But she wouldn't let him win. "Fine."

She unbuttoned the metal clasps on her vest and the leather fell away inch by inch to reveal her heated skin. Her fingers were steady despite the butterflies in her stomach. There were at least a hundred people on the other side of the glass. But it was the darkening of Nikos's gaze that spread desire like wildfire through her. Her small breasts felt heavy, her nipples rigid and chafing against the lacy silk of her bra.

The sound of his jagged breaths filled the room. "I can't wait to touch your breasts, Lexi. I have been going out of my mind thinking about them."

He ran his knuckle over the strap of her bra, his gaze hungry and hard. Without touching her, he bent and licked the upper curve of her breast. Lexi jerked and arched her spine greedily into his touch.

His forearm kept her against the wall, stopping her from leaning into him. "Sorry, *thee mou*. I forgot my own rules. Now if you want something…"

She looked up at him, every nerve in her tuned tight. Her mouth was dry but need triumphed over shyness. She pulled his hand to her mouth and kissed his palm. "I want—" she swallowed at the need rippling through her "—you to… touch my breasts."

A lick of fire burst into life in his eyes and a curse fell from his mouth. The sound of it cocooned them in the room.

He dipped his head again. His hair tickled her jaw, his fingers tugging the silky lace down. Rough fingers traced circles around her nipple, again and again, sending shivers of pleasure through her. Finally, he flicked the taut, aching buds, pinched them between his fingers. And the throaty sound of her moan filled her ears.

He took her mouth in a stinging kiss. "Next?"

"Suck…" She was wet just thinking it. If his plan was to drive her crazy with lust, he was succeeding.

He smiled against her mouth, before tugging her lower lip between his teeth. She clutched her legs tight together, a pulse of need vibrating at her sex. "Yes?"

She closed her eyes and shamelessly pushed herself into his touch. "Please, Nikos."

"What. Do. You. Want, Lexi?"

"Suck my nipples into your mouth."

In response, he tugged her up until she was straddling his knee. His hard arousal rubbed exactly where she needed it. She moaned and moved. And then his mouth closed over her nipple.

His tongue laved it and then he sucked it into his mouth. A white-hot shaft of pure sensation arched between her legs. She moved, needing more. He straightened his leg, and she would have crumpled to the floor if he hadn't been holding her up. She whimpered aloud, just short of begging.

"What next?"

She opened her eyes and looked at him. Twin streaks of color highlighted his sharp cheekbones, and his features were stark, his gaze ablaze with lust. He was just as far gone as she was. If she could reduce this powerful man to this, there was nothing she couldn't do. She felt absolutely, powerfully feminine in that moment. She widened her legs just a little and pulled her skirt up. "Touch me between my legs, Nikos," she said, owning the words, owning the desire she felt.

His nostrils flared, his eyes were the deepest brown she had ever seen. "No please?"

She shook her head, her pulse vibrating in her entire body. "No please anymore. You want to do it just as much as I want it."

The most gorgeously sinful smile curved his mouth, digging deep grooves in his cheeks. "Take off your panties."

She reached under her skirt and tugged her panties down.

He took them from her shaking fingers and threw them behind him, the sight of her white panties in his rough hands erotic.

She was not naked, but under his scrutiny, she felt hot and exposed and all kinds of sexy.

"Don't look down." Nikos whispered the words into the curve of her breast.

Every inch of her skin hyperaware, Lexi kept her eyes on him, the languid curve of his mouth, the tight cast of his features, the way his breath hissed in and out....

She could stand there and drink him in all night.

Slow, sinuous need tugged in her lower belly. The hot

rasp of his roughened palm on her skin was a searing brand as his fingers crawled up her thighs, his mouth trailing wet heat between her breasts. Her nipples knotted with need.

His long fingers finally found the folds of her sex. He stroked and tugged, pulled with a relentless pressure that had her moaning his name, tension coiling in her lower belly.

She clutched his shoulders and he traced slick, maddening circles around her nipple. "Now what, *yineka mou?*"

His voice was gravelly, coarse and deep with hunger. She sank her hands into his hair and pushed the words out. "I want you to move your fingers, Nikos," she whispered. Her wanton desire tightened her need.

His fingers pushed inside her and she threw her head back. It felt intrusive, erotic, nothing like she had ever experienced before.

It was unrelenting, intense. "What do you want now?" he whispered, his words abraded and slow.

"Faster, Nikos."

He laughed and increased the pressure.

Nerve endings she didn't know existed bloomed into life. He tugged and stroked her, whispered words in Greek that only added to the havoc he was wreaking on her.

He pinched the tight bundle of nerves at her sex, just as his mouth sucked at her nipple, and she came violently, the waves of her orgasm unending as he continued the combined assault of his mouth and fingers.

She shuddered against him, her breath hitching painfully in and out.

She opened her eyes and stared into eyes darkened to a molten black with desire. He licked one long finger and the sheer eroticism of the act sent another wave of jagged sensation to her sex.

She felt alien in her body, a fierce freedom running through her veins.

"What do *you* want, Nikos?" she said, more than a hint of brazen challenge in her tone.

He didn't answer her. Fingers digging into her hips, he lifted her off the ground. Her thigh muscles still quivering from aftershocks, she wrapped her legs around his waist.

She heard the sound of the zipper of his jeans, of a condom being ripped, felt the shudder that went through him as he sheathed himself.

And then he was pushing inside her with a guttural sound that seemed to have been ripped from him. She clawed her hands into his shoulders, pleasure and pain coalescing inside her, the walls of her wet sex clamping him tight.

She threw her head back and a long whimper escaped her. His breath stilled, a long shudder racking his powerful body.

"More, *agape mou?*"

How he was able to utter a single word, Lexi had no idea. "Yes," she whispered, her throat raw, her body aching for more.

He pushed in a little more, stretching her, making her achy and hot all over. He was big and she was tiny, and the most decadent pleasure pulsed through her sex.

He did something with his hips that sent a pulse of pleasure sputtering through her. And then, he was deep inside her—hot and throbbing. And it felt painfully good, intensely erotic.

She opened her eyes and caught him studying her, stark desire and something that was entirely Nikos.

His features stripped of all control, his breathing shaky, he was the most gorgeous sight she had ever seen. Every bone and muscle locked tight, his gaze devoured her. "You're so tight, Lexi."

He pressed a kiss to her forehead, and Lexi braced herself against the reverent touch. A frown rippled over his face, his shoulders hard knots under her fingers.

"I'm afraid to move."

She was hot, and tingly and possessed, and she never wanted to stop feeling like that. "I can't bear it if you don't, Nikos." She moved her hips and gasped at how deep he was embedded, at how mind-numbingly good it felt.

Clutching his shoulders tight, Lexi buried her mouth in his neck. He tasted of sweat and musk, an incredibly erotic taste. She clamped her teeth over his skin and sucked hard. Instantly, his hips moved, and an incredible fire licked along her aching core again.

His curse felt like the sweetest words to her ears.

His gaze never moved from her. His breath feathered over her, the raw sounds that fell from his mouth enveloped her. He pulled out slowly, the length of his erection dragging against the walls of her sex, teasing and tormenting her. Until she felt his instant loss, until her body cried out to be possessed again.

And then he thrust back into her. He moved slow, hard and deep, and she trembled, awash with jagged sensations, bursting to full with a raw awareness. Every square inch of her thrummed with a fever, shuddered with the influx of sensation.

And he did it again and again.

Lexi cried out his name as need coiled again and burst into a million lights. Her throat was raw, her entire body was raw.

His skin was slick under her palms, his muscles bunching and flexing, every inch of him rigid with want that was all for her. To have him inside her, to hold this powerful man shuddering in her arms, it was the most powerful, most freeing thing she had ever felt.

Every time, he thrust into her, Lexi felt his control snap, his finesse slip and his desperation take over. Until a hoarse grunt fell from his lips and he became utterly still.

Lexi pushed his hair from his forehead and pressed a kiss to his lips, unable to hold herself back. She had known that sex with Nikos would be fantastic, earth-shattering. But the tenderness in his eyes, the soft, slow kiss he pressed to her mouth, as if she had given him the most precious gift ever, seared through her.

She had no defense against it. Except to tell herself that she was imagining things, that it was her innate need to bond with him, to make this more than it was.

It was amazing sex, and she wasn't going to let her insecurities ruin it.

She could do this. In fact, she would not only do this, but she would have the time of her life doing it. Fears and doubts, regrets and tears…she would have the rest of her life to indulge in once she was back in New York.

CHAPTER TEN

LEXI HAD JUST returned to the mansion from the beach the next afternoon when Nikos returned from wherever it was that he'd been. Wraparound shades shielded his expression from her as he stilled in the foyer at the sight of her. But she still felt his scrutiny as vividly as if he had laid those big hands of his over her skin. Her neck prickled, every inch of her skin stretched taut at his continued perusal.

"I am going to the other side of the island where the new hotel is being built. If you would like to accompany me, meet me at the entrance in fifteen minutes. Ask Maria to pack a change of clothes for you."

"I can do that myself but...I... Why?"

"I might have to stay there overnight. Do you want to be here alone? If you wish to, that is fine."

"No, I want to go. I will be ready in fifteen."

She made her way to her bedroom, more confused than ever.

Instead of the smoldering sexual tension between them cooling off, it had only thickened once he had straightened his clothes and then hers last night.

She had just stood there on shaking legs, the aftershock of her orgasm still rocking through her, her body still quivering at the assault of unbearable pleasure. It was as though her brain circuits had gone haywire from so much pleasure. Only Nikos's gentle movements, as he'd held her in his arms for what seemed like an eternity had punctured the sensual haze.

The raucous gaiety of the nightclub, the quick ride to the private airstrip, she remembered nothing of it.

Her memories of last night were all of him—how he had felt inside her, how he had held her after and how he had her carried her to the waiting limo when her knees had threatened to buckle under her.

She had been glad that he hadn't commented on her silence, because she'd had no idea what she would have said. All she knew was that she had been buried under an avalanche of sensations and feelings. None of which she had wanted to examine or give voice to.

The next thing she knew, she had woken up in the vast bed in the Demakis mansion, a strange lethargy in her blood. Which meant she had fallen asleep on the flight to the island.

She walked back to the foyer and followed the sounds of the chopper. Clad in another pair of jeans and white T-shirt that fitted snugly against the breadth of his chest, he was waiting for her. She settled down in the helicopter, too absorbed in her own thoughts to complain about his silence.

His pants molded the hard length of his thighs. Those thighs, they had been like solid rock, clenching her tight, supporting her, cradling her.

A twang went through her belly at remembered pleasure.

She fisted her hands, a hint of regret swarming through her. She had been so lost in the sensations when he moved inside her, so lost in everything he had done to her, she had been nothing but a passive participant. The urge to touch the hot slide of his skin, to feel his muscles tighten under her was fierce.

The ride to the other side of the island didn't take more

than ten minutes. Blue water and golden sand stretched in every direction she looked. It was as close to paradise as she had ever seen. And a hotel would ruin the tranquility of it, bring tourists, puncture the peace.

But she kept her thoughts to herself as they landed and stepped out.

She stared around her with mounting wonder as Nikos had a word with the pilot.

The new hotel was nothing like she'd imagined. For one thing, it was, maybe one tenth of the size of the Demakis mansion. It was a simple, clean design with pristine white-washed walls, designed to reflect the Greek architecture.

She smiled at Nikos as he joined her. "It's not what I expected."

"Do you like it?"

She nodded eagerly. "I was worried that it would ruin the peaceful atmosphere, that it would be a noisy, touristy place."

"It's a new kind of approach to a hotel, really more of an authentic experience than just a place to stay. There are no televisions in any suite and the guests are guaranteed the utmost privacy. Even the meals are local Greek specialties. Every material that is used is environmentally conscious, and even the furniture and pieces inside are all one-of-a-kind specially made by local craftsmen using simple, organic materials. Kind of back to—"

"Basics," she finished, smiling widely.

She trailed after Nikos while he checked a few things, loving the idea more and more. There were no more than three suites in the whole building. Again, whitewashed walls created a cocoonlike environment. Each suite was open plan, divided into sleeping and living areas. Hand-crafted accessories and bleached wood furniture was everywhere. A large veranda offered a beautiful view of the Cycladic landscape.

A hammock made of the softest cotton hung in the veranda.

She went back down the steps and found the pool. Having finished his phone call, Nikos's gaze was back on her.

"I don't know the standard procedure for the morning after," she said, finding his silence unbearable. It weighed on her, poking holes in every comforting thought she came up with. "Do we shake hands and pat each other on the back for a job well done? Or is it beyond crass to mention it at all? Did I break the code by falling asleep on you in the car? I swear, I didn't see it coming. I mean, the only thing I can think of is that my body caved in at the influx of pheromones. You know, because what we did was…fantastic."

She grimaced at how idiotic she sounded as soon as the words left her mouth.

He turned toward her in the blink of an eye and clasped her cheek. "This is as new to me as it is to you," he said in a quiet growl.

The irises of his eyes widened as though he hadn't been aware of what he was going to say. He ran a hand through his hair.

"Then you better start thinking about answers. Are you done with me? Do you want me to leave and stay somewhere in the village? Was this a onetime deal? Because if it was, I would have liked some notice because there's a lot of stuff I wanted to do and I was so overwhelmed, I didn't get to do anything."

"Overwhelmed?" A curse fell from his lips, and he turned toward her. If any more hardness inched into his face, he would be a concrete bust. "Did I hurt you last night?"

"What? Of course not," she said, heat gathering like a storm under her skin.

"You were very—"

Hitching on her toes, she covered his mouth with her hand. The velvety edge of his lips was a sinuous whisper against her skin, the stubble on his cheeks making her wonder how it would feel against other places. Every little thing about the man sent her senses tingling. "I enjoyed every minute of what we did last night. The question is, did you?"

This time, a slow smile curved his mouth. "You couldn't tell?"

"Honestly? I can't remember anything except thinking I could die happily. And today, I'm drawing my clues from the fact that you've been gone all morning and now you're staring at me as though you wish I were invisible. With your wealth, you can probably make me. I did see an ad for an invisibility cloak on eBay last week, so—"

"You are talking nonsense."

"I think something in my brain got warped last night. Your presence now makes me think of nothing but sex, and I'm trying to cover that up—"

"With nonsense." He nodded. He pushed her against the wall, his jaw tight. "I had the hottest, most intense orgasm of my entire life last night. It took every ounce of self-control I possess to not wake you up just so I could have you again and again. Knowing that you had no panties on under that skirt...I don't know how I resisted you at all." The words hummed on the air around them, the feral intensity of it sending warmth stealing into places she didn't want to think of right then. His mouth took on a rueful twist. "Every time I closed my eyes since this morning, I can hear those long whimpers you make just before you come, taste you on my fingers.

"Is that clear enough for you?" He flicked his tongue

over the rim of her ear, his softly whispered words stroking her need hotter and higher.

Lexi would have crumpled to the ground if he hadn't been holding her upright. A rush of wetness gathered at her sex. And all he had done was talk. "Now if you'd just looked like a man who got laid last night and enjoyed it, then I wouldn't—"

"It was glorious sex, *agape mou.*" He let her go, his mouth narrowed into a straight line. "And I feel better than fantastic given that my sister is still missing, and my grandfather is using it as an excuse to deny me what I want."

The fever he incited instantly cooled, and Lexi took a staggering step back. Of course, Venetia. Her mouth felt clammy, her stomach tying itself in knots.

I'm so sorry, Lex. Just give me a few days and I'll bring Venetia back.

The small note that had been left on her side table under a cup of dark Greek coffee fluttered in front of her eyes. The shock of finding it, especially in Tyler's almost illegible handwriting, still pulsed through her.

Having read it close to fifty times in two minutes, Lexi had torn it up into small pieces, her heart in her throat. It was obvious Venetia didn't want to return and Tyler didn't want to hurt her.

Lexi felt a flare of anger at the both of them for doing this, for deceiving Nikos and for dragging her in between. This thing between her and Nikos, it was a temporary madness, she knew that. Still, she wanted to do nothing that would hurt him.

And she had a sinking feeling that that's what was going to happen in the end.

Pushing her hair back from her forehead, she caught the

sigh escaping her lips. There was nothing to do but wait. "What is your grandfather refusing you?" she said, her dislike of Savas Demakis a bad taste in her mouth.

"He and his cronies are refusing to vote me in as the CEO. The fact that I didn't protect Venetia is a weapon Savas is wielding to its full extent."

"I don't understand. Venetia and your company are entirely different things. How does he propose you stop your twenty-four-year-old sister from living her life, short of locking her up and throwing away the key?"

His pointed gaze told her she nailed the truth on its ugly head. "He must know you would never do that to Venetia."

Nikos shrugged. "What he knows for sure is how much I want to be in the CEO's chair."

"Do you?"

"Yes. I would do anything to be there finally. Except hurt my sister. Although really, Savas's suggestions are beginning to make more and more sense. In my desire to not hurt her, I brought you into this, and probably drove her even deeper into Tyler's arms."

She felt a shiver settle deep in her bones. "So he is pitting the two things you want above everything else against each other? Hoping that you are heartless enough to hurt your sister?"

"Yes."

Anxiety rampant in her veins, she came to a stop in front of him. "Are his... Do his assumptions have basis, Nikos?"

He traced his knuckles over her lower lip, and Lexi trembled for more than one reason. "You're trembling, *yineka mou*." She tucked her forehead into his shoulder, willing herself to let it go. She was courting nothing but trouble by asking, by digging herself in. Whenever this issue with Tyler and Venetia was resolved, she would walk away. She had to.

His long fingers gripped her nape, the pad of his thumb moving up and down. "What is it that you want to know but are so afraid to hear, Lexi?"

She looked up. "I think…no, I know that you will never hurt Venetia willingly. It's a different thing altogether that, with your twisted anger toward Tyler, you are doing just that…. But for your grandfather to blackmail you like this, to pit you against your own sister, to…see if you will take the suggestion and run with it…it means you—"

"It means that I have done things to remove any obstacles from my way before, yes."

She exhaled on a long breath, bracing herself. Whatever Nikos did, beneath the uncaring facade, she knew he had paid a price. "Like what?"

"My aunt's son, Spyros, he is a few years older than me and he was my grandfather's favorite when I first met him. He was everything I was not. Well-educated, smart and best of all, obedient. More than that, Savas had been grooming him, ever since my father walked out, to take over the reins of Demakis International.

"But it was not his right. It was mine. I had already slogged for a decade with little notice or returns for it. I realized following Savas's rigid instructions wasn't going to get me anything but the bare minimums. It was time to make him take notice of me."

"What did you do?"

"Are you sure you want to hear this, Lexi?"

Say no, walk away. "Yes."

"I went digging and discovered Spyros, beneath his perfect exterior, had a little secret. He had a wife hidden away that no one knew about, and he was struggling to get out of his engagement to one of Savas's oldest friend's granddaughters. I arranged for his wife to come to his engagement party. And despite Spyros's pleas asking for forgiveness, Savas kicked him off the board."

The quiet, matter-of-fact tone in his words only amplified the chill they caused. "You knew what your grandfather would do."

His gaze narrowed into an unflinching hardness, Nikos stared at her. "Everyone knew what he would do, including Spyros. He had made his choice. I just hurried along the consequences."

"I don't get it. It's not like you don't have money of your own." She pushed off from the wall, and walked the perimeter of the pool. "That yacht, the private jet, this new real-estate deal you have with Nathan Ramirez…you have nothing to want.

"Why is becoming the CEO so important to you, Nikos?"

He gave her a long look that said he wasn't dignifying her question with an answer. "It just is."

"Why can't you be happy with what you have? Why let your grandfather push you into anything?"

"Savas didn't push me into anything. I started on this path with one goal in sight. The moment I walked in through those electronic gates, clutching my sister to me, the poor little bastard that everyone pitied, I made a promise to myself. That I would do everything I can to become the master of it all. Do you realize what odds I have surmounted to get to this stage? I started with nothing, Lexi. And I won't settle for everything that he walked away from, until I'm everything he was not."

"Until you're everything he…" Her heart sinking to her shoes, Lexi finally realized who he meant. The bitterness in his words, it was only a superficial cover on a deeper cut. "Your father? Nikos, what he did was awful, but you have to forgive him. He may have started this, but it's your grandfather that brought you to his point. With every little thing you tell me about your grandfather, have you never wondered why your father might have turned his back on all this?"

"I don't care why he did it. Even before he died, we never had anything. He struggled in that garage, he barely provided for us and he stood by like a useless fool while my mother's health degraded and she eventually died. All he had needed was to call Savas, ask for help."

That garage, those cars, didn't he realize why it comforted him so much? "Do you believe Savas would have helped him? Without conditions? Would he have welcomed your father with open arms without a price?"

Not even a little of his anger waned. "Any price would have been worth it. It was his duty to look after her, to take care of Venetia. He not only failed in that, he then went and killed himself, breaking Venetia forever."

"And you."

Nikos shook his head, despising the glimpse of pity in her eyes. "He taught me a very valuable lesson early on. Love is a luxury only fools want and can afford."

His pointed look wasn't lost on her. "I'm not saying he was right, Nikos. But Savas never even gave you a proper chance to grieve."

"There was nothing to grieve. My father was a weak man all his life. He couldn't stand up to Savas—he couldn't live without my mother. He couldn't even keep himself alive for Venetia and I. I refuse to be like him. Becoming the CEO of Demakis International is the last step in that journey. And Savas can't stop me. I will find a way to that chair."

Lexi had no chance to answer, because the sound of a chopper slicing through the wind around them reached them.

Pushing the hair away from her face, she hung back as a

man of about seventy stepped out of the chopper, followed by a young woman.

Nikos shook hands with the man, and offered a polite smile to the woman.

Lexi turned away and walked toward the hotel. Judging by the jealous rage that took hold of her insides, it was better that she stay away. Leaving her backpack in one of the smaller bedrooms, she climbed the stairs to the next floor. The corridor was whitewashed with dark gleaming wood floors, with simple handmade crafts here and there. Among all the places she had visited with Nikos, she loved this hotel the most. And under the ambition and jet-setting lifestyle, she had a feeling he did, too.

She walked out into the huge veranda of one of the suites. Her breath hitched at the beauty of the Cycladic heaven. Orange bloodied the dusky sky, casting an ethereal glow over the strip of beach and the whitewashed hotel walls.

Intensely glad that Nikos had asked her to join him, she climbed into the hammock, her mind running over what he had said to her. One way or another, she needed to bring a resolution to this thing between Tyler and Venetia. And she had to do it without hurting anyone in the process, least of all, Nikos.

It was an impossible task, but she had to do it. Even with the childhood she'd had, she had known kindness, even if it had been in snatches.

Nikos had known none. She was damned if she had to see those shadows of despair in his eyes ever again.

She would do anything to keep them at bay. Anything.

Darkness fell by the time Nikos bade goodbye to Theo Katrakis. Savage satisfaction fueled through him. Finally, things were falling into their right place. The older man had, however, surprised Nikos by bringing his daughter to the meeting.

And one look at Eleni Katrakis had sent the blood rushing from Lexi's face. Did she really think he would be interested in Eleni after last night?

He found Lexi in the hammock, the quiet rasp of her pencil against the paper in her hand the only sound for miles. The feeble light from the adjoining bedroom was nowhere near enough for her.

Shaking his head, he plucked the sheet from her hands and walked back inside. With a huff, she rolled out of the hammock and followed him in.

He stuck out a hand to ward her off and studied the sketch. Surprise flooded him, and he laughed, the sound tearing out of him. A lightness, an amazement he had never known before filled him inside and out.

The sketch was extraordinarily detailed for something created with a pencil and paper. It shimmered with life, with the unique essence of the woman who drew it.

The drawing was of a woman, almost Amazonian in her build, big-breasted with a tiny waist, her long legs muscular and lithe, her dark long hair flying around her face a striking anchor of femininity. She wore a leather sheath kind of dress, a pistol hanging from the belt. The same sketch he had seen on Lexi's T-shirt the first time she had met him, a direct contrast to the beautiful, delicate woman who had drawn her, but just as dangerous.

Her legs planted apart, the woman was staring at something, a mischievous little smile curving her lips.

Here he had assumed that he had Lexi Nelson all figured out. But he couldn't learn everything about her if he spent ten lifetimes with her. A tightness emerged in his gut and he fought to dispel it.

"That's very insulting, Nikos."

He turned toward her, leaning against the huge bed. Her arms around her waist, she braced herself.

"This sketch…" He took a deep breath, the expectant wariness in her gaze causing him to choose his words carefully. "It's the most brilliant thing I've ever seen," he said, opting for unvarnished truth.

Her mouth curved in a wide smile. "Then why were you laughing?"

He waved the paper in her direction. "This is Ms. Havisham, isn't it? Your heroine? The one the space pirate kidnapped?"

She nodded, her gaze shining with a brilliant radiance. "She is a mousy little woman when he snatches her. But this is her true form. It comes out only when she or someone she loves comes under threat."

"And the space pirate has no idea what he has taken on," he said, frowning. He had a feeling he knew exactly what the pirate was going through.

Lexi Nelson didn't have to change into anything to send a shiver up and down Nikos's spine. Warning bells clanged inside his head and he kept the sound at bay. For now.

"Yep."

Nodding, he grasped her wrist and tugged her along with him. He settled her in his lap on a wicker armchair. His curiosity was far more feral than anything else he felt right now. "So tell me. Why does he kidnap her?"

She wrapped her arm around his neck and smiled. And again, Nikos braced himself. Desire and something entirely alien descended on him. It had to be the intimacy of their positions. He had never spent more than a few minutes with a woman outside of a bed or an office.

"He learns that she has the key to a time portal. And he needs it to turn back time. But she's not exactly what he had imagined. Nor is the key so simple."

Nikos stared at the picture again and caught the hint of sadness in Lexi's tone. "She is the key, isn't she?"

Shock spiraling in her gaze, she stared at him. "How did you guess that?" She didn't know what she saw in his eyes as she continued. "She is the key. Sacrificing her life will give him the power to turn back time, go to three different times in the past once."

"What is he going to do?"

She shrugged. "Right now, he's just learned the truth and is staggering under the weight of what he has to do. Because, you see, the space pirate—"

"Is beginning to like Ms. Havisham." He finished her thought. "But the realization won't stop him. He will try to kill her."

"Unless she kills him first," she said, laughing. At his disbelieving stare, the smile slid from her face. "Maybe you understand Spike, but Ms. Havisham is not like me, Nikos. Not weak or lonely and forever needing someone to make her feel like she matters. She's strong, independent, a survivor. She has no qualms about her sexuality or her place in the world. If Spike threatens her survival, she will kill him. As she has already killed before. And have no regrets about it."

He placed the paper slowly on the nightstand and turned her until she was straddling him. Having her this close was nothing short of torture. He held off the liquid longing at bay with sheer determination. This—this sexual desire, this situation between them, it was still under his control. *It had to be.* Never before had this kind of control been so important to him. "I don't think she's all that different from you."

"I clung to Tyler all these years. I let Faith walk all over me. All for what? For a few crumbs of affection, to feel like I have someone who loves me? Ms. Havisham is—"

"She might be packing in the boob and leg department,"

he said, using her words, and she instantly smiled and swatted his shoulder. "And she might be a badass with that gun, but all those are outward things, Lexi." He placed his palm on her chest, and her heart thundered under his touch. The words flew out of him on a wave, and he could do nothing to curb them. "Here, you're just as strong as her or even more. No one else could have lived your life and retained the good you have, the warmth you have. You don't have to rewrite your story, *yineka mou*. It is already an extraordinary one."

Lexi swallowed at the raw honesty that rang in Nikos's words, the tenderness shining in his gaze. She had been drawing for as long as she could remember. It had started as a comfort, and somewhere down the line had become more than that. It was her lifeline, her way of controlling things she couldn't change, her way of righting the things that had gone wrong in her life. In her bleakest moments, it had been the only way she could hold on to a life that had been nothing but lonely and sometimes, even cruel.

She had always meant for Ms. Havisham to kill Spike. But ever since she had begun the actual sketching, the story had taken on a life of its own. And the man staring at her with liquid desire in his gaze, with a tenderness that threatened to pull her under, it was him.

He had changed the course of her story and that of her own life.

How was she supposed to remember that this was just sex when he made her heart ache for more, when he looked at her as though she was the most precious woman in the world?

How was she supposed to walk away when it was time?

She threw her hands around his neck and kissed his jaw, choking back the tears catching in her throat. She breathed her thanks into his skin, explored the tangy taste of him with her tongue. The depth of emotion roiling inside her scared her.

She took a bracing breath, willing her heart to slow down, willing her mind to take control, willing herself not to ruin this glorious moment with this wonderful man with unwanted fears.

Only then did she realize the absolute stillness that had inched into Nikos.

He was so rigid in her embrace that she wondered if he was even breathing. Pasting a smile on her face, she pulled herself back and looked into his eyes. "Sorry," she whispered, forcing a levity she didn't feel into her tone. "Talking about my stories and sketches always makes me emotional." As cop-outs went, it was a good one.

She pressed her mouth to his, not waiting to see if he believed it or not. Because the desire she felt for him, the need that was already unraveling inside her—*that* she understood and she used it to root herself in reality.

With a groan, he dragged her closer until her aching sex rubbed against his erection.

She instantly parted her legs and moved over the hard ridge, wanton hunger rising to the surface. Her time was limited with him. And it made her desperate.

She tugged her T-shirt off with trembling fingers. He threw his head back and laughed. A gravelly sound that abraded her skin. Rising to her knees, she attacked the band of his black trousers. But he stilled her hands on them.

His large hands holding her immobile, he licked her collarbone. That small, almost-there-but-gone point of contact, her whole body gathered behind it. "I want to see all of you this time."

She nodded, her mouth dry. She slid from his lap, her skin tingling at his continued perusal. "I want to see you, too. On the bed," she added, forcing the words past the thundering beat of her heart.

He stood up from the chair and neared her. His smile cut grooves in his cheeks, making him look deliciously divine.

"What? I'm being outspoken, demanding what I want from life, from you."

"I can see that. And you look gloriously beautiful doing it." He ran his finger over the edge of her pink bra, and she willed herself not to step back. It was easy to speak the words, but to match her actions was something else altogether. Because she would always be amazed that he could want her, that the blazing desire in his eyes was for her. "Did you just think that up?"

"It's like my subconscious speaks up every time I am near you. You probably think the bed is boring but—"

He covered the distance between them and picked her up. She tucked her hands around his neck and pushed herself closer. "Nothing with you is boring, Ms. Nelson. Although, I think we can make it interesting."

He threw her on the bed, and Lexi thought she would expire from how soft the sheets were. "What do you mean, Mr. Demakis?"

Unbuttoning his dress shirt, he prowled to the other end of the room and grabbed a champagne bottle from the ice bucket.

Lexi moved to her knees. The dark desire in his gaze sent a tingle from her head to toe. "You should know I'm not much of a drinker."

He shrugged off his T-shirt and took a sip of the champagne. "Who said you will be drinking it?"

With his other hand, he reached around her back and unhooked her bra, while his tongue found the exact spot on her neck that drove her out of her skin and licked it. His hands tugged down her shorts and panties next.

She was naked and twin strips of color blooded his cheekbones. "Never say you're not beautiful again, *thee mou.*"

One hand snaked around her waist, his long fingers cupping her buttocks. Her nipples grazed against his chest. Throwing her head back, Lexi groaned, shivering all over.

He kissed her mouth, his tongue swirling the tender inside, licking, nipping, her hands roaming his back, desperate for more. His fingers sank into her hair and pulled her face up for his scrutiny. "Do you trust me, Lexi?" he whispered against her skin.

Lexi nodded, no words coming to her mouth.

"Then close your eyes."

Willing to do anything he asked, she closed her eyes. Words whispered in Greek and English, wicked promises, rained down sensation upon sensation. She gasped as he bound something around her eyes, and realized it was the tie he had loosened earlier.

He pushed at her shoulders softly and Lexi fell back, every inch of her trembling. She waited, the soft breeze from the veranda touching every inch of her. Desire coiled tighter and tighter in her lower belly as she heard the rustle of his clothes. The bed dipped and Nikos's hair-roughened leg rasped deliciously against her.

She gasped as something cold, the champagne she realized with a gasp, fell in a slow trickle over her collarbone. Then over her breasts, over her trembling stomach. She fisted her hands in the sheets as the cold liquid only heated up the rest of her skin even more.

Nikos's heated breath, the warmth of his body, swathed her. His lips met hers in a fusion of need and lust, the pressure of his mouth, the silky strokes of his tongue, every sensation amplified without sight.

And then he was licking the champagne off her body

in sure, lingering strokes, setting her on fire. He licked it from her breasts, his tongue rasping against the tight nipple.

"Champagne has never tasted better, Lexi."

Now his mouth licked it off her abdomen, and she sank her fingers into his hair with a shaking moan.

Sensation on sensation piled over her, her skin crackling with pleasure. The minute she felt his breath on her inner thighs, she clamped her legs closed, heat billowing inside her skin. "I'm... Nikos..."

His fingers kneaded her hip, his mouth opening in a smile against her thighs. "I want to see you, *thee mou*. All of you."

Her thighs trembled as she let him push them apart. He didn't give her another minute to think. His fingers separating the folds, he tasted her wet sex in a leisurely lick, and Lexi bucked off the bed with a long moan.

His forearm stayed on her abdomen, the hair on it tingling against her skin. Heat gathered in her belly like a storm, as he continued his torment. He made love to her with his tongue, and she climbed higher and higher, sweat gathering on her skin, throwing her head from left to right.

She sobbed his name, again and again, in search of a rhythm, in pursuit of relief. Her breaths were raspy, her body feeling like it would implode if she didn't find release soon.

He sucked the quivering bundle of nerves and Lexi orgasmed, in a shower of pleasure that had her shivering from top to toe.

With a guttural groan that pushed her over the edge, Nikos thrust into her.

Lexi trembled violently under him, the weight of his hard body knocking the breath out of her, her body twisting as he pulled out and thrust back in, setting a rhythm that told tales about his shattered self-control.

On the next thrust in, she felt his warm breath on her breast, and then his mouth closed over the hardened peak. The minute she felt his teeth on the tautly tender bud, she came again in an electrifying wave of spasms.

She dug her nails into his back, feeling the deep ridge of his spine stiffen, the hard muscles tightening.

With another firm thrust, Nikos came, his sweat-soaked skin rubbing against hers. Slowly, his breath evened out again, but he was still on top of her. She nudged the tie away from her eyes, but kept them closed, focusing on evening her breaths out, glad that he couldn't see her expression.

Only he kissed her again. Slowly, softly. She tasted his sweat, she tasted his passion and most of all, she tasted his tenderness in that kiss. And she sucked in a deep breath, trying to stem the avalanche of feelings inside her. He moved away from her, and she instantly turned to her side, her breathing still labored, but for a different reason.

Stretching behind her, Nikos pulled her close into the haven of his body. She felt the shudder in his body as he tucked her close to him. "Are you all right, *thee mou?*"

Running her fingers over his forearm, Lexi pressed a kiss to his palm.

She could talk as if she owned this affair, but she had a feeling sex was never going to be just sex for her. She didn't know whether to be happy or sad about it. But it was the truth, and she already had had a lifetime of shying away from it. She had wanted to stop hiding from life, to stop standing on the sidelines. But it also meant accepting herself as she was.

She was in this bed with Nikos because it was him, because for all his acerbic words and unfeeling facade, she liked him. It scared her—the little fluttering in her tummy when he looked at her, the way her heart missed a beat when he smiled. She couldn't lie to herself that it was just attraction or desire.

"Never better, Nikos," she said, speaking past the thump, thump of her heart. And felt his smile against her skin.

CHAPTER ELEVEN

VENETIA AND TYLER are getting married tomorrow morning.

From the minute Nikos had received the message from his security head, only one thought resonated incessantly in his head.

Had Lexi known all this time where they had been? Her concern for him—had it all been an act?

She hadn't denied his earlier accusation that she wouldn't tell him if Tyler contacted her. And yet, he wanted to hear it from her mouth that she had knowingly deceived him.

He thanked his pilot and swung his legs out of the chopper.

Pulling his cell phone from his coat pocket, he switched it off. Savas was going to call; he knew it in his bones. And he was not ready for another one of his grandfather's ploys. Theo Katrakis was going to make his move any minute now, and then Nikos would finally have what he wanted, and this time without paying Savas's price.

Walking through the marble foyer, he shrugged off his coat, suit jacket and tie. He mounted the steps to the first floor, and stopped outside Lexi's bedroom.

It was past eleven and by the absence of light under the door and the silence, she was sleeping. The last thing he wanted to do was scare her.

He turned the knob slowly. Moonlight filled the room

with a silvery glow. His heart thumping in that annoying way anytime he was near her, he reached the bed, only to find it empty.

A hushed whisper reached him from beneath the veranda, and he took the stairs down to the pool behind. A rented scooter lay against the wall next to the ivy at the back of the house and standing by the pool was Lexi.

In her white shorts and bright yellow spaghetti strap top, she looked innocent and young, as if she was incapable of deception.

Her slender shoulders stiff, she looked up at him. There was no guilt in her eyes.

He knew, and he had accepted as much as he could, that what Lexi shared with Tyler was indescribable. That he was her friend, family, everything rolled into one. He understood their relationship had been born out of the hardest time of her life.

Having known that bone-crushing loneliness, he was only glad that she had had Tyler.

But the consequence of that was that in her loyalty, her affection, Nikos would always only come second to Tyler.

Something flashed in her gaze as she took in his scowl. Fear? Shame? "Nikos, I've been trying to—"

He didn't let her finish. "Did you know where they have been all this time?"

Her luscious mouth trembled.

"Answer my question, Lexi."

"Yes."

The one word reverberated in his ears. His gut felt strangely hollow, his throat closing in, making it hard to breathe. Shying his gaze away from her, he turned and looked out at the blue surface of the heated pool.

There was a gentle breeze around them, the sounds of

the ocean beyond the estate walls soothing, and yet inside, he felt anything but.

He felt betrayed, hurt, he realized. And yet she had made him no promise, owed him nothing.

It was his own fault for forgetting what was important. Because five days of spending time with the woman, making love to her every which way, waking up with her slender form tucked tight against him, had warped his defenses, his armor.

Every time he had made love to her, it was as though she was changing him from inside out and he didn't know how to stop it. Sex had become something else, something he had never felt before.

His hunger for her knew no bounds, but it was the little things he craved to see that lingered in him long after he was away from her, the little intimacies they shared that sent a ripple of fear to brew within.

How else had the little minx gotten him to admit that Spyros worked for him in Athens? Her soft body cradled against his, her eyes had shimmered in the moonlight as she muttered about why he wanted to paint himself in the cruelest color possible with her.

She was determined to prove that he had a heart, and a kind, working one, at that. To stop her from going on, he had said that it had been to his own advantage to hire Spyros behind Savas's back, because he knew everything about the ins and outs of the business.

To which she had smiled, looking at him as though she had discovered a treasure, and kissed him, forcing Nikos to admit that Spyros at the end of it all, had been thankful to Nikos because he would have never had the guts to stand up to Savas and admit his love for his wife.

But she had drawn the lines now, had shown him his place in her life, like everyone else he had ever cared about.

The little realization sat on his chest like a boulder cutting off his breath. For all her claims, she hadn't given him another thought, while he…he had been planning to ask her to stay as long as she wanted, he'd had a studio prepared for her, he…

Hurt gave way to bitter anger that he had to choke back to speak. "Have you just been manipulating me, hoping I would learn about them too late?"

She looked at him with a stricken expression, shaking her head. "I didn't tell you when I thought they just needed time. I have been trying to rack my brain about what is best for everyone—"

"You mean what is best for *him*." The words barreled out of him on a wave of emotion that suddenly he had no control over. "Because everyone and everything else is secondary to you."

"This whole week…I've never felt more alive, I've never been happier. How dare you taint it with your ridiculous accusations?"

She sounded so uncharacteristically ferocious that Nikos stilled, his heart thundering loudly in his ears. Her gaze blazed with pure fury. "Then why didn't you…"

Tyler stepped out from behind the wall. Fierce emotion flooded through him, washing away the hurt, the anger, and he stood shaking in its wake.

Theos, what was happening to him?

Lexi clamped his fingers tight, refusing to let him retreat. "I know how much she means to you, Nikos. I… The moment I learned what Venetia was proposing, I have been going crazy with worry. I spent all morning trying to contact Tyler. I begged him to come clean with you."

He couldn't look away anymore. Their gazes met and the depth of feeling there rocked him to his toes. No one had ever considered his feelings before in his life, no one had ever wondered if he was in pain, that he could hurt and bleed just as anyone else, that he wanted to be loved and cherished and even protected.

Not his father, not Venetia and not Savas.

Until, one day, he had stopped feeling at all. He had turned himself into stone, starving everything else but his ambition. And he hadn't even realized until Lexi had showed up.

This feeling…it was gratitude, it was fear, and it gripped his body and wouldn't let go. But as warm and excruciatingly real as it was, he didn't want it. The only thing he understood, the only thing he could handle was his desire for her.

Nothing more.

"I care about Venetia," Tyler said, approaching him, his eyes welling with emotion. "And I don't know how to say no to her without hurting her, Nikos. But I can't marry her like this, not when I don't remember her, not when I have messed up every important relationship I've ever had." He took a step closer to Lexi and planted his hands on her shoulders, as though drawing strength from her.

Nikos had the most atavistic urge to push his hand off Lexi, to tell him that he had no rights to her. That she belonged to Nikos now.

There was such a ringing clarity to the thought that Nikos fisted his hands to not follow through on it.

"I trusted Lexi's word that Venetia's well-being is important to you, too," Tyler said in a gruff tone, "that you can find a way out of this without hurting her. I know you want me out of her life, but all I want is her happiness, Nikos. Venetia might very well hate me for this."

"Nikos? Please say something. This is the only way I could think of to—"

Nikos nodded, not trusting himself to say anything right.

He didn't know what was right or wrong right now. Only that the expression in Lexi's eyes—concerned, expectant— would stay with him forever. He held the answering desire in him at bay through sheer will.

"Where is my sister now?"

"At the inn. She was getting overexcited about the wedding tomorrow, and extremely anxious about not telling you, so I suggested she take a sleeping pill and take it easy for tonight. She is out like a light," he said with a wince.

Nikos nodded, once again surprised. Whether Tyler loved Venetia as he claimed or not, Nikos couldn't know. But he could clearly handle her well. "Go back to the inn now," he said, considering several scenarios one after the other. "Don't say a word to her about being here. I will be there in the morning at the inn. I was this close to locating you both anyway."

"And the wedding?" Tyler asked.

Lexi had been right. His sister was stronger than he had given her credit for. "I will convince her to not go through with it. For now. Which means I have to give her my blessing about you."

Lexi looked up at him. "Do you?"

He gave in to the urge and tugged her to his side, unable to keep himself from touching her. Her apparent happiness at the very thought, the depth of her goodwill toward two people who had caused her immense hurt, it was hard not to be transformed in a little way by it.

"I won't ask you to leave immediately," he said finally, meeting Tyler's eyes. "My sister has already suffered a lot. I don't ever want to see her hurt."

Tyler met his gaze unflinchingly. "Neither do I. Nor do I want to marry her until I remember everything, until I'm worthy of her. All I ask is that you give me the chance to try."

Still clasping her wrist, he pulled Lexi along with him. "You have it," he threw at Tyler, who stood looking at them with a nonplussed expression on his face.

Did she leave now?

The innocuous question attacked Lexi as Nikos pushed her into her bedroom and disappeared to answer a phone call. She knew the question had been coming, but she had shoved it away while figuring out how to handle what Tyler had told her this morning.

Now that everything between Tyler and Venetia was resolved, at least for now, the fact was that what she had come to do was no longer valid.

Tyler didn't need her anymore. Which meant her deal with Nikos was done.

Her stomach twisting into a painful knot, Lexi got off the bed and walked to the connecting veranda. She didn't want to sit there and let Nikos see the confusion in her eyes.

Because she didn't want to leave, she didn't want to walk away from Nikos. Not yet.

If ever, a sinuous voice whispered. Rubbing her clammy hands on her T-shirt, she leaned against the wall, fast tears gathering in her throat.

She would not cry, as much as it hurt. She needed to be grown-up about it. Deal with it like a holiday fling.

"Lexi?"

She heard Nikos's tread in the bedroom, drew in a deep breath and ventured back in. Feeling as though she was marching into battle.

Nikos stood beside the bed, his knees propped against it. Undoing the cuffs of his shirt, his gaze traveled over her pale face with increasing curiosity. By the time he was done, wariness entered his face. "I thought this was what you wanted for them—a real chance."

She wrapped her arms around herself, feeling inexplicably cold. "It is."

"It would have never worked out between you and him," he said in a soft voice full of emotion.

"What?" she said automatically, frowning. Realization dawned. "Nikos, I'm not moping over Tyler."

Reaching her, he took her hands in his. Her hands were the size of his palms, the rough grooves and ridges now as familiar to her as her own. She trembled as he ran one finger over her cheek and the circles under her eyes. "Thank you for trusting me with the truth today."

She smiled up at him, wondering if everything she felt was written in her eyes. And if he would run if he saw it. "I think you like deluding Venetia, your grandfather, and even yourself into thinking that you don't understand love or affection or any matters of heart. But I know that you do. I believed that in the face of Tyler's honesty, you would give him a chance."

He inclined his head and smiled. The warmth of it enveloped her. "Then why that look in your eyes?"

She tried for casual nonchalance and utterly failed. "You don't need me here anymore. It's time I returned to New York."

"Ahhh…so you won't want this then?" With his hand on her wrist, he tugged her from the room, giving her no chance to answer.

They walked through the corridor, went down the steps, through the lounge into one of the rooms to the side. It was the room she loved most in the villa. Very sparsely furnished, and during most of the day, sunlight filled the room.

They came to a stop in front of the closed door.

"Open it."

Her heart in her throat, Lexi pushed the door. Nikos

switched on the lights behind her. Tears clogged her throat, her stomach a mass of flutters at the sight that greeted her.

A huge drafting table stood at one corner, with a detachable drawing board set up on top, slightly angled and perfectly positioned for her height. A sleek silver laptop sat on a table next to it with a printer/scanner, a filing cabinet next to it. Reams of four-by-six paper, magnetic draw/erase boards, paintbrushes and boxes, pencils in every brand and size, erasers, everything and anything she could ever want was in the room.

It was a studio he could have plucked from her dreams.

Her mouth dried up, her chest filled with a lightness that should have made breathing easier.

Nikos stood leaning against the door, drinking in every expression on her face.

"Do you like it?"

"It's perfect," she whispered, her pulse hammering in her throat. "I… You have thought of everything. But I… It's just always been a hobby."

"Why is it just a hobby?"

She couldn't even answer for a few minutes for the tumult of feelings that flew within her. For years, she had wished for someone to think of her, to care about her. And in his own way, she realized, Nikos did.

"Your talent is beyond average, Lexi. You should finish your graphic novel and submit a proposal."

Her heart slammed against her rib cage. "For what?"

"For publishing it."

Trepidation swirled through her. He caught her hands in his, his fingers drawing circles on the backs of her palms.

"Or you can just scan a few teasers, and put it up on the web. There's a large community online that's much less scary if that's what you—"

"Wait. How do you know all this?"

"I've been researching it. People are going to love your work. Compared to everything that's out there, I have no doubt your work will stand out. The second way, you create a reader base, and the best thing about it is, knowing that people want to read it will motivate you to keep going."

Lexi blinked, unable to formulate a response. The fact that he had put so much thought into this, that he had researched it, the fact that he understood her trepidation, it sat tight on her chest. "I just… It's not going to be like Superman or Spiderman, you know. And I'm not that ambitious really, either. I just want to be able to do it more and support myself."

His long strides swallowed up the distance between them. His gray V-necked T-shirt delineated that broad chest gloriously. His long fingers clutched her shoulders as he looked down. "Then stay here."

"What?"

"Stay for as long as we both want this. It seems even your friend is going to be here for a while, right?"

She laughed at that last incentive and liked him a little more. He was making it so hard to say no to him, to refuse this chance. The little resistance she might have had was crumbling before his thoughtfulness.

"I can't accept all this…" She colored furiously. "I can't just live off of you, Nikos. That would just taint everything we have. Please try to—"

"I will respect your wishes," he said with such easy acceptance that shock robbed her of words. "The second half of your payment should be debiting even as we speak." He laid a finger on her mouth. "Before you argue, I am… I was the boss. All I wanted was to stop my sister from getting hurt. I think you did a great job. With that money you have, all I am offering you is a place to stay. It's nothing less than what I would do for a friend."

She scrunched her nose at him. "You don't have any friends."

He ignored her little quip. "Apart from this studio, I won't force anything else on you. You can even put in a few hours at the hotel when they need some help."

She thought her heart might burst open from her chest. It took every bit of self-possession she had to remain still. "This is what you want?"

He bent his head and kissed her nose. She smiled at the gesture. Over the past week, she had realized that while being an extremely physical man with an insatiable sex drive, Nikos really didn't do the little things like touching, or hugging outside the context of sex.

So every moment he touched her, or kissed her like this, was a precious gift she hugged to herself. "I want this, too…but I won't to be your sex stop of Greece." In this, she would not relent. She fought to force casualness into her tone. "I grew a monstrous, scaly, green head when that woman was touching you the other day. I'm not sophisticated like your other—"

His hands moved to her buttocks and tugged her off the floor until she was cradled against his groin, his arousal a hard, pulsing weight against the V of her legs. "I haven't looked at another woman since you began messing with my head. I don't want anyone else but you."

Something colored his voice—a resigned acceptance that this was different—and she smiled. It was not only her that was venturing into new territory.

She ran her fingers over his jaw. The rasp of his stubble against her palm was an intimacy that left her shaking. Equal parts excitement and fear raced through her veins. How long would they last? What happened when he was through with her? Wouldn't it be better to walk away now?

She hid her face in his chest, fighting the swarm of questions, fighting the urge to ask them. His heart thundered under her cheek.

He smelled like sex and warmth and…even with all his contradictions, he made her happy.

Being with Nikos made her happy, made her feel alive for the first time in her life. It was as simple as that.

Of course, there was her fear that he would end this suddenly, that she was already in too deep…and that gut-wrenching feeling in her stomach every time he reached for her in his sleep.

It was the time her every defense, her carefully constructed attitude to keep this uncomplicated, collapsed like a pack of cards. Just as she did then, she pushed away the fear again.

Nikos liked her. Every action of his made up for words he didn't speak. And that was enough for her.

When she was with him, she believed she was beautiful, that she was courageous and that she deserved the best that life had to offer. She loved what she became when she was with him.

She wouldn't let her worry about the future destroy her present like she had done for so long.

He had taught her to live, and live she would. She wound her arms around his lean waist. The hard muscles tightened for a second, but she held on, knowing that he was new to this kind of intimacy.

She looked up at him and smiled. "I'll stay."

He rubbed his thumb over her lower lip, his gaze full of…warmth and a light she had never seen before. "That's good." He spoke the words in a matter-of-fact voice, but the depth of emotion he was struggling to contain and failing to was enough for her.

A hundred things could go wrong in a day. But this moment with this man was perfect. She stood on tiptoes and pressed a hard kiss to his mouth. Teeth and tongues tangled against each other, and they were both out of breath in ten seconds flat.

Breathing hard, she laughed. "Can I give you my gift now? It finally got delivered yesterday, and I've been dying to show it to you."

"A gift?" He said the words as though she had pointed a gun at him.

She nodded, embarrassed. "It's not something as grand as this studio, but I thought—"

He cut her off with a finger on his lips. "Go bring it, *thee mou.*"

It took her all of two minutes to go upstairs, grab the package from her closet and run back down to him. She clutched it tight in her hands, suddenly feeling stupid. She had thought it a riot at the time.

But then what did she have that she could give him that he didn't have?

She had a gift for him. It was what normal people in normal relationships did.

Nikos stared at the colorful, cheap packaging in her hand and struggled to remain still against the shudder that racked his body.

He had lived through the most painful moments in his life without falling apart. He had cradled his mother's weak body, seen the life go out of it while his father had cried Nikos's tears, he had held Venetia through her silent screams when she found their father without succumbing to the grief and fury that had roiled inside him.

And yet that small package in her hands, the expectant expression on Lexi's face—it was the most dangerous moment he had lived through. Cold sweat drenched him inside out. He wanted to walk away from it, never lay eyes on the package even as another part of him was dying to see it. Like a child that he had never been.

Without another thought, he plucked the package from her hands.

"I used the scanner in your office upstairs."

Nodding, he tore the packaging aside and a T-shirt fell out. It was plain white, made of cheap quality cotton. He unfolded it and froze.

It had a sketch of the space pirate Spike imprinted on it. Like the one Lexi wore of Ms. Havisham, but this one was colored in, a contrast of black and white.

Spike wore black leather pants and a sleeveless leather vest. A gun hung from the holster on his side. It was again incredibly detailed but it was his face that caught Nikos's attention.

An arrested expression covering his features, Spike was looking at something in the distance. It was the moment when he found that Ms. Havisham was the key that would open the time portal—Nikos knew it.

He felt as if someone had pushed a hand into his chest and given his heart a quiet thumping to get it going. It slammed against his rib cage now and he felt his pulse everywhere in his body like a savage drumbeat. His breath choked in his throat, and his chest hurt.

It was the most precious thing anyone had ever given him and the most dangerous. Words failed him, and the cold dread multiplied a few hundred times. Suddenly, he had the most incredible urge to possess that time portal in his own hands, to turn back everything he had said to her in the past hour, to turn back to the time before Lexi had even entered his world. Before his emotions had been safely under lock and key, before he had begun to look beneath his bitter anger for his father. He fisted his hands and let a curse loose.

"Nikos?"

Shaking himself out of it, he looked at Lexi.

Her lower lip caught between her teeth, she didn't meet his eyes. She pounced on him, to grab it probably and he tugged his arm out of her reach just in time. "It was just a silly idea."

The wariness in her eyes propelled him out of his pensive mood. He would not shatter this moment for her. It was the only reason he was doing this. The thought rang flat and false within him.

Holding his arm out to ward her off, he pulled off his shirt. Her gaze followed the movement as he pulled the T-shirt on.

Warmth shone in her blue eyes. And something in him instantly recoiled against it.

"Perhaps Spike should kill Ms. Havisham," he said, emotion roiling in his throat. It was a warning, for himself and her. "He is a heartless pirate, isn't he? He's not going to miraculously fall in love with her and want to save her."

Something flashed in her gaze. "I never said they'll have a happy ending, Nikos. And as to whether Spike will kill her, I'd say you still underestimate Ms. Havisham. She's not going to let anyone kill her, least of all Spike."

Standing back, she held the edge of the material in her hand and pulled. "It's too tight, isn't it? I should have gone for XXXL instead of XXL." She winked at him and started pulling the T-shirt up. "Now it's going to be really hard to get it off."

He swallowed at the lick of desire in her blue eyes and at the relentless shiver that took hold of his skin. And let his own desire for her mute the warning bells clanging in his head.

CHAPTER TWELVE

IT WAS A whole week before Nikos had finally untangled himself from Lexi and made it to a meeting aboard his yacht with Theo Katrakis. A meeting that Theo had requested days ago. Nikos had deliberately locked himself out of any business matters but for the most important. Walking over to the glass bar that was the pride of the main deck, he was about to reach for whiskey when he saw an ice bucket with champagne. A note said it was from Theo, which meant he had good news for Nikos.

But instead of the fierce rush of satisfaction he expected, an image of Lexi, trembling with cold champagne over her skin, little mewls of pleasure falling from her mouth, flashed in front of him. He was instantly hard as rock, the strength of his desire unprecedented. That was the word for it. His desire, this ever-growing unease he felt right under his skin, everything about the situation he created with Lexi was *unprecedented*. And through each day, Nikos felt the doubts he experienced at night with Lexi solidify into cold, hard truth.

More than once, he had caught himself, weakening, wavering and shutting out the world and even work. Postponing this meeting with Theo when he had spent more than a year carefully cultivating this association, blocking out

Savas instead of finding out what his grandfather was up to even now...when and how had he become this man?

It was like watching himself exist in a different reality, as vivid as the one in Lexi's comic book, a happy one, a parallel one that seemed as fragile as it was fantastic. The ruthless life he had carefully built into existence slowly unraveled as Lexi wove herself into the very fabric of his life.

For a man who had never had a romantic relationship that lasted more than a few hours, having one with someone like Lexi was like sitting on a box of explosives. Because that's what he was doing. Only a week ago he had asked her to stay, and yet now, he felt the iron lid he kept on his control shake loose, and everything he had ruthlessly wiped from his life creep back in.

It was when he had caught himself panicking in the middle of the night because she hadn't been in the bed, wondering if she had left him like his mother had done, like his father had done, that was when he had realized he needed to get out of there. Cold sweat had drenched him just as his darkest fear rose to the surface.

If he let himself feel so much, there would only be pain. After everything he had survived to get here in life, he didn't want pain.

Hearing a sound behind him, he turned around.

Theo walked in, a frown on his craggy, old face. Silver glinted in his hair, the warm smile he wore belying the calculatingly shrewd light in his dark eyes. Shaking Nikos's hand, he subjected Nikos to a thorough scrutiny. Nikos brought him to the deck and they settled down on opposite sides of the table.

The sun glinted off Theo's skin, shadowing his expression from Nikos. "I was surprised to learn you wanted to postpone the meeting, Nikos. Your sister, she is safe, yes?"

Gritting his teeth, Nikos nodded. He couldn't fault the man for the doubts in his eyes.

"You still want to continue this alliance between us then?"

"Of course I do, Theo. Nothing else is more important to me."

Leaning forward, Theo smiled. "Then I have three more votes on my side. They will support me without doubt. Savas does not control the board anymore."

Nikos smiled. This was it. His dream was within reach now. He would sit in that chair, claim the prize of his hard work. He shook Theo's hands, his breath ballooning up in his chest. He wanted to celebrate with Lexi, he wanted to...

"There is one condition, though."

He had been expecting this. And Nikos was prepared. "Name your price, Theo."

Theo held his gaze. "Marry my daughter, Nikos. Join the Demakis and Katrakis name forever."

A buzzing filled Nikos's ears. He shot up from his seat and grabbed the railing. The sea glimmered endlessly blue in front of him. But he heard nothing of the waves with blood rushing into his ears.

His first instinct was to scream the denial that was struggling to be let out of his throat. Distaste coated his tongue at the very thought of Eleni Katrakis. He would find a different way to the CEO's chair. He couldn't even indulge in the idea of looking at any other woman except Lexi, he couldn't even...

All his thoughts came to a suffocating halt, his gut twisting into a hard knot. A chill broke out over his skin, despite the sun shining down. Was he actually considering walking away from his life's mission because of one woman? Turning his back on everything he had worked toward? To give in to the unknown, unnamed sensation in his gut that filled him with fear over tangible prize? To follow in the same path his father had trodden, leaving nothing but destruction in his wake.

Nikos did not want that life; he had done everything he could to get away from it.

He had nothing to give Lexi, not the kind of woman she was—kind, generous, affectionate. The sooner they moved on with their lives the better.

It was an affair—they both had known that from the beginning. And all affairs, at least his, came to an end.

Lexi had never felt more intimidated in her life. Even though, for once, she was wearing the right clothes, shoes and even makeup.

The blue cocktail dress was strapless and hugged her chest and waist and then fell to her knees in a playful skirt. Her hair was combed back and piled high, thanks to the stylist that Nikos had insisted on, leaving her nape bare. She had thought the classic lines of the dress would clash with her boyish haircut. But as the stylist had claimed, the blunt haircut made the small planes of her face stand out.

The inaugural party for the hotel on the other side of the island, the same hotel she and Nikos had christened so colorfully just two weeks ago, was open as of tonight. And from what she had overheard from Nikos's assistant, booked for the next five years through, just as Nikos had predicted. Apparently there were a lot of high-profile celebrities who were really into low-key vacation spots that were a slice of paradise.

Even the party today, set up under an elegant marquee on the beach was a low-key one. Lexi had spotted a celebrity chef that she was dying to tell Tyler about and even a famous underwear model. But more than the international celebrities, it was the presence of Savas Demakis that unsettled her.

With her heated imagination, she had imagined Savas to look cruel and scary. But he looked like any other man here tonight for the most part. Except when he had stopped in front of Lexi fifteen minutes ago and fired off questions without so much as a greeting, as if it was his privilege to be answered.

Cowed by his presence, Lexi had automatically answered. He clearly didn't like her presence here tonight, but she refused to hide like a dirty secret. With a sigh, she realized that more of Savas's guests had begun casting looks in her direction, their curiosity blatant.

She would have left for the villa on the other side if it hadn't been for the fact that she hadn't seen Nikos in three days. He had spent a week with her and Venetia and Tyler; curiously they had made a very peaceful foursome at the villa before urgent business had called him away. From the way his eyes had lit up, Lexi had known it had to do with the vote for the CEO position on the Demakis board.

She had wished him luck. Only he had told her that he didn't need luck. And he hadn't returned or even called her. She had swallowed her disappointment but couldn't stay away tonight.

According to Venetia, the board was present and was going to make an announcement. Her heart raced as Lexi heard the sounds of a helicopter. She dug her heels into the carpet laid on the beach, fighting the urge to go to Nikos.

She took a champagne flute from a uniformed waiter and joined Tyler and Venetia at their table. The moment Nikos appeared in front of the small dais, people mobbed him from every side.

Glad that she was sitting, Lexi took a sip, just to give her shaking hands something to do.

Surrounded by powerful men and women, Nikos seemed far from the man who had surprised her with the studio.

His gaze raked the crowd, and finding her, settled on her. Across the distance separating them, Lexi felt the weight of it as if he had walked up to her and touched her.

An older man claimed Nikos's attention and the moment was gone.

A few minutes later, the guests began to settle around the tables under the artistic handmade paper lanterns hanging from the roof of the marquee. And the speeches began.

She had expected Nikos or the American entrepreneur Nathan Ramirez to be giving the speech, but it was the older man who had come to see Nikos on the island a couple of weeks ago. He introduced himself as Theo Katrakis, a board member of the Demakis Board. He went on at length describing Nikos's achievements, and how his leadership had pumped Demakis International with new blood and money and that congratulations were due to Nikos.

Lexi's heart thumped hard. Finally, Nikos had what he had worked so hard for.

Nikos was the new CEO of Demakis International. The older man laughed and cracked a joke that Lexi didn't understand exactly but got the gist of when he invited his daughter Eleni Katrakis to the dais along with Nikos. With Nikos and Eleni on either side, Theo Katrakis beamed and made a comment to Savas.

The broad smile on Savas's face drove the truth home for Lexi.

Nikos was engaged to Eleni Katrakis.

Lexi's heart shattered in her chest, her breath hitching in her throat. Her head felt as if it was stuck in a space warp—all sounds and sights warbled in the background against the whooshing in her ears, against the chill on her skin. Like Tyler's curse and his hands gripping her, Venetia's shocked glance shifting between her and her brother. But they were all muted against the savage gleam in Savas Demakis's eyes.

He had stopped history from repeating itself.

He had demanded Nikos pay his price to be the CEO, and Nikos had paid it with his heart. And hers, too.

Because, despite her every effort, she was in love with him. It was the most terrifying truth yet that she had to face. Fear was a physical fist in her gut, a hollowness in her chest.

She had felt like this once before. The memory hit her hard, more sensations and feelings rather than tangible details.

She had been five and after her first day in the public school, she had realized that every other kid in her class had parents. That they didn't get shuffled from home to home, that they were loved. And that, her parents, for whatever reason, had given her up.

She had cried until her head had hurt, and Mrs. Nesbitt had hugged her hard and washed her face. That's how she felt now.

Like she had lost something valuable, something precious that she had never had in the first place.

Of all the times to realize how much she wanted him to love her, to hope that he had chosen happiness—hers and his—of all the times to realize that she would forever be alone in this world because she would never stop loving him.

Spike should kill Ms. Havisham.

He had told her how this was going to end.

She blinked back the searing heat behind her eyes. She couldn't bear to look at him, couldn't bear for him to see how much she loved him, couldn't bear for him to see how much he was hurting her.

She wanted to slink away and hide. She wanted to fly

back to New York this minute. If she saw him, she would surely break down, would probably beg him to love her as she did him.

Because she couldn't be sophisticated enough to not let this hurt, because she couldn't pretend, even for one second, despite his every warning, that she hadn't fallen in love with him.

She breathed in a deep gulp of air and fought the desperation.

She wasn't going to take it lying down. If she was going to lose him anyway, she was going to make him face what he had done. She was going to find the man who'd been kind under the brutal honesty, the man who had shown her what it was to live and make sure he understood what he was giving up.

It was hours before Nikos had been able to extricate himself from the night's activities. Every board member wanted to congratulate him; every investor wanted a piece of him. Through every minute of it, he had pushed himself to stay, told himself that this was the moment he had worked to achieve for almost fifteen years.

He searched for words to say to her, wondered about what to say and how to do it without hurting her. Like he had done for three days.

He had seen her, sitting quietly at a table at the back, dressed in blue silk that made her look as breathtakingly lovely as she was on the inside. Nothing else had registered in his mind until Theo had made the announcement.

She had looked shattered, and his throat, it had felt as if he had swallowed glass. Only then, did he realize what he had set in motion.

He stood outside her studio now—it would forever

be that in his mind—stunned to see her curled up in the recliner.

He had thought she would have fled in disgust. Maybe even hoped for it, like a spineless coward. He was about to step back out when her eyes fluttered open and instantly focused on him. Her knees tucked to her chest, her hands crossed over, she looked tiny, breakable in the huge recliner.

She offered him a small smile, nothing but sadness in her blue eyes. "Congratulations, Nikos."

"You're wearing the dress I picked."

She looked down and ran a hand over the silk. Moonlight threw just enough light to bare her slender shoulders to him. She met his gaze and the intensity of emotion in it skewered him. "I wore it for you. It made me feel different, confident. I wanted to look beautiful tonight. I had a feeling it was going to be special."

His heart beat a rapid tattoo, a part of him telling him to stay at the door, to not go to her, to act with honor. What little he had left. "I've never seen anyone more beautiful."

She took a deep breath as though to contain herself. "For once, I believe that."

Shrugging off his coat, he stayed leaning against the door. "I…had no idea Theo was going to announce it tonight."

Resignation curved her mouth. "Have you already slept with her?"

The profanity that flew from his mouth should have created a frost in the air around them. But it didn't wash away the bitter need inside to explain why he had agreed to this. He looked at her, and she seemed different. "*Christos,* I have no interest in her. I haven't even looked at her."

"Is that supposed to make me feel better?"

At his silence, she smiled. It was the most cynical thing

he had ever seen on her innocent face. And he was responsible for putting it there.

"Say it, Nikos. Tell me to be gone. Tell me to my face that you're done with me, that our little affair has come to an end. Tell me that you're moving on with more important things in your life."

"You know it's not—"

She shook her head and the words halted on his lips. Not that he had any idea what he was going to say. "Don't you dare say it's not like that. People have affairs with each other, and then move on, right? Whisper those little words you whispered to Emmanuelle that day. Tell me it is time to pack up my things. Do I get a goodbye gift?"

"*Theos,* Lexi. What are you doing?"

Hugging her midriff, she cast a furious look at him. Her face alight with color, her mouth mobile, she looked like an angry tigress and nothing like the woman he had expected. "Were you hoping I would just slink away in the night, heartbroken and pitiful? Or were you thinking I would be so desperate to be loved by you, that I would take you any way I got you, that I would accept what little you offer me?"

"I had to make this choice. This marriage is nothing but an agreement."

His jaw was tight like a vise, his cheekbones sticking out making him forbidden and stark. But Lexi wouldn't back down. The hurt continued to splinter inside her as if there was no end to it. As if this moment needed to be entrenched inside her, as if she needed to be changed.

Anger, red-hot and roiling, it was the only way to survive the moment and she clutched it to herself.

Because if she didn't, she would hear that voice inside her head. That little girl filled with hurt, filled with fear, the one that so desperately wanted to be loved.

The only way to drown out that pathetic voice was to

ride the storm of anger. "You think I can find solace in the fact that you're ruining your life along with mine?"

He shifted back, the expression in his eyes cycling from fury to desperation to a terrifying emptiness within seconds. "Don't say another word," he said through gritted teeth, every syllable bellowing around them.

"I won't stop." She wiped her tears and looked up at him, her heart breaking in her chest. "You have no idea how much the very thought of leaving you terrifies me. I can't breathe if I think about not seeing you ever again." She covered the distance between them, and he braced himself as if she was a weapon that would cause him damage. She reached for his face, and he immediately bent his head, his gaze a glittering pool of anger and something else.

Standing on her toes, she kissed his cheek, and he shuddered. Burying her face in his chest, she hugged him tight, learning and memorizing the scent and feel of him.

"I'm petrified that I will never see you again, that I'll never hear your voice again, never kiss you again. That no one will ever think me beautiful—" Her voice broke. "That no one will ever tell me to stand up for myself, that no one will ever think I'm extraordinary. I've never been more terrified that I'll never be loved, Nikos."

She pressed another kiss on his palm, and looked up at him. The pain she saw in his eyes stole her breath, knuckled her so hard in the gut that she swayed. But she didn't relent. She would say this to him, for herself. "I'm in love with you. I think I'll always love you. If you weren't so blinded by your ambition—"

Pulling his hands from her, he stepped back, a vein pulsing in his temple. "I've told you things that I haven't told anyone. This is not about ambition or greed. You have to understand..."

She wanted to shake him; she wanted to hit him for not seeing the truth that was right in front of his eyes.

"You still think this is victory over your father? Because it's not."

He flinched. The flash of pain in his eyes would have stopped her before, but now, she was filled with pure fury. He had shown her what it was to live and then he wanted her to go right back to being half-alive.

"This agreement you have made, it's your victory over your fear that you are like him. *Because you are,* despite your every effort to not be. You are his son...you feel something for me." She poked him in the chest. "You feel it here. You're getting attached to me. And it terrifies you.

"It terrifies you to realize that you might be exactly like your father, that you have the same weakness as he does, that if you let this small thing for me take root, if you accept it and let it grow, it will devour you from the inside, and that you will have no control over yourself.

"And your grandfather offered you the best way to beat it back, to keep it in its place, didn't he?"

"For the last time, Savas had nothing to do with this."

"Savas has everything to do with this. You and he are both terrified of the same thing. This way, you can tell yourself that I'm secondary to something else in your life, that your emotions have no power over you.

"You are breaking my heart and burying yours. And I hope to hell you've just as miserable a life ahead of you as I do."

CHAPTER THIRTEEN

NIKOS SAT IN the leather chair in his new office in the Demakis International tower in Athens. He had been in this
room countless times, stood on the other side of the vast
desk as Savas spelled out more and more conditions that
defined Nikos's survival.

And he had conquered every obstacle Savas had thrown
his way. This moment, this chair was his prize after years
of painstaking hard work.

Except it didn't feel like a moment of triumph. It felt
hollow...it felt tainted. Frustration boiled inside him. He
didn't want to think of Lexi.

He had thought she understood why he needed this. He
didn't need her any more than he needed her analy-
sis. Wherever she went, or whatever she did, she would
be loved. It was a matter of comfort and intense envy inside him.

He picked up the champagne bottle from the ice bucket
and popped the cork just as Savas walked in. Curiously, he
had stayed away from Nikos since the party a week ago.
As if he knew that Nikos had been like a wounded animal,
rearing to attack anyone who ventured close.

But he couldn't. Savas understood nothing of emotions.
He shouldered enormous responsibility without complaint.
Nikos's father had been a late child, and by the time he had

turned his back on this wealth, Savas had already been close to sixty. But Savas had gone on with his life, with his duty, shouldered his company, his family.

"Congratulations," Savas said, taking the champagne flute from Nikos. "You've proved yourself worthy of the Demakis name."

Nikos nodded and took a sip. But one question lingered in his throat, clawing its way to his tongue, refusing to be silenced. He had never before asked Savas about his father. Ever.

There was no need to do so now. Yet the words fell from his lips and he didn't stop them. Maybe if he asked, maybe when he knew, there would be no more wondering. He could put all the dirty questions Lexi had raised to peace finally.

"My father...did he come to you for help when my mother was sick?"

His eyes widened under his dark brows for an infinitesimal moment before Savas could hide the flash of emotion. But Nikos had seen it. "You gain nothing by delving into the past, Nikos. You have done remarkably well until now, beyond my expectations. Don't look back now."

Nikos dropped the flute onto the table, his heart slamming against his rib cage. Savas turned around, leaning heavily against his cane.

Panic robbed his breath from him; his gut heaved. Nikos planted himself between Savas and the door. "Answer my question. Did he come to you for help?"

This time, there was not a flicker of doubt in his gaze. "Yes, he did."

Nikos exhaled a jagged breath, pain twisting hard in his gut. Everything he had assumed about his father, it had been colored by the excruciating hurt that he hadn't hung on for him and Venetia, that he had been weak.

"What did you do?"

If he felt anything of the vehemence in Nikos's question, Savas didn't betray it by even a muscle. "I presented him with a set of conditions, just as I had done with you."

A cold finger climbed up Nikos's spine. He knew what was coming; he finally understood what Lexi had meant when she had said it was Savas that demanded a price from Nikos. A price he had paid willingly, crushing his own heart in the process. He licked his lips, pushing the words out through a raw throat.

"What were the conditions?"

"I told him I would give her medical care, enough money to live out the rest of her life in comfort. In return, he had to walk away from her. And instead of taking what I offered, your father decided to remain a fool."

Exactly what Nikos had thought him to this day.

A sudden chill settled deep in Nikos's chest, filling his veins with ice. All his father had needed to do was to walk away from his mother. And her last days would have been in comfort.

And yet, he hadn't been able to make the ruthless choice, hadn't been able to leave the woman he loved.

Had the guilt been too unbearable to live, knowing that his love for her had caused her suffering? Powerlessness transformed to rage, and Nikos turned toward Savas. They both knew he had been a weak man. "Why? Why did you ask that of him?"

Savas rocked where he stood, his head erect, his gaze direct.

"She stole him from me. My only son, the heir to my empire, and he ran away the minute he met her. She weakened him even more. And what did she gain in return? Poverty, starvation, failure?"

"She did not weaken him, Savas. He was already weak."

Savas flinched. The tiredness he must have held at bay, the pain he must have shoved aside, crept into his face. There was unrelenting grief there, and to Nikos's shock, regrets. Savas had never meant to push his son to that bitter end he had finally sought. It had been nothing but stubborn pride that had motivated Savas.

Instead, in the blink of an eye, Nikos's father's cowardly step had shattered so many lives.

"Eventually, he let her down just as he did me. And I could not let you make the same mistake. I held you at arm's length. I put you through so much—my own blood. I could not let you become weak like him, incapable of doing your duty."

And it had cost Savas to see Nikos suffer as much as it had cost Nikos himself. Nikos shuddered at the weight of that realization. "So you manipulated Theo into making a deal with me. My marriage to Eleni Katrakis—that was your idea."

"Yes. I heard about that American woman, about how wrapped up you were in her, about how she had changed your mind even about Venetia. This time, I couldn't not act."

And as before, Nikos had walked right into his own destruction. "Neither of you was right. Do you understand, Savas?

"If he was irresponsible, weak, you were bitter, abusive. When he died, Venetia and I needed your love, we needed your support. Instead you turned my anger for him to your advantage. You made me loathe my own father. But I am not weak like him or bitter like you."

And neither would his love for Lexi weaken him.

His body shuddering at the realization, Nikos sank into his chair.

He had a heart, and it hurt, and it bled, and most of all, it loved.

And he had pushed the woman who had shown him that out of his life without second thought.

Even with her heart breaking, even with the fear that she had lived with for most of her life rioting through her, she had still fought for him, for them. She had tried to show him what they had and what he was so intent on destroying. Because the love she felt for him, it had given her that strength, that courage.

I will always love you.

Now he understood how easily, how perfectly those words had come to her, and why she had been so furious about what he had chosen.

Picking up the papers of his appointment as the CEO with shaking hands, Nikos brought them over to Savas. He dropped them on the table and met his grandfather's gaze. "Whatever you did, I realize you did it out of a twisted sense of guilt and love. You sought to make me stronger than him." He swallowed the thick lump in his throat. "And I am a stronger man than he ever was. I have never shirked my duty toward my sister. I will never betray your trust in me. But Lexi…she's a part of me, Savas.

"She makes me stronger. She fills my life with laughter and joy." He took a look around the office and sucked in a deep breath.

"I have proved my worth a hundred times over to you. I deserve to be the CEO of Demakis International. But I will not pay the price you ask of me anymore. I will not lose the woman I love any more than I will shoot myself mourning her loss. You want me to run this company…you want me to be your legacy? Then I will do it with her by my side. That's the only way I can do it. I'm through living my life based on you or him. I have to be my own man now."

Without waiting for Savas's answer, Nikos closed the door behind him. Fear-fueled anticipation flew hot in his veins. He couldn't wait to see her, couldn't wait to hold her in his arms.

Because this time, he didn't feel resentment at the thought of the woman who had been through so much and yet had such a capacity to love. This time, he wanted that love. This time, he wanted to love her as she deserved to be loved.

Lexi was opening a can of mushroom soup when a knock sounded on the door. She knew it wasn't Faith, because Faith was playing the adult, much-less-fun version of hide-and-seek with her. Tired of putting up an elaborate pretense when she was already feeling fragile, Lexi had given it to her straight—everything she had learned about her and Tyler, all the lies that Faith had told her.

And then burst into tears like a raving lunatic the moment Faith had asked about Nikos. To give her credit, Faith had stayed back a full day, looking after Lexi before splitting.

Lexi knew she wasn't gone forever, and with Tyler staying back in Greece for the time being, Faith was the only friend Lexi had. But she had told Faith in no uncertain terms that she wouldn't put up with any kind of nonsense.

But rattling around in the apartment that she had shared with both Tyler and Faith all by herself wasn't helping her already-vulnerable state. More than once, Lexi had indulged the thought of calling Nikos, had wondered how he was. But the next moment her thoughts turned to his engagement, and the vicious cycle circled back to fury at him.

That fury, it was the one thing that was holding her together. She couldn't bear to think about what would be left when it was gone, too.

The knock sounded again.

With a sigh, she took a peek through the peephole and jerked back as though bitten.

Clad in a long coat, his mouth set into a tight line, Nikos stood on the other side of the door.

Her heart, if possible, might have jumped out of her chest. For a few seconds, she forgot to breathe as panic flooded her muscles. Tears hit the back of her eyes with the force of a thunderstorm.

"Open the door, Lexi. I know you're in there."

The nerve of the man to think she was hiding from him! Sucking in a sharp breath, she undid the dead bolt and opened the door.

And felt the impact of his presence like a pealing pulse everywhere in her body. His tie dangled from his throat, his dress shirt unbuttoned and crinkled. He already had stubble—which meant he had shaved only once today—the very sight of which gave her tingles in the strangest places.

She had complained once that it rasped her skin, and he had begun shaving twice. Then she had complained that she missed it. He had grown it in the next day and tickled the inside of her thighs with it.

Dear God, the man could turn her inside out.

Fighting the upsurge of color, she stood in front of the door and eyed him nervously. "If this is about me taking that laptop, I'm sorry, but I'm not returning it. Put it under damages that were due to me." She had to keep this light, self-deprecating, or she would collapse into tears right there.

"That's what you think I came over for? Because you took a laptop?" He threw her a narrowed look before striding through the small gap and entering the apartment. The quiet brush of his body against hers made her tense.

With a sigh, she closed the door and leaned against it.

Cursing, she ran a nervous hand over her abdomen. Even with clothes mussed from the flight, he looked breathtakingly gorgeous and effortlessly sexy. It was not fair that one man had everything—looks, sexuality and the arrogant confidence to carry it off so easily.

She couldn't think like this about him. He was engaged to another woman. There were a few lines she wouldn't cross, even in thought. But the sight of his sunken eyes, and the protruding cheekbones, the tired look, gave her immense satisfaction.

Really, she needed to channel Ms. Havisham more.

"Where is your fiancée?"

"In Athens, I assume, with her lover."

"If this is a pitch about sophisticated open marriages and New York sex stops—" she wasn't going to break down again, at least not until he left "—then get out. I have work to do."

He shrugged his coat off and threw it on the couch behind him. Pushing the sleeves of his shirt back, he picked up a sketch from the couch. And casually rolled the grenade onto the floor. "The engagement is off."

Her mouth fell open. For a few seconds, she wondered if she had imagined the words, if she was, once again, lapsing into an alternate reality in which he came back to her and professed undying love.

"Lexi? Are you all right?"

When she nodded, he went back to poking around the living room that she had converted into her studio. The wide wood table she had found in a flea market stood tilted to catch the sunlight from the sliding glass doors. And taped to it with a clip was the penultimate chapter of Ms. Havisham's story.

With hands that were obviously trembling, he ran a finger over the last box on the page. The one where Ms. Havisham was standing over Spike's immobile body. He looked at her then, and the stark expression in his eyes knocked the breath out of her. "She has killed him then?"

Swallowing the tears catching in her throat, Lexi nodded. "In this draft, at least."

He frowned. "What do you mean?"

She rubbed the heel of her palm over her eyes. "I can't decide on an ending. I'm meeting a freelance publisher guy in two days, but I'm still not sure. She has to show Spike what she's capable of so that he doesn't underestimate her ever again, but maybe she'll just maim him. Maybe she will turn him into her sidekick, who knows?"

He blinked. And she realized it was to shield his expression from her face. "You're enjoying this immensely, aren't you?"

"Yes. I have totally embraced the fact that Spike's life is in my hands and I can inflict whatever damage I can on him." She raised her thumbs up, a parody to cover up the misery she felt inside. "Once again, it's delusional fantasy to the rescue."

Shaking his head, he picked up the rest of the pages of the strip from the table and flicked through them. "You have done a lot in one week."

She shrugged. "The money you paid me will tide me over for a few months if I work minimal hours. I decided it's now or never to give this a proper shot."

"That's fantastic." His gaze lingered on her hungrily before he resumed pacing again, a restless energy pouring off him in waves.

She fisted her hands, stifling the urge to pummel him. How dare he just dangle the announcement that his engagement was off but not say more? But she would not ask for details.

Her sudden movement caused his hard chest to graze against her, and he jerked back like a coiled spring.

"Will you stop the pacing? You're beginning to scare me, Nikos. What happened? Is everyone okay?"

"Yes, they are all fine. Venetia is driving Tyler and me crazy planning the wedding of the century."

Lexi's heart sank. Venetia and she, despite all odds, had struck a weird sort of friendship. They both loved Tyler, and it created a surprisingly strong connection despite their different temperaments. But because of the inconsiderate, intractable brute in front of her, Lexi was missing all the fun. "They have set a date?"

"Yes. For eighteen months from now. You would think she was the first woman to get married. I have renewed respect for Tyler that he was able to persuade her at all to a date so far away."

She hadn't spoken to Tyler in a week, and even before that only to assure him that she had reached New York safely—like a flight on a private jet would be anything but—and that she was fine. He knew she was not fine. But she hadn't wanted to linger for an extra day, so she had promised him that she would take care of herself. But she couldn't talk to him over the phone. Because if she did, she was going to start crying, and she didn't want to alarm him.

Because more than the threat of loneliness, it was the shadow of the happiness, the joy she had known with Nikos that remained behind, making her ache. And now he was here again, setting her back to square one. Not that she had made much progress in moving on.

She still had a couple of weeks before she went back to work and she had been eating greasy takeout, drawing and crying herself to sleep.

"So your sister is fine, you are still the CEO—" she had

never heard so much bitterness in her voice "—then why are you here?"

He stood rooted to the spot. She watched him swallow, watched the dark shadow that fell over his face.

Suddenly she felt exhaustingly fragile. Being in love was so hard. She would have given anything to make it stop hurting so much.

Nikos was looming in front of her before she could draw another breath, running a finger over the bags under her eyes. There was such desolation in his eyes, such open need that she trembled from head to toe. "There's this tightness in my chest, *thee mou,* like someone is relentlessly carving away at it. It hurts like nothing I have ever felt before."

Lexi felt dizzy from the emotion in his words. "You don't have a heart." She wanted to sound cutting, instead she sounded immensely sad.

His mouth closed; he smiled without warmth. "Apparently I do. You kick-started it when you blazed into my life."

"I didn't blaze anywhere. You manipulated me." Tears filled her throat. "You forced the truth on me and then you—" She hit him in the chest. "I have never been so angry with anyone in my entire life, Nikos. I hate you for you doing this to me."

His arms came around her, his grip infinitely fragile. She felt his mouth on her temple, felt his sharp hiss of indrawn breath. "Not as much as I hate myself, *thee mou. Theos,* there isn't a single name I haven't called myself these last few days. I had a whole speech prepared, liberally infused with begging. And I don't remember a word of it.

"Every time I come near you, you unravel me a little more. You show me how much I can feel, how much I can hurt. It's a little scary, Lexi."

Tears came fast at her and spilled onto her cheeks. She had no defense left to fight him. Not anymore, not when he said things like that, not when the heat of his body was an incredible fortress of warmth around her.

His mouth compressed into a line of pain, he gathered her closer. And she cried. She thought it wasn't possible for her heart to break again. Apparently it still could. The pain was as sharp as ever.

"Don't cry, *agape mou*. I can't bear it." He tucked her chin up gently, a flash of indecision in his gaze. "I'm desperately in love with you, Lexi. You were wrong about one thing. This thing…it's not just taken root inside me, it's consuming me whole. My life is terrifyingly empty without you. The power you hold over me, over my happiness—I'm not scared of it anymore. I want to spend the rest of my life loving you, *yineka mou*."

Lexi's heart beat so fast she wondered if she was having a heart attack. His hands around her waist, Nikos held her tight, a shudder racking his powerful frame. "You mean it?"

Nikos nodded, his heart shining in his eyes. "I do. I can't stop giving thanks for the moment that brought Tyler into Venetia's life and you into mine.

"You are the most wonderful woman I have ever met, and I want to live my life with you. I want to have a family with you. I want to make love to you every night and every morning. I want to hear your incredible stories about space portals and time warps. I want to be the first one who sees every sketch you ever draw. I want to take care of you, and I want you to take care of me. The number of things I feel for you, they are dizzying and invigorating.

"Please tell me you don't want to have an extremely elaborate wedding like Venetia because that would just about kill me."

"What?" Her heart pounding harder, it seemed all she was capable of was asking inane questions.

His thumbs moving over her cheeks, he pressed a kiss

to her forehead. "I want to marry you, *yineka mou,* as soon as possible. We will honeymoon on the yacht, I think. I promised Savas we would return in a month so that I can officially take over and be the new CEO."

Her gaze flew to his. It was too many shocks for one day. "He agreed to this?"

"I didn't give him a choice. I told him that the CEO position meant nothing to me without you." He pushed her hands behind her with one hand and tilted her chin up. "Tell me this is what you want, too. Tell me you love me."

Lexi smiled, but she still couldn't stop crying, either. "I do love you, Nikos. You helped me discover that I'm just as cool as an imaginary action heroine with a penchant for killing. Or even better—" she choked on the tears again "—you made me want to live my life. And then you left me to do it all alone. It's a good life, I have realized. It's just that it's a lot happier with you in it, and I don't want to spend another minute of it denying myself that happiness."

He touched his forehead to hers and whispered the words into her skin. "Then you never will. Your happiness, our happiness together, that's all I want now, *thee mou.*" He sealed his promise with a kiss, and Lexi felt the stress and tension leave her body. Her heart thundered inside her chest, and she trembled in his arms, bursting with happiness. "Although I think I have to kill whoever Tony Stark is."

"What?"

"It says I Love Tony Stark on your T-shirt, *agape mou.* You're not allowed to love anyone but me."

She laughed and stepped back from him, loving the jealous glint in his eyes. She loved him like this—playful and willing to show what he felt for her. It cost him a lot, and she loved him all the more for it. "Sorry, but that's an occupational hazard of being a comic artist, Nikos. At any given time, I'm in love with at least two to three fictional heroes. Recently, it's been Iron Man. And it's not like you can compete with him, so it's better—"

She squealed and turned as he reached her in two quick steps and pressed her to the wall behind her with his huge body. She saw his hunger in the tight lines of his gorgeous face, in the way he clenched his muscles hard holding the lust at bay. "By the time I'm through with you tonight, you won't remember your own name much less another man's, *thee mou*. My name, that's all you are going to say, or scream."

She trembled at the dark promise in his words, her body already thrumming with arousal and anticipation. She choked back a laugh as he picked her up and moved toward the couch.

She shook her head and pointed him in the other direction. "The bedroom is that way."

Desire roared into life in his eyes.

"Three hundred and sixty hours and forty-three minutes."

"What?"

"Since you made love to me."

"I think you're addicted to sex, Ms. Nelson."

"Nope." She tucked herself tighter around him and smiled up at him. "I'm addicted to you, Mr. Demakis."

* * * * *

MILLS & BOON®
By Request

RELIVE THE ROMANCE WITH THE BEST OF THE BEST

A sneak peek at next month's titles...

In stores from 14th December 2017:

- **Bound by a Baby** – Maureen Child, Tessa Radley *and* Yvonne Lindsay

- **A Proposal Worth Waiting For** – Raye Morgan, Teresa Carpenter *and* Melissa McClone

In stores from 28th December 2017:

- **The Montoros Affair** – Kat Cantrell, Jules Bennett, *and* Charlene Sands

- **New Year, New Man** – Michelle Major, Ally Blake *and* Natalie Anderson

1217/05